The Face of the Dead

The face twitched. The nose wrinkled and the mouth opened and closed. The chained prisoner's eyes bulged as he watched the mask continue to make a pretense of life.

G'Meni allowed him to gape for several seconds. "It is fascinating, is it not? The power of magic and the knowledge of science combining to create this!"

"Mother of God . . ." the peasant was finally able to whisper.

"You will be Viktor Falsche, my loutish friend, and you will be as he was . . . until he died."

G'Meni pressed the underside of the mask against the peasant's countenance. There was a muffled scream that quickly faded.

The false face stretched and remolded, shaping to conform to the contours of the host and still retain the features with which it had been instilled.

At last, the rippling and twisting quieted, leaving what seemed an entirely different man. Even unconscious, the figure chained to the platform shifted to a more defiant, arrogant position, as if ready to fight even in the land of dreams . . .

RICHARD A. KNAAK

THE

JANUS MASK

ASPECT ®

WARNER BOOKS

A Time Warner Company

WARNER BOOKS EDITION

Aspect is a registered trademark of Warner Books, Inc.

Cover design by Don Puckey
Cover illustration by Den Beauvais

Warner Books, Inc.
1271 Avenue of the Americas
New York, NY 10020

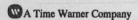A Time Warner Company

Printed in the United States of America

First Printing:: September, 1995

10 9 8 7 6 5 4 3 2 1

Dedicated to my mother, Anna,
who believed in both me
and my success from the beginning.

I

It was, G'Meni had to admit, a handsome enough face by present standards. The nose was perhaps just a tad too big as far as he was concerned and the mouth had a mocking cast to it that still unnerved him after more than a decade, but those very features were considered aristocratic by the standards of most, the type that leaders and lovers wore. Eyes of forest green and a head of stark black hair would have completed the picture of the man and soon they would again, now that the baron had chosen at last to make use of his greatest triumph.

He opened the top of the small glass case and removed the face from its container.

The mouth opened and closed once, a reflex that the squat, mustached alchemist was long used to seeing. All of the faces moved when one touched them. Sometimes the mouth worked or the nostrils flared. Once in a while, the eyelids opened, revealing the empty space behind them. G'Meni had made a long study of the properties of the dormant faces, determining what made one more mobile than another. He had come to the conclusion that it was the personality of the one from whom the face had been cast that dictated the random movements. The more vibrant the life, the more active the face.

Ten years had done nothing to render this particular face passive—but then, Viktor Falsche had never been what one would have called passive. Bloodthirsty and impetuous, yes, but never passive.

Still holding the face in his hands, G'Meni looked

about the chamber, long oily mustache whirling wildly. "Where are they? They are late again! This will never do!"

His view took in walls overburdened by half-completed experiments, notebooks, jars of samples, and, on one side, the special ceiling-high case, normally locked, from which the container holding the lifelike mask had been drawn. It was a pleasant enough place, to his mind, but it revealed no answer to his question. Before he could repeat his query, however, there came the sound of marching, boot-clad feet. The pace with which the newcomers moved indicated that they knew very well that they were late.

G'Meni scratched the scarred wreckage that was all that remained of his nose, the end result of long ago leaning too close to one of his more explosive experiments, and chuckled at their evident fear. Their fear was a triumph, a major one, in his constant war of bickering with General Straas. To put fear into the minds of the general's men was to put a trace of fear into their commander's own mind, for were they not an extension of the bearded, arrogant soldier himself?

Yes, indeed, they were. Very *much* so.

There was a knock on the door. G'Meni rose to his full inch below five feet, used one hand to straighten his black robe, and tried to look as menacing as possible. "Enter and be damned quick about it, you slow-witted zombies!"

The door swung open and a soldier clad in the blue and gray half-armor of the Guard stepped inside. He saluted. His pale features were rough-hewn and, save for the sleepiness hinted in his eyes, the clean-shaven face was that of a butcher, a methodical killer. But for the lack of a beard, he perfectly resembled General Straas as the general had looked some fifteen years earlier.

A second soldier clad like the first entered. He, too, saluted. His features were identical to those of his companion. Only the color of their eyes differed, one man having blue and the other hazel.

"Well? Did you bring the one I asked for? He must be just right for Baron Mandrol, you know! This is a special occasion."

"Someone put him in the wrong cell," answered the first, in a tired drawl that was typical of his kind. "It took us several minutes to find out just which one, Master G'Meni."

The face in the alchemist's hands began to twitch. "Well, don't just dawdle, then, you idiots! Bring him in!"

The first man snapped his fingers. Two more guardsmen, copies of the rest, entered the laboratory with a third, much abused figure stumbling between them.

"Be careful with his arms, dolts! He won't be much good if you break them just yet! Save that for the masque!"

Looking rather chastened, the two soldiers loosened their hold a bit on the prisoner.

G'Meni eyed the four members of the baron's Guard. Perhaps it was time to ask the general for a new fitting. These men were becoming sloppy, not at all like the warrior whose visage they wore. It would require some work with the special acid he had prepared for such eventualities, but the wounds would be minor. He would broach the subject with the baron first. Straas was not going to be at all pleased to be forced to shave his beard after five years. He had grown it specifically to erase some of the unsettling resemblance between himself and his drone soldiers.

"But that can wait," the alchemist mumbled. With his chin, he indicated a long, angled platform fitted with manacles. "Put him on the table. Quickly, now! Your ineptitude means that I will be preparing him nearly up to the time of the masque!" He shook his head at the need for such rushing. G'Meni was a believer in quality workmanship where such a task was concerned. He wanted this to be the crowning masterpiece of his career, the focal point of the greatest of the baron's masques.

"And who better than you?" he whispered, gazing down at the flattened visage. The mouth worked again, followed almost immediately by a flaring of the nostrils. *Eager for life again, Viktor Falsche? Enjoy it while it lasts! If you only knew of the revenge I have taken . . .*

"He is ready, Master G'Meni."

"Then step back so that I can take a look at this one."

The prisoner, some peasant from the cells, was of the right height and build and his hair was only slightly lighter than desired. A little dye would take care of that. The eyes were green, but more emerald than forest. Still, they would do, too. The man looked and stank of several days in the company of the other refuse that populated the baron's dungeons, but a thorough cleaning would deal with that. The cleaning could take place *after* this part of the process.

G'Meni blinked, leaned a little closer, and studied the battered countenance of the peasant. "Give me a little more light."

One of the guards seized a lit oil lamp and brought it forward. In the increased illumination, the prisoner's features became clearer. The alchemist chuckled. He would have recognized those features anywhere. The long face, the broad, flat nose, the extended cheekbones . . .

One of your earlier trysts, my baron? He has to be one of yours with a face like that. An idea formed, one that the bent figure quickly quashed. He dared not risk such a feat; it could very well undo all that he had accomplished these past several years.

The guards would have noticed the resemblance to the baron, but they knew Mandrol's feeling toward his bastards. The children were a symbol of mortality to him, a symbol that he, too, must pass. The baron did not like being reminded of that, and so such children were to be removed when discovered. No one in Viathos Keep would think it amiss to make use of this one for the coming masque. In fact, the more G'Meni thought about it, the more it would be the crowning touch to the event. Two birds with one stone, so to speak.

He realized that the peasant was staring back at him, cold fear evident in those green eyes. "What is your name, my boy?"

The "boy" was in his mid-twenties, a tad too young for G'Meni's preference in this, but old enough to make do. He hesitated, as was not surprising in the presence of the baron's most trusted adviser and the land of Medecia's second most feared name, then finally croaked, "Emil."

"Emil." Typically dull peasant name. "Well, dear Emil, you have been chosen for a great honor, you have. *You* are going to be a guest, a very *special* guest, at the baron's great ball tomorrow evening. Isn't that wonderful?"

From the shudder that visibly coursed through the peasant's rank body, G'Meni gathered that Emil knew some of the tales that surrounded the monthly masques held in the grand ballroom of the castle everyone still insisted on calling Viathos *Keep*. It was to be expected. Had he not received such a reaction from the peasant, then the alchemist would have truly been surprised.

"Yes," he continued, holding up the unsettling visage in his hands for the chosen one to see. "You are going to attend the ball just like the nobles and courtiers. You will even have a special place of honor, one reserved for only the greatest of the baron's associates."

As if in response, the face twitched. The nose wrinkled and the mouth opened and closed. The chained prisoner could not help but be attracted by the movement. His eyes bulged as he watched the mask continue to make a pretense at life.

G'Meni allowed him to gape for several seconds. "It is fascinating, is it not? You have heard stories about this, haven't you?"

The peasant managed to nod, his eyes still fixed on the horrific thing his captor held so gently.

"I cannot take credit for the design, although I can take credit for the perfection. The baron himself is to be congratulated for this creation. It is, I can easily say, his crowning achievement." All knew of the baron's lifelong delving into sorcery and alchemy. "The synthesis of two astonishing schools! The power of magic and the knowledge of science combining to create *this*."

His audience did not seem as admiring of this marvel as G'Meni was. In fact, the peasant muttered something under his breath. At first the stooped figure could not make out what it was. He had the frightened Emil repeat the words, encouragement given in the form of a slap by one of the gauntleted hands of a guard.

"Death . . . mask . . . the death mask . . ."

The words were an offense to G'Meni. "Death mask, indeed! This is a symbol of the continuance of *life*, not death! This is, in its own way, an honor!" Balancing the face in one hand, G'Meni indicated the great case. "Each of those slots contains the perfect reproduction of the baron's most worthy adversaries through the years. Each of those faces was taken with great care and respect from their dead or dying forms in such a way that there remains a reflection, a hint of personality, of the original! Do you know the intricacy involved in such a feat? All of our work through the years!" The alchemist shook his head at the sheer ignorance of the masses. "It is ever the fate of the learned to be misunderstood and misjudged by those who do not know better."

His audience did not seem convinced. G'Meni looked up at the guards and saw little more comprehension despite the fact that they of all people should have understood the complexities of what he and his patron had accomplished. He wondered why he always tried to explain to such obviously unfit audiences as this bastard son of the baron. Better to get on with the process. Time was already slipping past.

Still, he could not help talking as he proceeded. It was the part of him, G'Meni always believed, that desired to educate and illuminate the ignorant despite their never seeming to *appreciate* his efforts that made him do it. That and his affection for the sound of his own voice.

"The highlight of the ball is a morality play of sorts, you must understand. A retelling of events in the great life of our baron. You have been given the honor of portraying a central figure in that play, one who certainly has earned a place of respect in *my* heart."

The prisoner shook his head, his eyes unable to turn long from the otherworldly object resting in G'Meni's palms.

"You do not feel up to the role, I am sure." The alchemist raised the wrinkled face up to the horrified visage of his subject. "Rest assured, it will seem more like a dream. The mask will guide you. I believe you may even *sleep* through it. I've never been quite certain of the extent.

Depends on the personality of the mask, you know."

"Mother of God . . ." the peasant was finally able to whisper. G'Meni already had the face mere inches from Emil's own.

"You will *be* Viktor Falsche, my loutish friend, and you will be as he was . . . until he died."

He pressed the underside of the mask against Emil's countenance.

There was a muffled scream which quickly faded. G'Meni paid little mind to the reaction save to note that it was part of the normal chain of events for the process. That pleased him; the mask had been waiting for so long that, reflex actions aside, he had still been a bit afraid that it had lost some of its potency. *Should have known . . . Viktor Falsche was always so lively.*

The false face stretched and remolded, shaping so as to conform to the contours of the host and yet still retain the features with which it had been instilled. The alchemist watched the process take place with pride in his heart. The masks were as much his children as they were the baron's.

At last, the rippling and twisting of the features quieted, leaving in their wake what seemed an entirely different man. G'Meni noted that even unconscious, the figure chained to the platform shifted to a more defiant, arrogant position, as if ready to fight even in the land of dreams.

"It has melded well," he informed the guards. "Inform the baron that all will proceed on schedule. He shall have his special anniversary masque tomorrow and there he shall reaffirm his position with a replaying of his greatest triumph . . . the humiliation and death of Viktor Falsche, rival and pretender."

"Yes, Master G'Meni." The identical soldiers departed, save for the first who had entered.

It took G'Meni a moment to notice the presence of the remaining guard, so absorbed was he in examining the fine, almost invisible line revealing where the mask ended. "What *is* it? I am extremely busy!"

The soldier indicated the prone form. "Is it safe to leave you alone with this one? I remember Falsche. I remember how—"

"You remember *nothing*. Your general recalls, and that memory is of years past. Forget it. If this were truly Falsche and not simply a shadow mask of him, I would perhaps worry, but there is no reason to fear. This puppet is mine to lead, mine to direct. He will play his role and then he will die. Is that too much to understand?"

"No." Despite the response, there was still a hint of unease in the face. Even the eyes looked less sleepy.

G'Meni waved him away. "Your concern is noted. You may depart now."

The soldier saluted, then disappeared through the doorway.

When he was finally alone, the squat alchemist delved once more into his work. There was so much to do. The guards no doubt believed that once the face was in place, the rest was simple, but that was not how G'Meni saw it. He was a perfectionist, an artisan, when it came to the process, and that meant that he had to put the ensorcelled figure through a series of tests in order to ascertain just what level of possession had been attained. This Viktor Falsche had to be perfect, save for the flaw that would lead to his downfall tomorrow.

"You shall need a washing, too." He sniffed, looking over the figure. That would be the first test. A full head-to-toe cleansing would require extensive physical activity, which would inform G'Meni as to the strength of the link between the mask and the host. "Then, I have a *special* series of experiments designed just for you."

He paused then, noting something amiss just before the left ear. A crease. There should have been *no* creases, but there it was. "This will never do, you know! We cannot have you losing face before the climax!"

Chuckling at his own jest, the robed figure turned away to search for the adhesive he had created for just such emergencies. It was not as permanent as the liquid that was applied to the faces of Straas's drone soldiers, but it would hold for the length of the morrow's ball.

"No, indeed." He chuckled again, still very much amused at his humor. "We want you just perfect tomorrow when you face Baron Mandrol and the Lady Lilaith DuPrise."

As he finished speaking, a chill coursed through him, nearly causing him to drop the container he had just picked up. Not knowing why he did so, G'Meni whirled around and stared at the figure on the platform.

The prisoner had not moved. He still lay as the alchemist had seen him last, sleeping the slumber of the deeply entranced.

Master G'Meni's mouth curled slightly upward into a rueful smile. "Only you could do that to me after ten years of death, Falsche! Hmmph! I wonder how you will affect the Lady DuPrise."

He turned back to the table and the container and began measuring out a proper amount of the adhesive. Too much would be almost as detrimental as too little.

Behind him, the eyelids of the figure slowly opened, stared momentarily at the alchemist's hunched back, and then slowly closed again.

II

All about him, they moved as if part of a dream, yet he could not help feeling that it was *he* who was the dream and they who were the dreamers. People spoke and moved as if all were normal, despite the fact that he was certain that something was out of place, something was not as it should have been.

It matters not, Viktor Falsche chided, suddenly furious at his inability to focus on the world and the deed at hand. *Only Mandrol matters!*

Yet, his irritation with himself served only to underline his sense of anxiety. It was as if he were trying to convince himself that the deed had to be done. Of *course* it had to be done. Why would he question both his reasons and his plan, a plan that was finally coming to fruition after too much sacrifice both on his part and that of his love?

Still Viktor hesitated.

He had peculiar memories of a time spent in a dimly lit sanctum and of the face of the damnable G'Meni, Mandrol's pet alchemist, leaning close to his own. Yet, if such memories had been real, he could not be standing where he was now, plotting the foul baron's death.

There were other memories, too, of peasant life, something that was not part of his high-born heritage.

What was happening to his mind . . . and why now?

Cloying laughter from across the ballroom served to remind him once again why he had come here. Viktor Falsche stared at the dapper and haughty figures moving about as the musicians played, and swore not for the first time that this would be Baron Mandrol's last masque. He owed Mandrol for many things; that, at least, was fresh in his mind, if much else from the past few days seemed murky. Even the baboon-faced baron's own destruction had had its price. Lilaith had made a greater sacrifice than Falsche in agreeing to do her part. Viktor would not have gotten this far without her, but to have her play such a role for *Mandrol* . . .

Tonight, we shall all be free of him! It sounded hollow, whether true or not. Both of them would be forever changed, regardless.

Like the rest of the revelers, Viktor wore a fanciful mask, in his case that of a grinning badger, that covered all but his eyes and his mouth. The mask had been one of the trickiest parts of his plan, for Mandrol kept them under lock and key for reasons apparent only to him and possibly his lackey, G'Meni. It had been up to Lilaith, faithful Lilaith, to procure one for him.

Another debt he owed the baron. Viktor Falsche hoped that both he and Lilaith would be able to forget the past several months once this was all over. Of course, they had to survive the assassination. There would also still be General Straas and G'Meni to consider, but Viktor was not so worried about them. As strong as the duo were in their own fields of expertise, they did not have the ability to rule, to oversee the complexities of leadership, that he had to admit Mandrol did. Straas could command armies, quite ably, but civilian governing was beyond him. G'Meni . . . out of his laboratory, the alchemist was lost.

Baron Mandrol's assassination would mean the end for both of them, especially if Lilaith had succeeded and discovered the one key element Viktor needed. She should have been here by now, in fact, and that she was not was one more fear to add to the rest.

"Excuse me, please, is it not Squire Robiere behind that mask?"

The musical, slightly accented voice sent his mind to work even as he turned and replied, "No, my lady, I am not that august gentlemen, although if it would please you for me to be, I will do my best."

The woman who joined him was nearly a foot shorter, but she radiated a presence that made her seem taller and formidable. She was certainly the latter, and that was simply one reason why he loved her so. The billowing ivory gown she wore made her look every inch the queen she should have been. The top was off-shoulder and cut deep to reveal much too much as far as Viktor was concerned. The gown, however, had been designed for Baron Mandrol's tastes, elegant yet enticing. It had worked its own magic on the dark aristocrat.

The woman who allowed such clothing to grace her exquisite form was a night-tressed aristocrat with the brown, gleaming skin of the south lands, full lips speaking of some western ancestry, and oval eyes that twinkled gold. The contrast to her ivory gown only served to amplify her unique beauty. Even among her own people, she was matchless. That she had come to love him was more honor than Viktor felt he deserved.

As elegant as his own blue and silver courtier's suit was, Viktor felt like a piece of coal set beside a glittering diamond. When the time had come to find the one path into Viathos Keep, they both had swiftly realized that she would be the key. Mandrol lived to collect the beautiful and the unique for his treasure trove, and Lilaith DuPrise was both.

"Why do you stand there staring at me?" she whispered. For the first time, the anxiety in her voice caught his attention.

He made certain that no one was near enough to notice, then took her in his arms. They dared not let the embrace last for more than a moment, but even that was long enough to help rebuild some of his sagging resolve. For her alone, he had to kill Mandrol. Other past debts paled in comparison.

"Are you all right? Did he *touch* you again? After he's dead, Lilaith, I will carve him into small pieces and feed him to his own Morags."

"Please! We have no time to speak of anything but the plan, Viktor!" She produced a small vial from within the confines of her gown. "Here is what you wanted!"

"This is it?" The would-be assassin eyed the tiny

vial dubiously. "This is all I need to stop Mandrol's Guard in its tracks?"

She gave him a smile that the mask she wore partially obscured. "Whatever else we think of Master G'Meni, he *is* an alchemist of great skill."

The vision of the ugly, warted alchemist leaning over him returned to Viktor. He shook his head, sending the image away. This was a time when he could ill afford to let his thoughts drift. It would be difficult enough to do this, considering the state of his mind already. Things still had a slight dreamlike quality to them. Even Lilaith. Her voice sounded as if she spoke from a short distance away in some tunnel.

Viktor focused on the vial, the key to his success. "I'll need a few minutes to prepare this, then. If it's as potent as you say, then Mandrol may end up gutted by his own slave soldiers." He allowed himself a smile. "I think that I could live with that."

"There is a chamber across the ballroom." Lilaith pointed at a large wooden doorway. It would require Viktor to cross the entire floor, but it was doubtful anyone would recognize him in his disguise.

Yet . . . he found himself suddenly unwilling to go that way. The door, the act of walking among the crowd of Mandrol's boot-lickers, sent warning signals through his already uneasy mind. Viktor was adept at what other men termed sorcery, but not so much that he could have premonitions. *Nerves. It must be nerves. I simply grow too anxious in anticipation of Mandrol's death. That's all it can be.*

Why, then, did he feel as if he had already crossed the floor? Why did he feel that stepping through the doorway would mean his death . . . and already *had?*

"Godspeed, dear Viktor!" whispered Lilaith suddenly, leaning forward and kissing him lightly on the cheek. Her hand briefly touched his own, then the dark-haired woman turned and walked away, acting as if the conversation had never taken place.

She was even more nervous than he was. The anxiety he had felt in her touch had been unsettling. Viktor stared at his hand, wondering if this should all be taken as some sign. Unlike many of his calling, he did not believe in astrology, but he did now wonder just what the stars would have foretold about tonight. Viktor was aware that he stood a good chance of dying in this, but it would be worth it to be rid of Mandrol. Whatever the outcome, Lilaith would be safe. Dré was secreted below, ready to help them . . . or simply her . . . escape through one of the kitchen areas.

Dré. Again that sense of distance caught up to Falsche. He had *forgotten* about his oldest friend, astonishing as it seemed, and now he was even having trouble conjuring up his friend's face. Try as he might, Viktor could summon only a vague, blurred image of Dré Kopien. Dark brown hair, clipped mustache . . . that was all he could recall with any confidence.

Sometimes your mind dances around too much, Viktor, Dré had often said. *It's a wonder, it is, that you get anything accomplished sometimes.*

If you knew what I was like right now, Dré. . . . Gritting his teeth, Viktor Falsche tried again to focus on the vial. His position kept him out of sight of all but the nosiest revelers, for which he was now extremely grateful.

I am one. I am focused. I am in command of myself.

Some of the fog cleared from his mind, but he found himself not at all comforted by that, for now things seemed even more amiss than he had first felt they were. In his mind, he saw the plan unfold as he and his companions had predicted, save that when he tried to use the vial, the contents proved to be other than what Lilaith had said they were. Instead of freeing Mandrol's drones from their ensorcellment, the potion within rose up as a gray mist and stole his strength.

He could see Mandrol's face, a triumphant visage surrounded by the flowing mane of hair that had always struck Falsche as so ostentatious. Mandrol, smiling and saying something that he could not hear. Lilaith by his side, arm around him and also smiling, although *her* smile held a certain sense of lost hope.

G'Meni.

G'Meni reaching toward him with some foul toy of his own, covering Viktor's face, *smothering* him—

Viktor Falsche inhaled sharply, returning to his present world. He glanced in the direction that Lilaith had gone. She could *never* betray him to Mandrol! Never!

Across the ballroom. To the door, his mind suddenly insisted, ignoring his turmoil. *You must be in the other chamber when the baron enters. You must take the vial, whisper the words of the earth and wind to it, and open it.*

That was what he had intended to do . . . but now he was certain that if he did, it would not be Baron Mandrol who died this night.

"Lilaith . . ." Viktor whispered. He put the vial in the pouch that hung from the waist of his splendid garment. All thought of revenge, assassination, and triumph faded. Now he was interested only in finding the dark-skinned woman and stealing away with her. The plan had gone awry somehow; he was positive. The images in his mind were too real to him. Viktor almost felt as if he had already *lived* that utter failure; even the sense of death was tangible. Viktor shuddered. He was a brave man, considered brash and a risk-taker by both his friends and adversaries, and the possibility of death had never bothered him much in the past, but now the sorcerer and would-be assassin felt as if he had not only put one foot into the grave, but had been both buried and exhumed.

Viktor started after Lilaith . . . and found himself turning instead toward the now dreaded doorway across the ballroom floor. He had to hold himself back. It was almost as if there was a geas upon him, but he could sense nothing. He had so far dared not summon up his power for fear that Mandrol would detect his presence in Viathos. He and Lilaith had to try to escape without any use of illusion or wizardry.

Again he thought of loyal Dré, waiting near the kitchens.

Was Dré even there? The question did not seem so ridiculous as it might have if he had asked it a moment before.

His gaze drifting, Viktor fought within himself to come to terms with the contradictory images and desires. He was here to kill Mandrol . . . but he had failed . . . but he could *not* have failed because he had not yet tried . . . but it felt very wrong . . . somehow the plan . . . and Lilaith . . . had been compromised.

Then his eyes caught sight of a familiar and foul form stalking the upper level and peering down at the guests as if seeking one in particular.

G'Meni.

In that instant, Viktor knew what he had to do. He eyed the faraway door and reached for the vial in his pouch.

"I wish you would reconsider this, Baron."

"Your loyalty and concern touch me, my dear General Straas, but I have waited long enough. I can understand your distaste, but rest assured, I will have the mask burned after this one time. I *must* do this tonight, though. There is no choice and you will simply have to live with that."

Baron Mandrol rose from where his servants were putting the final touch on his appearance. Mandrol did not condone the perfumes and makeup that many of the aristocracy, both female and male, made use of these days. He found it effeminate. Mandrol was proud of his appearance and flaunted it. His long, proud face, accented by his mane of dark, only slightly graying hair, made him look, so he believed, like a shadow-tressed lion. Anyone who suggested that he more resembled a baboon would have found themselves quickly bereft of the ability to make any future suggestions.

His black and silver dress uniform, an extravagant variation of that worn by Straas and the officers of the Guard, fit the baron perfectly. His tailors had worked hard to make it so, but even Straas, a man who lived for the military, would have been willing to admit that Mandrol kept himself as fit as any man. Of course, some of that supreme fitness was due to magics and elixirs, but it was the end result that counted, was it not?

A long silver and gray cloak and knee-high black boots finished the effect. Mandrol stood for a time and admired himself in the full-length mirror. Although there was no visible reason for doing so, he reached up with both hands and ran his fingers along both sides of his face where the hairline began. Straas had long decided it was some mental ritual his master had picked up in the past several years, perhaps a way for the baron to organize his thoughts.

The baron glanced at the general's own rather subdued uniform. While it was wise of Straas not to compete with the wear of his master, Mandrol wished that the general would add a little more decoration to his own outfit. Straas wore a few medals, but that was all. There was also a slight bulging to the upper part of the suit, indicating that the soldier was wearing a metal vest underneath. Straas was never one to relax.

"At least take your helmet off."

The general obeyed with evident reluctance. "Baron. I must insist again. Just burn the bloody thing and forget it! Viktor Falsche had many, many supporters and his return, even for this, will stir them up. For that matter, while we've never found Dré Kopien, I'm certain that he is still in Medecia. There are others, too."

"Ten years is long enough, Straas." The baron's previously smooth voice caught. "I have nothing to fear from either a dead man or his shade! Tonight, we will all relive the humiliation and execution of Viktor Falsche, reminding everyone—for you and I both know the story will spread to the city and countryside as well—that *I* am the hand of Medecia. *I* am the power that rules."

Straas backed down. "As you say, my baron."

"Do not irritate me, Straas," Mandrol said in a companionable tone. "We are nearing the point when it will be time to take Wesfrancia. You have been waiting for that, haven't you? You have missed your old home, haven't you?"

"I look forward to greeting my old master, King Leopold, yes."

"And cutting his head off with your own blade, I

know. It will come soon enough." Baron Mandrol flourished his cape. "I am ready to descend. My scepter, please."

The scepter in question was more a decorative mace. Mandrol had used it more than once to show his displeasure at failure. Those who had committed those failures did not generally rise again.

A dozen soldiers surrounded them as Mandrol and Straas made their way to the masque. Unlike so many others, these men wore faces of their own. They were part of the general's personal staff, paid and loyal men like himself. It was well known that Straas trusted them more than he did even his own copies.

Mandrol always found that fact rather droll, but since the general was one of his most valued followers and slightly temperamental, too, it was one point upon which he did not press. He would have hated to have to kill the man for something so minor as growing too angry in the presence of his lord.

The baron's throne was situated between two vast curving staircases and it was from one of these that he and his guards would descend. Whether it was the one on the left or the right was a matter of Mandrol's whim. Tonight, however, it had to be the one on the baron's left. That was the staircase from which he had descended on the night Viktor Falsche had made his foolish attempt to murder him before his very supporters. The audacity of the plan had nearly made it workable, something the baron never allowed himself to forget. A wolverine had made its way into his den without anyone noticing.

Straas had made certain that there would be no repeat of that. The passage below the kitchens, an old escape tunnel from the days when Viathos had been only a keep often under siege by barbarians from the east, was now sealed. How Falsche had discovered it was still a mystery. Kopien had escaped, but without Falsche to guide him, he had become nothing. This night would prove to everyone that only luck had brought Viktor Falsche so close to success. Now everyone would see that Mandrol had not been in any true danger.

It had taken him ten years to dare to prove it to himself.

The heralds announced his coming and the horns proclaimed his glory to all those in attendance. Gazing at his followers, Mandrol could not help thinking what fawning sycophants most of them were, but they served their purpose, their infighting especially keeping any serious threats from reaching him. There were some here he knew who had probably supported Falsche, but it was impossible to say for certain who those might be. The obvious allies had all been dealt with after Viktor Falsche's own execution.

"Where is G'Meni?" he whispered to Straas.

"He was to keep an eye on both Falsche and Lady Lilaith from the upper floor there."

"Lilaith? Does he expect something amiss?"

Straas pretended not to notice the touch of jealousy in his baron's voice. "He merely wishes to make certain that she performed as she was told to perform. Seeing Falsche could upset her, you know."

"It will begin soon, will it not?" snarled Baron Mandrol. "I want it to begin *very* soon."

They reached the throne, the general's men flanking Mandrol. Members of the Guard stood at attention as the baron finally acknowledged his guests and seated himself. Straas sat next to him in a lower and much less elaborate chair. He eyed the ballroom as if marking each reveler as a potential enemy.

A servant brought forth a tray with a single golden goblet positioned in the center. Others with fuller trays waited behind him. He proffered the goblet to the baron, who did not seize it immediately but rather raised a hand over it. Mandrol drew a circle with his index finger, muttering words that even Straas, who sat nearest, could not make out. When he was finished with his own drink, he drew further circles in the direction of the other trays.

Nodding at last, Mandrol lowered his hand and took the goblet. He sipped long from it before finally dismissing the servant.

The sip was a sign to the rest that it was permissible

to renew their activities. The other servants brought wine to the general and his staff even as the musicians began to play again.

Straas drank lightly from his own goblet. He was unconcerned about the possibility of poison now that the baron had checked for it, but was unwilling to let the strong drink muddle his thoughts.

Despite the resumption of festivities, the air was filled with anticipation. Everyone knew that tonight was to be a special presentation. The baron had made his enemies dance and dance for him time after time. There had been Proloff, who had challenged him to a traditional battle of sorcery and failed, his remains little more than a burnt crisp. It had been tricky creating a mask of him. The re-creation of that confrontation had forever left a scorched mark on the western wall of the ballroom now covered by a great tapestry of Baron Mandrol. Then there had been Master Gingrich, who had assumed that the distance from his sanctum in Wesfrancia would protect him from the arm of the baron. His face, too, was a part of the collection.

So many others . . . but no one knew me like you, did they, Viktor? No one had reason to hate me the way you did, hmmm? The baron's free hand balled into a fist. He glanced impatiently around, then leaned toward Straas. "I am growing *impatient* with G'Meni. I want this to begin now, do you understand?"

"Lady DuPrise is not yet here, my baron, and it *cannot* begin before she—"

"I apologize for my delay, my love," came a voice from the baron's other side.

Both men turned, Straas barely hiding a sour expression. Lilaith DuPrise curtsied for Mandrol. She had removed her mask and now carried it in her hand.

"Lilaith." Her name tumbled from his lips. There was both desire and resentment in that one spoken word. "You are late."

"I am sorry." With her formal gown, it was impossible for her to sit in a chair like that used by either man, but a pair of servants quickly brought her a plush, padded bench over which her dress could rest without causing any embarrassment. Lilaith normally wore less bulky gowns and dresses, but this one was a perfect imitation of what she had been wearing that night and it was important that all the essential elements of the play remain consistent. Baron Mandrol demanded that. Lilaith DuPrise had been an irreplaceable part of that night.

From her hand had come the means for Viktor Falsche's destruction.

"It's done?"

She nodded in silence, turning away to accept a goblet of wine before the baron could study her face long.

"And what of our Master G'Meni? Is he in place?"

"Yes."

"It can begin now," General Straas announced quietly to his master.

"No one has neared the doorway."

"This is the shade of Viktor Falsche. He will find a way into the chamber. Unless Master G'Meni has for some reason failed to give him his commands, your puppet *must* follow through. He has no choice. So the alchemist keeps insisting."

Mandrol turned a darkening countenance toward him. "I *know* my creations, general. Do not seek to lecture me on their abilities and limitations."

"My apologies, my baron."

The next few minutes passed with a slowness that ate away at the baron's resolve. Mandrol's impatience began to affect Straas and, through Straas, his officers. The crowd, too, grew more and more tense. Laughter was tight and uncertain; the music was hesitant.

In an effort to calm himself, General Straas finally took a second, much deeper sip of his wine.

Something rattled lightly in the bottom of his goblet.

The dark wine did not allow him to make out what it was. Signaling one of his men, Straas took the other officer's chalice and began pouring his own wine into it. Baron Mandrol and the Lady DuPrise turned their attention to his deed, neither at all certain what to make of the soldier's peculiar act.

His goblet was over half empty before the general was able to identify the small object within.

A vial.

A tiny vial still—he exhaled in relief—sealed.

He rose from the chair, his gaze sweeping over the ballroom. A few of the masked guests glanced up, but none of the half-hidden faces before him was the one he now sought.

"Straas! What—"

The general thrust the goblet and its unusual contents toward the baron even as he turned to his officers. "I want Viathos sealed tight! I want all servants searched and anyone wandering around with a mask to be brought here! No one, absolutely *no* one, is to be allowed to leave this ballroom without my permission!"

By this time, Baron Mandrol had recognized the tiny object rolling around within the chalice. "This is . . ." His eyes sought those of the general. "Falsche!"

"Where is G'Meni?" roared Straas, ignoring the sudden hush his cry left in its wake. The guests and servants all stood staring, wondering what was amiss and whether it meant danger to themselves.

"Here!" G'Meni burst through one of the doorways. "Something is amiss! I feel it!" He turned on a drone soldier standing near the entrance through which he had just come. "The room! Check the room, dolt! He should have entered by now!"

Baron Mandrol looked at Lilaith, but her expression was one of honest confusion. He turned from her and rose.

A gloved hand stayed him. "No, my baron. It would be best if you remained here in case it is a trap."

Two soldiers had already made their way to the wooden door. One held his sword ready while the second pushed. The door swung open with ease. The soldiers, now joined by another identical pair, did not hesitate.

"They will find nothing," decided Mandrol before the last of the foursome was even through the doorway. "He is elsewhere in Viathos!"

"But I gave him specific commands!" insisted

G'Meni. "There was no possibility of diverging! He should have followed them to the letter."

"This is Viktor Falsche!" Disregarding the murmurs of the stricken throng, Straas loomed over the alchemist. "I warned you about thinking that anything involving Falsche could ever be trusted to follow as it should!"

"Never mind." Baron Mandrol ran his fingers along his temples. His voice grew almost calm, save for a little catch whenever he finished a sentence. "I should have known. I, of all who knew him, should have known that Viktor would ever play the hand his way and no other."

"Baron, the mask, it won't last forever, you know. It wasn't a permanent seal."

"Permanent enough, G'Meni, for him to kill me. I doubt that it will come off in the next minute or two. Straas, the patrols must also be alerted. Send forth the Morags as well."

"My baron, he is in Viathos! The way the original Falsche would have used is no longer available. Certainly it is not necessary to expand the search out—"

The look the dark-maned aristocrat gave the soldier was enough to silence Straas. "I can think of a dozen different ways that he could have used that vial in an attempt to complete his quest, but he chose instead to use it as a message." Mandrol studied the three figures around him, lingering longest on the strained countenance of Lilaith. "He intends to depart Viathos and lose himself in either the city section or the wilds beyond. *That* is why you must alert your forces beyond this wall. Perhaps we may still catch this makeshift creature within Viathos, but I want every possibility covered."

Straas, only a soldier regardless of his abilities, did not see what it was his baron saw. He did not know Falsche as his ruler did. "Why flee when his obsession is your death? Why run away to the city or the countryside?"

"Because he is now Viktor Falsche, Straas." Mandrol's expression hardened. "And Viktor Falsche would leave now so that he can return at a time of his own choosing . . . the better to complete the task *we* have given him a second chance to fulfill."

III

The path out had been sealed. No, more than that, the path looked as if it had been sealed for many years.

Viktor Falsche had not dared let that stop him. Whatever had happened to Dré and the exit, he still had to escape from Viathos. Although he had never expected the assassination attempt to become a trap for him, Viktor had been wise enough to assume that he might need to adapt to suddenly changing circumstances. If his means of escape was blocked off, then he would find or create another path.

Fortunately, a place as large as Viathos made it certain that a skilled and cunning person like himself would be able to find *some* avenue. It was all a matter of avoiding Mandrol's soldiers until then. Places like Viathos were designed to keep intruders out, not hold them in unless they were already prisoners in the dungeons below.

He thought of the dungeons and the possibility that Dré was a prisoner down there. Still, Viktor could hardly help him until he was free to make plans. His mind was still in turmoil, both because of Lilaith's evident betrayal and the peculiar memories that did not belong.

Viktor forced the confusion back as he wended his way through the stables. The information about Viathos for which he had paid so heavily included knowledge of an area near one of the gates where the roof of the stables rose almost high enough for an athletic man to make his way over the wall and into the city. There was nowhere to hook a rope, but Viktor did not need one; he had a tool that most ordinary assassins did not.

Sorcery.

It did not take him long to find the spot. The masque had actually worked in his favor, for with so many of the baron's toadies present for the event, the hands had their work cut out for them this evening. Grooms and stable boys had to make certain that every horse was cared for. They would pay little attention to him as long as he remained in the background. He had discarded the badger mask and removed much of the decor from his garments, making them much more subdued. Anyone looking close would notice the minor rips and strings, not to mention the fine tailoring still evident despite the dirt and grime that now marked the outfit, but from a distance, he could pass for a servant from the kitchens. Viktor only needed to do so for a few minutes, anyway. He had a cloak bundled under one arm, stolen from the chamber where the guests turned their outerwear over to Mandrol's servants, and would put it on once he was outside the walls.

As he climbed onto the roof, the first sounds of alarm reached him. A trio of soldiers darted into the open area before the stables, calling out to the sentries along the walls. Their words did not carry to him, but he knew what they were saying. There remained but another minute or two before he risked discovery.

Looking up, Viktor Falsche saw that his information was correct. Here, the wall was only another nine or ten feet higher than he was. The top of the wall was rounded at this point, which would have prevented most leapers from gaining a handhold even if they were capable of jumping so high from the creaking and angled stable roof.

It was time to make use of his power. Mandrol himself might be protected by a variety of spells and wards, but it was very doubtful that he had wasted energy warding his entire citadel.

Viktor concentrated . . . and found himself no closer to the top than he had been before. Almost there had been the familiar tingle that marked the usage of sorcery, but for some reason successful completion of the spell had evaded him.

Now he worried about the sentries.

More and more men were spilling out into the open from every doorway and passage within Viathos. Shouts had gone up everywhere in the edifice.

Viktor tried again.

Still nothing.

The creaking behind him was just enough warning to save his head.

A guardsman with the face of General Straas confronted him. Viktor felt both compassion and anger and knew that he dared not let the former emotion prevent him from doing what needed to be done. He had been forced to discard the ceremonial weapon he had worn in the ballroom, but that did not mean he was helpless. As the drone soldier slashed again, Falsche dropped and kicked out with his foot.

His reflexes were horribly slow compared to what he was used to, but there was more force behind the blow than Viktor expected. Struck near the knee, the armored figure stumbled. With a grunt, the pale soldier tried to regain his balance, but he was already slipping. Viktor reached out and helped him on his way.

Even as the man slid off the roof, the escaping assassin once more attempted the spell that would levitate him over the wall. It should have been a reasonable but not difficult effort for him, but success still refused to embrace him.

Below, he could hear the sounds of other soldiers entering the stables. Gritting his teeth, Viktor Falsche began muttering the words of the air, the litany that would call the spirits of the wind to aid him in rising. He called upon them to lift him, to free him of the shackles their earth cousins demanded of all humans. It was only a small favor that he desired, for once over the wall they could return him to the earth.

Slowly, at first almost imperceptibly, he rose.

It was an unsteady, unnerving ascent. Twice his climb faltered, but at last Viktor crossed over and began his descent. The earth below was much farther down than he had anticipated and the thought that he might plummet to his death grated on him. He did not dare hasten the journey down, however, for fear he would succeed in doing so all too well.

Even still, he was more than ten feet from the ground when the levitation spell suddenly faded.

Forewarned by the precariousness of the ascent, he was as ready as he could be. Viktor struck the ground in a crouched position. Nothing was broken, but every bone in his body shook from the impact. Viktor Falsche was glad that the night had shielded him from prying eyes; his pursuers notwithstanding, he would have been shamed had someone witnessed his poor, feeble spell.

Something must have happened to him while he had been biding his time preparing for the aborted assassination. Perhaps it had been something to do with the vial. Maybe he had not had to open it for the contents to affect him. Maybe all it had taken was for him to touch it. Mandrol and the others wanted him not only helpless but humiliated as well, and dampening his sorcery might well have been a step they had taken to achieve the latter.

As Viktor donned the cloak and pulled up the hood, he allowed himself a sour smile. Hindered he was, yes, but Baron Mandrol should have realized that even without his power, Viktor Falsche was by no means helpless. He would return for his enemy when he was ready to take him . . . even if it meant seizing Mandrol's throat in his bare hands and squeezing the life out of him.

He found the horse where the owner had carelessly left it, evidently not realizing that Medecia had its share of thieves. Viktor talked to the animal in soothing, understanding tones as he untied it and mounted. Not a moment too soon, either, for the patrols were starting to range farther and farther from Viathos. Three times he had slipped past riders and twice he had been forced to hide from men on foot. One soldier lay dead in a back alley, a life uselessly shed because Viktor had had no choice. Slave or drone soldiers the creatures with the general's abominable features might be called, but behind the masks were men torn from their families and friends, men who had ceased to exist the moment Straas's brand had covered their faces. They would kill Viktor as willingly as the mercenaries and officers who had no false faces with which to excuse their atrocities. Therefore, he, in turn, had no choice but to kill them first.

Under the shroud of night, it was difficult to make out every detail of the city as he rode toward the eastern gate, and such trivial matters should not even have bothered him, but Viktor kept sensing something unsettling about his surroundings. Things were out of place that should not have been and other, familiar landmarks appeared slightly altered. It was as if someone had rebuilt part of the city while he had been plotting within the walls of Viathos. That was preposterous, however, for even Mandrol's sorcery was not capable of making so many detailed changes. Viktor finally came to the conclusion that he was taking a slightly different path than the one he was familiar with, but although that answer was the more reasonable one, it still did not alleviate his anxiety.

"You there! Halt! Show your face!"

He brought the horse up short as a pair of the baron's men, one bearing a torch and both armed with blades, stepped out from a side avenue. The torch bearer wore the face of Straas, but not only did the other bear features of his own, he was also clad in an officer's uniform.

The ride had given Viktor the opportunity to recuperate after his near-disastrous levitation spell, but he was not certain that he had the strength for anything major. Sorcery still seemed alien to him somehow, a most peculiar sensation.

It did not matter. The officer's eyes suddenly widened in recognition and he raised his sword toward the figure on the horse. "It's him! It's Fal—"

The last was cut off as Viktor urged the horse into the pair. The officer tumbled out of the animal's path, but the drone soldier, not quite so agile, was bowled over. Unfortunately, Viktor's borrowed mount grew excited by the activity and attempted to fight his control. Falsche cursed and brought the animal back under sway, only then to have to quickly shift as the officer tried to thrust the blade into his side. He kicked at the man, but missed.

Viktor slipped off the horse on the opposite side, but

retained a grip on the reins. Maneuvering the horse so that it stood between him and the soldier, he sought out the sword of the other attacker, who was still struggling to rise.

Another sword thrust nearly pierced his left leg at the knee just as he stooped to pick up the weapon. Fortunately, the officer had still not thought of the obvious and simply killed the horse first, leaving Viktor with no moving shield. Sword ready in one hand, Falsche suddenly threw himself over the saddle and swung in the direction of his adversary. The officer cursed as a lucky stroke caught him on the side of the face. Cheek bleeding from a two-inch slash, he stumbled back but still kept his own blade at the ready.

From the other side, the second attacker grabbed Viktor's leg and tried to pull him off. Viktor tried to push him away, but succeeded only in tearing the man's helmet from his head.

The officer chose that point to lunge. He had miscalculated his advantage, for Viktor saw him with his peripheral vision and brought his sword down. It was more by luck than skill that this time he caught the man full in the face. The officer screamed and collapsed, his head a bleeding wound.

A kick threw the remaining soldier back. Unarmed and alone now, he chose instead to do what Viktor would have done in the first place; he shouted the alarm. It was likely that the battle had already alerted others nearby, but the cry now left no doubt as to Viktor Falsche's whereabouts. He cursed and urged the anxious horse on, not even taking time to toss away the helmet.

All around him, Viktor heard people shouting and horses running. Lanterns in homes were lit and confused civilians wandered out from various buildings to see what was happening. The sound of metal against metal warned him that other soldiers were already drawing near. He turned down a darkened, more narrow street, hoping that it would slow any pack of pursuers on horseback while at the same time praying that he had not just steered himself into a cul-de-sac.

He had not. Fortune was with Viktor for the moment, for the street proved to be a shortcut. He could see that the gate was not that far ahead. He also knew that the sentries there would be alerted to the news that a deadly fugitive might be racing their way. There was no possibility that he would have the strength to levitate himself again, which left him only with a few less savory options. Viktor cursed and started to throw away the useless helm he realized he still clutched in his hand, wondering why he had held on to it even this long.

He kept his grip on it only by the sheerest chance. An idea formed, one that would only work *because* of the helmet. Viktor prayed that the officer he had killed had worn it for quite some time. If it was new or even fairly recent in age, he was about to betray himself.

Only a short distance from his destination, he quickly forced the helmet on. It was a tight, almost unbearable fit, but he ignored the pressure and began to concentrate. No one was around at the moment, which also gave him the privacy he desperately needed. His plan could not work if someone was there to observe its unveiling.

This time, he whispered no words, simply tried to picture the man who had owned the object. He tried to recall everything that he could about the soldier's appearance and hoped that he would not mix that image with the one of the officer dying. It would not do to arrive at the gate looking like a bloody corpse.

A wave of nausea nearly sent him falling from the horse, but Viktor prevailed. He either now looked like his late foe or like himself. There was only one way to be certain.

There were more than half a dozen men standing in front of the gate. Several others, many of them archers, mounted the wall. Everyone was looking at him. That they had not yet charged or pierced him like a porcupine with their arrows was promising.

"Who goes?" cried one.

"Open the gate, you damned fool!" Viktor Falsche snarled. "I have to get out there to warn the outer patrols!"

"Someone went through only a few moments ago!" The speaker, a bearded, heavyset, but quite efficient-looking veteran looked the rider over with the one eye remaining to him. Viktor took him to be the captain of the gate. "We've no orders to let anyone else through."

"And you think there was time to let you know everything? We've word on the criminal! I have to reach the others before it's too late, man! Do *you* want to explain to the general why I never contacted them? Do you?"

Invoking Straas proved to do the trick. Without another glance at the mysterious officer before him, the captain turned to his men and waved for the gate to be opened. Viktor waited impatiently while they slowly unbolted and swung open the massive wooden doors. As soon as the opening was wide enough to permit him through, he urged the horse forward.

"Move aside!" he roared. Two of the soldiers had to scatter quickly to avoid being run down. As Viktor charged through the open entrance, he twisted around and shouted to the captain, "No one else gets through without the general's authority! No one!"

The veteran officer replied, but his words were lost to Viktor Falsche, who had to struggle to maintain control of not only the illusion he had cast, but also both his mount and the growing nausea within.

Again, this latest ploy would buy him only minutes, but that would have to do. Someone would soon realize what had happened. By that time, Viktor would be well on his way to the wild lands, where he stood a better chance of completing his escape.

Paradoxically, reaching the wild lands would also increase his chances of being killed.

He did not realize that he had passed out until several seconds after he had woken again. Only when Viktor took a careful look at the darkened landscape around him did he discover that he was now on the very edge of the wild lands. The last of the farms was behind him now and the hills and woods were beginning to dominate. That meant a substantial amount of time wherein he had ridden without knowledge or care of his path. It was fortunate that he had not fallen from his mount.

Thankful as he was that he had still somehow managed to make it this far, Viktor was disturbed by his weakness. The nausea, the headache, and the lack of strength were all disturbing signs. It was almost as if his body were repelled by the act of sorcery. Toward the end, he had barely been able to maintain the illusion.

Thinking of that, Viktor Falsche reached up. The helmet was gone, lost somewhere behind him. He was grateful for the relief, but now the illusion was definitely lost to him. There would be no deceiving the patrols with that trick.

Not for one minute did he think that he was safe. There would not only be pursuers on his heels but also the outland patrols. Whether Straas had some means of alerting them other than riders, Viktor could not say, but they would be wary of a lone traveler journeying through the wild lands in the middle of the night. Only fools and folk with dark deeds on their minds would travel at such a time.

The nausea was still with him, although his unexpected slumber had eased the sensation. He was not naive, however. Another forced use of sorcery would increase the sickness tenfold again, possibly causing him to pass out once more. If that happened, he was surely dead.

He could *not* die, though, not until he was certain that Mandrol was also dead.

The wild lands were actually beautiful in their own way and perhaps if things had been different, Viktor Falsche would have admired that beauty, but he was too aware of the fact that he now faced threats beyond simply that posed by his pursuers. There were things that haunted the woods and hills, things older than the power of Baron Mandrol or himself. There were the typical wild creatures, bears, cats, meredrakes, and such, but there were also the trolls, the water fairies, and, of course, the Morags.

As if to punctuate his thoughts, he heard the sounds of several horses galloping toward him. Suddenly alert, Viktor urged his mount to a gallop. He did not know how long he could expect the already-abused animal to keep up such a pace, but if the horse got him into the deep woods, that was all he could ask.

A cry warned him that either he or his trail had been noticed.

The sounds of the wild ceased abruptly as the chase entered the land. If men were wary of this region, then the creatures here had just as much cause to be wary of them. Only a Morag or a high drake would consider remaining in the vicinity of an armed party of Mandrol's soldiers.

The woods thickened and the ground grew more uneven. The path that Viktor had chosen became more and more simply a forest trail, then even less than that. His horse began to stumble and often he had to steer through narrow gaps between trees. Behind him, the patrol pursued, silent hunters save for the occasional curse as some low branch snagged a helmet or some horse momentarily lost its footing.

They were catching up. He would never make it unless . . .

He slowed his mount enough so that he could leap off. The animal slowed after that, but he gave it a hard slap on the hindquarters, which set it off and running again.

Viktor ducked low and ran to his right. He crouched down, the cloak pulled over him, just as the first of the baron's riders raced past. The man did not even pause, nor did the two that followed after. Viktor had neither the strength nor the stomach to cast another illusion, but the night hid him well enough, for each rider that materialized continued on without hesitation. They would discover before long that the horse they followed was running free, but by then he would be deep into the wild lands. The darkness was his ally and by the time the sun rose, he would be well on his way to his destination.

That confidence lasted just long enough for the Morag to find him.

He was several minutes from where he had abandoned the horse when he first noticed that one of the massive, tall shadows in the forest was not a tree. It did not move at first, but what he could make out in the dark was enough to tell the sorcerer that it was likely one of Baron Mandrol's monstrous servants. Viktor Falsche stopped in his tracks. Sight of the beast sent an unfamiliar shiver through him.

Morags were a terrible danger, but he had never felt like this before. The urge to run, to put as much distance between himself and the stalker was too great. Viktor struggled, knowing on one level that it was far safer to stand still until the Morag itself departed, but in the end he turned. It was as if a different person controlled him.

The Morag, with its vast, batwing ears, could not help but hear him crashing through the woods.

Dull thuds announced each heavy step of the creature. It moved at a slower pace than a human, but that was made up by the length of its stride. Morags were nearly twice the height of men and about four times their mass, most of it muscle. If this one was like most, it wielded either a two-handed ax, for which the monster required only one hand, or a wooden club about Viktor's height.

Now that he had no choice but flight, Viktor put his mind to seek out the path that would least hinder him but put obstacle after obstacle in the Morag's way. The same sort of narrow gaps that had hindered his riding were now his only hope. The Morag was two or three times wider than a normal human and could not squeeze through such confined places. Unfortunately, Viktor quickly discovered, the monster simply *crashed* his way through. Trees were sent flying. Worse yet, even despite the Morag's need to pause whenever the path was blocked, Viktor Falsche was still losing ground.

Now exhaustion threatened to defeat the sorcerer. He came to the point where cramping nearly made him tumble. The Morag was so close now that he could hear its breathing, a harsh, raspy noise that did not indicate any exhaustion on the creature's own part. For the first time, it uttered a sound, a swift procession of staccato grunts; Morag amusement. It knew it had him.

The unreasoning fear that had made him flee in the first place overwhelmed Viktor once more. He leaped without caution over a tangle of upturned tree roots.

His foot caught on one. Arms akimbo, Falsche tumbled toward the ground. He was barely able to keep his face from slamming against the hard earth, nearly breaking a wrist in the process of saving himself.

Viktor freed his foot and rolled onto his back.

Smiling horror loomed over him, the black shape of an enormous double-edged ax in one head-sized fist.

The ears flickered back and forth much the way a dog's might, but there was nothing canine about the Morag. Morags were distantly related to trolls, but it generally meant death to the troll when the two met in confrontation.

Even in the black of night, Viktor Falsche could make out the basic details of the monster's grotesque features. The Morag had a squashed, almost flat face that looked as if someone had then stretched it wide just to make it that much uglier. Its nose was a narrow bridge that stretched across its face. The almond-shaped eyes lacked any visible pupil and in the dark glowed purple. Morags had no eyelids.

Below the stretch of nose was an even wider stretch of mouth ever curled toward the ends into a smile. The mouth reminded Viktor of that of a frog, save that most frogs did not have three rows of jagged teeth each the size of his index finger. Now and then, a long, dripping tongue darted out.

The staccato grunts began again. In the light of day, the Morag would have been a slight orange in tint, but in the night, this one looked as pale as the dead. The Morag wore a horned helm, a meredrake-scale breastplate with shoulder guards, and a kilt. Since Morags in the wild wore only kilts, it was obvious that this was one of those monsters who obeyed the edicts of Viathos.

"Morag meat . . ." the huge monstrosity rumbled. It was an impressive speech for one of its kind. Morags did not have proper vocal cords; their native tongue consisted of an astonishing variety of grunts and snarls.

Viktor stared at his doom, wishing he had the strength to summon light. Morags had trouble adjusting from daylight to darkness to daylight again. It took them quite some time. Even the light of a single torch would have bought him a moment's reprieve. Amid his fear he also felt anger that *he*, Viktor Falsche, should die cringing before this beast. It was an ignominious end. Better if he had died trying to assassinate Mandrol. At least that would have been a worthy death.

The Morag reached down with its free paw. The helpless sorcerer expected his head to be crushed, but instead his horrific captor lifted him by the front of his shirt and raised him into the air without any visible strain.

It sniffed him. "Smell funny." A shrug. "Still food."

Viktor Falsche stared at the opening mouth.

It was fear that saved him, the same fear that had led him to this predicament. The strength he had lacked only a moment before now filled him, as the unreasoning fear that did not seem his own nearly overcame him again. Only by the greatest effort was he able to channel that strength, but channel it he did.

A tiny sun burst before the eyes of the Morag. Viktor shut his eyes and braced himself.

The monstrosity shrieked, its lidless eyes seared by the brilliant light.

Mindful of nothing but its agony, the Morag tossed aside its prey, dropped its ax, and tried to wipe the blindness from its eyes.

The landing was harsh, but not nearly so harsh as the nausea and throbbing that struck Viktor the next moment. Nonetheless, he stumbled to his feet, arms wrapped around his stomach, and wobbled away as fast as he could from his stricken captor. The Morag ignored him, caught up in its own misery.

He doubted that its blindness was permanent; the beasts had resilient orbs. Viktor only hoped that he would be far, far away when it recovered. Better the patrol on his heels than an enraged, wounded Morag.

Thinking of the patrols, the sorcerer quickened his pace as best he could. With soldiers everywhere, it was likely that someone had heard the Morag's cry. A patrol would be along to investigate. Of course, then they would have to deal with the agonized creature, which meant that they would have their hands full. Viktor pitied the men who first came across the beast. This Morag would not be able to distinguish between friend and foe for some time.

He ran and ran and when his body cried that it could run no farther, Viktor Falsche forced it on. At least twice he heard the clatter of horses and once the movements of something large in the woods close by. The ground grew more uneven, a sign that he was entering the high hills. Vaguely the worn sorcerer understood that he was near his destination. Yet, there were growing doubts in his mind concerning whether he would make it. It was his body, he decided; it was not behaving as it should. He was a sorcerer in fit, nearly perfect health. His was a body long-trained in the arts and well used to the rigors that those arts entailed. He was also a swordsman, a warrior, who kept his body fit for the trials of physical danger facing Mandrol would require.

Why, then, had his body turned on him? What had happened during this long night in Viathos?

It took him minutes to discover that he was no longer running, that he was, in fact, facedown in the hard, rocky soil of a hillside. How long he had been sprawled here, Viktor could not say. He tried to rise, but it felt so much better to simply remain where he was.

The minutes blurred together. At last Viktor Falsche heard the stomp of boots. He had failed. Mandrol had him. It had taken more effort than the good baron had no doubt expected, but he at last had his hated adversary in his hands.

A hand that was not the baron's took hold of his shoulder and carefully turned him over. Through eyes nearly shut, the beaten sorcerer caught glimpses of a dim, red glow and a head, only a silhouette in the dark, leaning over him.

"Eyes of Ariela! *Viktor?* You . . . it can't be!"

With what little strength he could muster, Falsche managed a smile and gasped, "What . . . went wrong . . . Dré?

IV

Baron Mandrol did not sleep that night. Instead he paced the length of his chamber, hoping more than expecting that at any moment a messenger would arrive to say that the patrols had either captured or killed the runaway. Straas would present him with the infernal mask, and before the general and the others, especially Lady Lilaith, Baron Mandrol would burn the offending horror, putting an end to the legacy of Viktor Falsche.

No messenger arrived. Straas did not even come to inform him that the patrols, including the Morags, were still searching. After a time, Mandrol tired of the useless pacing and departed from his chamber.

G'Meni was at work when the baron pushed the door aside and entered. It seemed that the alchemist never slept, which for once infuriated his master.

The chill in Mandrol's voice was enough to make G'Meni straighten in sudden fear for his continued existence. "Tell me why you are here, tinkering with your experiments, when a cretin who thinks and acts like Viktor Falsche is still at large! Tell me why and tell me good, so that I can decide whether to have your hide peeled from your body or simply have your head cut off."

"I am . . . I'm endeavoring to do what I do best, Baron, in order to understand what happened and how to rectify it." The misshapen alchemist recovered some of his poise. "I am no use to Straas. He knows that and I know that. I may best serve you by what I do now, baron."

"And what's it you claim to do here? I think, as I

created the first mask, that it might be of interest to me, don't you?"

"This." Master G'Meni stepped aside so that Mandrol could see his latest project.

It was a mask . . . one of *those* masks. The baron was so repelled that he stepped back. The face, one whose name he could not quite recall at the moment, stared at the ceiling with empty eye holes. The mouth moved once, but that was the only sign of activity. "Why did you bring out another of those things? I should have them all destroyed, now that I think of it! How many more are there like Falsche? How many more?"

"None."

"What's that you say?"

"This is the sixteenth mask that I have tested since the notion occurred to me. It reacts exactly as it should. There are no deviations and I have made a careful scientific record to back up this statement, you know."

Mandrol was not convinced. Suppressing his sudden fear and dislike of the very collection that he had created, the master of Viathos seized his adviser and dragged him close enough so that his wide, flat nose nearly touched the remnants of G'Meni's own.

"The mask of Viktor Falsche *also* behaved as expected. I seem to recall those very words from you earlier, yes?"

G'Meni attempted to disengage himself from Mandrol's clutches, then thought better of it. Meeting the dark gaze, he sputtered, "But none of the others were created under the same circumstances."

"Meaning?"

The alchemist swallowed. "Meaning that Viktor Falsche was *not* dying when the impression was taken."

Lowering the ugly figure, Baron Mandrol eyed the mask resting on the table. He had created the masks, true, but his memories had grown hazy over the years concerning their limitations and development. In truth, he had come to rely on Master G'Meni too much. Still . . . "The life was still strong in Falsche?"

"He would have survived if the mask had not been made. Instead" —at last G'Meni untangled himself from Mandrol's grasp— "his greater strength, his greater will, was *absorbed* into the impression."

The baron stared into empty space. "The mask is nearly as much Viktor Falsche as Viktor Falsche himself was."

"That is the essence of it, yes, Baron." Master G'Meni turned back toward his work. "But always recall that he *is* a mask, a face without a man. Either the general will hunt him down or the ghost of Viktor Falsche will fade away as the mask loses its hold on its host. The sealant will not last long out in the wilds, where the dampness and cold will weaken it. We can outwait him, Baron Mandrol. He has no sorcery at his command. He does not even realize his time is so very short. *We* do."

Not at all mollified but unable to deny the alchemist's words, the baron exhaled. Wait he would, albeit not by choice, but Mandrol had not risen to his position by depending solely on others. There *were* measures he could take on his own, measures that only his sorcery could make work. Baron Mandrol would end this thing with Viktor Falsche as it should have ended those many years before, even if he had to kill him a thousand times again.

He turned to the door, intending to depart, when a matter of some question occurred to him. "G'Meni, who was it who took the impression?"

Although his back was still to the alchemist, the sorcerer baron could sense G'Meni turn and stare at his back. "It was I, of course."

"I cannot recall what we did with the corpse."

"It was burned and the ashes spread to the winds, Baron, as per your commands."

"Ah, yes. Of course."

Mandrol stalked out the door, shutting it behind him and therefore not noticing the fearful glance that played briefly across Master G'Meni's horrid countenance.

"Who are you?"

He was surrounded by a gray haze. The voice that questioned him floated from every direction.

Slowly his mouth worked. "Viktor Falsche."

"Viktor Falsche is dead."

"Dead?" He was not. He could not be. Did he not stand here before—

He did not. Viktor tried to raise a hand and found he had none to raise. He was as bodiless as his inquisitor.

"I am not dead." His words sounded hollow to him, but he refused to accept the alternative. "I am alive!"

"You are not Viktor Falsche."

"I am!" He reached out again with his nonexistent hands and somehow caught hold of something. A savage smile crossed his face. He had control. "I am Viktor Falsche."

The gray haze became the inside of a small, dimly lit chamber carved out of the earth. His hands clutched the neck of the tunic worn by a graying, mustached figure with wide, fear-struck eyes.

"For the love of Ariela, Viktor!"

"Dré?" His fingers uncurled, releasing the other. Only now did Viktor notice that he had been lying in a bed of furs and cloth. His legs were bound and the tattered pieces of leather straps dangled from his wrists. He eyed the straps, then glared at the figure he had first thought was his friend and confederate. The man looked much like Dré Kopien, but he was too old, too unkempt. This was not Dré, then, but rather someone who had made use of his resemblance to attempt to trick Viktor.

He raised a hand, summoning up what power he could.

"Viktor! Gods, man! Don't you recognize your old friend? It's been ten years and I thought you dead, but—"

The power was slow in responding. The same touch of nausea threatened to overwhelm him again, but he tried to ignore it.

The other's words finally registered. Viktor's hand froze. He glared at the false Dré. "What did you say? Ten years? Ten years since what?"

"Since you never came out of Viathos, man!" The graying figure scratched at a short, scraggly beard. "Since I thought you'd died at Mandrol's cursed hands—"

"There's been no ten years passing and you are a fool for trying such an idiotic trick!" Viktor tried to bring his sorcery into play. It was coming, but slowly. He was also not certain just how powerful his spell would be. "Try something a bit more realistic!"

"Look at me, Viktor!" The bearded man planted his hands on his chest. "Darken the hair, cut the beard, and dress me in garb that doesn't look like that of the shepherd I'm forced to play!"

His captor did resemble Dré, but that could easily have been thanks to the work of Mandrol and his toady, G'Meni. That likely meant that Dré was dead.

Before he could do anything, the other man started talking as quickly as he could. "Remember Wesfrancia! Remember what we did when we found Mandrol's man Hesprin! He had the bag with him, the one you and I had been searching for, man! You gutted that devilish south-lander without giving him a chance to fight, which was still too good for a sorcerer trafficking in soul-snaring!"

Viktor paused. The scene flashed before him. Hesprin, almost as dark as Lilaith in skin color, but far, far darker than her in spirit. The bag he had been ferrying to his master was the reason for Falsche dropping all else and beginning the hunt. Mandrol had gone too far. He had chosen one victim too many, a woman named Cordelia who had not even been his enemy, but who had made the mistake of marrying the son and heir of one.

She had been spirited away to Wesfrancia to seek refuge with her brother, but had been taken within sight of his home.

Viktor's home.

He blamed himself for his sister's death. He should have heeded the warning signs, but like many Viktor had not realized the distance Mandrol's tentacles could stretch. In his mind, that did not excuse him. He was a sorcerer of standing and prowess; such a tragic error should have been beyond him. Cordelia had died because of his failure as much as the baron's evil. Not even the most adamant arguments of Dré or Lilaith had ever been able to convince him otherwise.

There had been three boxes in Hesprin's bag. Two had been empty, but Viktor knew that he and Dré had been marked for them. The third, the only part of his mission in which the lanky sorcerer had succeeded before *he* had become the hunted, had held the still-beating heart of a young woman.

All Viktor's power had not been sufficient to bring Cordelia back, but at least he had had the satisfaction of guaranteeing that no one would find enough of Hesprin to try to summon his ghost. The foul sorcerer was spread across a dozen distant lands now.

The memories were enough to give him the will he needed to destroy the man before him, the man who had dared remind him so fully of how he had come to these straits.

The false Dré must have read the darkness in his eyes, for he raised both hands in a gesture of absolute surrender and cried out, "We burned the box in the temple of Ariela, to whom she had pledged her faith and to whom I swore mine that night because of that horror! Cordelia's ashes we spread across the Wesfrancia River, as is the custom of Ariela's faith in that region! There was only the two of us, man! You and me! Who else would know?"

"Mandrol *might*," Viktor replied, but he lowered his hand. It was not the tale, horrible as it was, that moved him to believe, but the distress, the despair, in the other's every word and breath that convinced him that this was Dré Kopien. Each inflection, each quiver, bespoke the man who had been Viktor's constant companion and the one who had lost the woman he loved first to another man, then to a terrible death.

"Mandrol could, I suppose." Dré slumped. "Mandrol's been capable of everything else, hasn't he? He even had you . . . I thought."

"Dré?" He had to repeat his rescuer's name twice

before the graying man looked up. There was a darkness in Dré's eyes. "Ten years, you said. Tell me. Prove it to me."

"Look at me, man. Look at how far I've fallen from our days in school. Do you think I'd be doing this to myself? This is ten and more years of dodging soldiers and Morags and trying somehow to find a way to complete what we began." Dré shook his head. "And all I've done is grow older and more useless while Mandrol extends his power beyond his borders and forces your Lilaith to dance his tune."

Lilaith. "She was there. She betrayed me, Dré! She gave me over to Mandrol as easily as breathing. I never suspected her."

"She had no choice, Viktor. Mandrol's directing her. He broke her will and made her his smiling slave. She's suffered worse than me these years, I'd say."

Something did not make sense. "But it only happened this night, Dré. I only tried to assassinate Mandrol *this* night, do you understand?"

"Your mind's still addled. It was ten years ago, Viktor. I waited in that kitchen area until the guards were nearly on me. I barely escaped them as it was. It was ten years ago . . . this very night, I think . . . and you never came out of Viathos."

"It was *tonight*, Dré." Even as he repeated that, the visions he had suffered while preparing for Mandrol's assassination returned. Again he saw himself cross the floor, work his way through the crowd of vermin gathered to honor the devil baron, and enter the opposing chamber. He saw the vial opened, his words cut off, and his body collapsing.

He saw G'Meni leaning over him, covering his face.

Despite himself, Viktor shuddered.

Had it not been a vision, but rather a memory? Had he indeed failed in his quest ten years prior?

"And where have I been, then?" he whispered.

Dré had moved away and therefore had not heard the whisper. The graying figure returned with a small bowl full of hot stew, which he handed to his companion. "I think that you should eat some of this."

The smell of food made Viktor Falsche realize how famished he was. He seized the bowl from his friend's hands and began wolfing the stew down. Only when he had devoured several mouthfuls did he look up again, and that was to find Dré studying him with a quizzical look.

"What is it?"

"Must be ten years of weariness." Dré forced a smile. "I would swear that your eyes are different. Still green, but not the green I recall. You look a little broader, too."

Viktor stopped eating. His eyes narrowed. "I am me, Dré. Make no mistake. This is no illusion."

"I know Viktor Falsche, man. I know him better than anyone. You're different than before, but I cannot deny that you're you. Let it rest, Viktor. I apologize for bringing it up."

"I have ten years that I can't account for, Dré, so the apology is mine. Consider this just one more thing that Mandrol owes for, one more reason to drag him down."

"You still intend to return to Viathos? You still intend to try to kill Mandrol?" Dré Kopien's voice was tinged by years of futility and a growing sense of regret. "The last time, neither you nor Lilaith returned."

"Lilaith is still inside." Viktor studied his friend. There were hints of what the past years had been like. For Viktor Falsche, the ten years had passed without notice; for Dré Kopien, they had been long and hard, each moment a reminder of the failure that had left him bereft of his two friends. "*Mandrol* is inside. Do you think that I could walk away from Viathos?"

Dré sighed and reached for a water sack. Neither of them needed to speak, for they both knew the answer to Viktor's question.

Now it was only a question of *when* he would return . . . and what would happen then.

It was dark again when Viktor next rose, the hot meal having lulled him to sleep but minutes after he had finished it. The darkness was not confined simply to the earthen sanctum he and Dré had created so long ago, but also the world outside. Viktor wondered how long he had slept.

The sanctum had been dug out of earth and rock and over it was created a false impression of more rock and shrubbery. Trees and a careful casting of illusion also aided in its disguise. All in all, it was a difficult place to find unless one knew exactly where to look, and even more difficult to locate for one who had not seen it in ten years. There was enough moonlight to inform Viktor that the landmarks he recalled had altered some. The trees were taller, the shrubbery thicker, and the rock formation had shifted. Left to his own devices, he probably would have never noticed that he had reached it.

The interior had already existed, some natural formation that the ages had dug out of the hill. It had been lived in at some time in the past, probably by a Morag if the broken and chewed animal bones they found were any indication. Dré had been the first to suggest its use as their base. In the end, it had become their home.

Dré knew the place all too well. Viktor had more trouble accepting the idea of ten years of hiding than accepting the same period simply erased from memory. If his old comrade wondered where Viktor had been the past decade, then Viktor, in turn, wanted to know what Dré had actually been doing with his own time.

Ten years lost to both of them. Ten years too many for Baron Mandrol to have lived. Ten years too long for the ghost of a young woman to wait for justice.

And ten years too long for my vengeance! He turned in the direction of the city and Viathos. Lilaith was also there. If what Dré said was true, she had suffered even greater than the rest. What had she been forced to do in the name of Mandrol?

Revenge and justice intermingled in his mind, becoming so entwined that Viktor Falsche had trouble telling which was which. It did not really matter to him as long as the outcome was the same. He knew that Lilaith, Dré, and his sister would have fretted over such thinking, but he considered himself a pragmatist.

A harsh whisper shattered his thoughts. "What are you doing out here, Viktor? Suppose a Morag is nearby!"

Dré Kopien no doubt would have said more, but his mouth clamped tight when Viktor turned his gaze on him. The dim light of the moon was still sufficient for the two men to see one another's features.

"Thinking. Wondering. What have you done all these years, my friend? Why is Mandrol still reigning merrily in Viathos while you are out here wasting your life? Why isn't one of you dead? We both swore to see this through to the end, whatever that end was." His voice was a dangerous rumble. "Lilaith is still in there, too—"

"I *know* Lilaith is still in there! I also know that it finally became pretty damn clear what that end would be!" snapped his companion. "It took your disappearance to teach me that, man! This is more than simply a blood price between ourselves and him! This is about *Medecia*. It isn't enough to bring down Mandrol! Straas will do what his kind always does; he will strike out at the population, slaughter innocents, in order to teach some lesson they will never understand. In the end, they will curse your name as much as his, for you will cause them to suffer more."

They both knew the general and they both knew that he would do exactly as Dré had said. "There's nothing I can do about that," Viktor replied. They will still be better off without Mandrol in the long run. Lilaith will be better off."

"Tell them that as they watch their children and mates slaughtered by their own kin. Tell them that as Straas sends his unholy drone soldiers through the city and countryside. He'll know that all's lost, man, and he'll be taking everything he can before he either escapes or falls. Maybe even Lilaith." Dré stared at him, waiting for some kind of acknowledgment. When none seemed forthcoming, he exhaled bitterly. "I forget. You haven't had ten years to come to this conclusion."

"And have you done more than come to a conclusion?" pressed Viktor.

"Have I done anything? Oh, yes. We have supporters everywhere. Quite a network of spies, too. Safe houses in the city. Groups that harass the merchant caravans of anyone loyal to the baron. More than one attempt to try to free Lilaith from Mandrol's spell . . . and enough deaths of good men during each failure. Oh . . . and trying to start a revolution, too, one that won't leave Medecia a burning, raped land." A pause. "But I suppose nothing that means much to your plans."

A curtain of silence hung between them for several seconds, then the sorcerer forced a smile and put a companionable hand on his old comrade's shoulder. "You would be wrong there. You would be very wrong. What you've done is given me some food for thought."

"I have had enough feasting on such fare. I am weary of it, Viktor. Each night I fight with nightmares. I see Cordelia before her death, Lilaith in Mandrol's arms, and until tonight I even saw you as our dear friend the false baron had his executioner prune your head from your body."

"Which he has not done yet. Mandrol will be ours and Medecia freed with no further bloodshed than there must absolutely be. I will see to that."

"You cannot even recall where you have been the past decade, man! There's something else wrong, too, but it's something you've not chosen to share with me. You still think you can fight Mandrol?"

Viktor started back to the hidden sanctuary before replying, "Yes."

Growling, Dré leaped after him. "And how do you plan to do that? What's your secret, Viktor? Face me and tell me this wonderful news, won't you, man?"

The sorcerer opened the entrance just enough for them to slip through one at a time, then confronted his comrade. "Actually, it does concern faces, but for now, I won't say any more. Just trust me, Dré. There are a few more things I need to do. One more step to take."

"I still remember that you mentioned some other plan that night you left. Is that what you're talking of? You wouldn't tell me of it then, either. Are we friends or not?"

Viktor Falsche steered Dré past him into the hidden sanctum. His old companion, could no longer see his features, for which the sorcerer was grateful. "Yes, we are and, yes, that's the one, Dré . I was never able to finish preparations. Now I have the chance."

"Well, I hope you bother to tell me what it concerns some day, man. I've always wondered."

Viktor began to seal the entrance. He was only mildly concerned about patrols and Morags. At the moment, his thoughts concerned his plan for returning to Viathos and completing his mission. He had been bluffing when he told Dré that he had something in mind. Until his companion had mentioned that Viktor had already had another plot prepared, he was simply hoping something new would occur to him by morning. Now reminded of his prior intentions, he wished that he had discussed the older plan with Dré, especially its more intimate details. It would have been good to hear the other's opinion . . . not to mention just exactly what those details had been.

An itch developed along the edge of his jaw. Viktor absently scratched it, trying to resolve this new crisis. Yes, there was a plan, but what it was remained shadowed. It was almost as if it had been a plan wrought by someone else and not him. His memory had always been sharp; now he could not even recall yesterday.

Mandrol was to blame. Mandrol had done something to him, that was it. It was some spell or blow that made his mind so hazy. Nothing he could not eventually counter.

The itching faded and with it some of his anxiety. If his original plot was lost to him, he would simply devise another. After all, he *was* Viktor Falsche. Mandrol could do nothing to change that fact, nothing short of killing him, that is.

The aggravating itch returned. Viktor scratched the annoyance away again, then returned to his resting place, confident that the coming day would bring him the answers he desired.

From where he rested, Dré Kopien peered at the

other through slitted eyes. Only when he was at last certain that the man across from him was asleep did he allow himself to drift to slumber. Even then, the older man kept one hand near the short blade hidden by his form.

V

Baron Mandrol leaned over the balcony's edge, surveying his domain. Somewhere out there was a mask that thought itself a man, a mask that had already proven itself *more* a man than the combined force searching for him . . . it . . . them.

A week, G'Meni finally decides. A week before the mask begins to slip and we are left with but a confused farmhand and a new legend born. Viktor Falsche's ghost wandering Medecia.

Within that week, Mandrol knew he might be dead. A week was longer than he had first been informed; Master G'Meni had failed to inform him of the improvements he had made on the adhesive used to hold the monstrosities in place. The alchemist's tests on several of the other masks had proven that his skills had not yet waned. The superiority of the new adhesive was far greater than the squat figure had calculated.

Are you down there, dear Viktor? The soldiers still searched the city. Patrols and Morags scoured the countryside. It could not go on much longer. The entire domain was unsettled. The people knew that something disturbed the master of Viathos. There would be incidents. There would be need for Straas to suppress those incidents.

He sensed rather than heard the entrance of a second figure. It could only be one of two people and the other was not due just yet. "You have come to give me another report reeking of futility, have you not, Straas?"

Mandrol could imagine the pinched expression on

the general's face as the latter replied, "He eludes us for now, my baron, but the searches will continue, the patrols will sweep through the farmlands and countryside, and the Morags will listen and sniff for him in the hills. Even if he evades capture, he will have little opportunity to enact the original Falsche's plots."

"Can you be so certain?" The baron turned to face Straas. "Viktor Falsche nearly succeeded the first time he sought to assassinate me, General. You still haven't explained to me how this misbegotten mummer escaped over the walls and into the city."

"You should ask that foreign gargoyle of yours, my baron. We know that he got through the city gate with a disguise and the shroud of night, but how he got out of Viathos itself is still a mystery, I agree. Smacks of sorcery, in my opinion."

"Don't be ridiculous."

"Am I?" Straas tugged at his beard. "Someone entered the stables and climbed to the roof. We found the body of a soldier who had evidently been thrown off the roof lying behind the building, his neck broken. I say thrown off because of the signs of violence we discovered on top. The hands in the stable recall someone heading that direction and the soldier following suit a few moments later."

"He climbed back down, then. No sorcery."

"A party of four soldiers entered soon after. The hands, under strict questioning, I might add—all affirm that no one could have come back down. There was no other way out except over the wall."

"A *rope*." Mandrol ran his index fingers down his temples. "He used a rope."

"There was no sign of it, and the one stranger who entered carried only a cloth bundle not large enough for a rope of sufficient length."

The baron was growing very tired of the general's thorough dismantling of all other suggestions. "What you are proposing is entirely out of the question, General Straas. The masks do not work that way. You may consult Master G'Meni on the specifics, but I know that for a fact."

"I am not certain that even Master G'Meni understands as much about the masks as he claims." The soldier shrugged. "I might also be interested to know his choice of hosts, too. What criteria must they pass? What safety measures are taken?"

That was a thought that had not occurred to Mandrol. He always left the choice of hosts up to G'Meni. Over the years, the alchemist had made the masks his own and that had suited Mandrol, who had far too many other matters as baron to attend to. Now he was wondering if he had made a grave error.

"If you will excuse me, my baron," concluded Straas, a satisfied glint in his eyes. "I must return to coordinating the search. There has been some slight trouble with the Morags. I do not wish them to get too enthusiastic in their work. It wouldn't do to have them start attacking caravans who've paid their tolls. Wesfrancia would make much use of that news."

Even as the general bowed, Baron Mandrol sensed the other he had been expecting. He decided to forgive Straas his insinuations this time, especially since they *had* added rather unappetizing food for thought. He would have to speak to the alchemist later.

General Straas backed away just as Lady Lilaith entered. The two would have collided if not for the officer's swift reactions. A look of mutual distrust passed between the pair. Mandrol's enchantment did not include making the Lady DuPrise more than tolerate either of his subordinates. Straas, on the other hand, did not have the faith in sorcery to trust that the enchantment still held full sway even after so long.

"You are free to go, General," the baron pointedly reminded him. "I have need to talk with the Lady DuPrise."

Lilaith watched Straas depart before turning back to Baron Mandrol. "You desired to see me, my love?"

Her face was all innocence, all desire to please him. With her, Mandrol had found the woman he had dreamed of and more. She did his bidding and gave him her care. Lilaith was his constant companion and obedient servant.

Over the years, Mandrol had come to resent her with such force it came close to loathing.

She was not his. She had never been his. The enchantment was all that kept her so pliable, so adoring, yet even that could not erase *all* of her feelings for Viktor Falsche. If he were to release her this instant, give her back her own mind, Lilaith would flee to her old lover . . . if she did not first try to thrust a dagger into her enchanter's heart.

"I have a task that requires your cooperation, beloved." The last word tasted bitter. She sat with him during the masques and the various meals, even joined with him on his projects and personal activities, but it might as well have been Straas or G'Meni beside him during those times. The Lady Lilaith now spent most of her day in her own chambers, surrounded by her servants. It was not out of her choice; the enchantment demanded otherwise from her. Yet, if what her baron desired was her presence elsewhere, she would obey.

Her face lit up, as much a mask in its own way as the ones worn by his soldiers. *We are the children of Janus; two-faced each and every one of us,* he reflected, not for the first time. That, too, was a sign of his lax attitude. In the old days, Mandrol would have never spent so much time on reflection; he would have acted.

It was time to return to those days, time to seize the reins and remind the populace who was master here.

"I am yours to command, my love." Lilaith curtsied.

"Of course you are." He thought of dismissing her there and then, but he needed her for this. She knew Viktor Falsche as well as anyone could have. Knew him intimately. That was what the baron required now. "Come, sit with me."

They moved to a couch in the room. A carafe of wine, personally inspected by Mandrol, waited on a table near the couch. Once they were seated, the baron poured both of them a goblet of the fine, crimson liquid.

He watched her as she drank trustingly, then muttered, "Damn you for loving him so much. . . ."

Lilaith lowered the goblet and gave him a dazzling smile. "But I do not! 'Tis you I love, Mandrol."

Grunting, the sorcerer put aside his untouched wine. "Then you will help me find him, won't you? You want to help me track him down and prop his head on one of the spikes near the city gate, don't you, Lilaith?"

"Of course. Just tell me how I can help you!"

Her enthusiasm grated on him, but he proceeded. "All you need do is remember everything you can about Viktor. His mannerisms. His voice. Words he spoke to you. The . . . the touch of his hand on your—"

"Must I think of that? I'd rather not."

"It will serve to bring him sooner to the headsman's ax, my love."

That was reason enough for the ensorcelled woman. Lilaith straightened and stared proudly at the baron. "Then I shall do it. I will prove to you how much I truly love you, Mandrol!"

"I'm certain that you will." He snapped his fingers without warning.

The Lady DuPrise froze, eyes caught in mid-blink.

"Give me your hands," Baron Mandrol commanded. Transfixed, Lilaith placed her small hands into his own. He gripped her fingers tight, then stared into her blank gaze. "Unlock the gates of your mind to me, Lilaith. Open the path to your thoughts to me."

He sensed her will bending. In a moment, she would be a part of him, enabling the baron to use her intimate knowledge of Viktor Falsche to strengthen a magical search for the missing assassin. Lilaith's memories would attune the probe that much more. If the man who thought he was Viktor Falsche was near enough, Mandrol would be able to detect him.

Her natural resistance to the invasive probe collapsed. Baron Mandrol pushed deeper, preparing to entwine her thoughts with his own.

"Baron! What are you doing?"

The walls of Lilaith's mind rebuilt themselves. Mandrol's probe dissipated. He blinked, cursing whatever fool had interrupted him at such a crucial time.

It was G'Meni, of course. No one else would have

the nerve, the gall. The squat alchemist peered anxiously at his master.

"Damn you, you grotesque little roach! How dare you interrupt me at this time! I was just going to—"

"Make a terrible mistake, you see," finished G'Meni defiantly. He shook his head. "Baron, it is dangerous entering the mind of the Lady DuPrise. You know how she feels deep down, don't you? You know that to allow those thoughts even a remote possibility of escape could break the carefully bound enchantment you placed on her?"

It was galling to think that Master G'Meni was correct, although Baron Mandrol was not about to admit that to the man. "*I* am the sorcerer here, am I not, G'Meni?" The baron abandoned Lilaith, who still sat silent. The alchemist's cry had shattered the spell that Mandrol had been trying to shape, but the ensorcellment that kept her frozen still held. "Do not presume to tell me how enchantments work. You have a habit, of late, of assuming that you are the only authority when it was I who taught you. It was *I* who first showed you how sorcery and alchemy could be combined. Remember that if you value your head!"

Under his lord's grim gaze, the alchemist retreated a step. Yet he was not cowed. G'Meni rarely was, especially when he knew he was correct, which was most times. He bowed as best he could to Baron Mandrol. "My humblest apologies, Baron. I meant no insult. I'm only aware that you are under much pressure and so perhaps you are a little hastier in your decisions than normal. In fact, I came here now for that very reason."

There were times when Mandrol found it hard to follow the alchemist's words. If G'Meni had not been so useful to him over the years, the sorcerer would have dismissed him long ago. "You have some news? You've found something?"

"Not yet, but I will, you know." G'Meni waddled over to him as if their confrontation had not taken place. He leaned close to the baron and spoke in a whisper, as if both men were conspirators in some plot against the Lady DuPrise. "I have conducted my own research into various probes and searching devices and believe I may come up with something, but I need a few essential ingredients that I was hoping you . . . and now that I am reminded of her, the Lady DuPrise . . . could provide."

Now and then, the disfigured alchemist collected various items for his work, items that, in great part, made the baron happy that he had chosen sorcery instead of G'Meni's trade. It was not uncommon for people in Viathos to find the alchemist rummaging through the trash piles or wandering around the stables, gathering unsightly and unspeakable things. Only Mandrol's demand that G'Meni keep his stenches confined to his laboratory kept the keep from smelling like the pits of Hell. There was, however, no denying that the squat man was ingenious, failing only when confronting the legendary search for the Philosopher's Stone.

"What is it you need?" Mandrol finally asked, curious despite his earlier anger at the interruption.

"Simply a few hairs from both of you, Baron. A fingernail clipping from you would also aid, but only if it would be no trouble, you know. I can make do with other things."

Hair? Fingernail clippings? Witches utilized such items for their hexes, but what an alchemist would do with them the baron could not say. "What is this for?"

Master G'Meni spread his hands in complete innocence. "It would take long to explain the intricacies of my project, Baron, but it will help us locate the false Viktor, I promise you. I must take these and mix them with—"

That was enough for the baron. "Take them then and spare me the listing of your unsavory ingredients."

The alchemist produced a short cutting tool from the folds of his robe, then pulled out two small vials. "Shall I begin with you or the lady?"

"Just be done with it."

In short order G'Meni had the two hair samples. He started to reach for the baron's hand in order to take a clipping, but Mandrol pulled away.

G'Meni looked hurt. "It would help our chances of success, Baron, if I could take the nail, too."

For some reason that was not clear to him, Baron

Mandrol did not want to give the alchemist any more. He was already regretting the hair. If Master G'Meni was fairly certain of success, then it behooved Mandrol to give the alchemist what he needed. Yet something prevented him from doing so. "The hair will have to do. Take a few more strands if need be, but that's all. Take a clipping from Lilaith, if you need one so badly."

Glancing at the entranced woman, G'Meni shook his head. "No, I think that the hair will do."

Every moment near his second was making the baron edgier, although there was still no clear-cut reason why. "Then begone with you. The sooner Falsche's doppelgänger is captured or dead, the better."

"As you wish . . . ahh . . . I ask again that you heed my advice concerning Lady DuPrise, Baron. If she awakes, you may have to kill her."

Before she kills me? "Very well. I will hold off for now. There are other methods at my disposal."

"If I might ask what—"

"*G'Meni . . .*" The baron stared at the alchemist.

The hideous figure fell to his knees, his face growing pale as he struggled to rise. "My . . . baron . . . "

"Never forget who is master of Viathos, G'Meni. I am the one who rules here, not you. I take your advice, but I answer to no one. Without me, you are nothing, do you understand that? You would be burned at the stake or bound and tossed into the nearest lake if not for my protection. Do you understand that?"

He released the alchemist, who attempted to nod as he drew in lungfuls of air. Mandrol felt a surge of pleasure. G'Meni had allowed him to unleash some of the energy pent up within since the false Viktor's escape. He was almost grateful to the little man.

G'Meni continued to kneel even after his breathing had returned to normal. The alchemist gazed up at his master. "I meant no harm, Baron! Your life is my life! I would do anything to see that you remain lord of Viathos!"

"Enough of your toadying! You have work to do, don't you?"

"Yes, Baron."

"Then do it and do it right." As the alchemist rose and began bowing his way out of the chamber, Mandrol added, "Fail and your head will replace the imposter's on a pike."

"I will not fail, Baron!"

It felt good to hold such power over another, even if in this case it was only the already-subservient alchemist. G'Meni was very aware that without his master he was dead. Straas would certainly not protect him; the general would, in fact, probably order him killed. G'Meni needed Mandrol alive if he was to survive. Wesfrancia and the other neighboring lands kept lists of those they deemed necessary to eliminate for past crimes, and the alchemist was on the top of most of those lists.

With Master G'Meni gone, Mandrol turned his attention back to the unfortunate Lilaith. She still sat where he had left her; even the alchemist's work had not broken the ensorcellment. It was possible that she was so deeply trapped that even his delving into her subconscious would not wake her.

He snapped his fingers.

Lilaith stirred, blinking in surprise when she found Baron Mandrol no longer sitting beside her. Her frown was replaced by a warm smile when she finally located him. "Did it go well?"

"I've decided to forgo that for now. Other possibilities have presented themselves that make it unnecessary at this time."

"I would gladly endure it again if it means success, Mandrol. You know I would."

He reached out and cupped her chin in his hand. "I know you would. I know how much you love me."

She did not catch the inflection. "Of course I do."

Mandrol lowered his hand and turned from her. He could stomach her nearness no longer. "You may leave now, Lilaith. I will see you at dinner."

"Must I go?"

"Yes."

The rustling of her garments was the only sound she made as she obeyed. Mandrol cursed silently. Sometimes he wanted to abandon Medecia and begin anew, but he had become too entrenched here. If he departed this land, his enemies, Wesfrancia and the rest, would renew their manhunt for him. Here he was safe . . . from all save the ghost of Viktor Falsche.

For now he would allow Straas to march his little toy soldiers and G'Meni to mix his foul ingredients. One or both of them might prove fortunate in locating the pretender. If not, then Mandrol would turn to the mind of Lady Lilaith DuPrise regardless of the alchemist's warnings.

In the meantime, there were still those other paths the baron could follow, other spells. The baron's mood brightened as he recalled one long forgotten. This one in particular had proved useful time and time again in hunting down especially crafty quarry. Once unleashed, the Amantii did not quit until they had found their prey, no matter how long or at what great odds. They were tenacious, to say the least.

"The Amantii . . ." he mused. "How appropriate. They must be very hungry by now."

Viktor Falsche dreamed, but the dreams confused him even in his slumber. He was himself, yet he was also working the field, trying to help a man who was his father yet not his father keep the family alive. The field was large enough, but too much of its bounty went into the coffers of Viathos in the form of tax collection. The baron had many more important people to feed.

The same surge of panic that had hindered Viktor during his escape overwhelmed him now. Soldiers were riding toward the farm, the foul countenance of General Straas on all but the lead rider. Father ordered all inside, but the doors could not hold under the attack of heavily armored warriors.

They stalked into the simple house, their expressions identical. His sister . . . Cordelia? . . . no . . . not Cordelia . . . this girl was too young . . . .screamed as one of the drones reached out and plucked her off the floor. The tip of his blade brushed against her throat in warning to the rest of the family.

The officer entered. He wasted no time, stomping toward Viktor himself. The officer's face, being his own, was more animated than those of his men, but the sadistic pleasure in his expression made him the most frightening of the invaders.

Here the dream shifted, becoming Viathos Keep. Here he saw the dungeons of the baron and the refuse left almost forgotten there by Mandrol.

The dream shifted again. He was strapped to a table. There was someone standing before him and at first he thought it was the officer again.

It was not. It was Master G'Meni.

The alchemist had something in his hands, but when Viktor tried to look at it, the dream began to fade. He only knew that whatever it was squirmed in the horrific figure's hands as if trying to escape.

His last image was that of the devilish alchemist raising the dark shape toward his face, then all became darkness. The darkness smothered him, though. Viktor tried to breathe, but it was nearly impossible. The thing had wrapped itself over his mouth and nose.

He started to suffocate . . .

. . . and woke to find a hand over his mouth.

"Be still!" hissed Dré before he could react. "They're all around us, man! No loud noises!"

Viktor nodded. Dré removed his hand and signaled his companion to join him over by a small bench. Something round and glittery was perched on a makeshift table next to the bench.

It was not quite a crystal ball, but Falsche had no other name for it. He remembered the artifact now, an old device created by some forgotten sorcerer and eventually sold to Dré Kopien by a merchant who could not have understood its great value.

The ball was completely transparent, but the moment Dré passed his hand over it, an image materialized.

Mandrol's hunters . . . and a landscape that was identical to the region only a few paces from their hiding place. The soldiers were scouring the countryside. Men on horseback urged their mounts around trees. Foot soldiers prodded at every large growth of foliage. There were even dogs, baleful hounds straining at chain leashes while their handlers cursed them on.

The face of Straas materialized again and again, as the search was coordinated by a handful of officers, the general's mercenary companions.

A huge form lumbered by, briefly blotting out all else.

Dré kept his voice a whisper. "They'd dare risk a Morag during the daytime just to find you, eh, Viktor? Those devils can get surly even with their own kind if they're out in the sun too long."

Viktor Falsche said nothing, at the moment brooding over the fact that he was responsible for Mandrol's soldiers coming so close to finding their hidden lair. He had stumbled through the area after the struggle with the Morag, no doubt leaving a trail so obvious that even Straas could find it. Now he had not only endangered himself, but his oldest and dearest friend as well.

What was worse was that his sorcery was no longer his to command, not without great cost, anyway. Viktor stared at his hands, as if discovering them foreign things. The hands represented to him his power, for many aspects of his art required their use. Now they were good for holding a blade and nothing better, which would do neither of them much good against either a squadron of soldiers or a single Morag.

"The hounds are near the entrance."

Viktor looked up. Two fierce, black dogs snuffled the earth as they no doubt followed the trail left by the two men. Dré had certainly had no time to cover his tracks, not with Viktor's body to carry back.

"This should be interesting," Dré Kopien cryptically remarked.

The dogs abruptly paused in their search to sniff at a small patch of wildflowers only a few yards from the entrance. The hounds seemed perplexed at first, then both wagged their tails with such frantic energy that their handler began pulling at their chains. The two huge creatures ignored him, however, now intent on inhaling whatever they could of the flowers' fragrance.

This baffling act continued for nearly a minute, then the pair suddenly lost interest in the flowers and started sniffing for the trail again. However, the dogs now seemed confused. One started back the way they had come, while the other headed toward a point beyond the underground shelter. Caught between the shifting beasts, the handler squawked a demand which both dogs completely ignored. He tried tugging on their chains, but could not fight both at once.

A look of pride crossed Dré's worn face. "A bit of alchemy I picked up from a turbaned easterner who probably smelled worse than the pit those two beasts live in. A few ingredients mixed together and sprinkled here and there on various plants. Supposed to be used to keep animals and bugs from eating one's crops, but I think that this is just as good, eh, Viktor?"

"What did it do to them?"

"Addled their minds and senses just enough to confuse them. No more. I don't have your abilities, man, but I try to make do."

As if the dogs' contrary opinions had some effect on the rest of the hunting party, the search began to head away. Within minutes, the last of the soldiers had faded into the distance.

Dré leaned back, looking exhausted now that the danger was past. "That was the closest they've come in seven years and I wasn't half as nervous then. I'm getting old, I am." He twisted his head to the side and studied Viktor. "Unlike you, man."

"I have no explanation, Dré'. Nothing to give you except my word."

"I'd rather trust my own sense, which tells me that you're you although definitely a bit changed . . . and unchanged. That bastard Mandrol must've done something to you, locked you away somewhere until you finally escaped. Either that or . . ." Dré let his voice fade away, his eyes fixed on Viktor's own.

"Or he let me out purposely? Is that what you mean?"

A sigh escaped the other man. "I thought that last night, but you could have bespelled me at any time, eh? Besides, I can't see any reason that Mandrol would ever let you go; he'd kill you before he'd ever consider making you one of his toy soldiers. He'd have to keep watch on you all the time just to make certain that you didn't break free of his enchantments."

It was true. In his place, Falsche would have done the same. Both he and Mandrol were too strong-willed to be made permanent slaves. Enchantments were not perfect and if they weakened even a little, it was possible for those people of great will to free themselves.

It was knowing that which made Viktor fear for Lilaith. Her will had also been strong, but she was still the obedient consort of his foe. Dré swore to her loyalty to Viktor, which left the question of just what Mandrol had done to her to keep her so deeply under his control.

He was almost prepared to leave the sanctum there and then in some mad, one-man assault on Viathos. If *only* he had taken her with him; but he had thought her a traitor.

The itch from earlier returned. Viktor scratched it away, irritated by more than its presence. He had no plan, no memory, and no power. He had one aging man besides himself, a man who he knew did not completely trust in him. To even consider returning to the city and Viathos was madness.

And yet . . .

Something, a memory that was only a vague hint, stirred then and urged him to return. There was something he had left in the city, something he knew was important. What its importance was, Viktor could not recall, but that was enough. There was nothing else but this slim hope.

"Come the night, we go to the city," he announced.

Dré, still intent on searching the countryside for any lagging hunters, shot him a startled glance. "The search parties will still be out, man! We shouldn't be leaving here for another three or four days at least."

"It has to be tonight." He could hardly restrain himself for yet three *more* days. The chamber already felt much too cramped and, more important, Mandrol had lived much too long. "Time to set the plan in motion, Dré."

"The plan, is it?" His companion leaned back, reluctant but interested. The images in the artifact faded the moment the man's interest turned to the new subject. "It's still that ready after ten years? We can just start it up again now?"

Viktor hated lying to his friend, but consoled himself with the thought that he was certain to remember everything once he returned to the city. More and more he was positive that it was important for him to return . . . to locate a particular . . . *building*. Yes, it was slowly coming back to him. Bit by bit. The city would give him the answers. Then he could explain to Dré the truth of the matter.

"Yes, exactly as you said."

"Can it not wait? The Morags will surely be out searching even if the others return."

"Tonight." Viktor pondered the trouble he was having with his sorcery. He would have to use the remaining hours to either overcome this sudden handicap or discover another way around the difficulty. Dré's life was at risk, too.

"All right. Tonight. Can you tell me what it concerns now?"

"Better to wait until you need to know."

That caused the frown on the other's face to deepen, but Dré nonetheless nodded. "All right. Have it your way."

Dré might die because of him, because of the gaps in both Viktor's memory and power. However, even knowing that did not dissuade the sorcerer.

"Well," continued the graying man. "If I'm to go on some insane midnight jaunt, avoiding wolves and Morags on the way, just so that I can return to a city where they want to parade my aching head on a pike, then I think I'll grab a little more shut-eye." He grimaced at Viktor before adding, "I will never understand why I choose to remain your friend."

Viktor almost told him the truth then. Instead, he watched Dré Kopien wander over to a pile of furs and old blankets and lie down with his back toward his companion. Viktor Falsche wanted to thank the man for his loyalty and his love, but the sorcerer knew that doing so would only make him sound patronizing or sarcastic. Dré did not deserve that.

When they reached the city, Viktor would make amends. When he finally remembered the rest of the other plan, he would tell Dré everything.

Returning to his own sleeping place, Viktor sat down and waited until he heard snoring. He counted silently to a thousand just to make certain, then crossed his legs and cleared his mind of troubling thoughts as best he could.

The nausea would strike the moment he began his first attempt at sorcery, but he would have to overcome it. If he did nothing else in the few hours remaining before their departure, Viktor Falsche would finally overcome the horrific nausea. He dared not drag his old comrade through this deadly quest unless he had at least some hope of protecting him from both the natural and unnatural forces at Mandrol's command.

Best to start as simple as possible. Work my way up. The greater the feat he attempted, the worse the nausea. If he could build an immunity of sorts . . .

Gritting his teeth, he gathered his will and began.

The sickening sensation in his stomach commenced almost simultaneously.

VI

As sunset approached, riders from Viathos raced throughout the surrounding lands, seeking out the various hunting parties with commands from the baron himself. Some few of the officers hesitated after reading the missives, but all obeyed the new commands to the letter. They knew better than the people of Medecia just how true the stories concerning Baron Mandrol were.

By the end of the first hour of darkness, the vast majority of the patrols had retreated to within a two-mile radius of the city walls. The remainder hurried along, the drones in silent obedience and the mercenaries with nervous mutters.

Not long after, a light mist began to settle on the outer lands. The sounds of the night, the calls of animals and the cries of birds, stilled.

One of the general's mercenaries who had fallen behind due to a horse that had thrown a shoe was the only witness to a strange sight, but as he had never had a reliable tongue, few truly believed his tale . . . which of course did not keep the story from spreading.

As he hurried his mount along, the mercenary had suddenly noted three forms that seemed to take shape from the mist itself. The shapes were hard to see in the dim light of the moon, but they resembled cats.

Cats as large as half-grown horses. Cats with glowing eyes of a dreadful blue-green who glanced at the mercenary, seemed to catalogue him as not worth their time, then separated as they raced off into the wild lands.

General Straas, still much put out by the baron's sudden counterorder to his own soldiers, gave no explanation to his officers, but there were those who swore that as he departed the hastily called meeting to discuss the reorganization of his troops, he was heard to mutter about "the damned Amantii come again."

Ensconced in his laboratory, Master G'Meni heard nothing about the mist or the creatures men thought they had seen. He, instead, worked steadily on a device involving a magnetic rock, several of his own chemical concoctions, and the hair samples taken from the baron. The samples he had snipped from the beautiful head of the Lady Lilaith DuPrise he stored away for another time, they being of no use in this experiment.

He could not have told Mandrol that. Mandrol would have wanted to know why *his* hair was needed but not hers, and G'Meni could not have told him the truth.

The truth would have meant his head.

The dry mist that hovered over the entire countryside touched Viktor Falsche in such a way that he knew it was not a natural creation. There was sorcery afoot and it made sense that the source of the bleak, unsettling mist was Viathos.

"We're in luck with the weather, at least," whispered Dré, scratching at the rough peasant clothing he wore. Both men also wore worn cloth cloaks with hoods. Their faces were smudged, as if from many days traveling. "This mist will help more than hinder us. Mandrol's unholy drones grow a little confused in the mist, though I can't say why."

Drone soldiers and mist. There was a connection there, another link with the plan that Viktor sought desperately to recall. His spirits rose for the first time since the two had departed the hidden sanctum for the city.

Although he walked as if rested, the sorcerer's body screamed at him for a chance to recuperate from his attempts to conquer the nausea. The only thing that made the trek possible now was the knowledge that the last three castings had been, if not pain-free, then at least tolerable. More to the point, Viktor felt as if he were capable of more difficult or stronger spells. He was still very limited in what he could do, but he was improving.

With such progress made, it would have made more sense to wait another three or four days before beginning this insane journey, but Viktor had been more eager than ever to start out the moment Dré was ready. That he had not had more than an hour's slumber himself did not matter; sorcerers learned to make personal sacrifices early on. Sorcery granted much, but it also demanded in return.

When we reach the city, I know a safe dwelling where we can rest. We'll also be able to get some food there. Dré had promised that just as they left, and now Viktor was using those words in addition to his own desires to keep himself going. He would get the food and rest he needed when they reached their destination.

By then he would surely remember the entire plan.

"Stuff smells a little foul, almost like smoke," his companion added. "That'll make it harder on dogs or Morags what with their sensitive noses."

Dré still did not understand the nature of the mist. Viktor could hesitate no longer. "We might have more to worry about than dogs or even Morags. This is not a natural fog."

The other man stopped dead in his tracks. "This is Mandrol's doing?"

"I would assume so."

"Do you know what he's trying to do with it? Is it dangerous to breathe, do you think?"

"That would be too clumsy, not to mention too risky. He would endanger Medecia too much that way, and while Mandrol is a tyrant, it is difficult to be tyrant of a dead land. No, he has something else in mind."

"Lovely."

The mist hung oppressively low, turning the wild lands into a dreary tract suitable as the domain of restless spirits. Viktor's imagination changed swirls of mist into half-human forms, all of them resembling Cordelia. Dré Kopien was silent beside him, but Viktor's companion, too, looked around as if seeing ghosts.

It was a long trek toward the city, due in great part because of their need to remain off the most obvious paths. They could especially not follow the sorcerer's escape route back, for that would be the path most searched by the hounds and Morags.

At one point they heard the heavy steps of one of the huge trollish creatures, but the Morag never drew nearer. In fact, the Morag sounded as if it was moving in great haste away from them. Since there was nothing capable of bringing down one of the monsters save either a band of soldiers or one of its own kin, its haste made little sense unless it had found some other quarry. Neither man cared, being much too pleased when the Morag finally moved out of hearing.

"Definitely strange, this haze," Dré commented some minutes after their near encounter with the devilish monstrosity. "I'd swear that even the Morag wanted nothing more than to get away from here. I suppose only madmen and fools would be out in the midst of something like this . . . and that pretty much describes us, don't you think?"

Viktor did not answer, for suddenly he was aware of another presence nearby. It was not human, not in the least. There was something familiar about what he sensed, as if he had come across its kind before. He tried to prepare himself, although he was not at all certain that his sorcery would be sufficient for the task. It had to be, though, because if Viktor Falsche was correct, the thing was both powerful and magical in nature.

It was also moving steadily in their direction.

"What—?"

He waved Dré silent. Likely whatever it was that stalked them did not need to hear them, but Viktor needed every advantage if he was going to deal with the creature.

Then, even as the sorcerer began to summon his power, the queasiness in his stomach aggravating but acceptable, the same panic that had nearly undone him earlier returned. This time it was worse. Viktor Falsche wanted to turn and run for the safety of . . . the farm? This only added confusion to his panic, for he had never lived on one. He began to edge back, all thought of defense gone, and probably would have fled a breath or two later if not for Dré noticing his movement.

"What is it? What's wrong, man?"

What *was* wrong? He was Viktor Falsche, sorcerer of high esteem and ranking, yet here he was shivering uncontrollably. Fear would only lead to his death . . . his death and Dré's.

Snarling, he fought back the panic even as the shadowy form before them started to move at a swifter, more determined pace.

"Get back!" Viktor demanded through clenched teeth. He vaguely noted his companion—who wrongly assumed that *he* was the one to whom the sorcerer spoke—obey.

The thing, a huge, nearly feline shape, slowed but did not stop.

"We are not here!"

It hesitated, for the first time emitting a sound. The sound reminded Viktor of a blade being slowly dragged across a stone floor.

"There is someone running in that direction!" He pointed to his left. "It's probably the quarry you seek!"

Blue-green eyes, which threatened to inspire Viktor's fear once more, blinked and shifted to the direction Viktor indicated. The shadowy monstrosity sniffed the air, then started in that direction. Its pace increased as it moved. Despite its bulk, the unholy creature barely made a sound when it ran.

Only when it was gone did Viktor nearly collapse from the effort. He had cast a glamour on Mandrol's pet and while the work had been of a subtle, almost quiet nature, it had cost much. The sorcerer was frankly surprised that the glamour had even held.

"Viktor!" Dré caught him before the sorcerer's legs could buckle. "Ariela, man! What was that ghastly apparition and how did you get rid of it?"

"I . . . I'm not certain, but I think it was an Amantii."

"What the devil is an Amantii?"

"What fairy tales in Wesfrancia called hellcats . . ." Viktor finally regained the energy to stand without support, "but not nearly so whimsical as in the stories."

"Mandrol's doing?"

"It could . . . only be." The sorcerer still breathed in large gasps, but this was due to the earlier panic as much as the spell he had cast. "They're hunters and trackers. They learn as they chase. If a quarry escapes or tricks them, they only come back stronger."

Dré looked after the vanished horror. "You mean it'll come back?"

"Not right away, I hope. The glamour *should* remain on it for a while, but eventually it will overcome the spell. A second glamour would then fail, because that Amantii would have built resistance. We can only hope that the Morag does some damage to the Amantii before the hellcat kills it."

"The Morag?" It took the other man a moment to grasp the meaning. "You sent it after the Morag we heard before."

"It will track the Morag down; there is no doubt about that. By that time, we will be gone and it will have lost our trail."

"So we're safe?"

The queasiness becoming more tolerable, Falsche renewed the journey. "From this one, perhaps."

"There are others?"

"Probably two. That was a female . . . I believe. There will be another female and one male."

Dré caught up to him. The older man's gaze darted this way and that as he searched for other sinister shapes in the misty darkness. "Lovely."

They moved on at a quicker pace, their decision encouraged in part by a desire not to repeat their encounter with the Amantii. Viktor believed that the other two were far away, but did not voice the notion for fear he would put Dré off guard should one of the other beasts actually be nearby.

He had just begun to relax when a tingle of fear rushed through him. Viktor pretended to stumble, taking advantage of the action to peer into the darkness behind them.

"Are you all right?"

The cause of his fear was not readily detectable, but the sorcerer was certain that it was out there. In a whisper, he replied, "The Amantii . . . is back."

It was to his companion's credit that his body did not betray his surprise. He helped Viktor straighten. "The same one? Not one of the others?"

"Yes. It shouldn't be, but it is."

The glamour should have held. It had always held in the past, even against creatures fouler than either the Morags or the hellcats. His power had failed him once more. Viktor doubted his strength was sufficient to ward off the Amantii again, much less destroy the beast.

They kept walking, forcing themselves not to quicken their pace lest the Amantii know that it had been noticed. The tendrils of mist twisted around them as they journeyed, seeming to taunt them now as they sought some rescue from the stalking form.

We cannot continue this charade much longer! Despite that thought, however, Viktor Falsche could not think of any way of escaping the magical predator. His stomach still churned with the effects of his last effort and while he was now able to endure that, added attempts would increase the pressure on both his body and mind.

Dré will die because of me . . . and Mandrol will still have Lilaith.

"This is ridiculous!" Kopien breathed between clenched teeth. "There must be something we can do, man! I'll not go down its gullet like a rat to some overgrown farm cat! Don't the blasted things have any weaknesses?"

That question had been plaguing Viktor Falsche since their first encounter with it. He felt he knew more about the Amantii than he could recall. Mandrol had used them before. That was something newly dredged from his poor memory and the realization stirred his hope. Not only had Mandrol utilized the fiendish felines before, but Viktor *did* know their weaknesses. He could just not summon the knowledge yet. A little more time, though, and he was certain that—

A quiet snarl from behind them informed the desperate sorcerer that the Amantii was not going to give him that time.

"Don't turn!" he called, but Dré was already spinning around, his hand on the hilt of his blade.

"Ariela!" His arms dropped to his sides, hanging limp. His face grew pale and lifeless. Dré Kopien was a corpse still breathing.

The hellcat had him in a death trance. It was how the creatures played with their prey before taking them. They had been fortunate the first time that the Amantii had not snared both of them before Viktor had placed the glamour on it.

Falsche fought the great desire to repeat his friend's mistake and turn to face the demonic beast. Instead, he sought in his pockets, for what he could not say, and tried to summon again the knowledge of the cat's weaknesses. It did not help that he was aware that even recalling those weaknesses might not save them. What if the Amantii was afraid of firegrass, for instance? Viktor could hardly run to the vast seas of the south and carry back a bundle of the fiery plants.

Although the great cat moved in silence, the sorcerer could sense that it was edging closer. It was wary of the one human who had sent it away once and did not now fall prey to its power. The hellcats were not foolish.

If only it would rain! he thought . . . then wondered why. The notion of rain sparked more than one thing in his memory. It had to do with more than just the Amantii; rain had also something to do with his ultimate plan, which did him no service now.

Rain. Like the cats to which it was distantly related, the Amantii hated it. There was more to it than that, however. Rain was . . . was *lethal* to it somehow.

His hand went to the small water sack at his belt. It was not large, perhaps only worth three, maybe four cups of water, but it was not the quantity that counted. Rather, it was how he made use of it.

The Amantii paused. Any other person it would have charged by now, but because its master considered Viktor Falsche a most deadly threat, it wanted to snare his gaze and freeze him in place. The human was not cooperating, however.

Viktor opened the sack. He hoped he had the wherewithal for one more spell. It only needed to be one of similarity. Create the effect of something from something like it. He poured a handful of water even as the hellcat appeared to be making up its mind whether to pounce or not.

"Mist-spawned feline," the sorcerer whispered as he tossed the water into the air. "Hellcat. Much too nasty a night for you. Yours is a dry mist. You are a thing of heat, more smoke truly than fog."

The air around Viktor grew damp and the Amantii suddenly snarled uncertainly.

The desperate sorcerer felt his insides turning, but he continued. Another handful of water went flying into the air.

"Wash away the smoke, wash away the fog."

Droplets struck the earth from above them. A few touched the murky form of the beast.

Sizzling, the water burned through the Amantii. The hellcat roared. It crouched low even as Viktor tried to pour more water.

He brought up his hand even as the furious Amantii committed itself to its pounce.

A downpour caught the two humans and the beast together. The hellcat shrieked as its form burned, but it did not falter. Viktor threw himself to the side, the sack falling from his hand, and tried to roll out of the monster's long reach.

Somewhere in the dark Dré cursed as he woke from the Amantii's spell. The cat continued to shriek. Savage claws tore at the ground just inches from Viktor. Oddly, the rain made it difficult to see anything *but* the Amantii, which was outlined in a fiery halo. The demonic beast was a tattered shape now. Yet the danger was far from over, for despite its great injuries, the monster still stood.

It slashed again, tearing at the earth, trying to rip Viktor's body apart. He rolled, but the gap between himself and Mandrol's demon was shrinking.

The magical downpour began to falter.

The cat swiped at him and although Viktor Falsche again rolled away as fast as he could, this time the monster snagged his left arm. The sorcerer did not scream, but his body shook with pain. The Amantii's claws had barely cut the skin, but the angle the creature was bending his arm threatened to tear the limb out of the socket unless Viktor found some way to free himself.

One more handful would have destroyed the hellcat, but the sorcerer had not been able to remember the Amantii's weakness soon enough. Now it had him. The rain was now only a light drizzle. The monstrous form shivered in pain, but still had the strength to crush him.

The Amantii roared and lowered its head so close that it was impossible for Viktor Falsche to escape its baleful gaze this time.

Water abruptly drenched both beast and man.

The hellcat howled and, still trying to shake the moisture from its wavering form, *dissipated*. A last mournful call cut through the night as it faded away.

Viktor gazed up to see a bedraggled Dré Kopien holding an empty water sack and looking almost as monstrous as the demon he had just vanquished. The other man gave a weak smile. "I saw your sack and knew the rain couldn't be natural, so I figured you had a reason for wanting it wet."

"That should not have worked," grunted the sorcerer as he struggled to his feet.

"But it did. Don't go complaining about miracles, man. Speaking of which, you look pretty fair. Are you all right?"

"Thanks to you." Viktor would have replied further, but he then recalled that there were two more of the monsters loose upon the land. With the water sacks empty, the travelers had no defense against them. "We need to move on. The others might have heard this one."

"Think so?"

"There is a good chance of that." Viktor started forward, but began to wobble after only a few steps.

"Are you sure you're all right, man?" Dré hurried to his side to steady him. "Did that devil wound you?"

He could not tell his comrade just how weak his conjuring had made him. "A little shock. That is all, Dré. I will be all right. How much farther to the city?"

"We're about halfway there. Can you make it?"

Viktor Falsche bristled and shook off the other man's support. "I can."

Dré retreated a few steps, but not before giving the ungrateful sorcerer a glare. Viktor knew that he had overreacted to the question of his health, but he dared not let the truth be known. That would lead Dré to ask too many questions. So long as Mandrol lived and still held sway over Lilaith and Medecia, Viktor could not spend the time answering those questions.

"Let's go, then," Dré Kopien finally muttered, picking up the remnants of Falsche's own water sack and tossing it to him. "Here, you might need this if we come across a stream. I always did think it wise to carry a little water along."

From there on, the trek became a silent one. Both men watched the land around them, but rarely looked at one another. Viktor could not blame Dré, but felt it was better this way until they reached the city. The silence allowed the sorcerer to concentrate more fully on fighting the pain.

They did not encounter any more Amantii, although once they heard a cry that did not sound as if it could have come from any natural creature. The cry came from far off, however, so while both men remained wary, they did not panic.

At last they reached a point where they could see the torch lights of the city. Unfortunately, that also meant they could see the encampments and patrols that dotted the landscape nearby.

"Mandrol must have half his men out here," muttered Dré.

"There was not much else to do, not with the Amantii out there."

Dré shook his head. "I don't know if we can make it inside now. I wasn't expecting them all to be out here between us and the walls."

Viktor, too, studied the armed might of his nemesis with some degree of doubt. "Tell me again where we have to go to gain entry."

"Around the eastern side is a gate used by the city to dump out the biggest garbage . . . the stuff too big to walk or ride a horse over when it falls into the streets. I have friends there, men and women who drag the refuse out. They'll let us in. I don't know what else the gate's ever been used for, but that seems to be its function now. They do guard it, but the guards aren't the cream; these're the ones who've gotten in bad with their commanders."

"Not drones?"

"Why waste loyal men for this detail when there's always some mercenary who's gotten too deep into his cups or picked one fight too many?"

That was the way Straas would think. Viktor nodded.

"Trouble is, we have to go through all of those to reach it."

The sorcerer studied the flickering fires and black shapes moving about. "Their numbers may work to our advantage."

"So we *are* going through with this?"

Viktor glanced at him.

Dré nodded. "I was just wondering." He sighed. "Just when I start to worry, you act just like I expect you to."

Exactly what that meant, Kopien did not elaborate. Instead, he began the climb down from their vantage point. Viktor scratched his cheek absently, then followed.

They would make it into the city, of that he was now certain. Oh, there was risk, but entering and leaving Medecia was, in the long run, hardly that great a feat to him. Even the Amantii, while a substantial threat, were surpassable.

It was Viathos that offered the true challenge, the true danger. He had escaped the citadel once; he would not be able to do so again. To enter Viathos again meant that this time the sorcerer *had* to kill Mandrol. The only way Viktor would leave a second time would be when his torn and gutted remains were tossed by the garbage handlers into the rotting pile that was the trash dump of Medecia.

VII

The door to Master G'Meni's laboratory shook as someone tried to pound a hole in it. The alchemist finally stirred and pushed himself away from the table where he had fallen asleep, but it was too late. The door finally flew open and an officer stepped inside, to be followed but a moment later by General Straas.

"Don't you ever keep normal hours, alchemist? Or use a bed, for that matter?"

G'Meni was awake enough to counter his adversary's barbed questions. "My work knows no normal hours, General, and I, at least, find beds to be generally too soft, although I understand those who have grown infirm find them comforting."

The general, who did sleep in a bed, did not respond to the verbal attack. Instead, he said, "I have some questions that I must ask you, alchemist."

"By my reckoning, it is not quite sunrise. Peculiar time to come asking questions."

"You must forgive me. I am younger and in need of less rest, I suppose, than one of your years."

G'Meni grunted. He turned his attention momentarily from the general to his experiment. Everything remained as it had been since he had quit in order to rest for a few minutes . . . which had evidently become a few hours. The alchemist had worn himself out more than he had thought.

Unused to being ignored, Straas marched over to the area where his counterpart was staring and studied the experiment with a complete lack of interest. He toyed briefly with one edge of the bowl, nearly sending the squat figure into fits.

"I do not presume to order your little toy soldiers around, General. Kindly refrain from playing the alchemist. You might very well blow us all up that way."

Straas removed his fingertips from the bowl with just a hint of trepidation. G'Meni held back a smile; the mixture was not explosive, not even if heated, but had the general shaken the contents, he would have set the alchemist's work back a full day.

"As I said," General Straas began again, stepping toward the bent man, "I have some questions."

"I am always willing to aid in your education, General."

Straas removed his helm. It became clear to G'Meni that the other had not slept that night. Foolish, in the alchemist's opinion. A rested mind was a quick-witted one.

"I have some experience with the masks, of course, so I understand some of the principles, but it occurs to me that you've made some changes from our lord baron's original designs."

"With his permission," G'Meni nearly snapped. Straas had no idea just how much the alchemist had altered the original designs. Sorcery left so much uncertainty. This and that power was called into play in fashions often nebulous at best. Sorcery was not clear-cut, like science.

"I'm sure that you did. Was there anything different about the makeup of this particular mask? It might give some clue as to what to expect."

"No. Nothing. The only difference is the one you know about, the fact that the life force of Viktor Falsche was still strong when the image was taken. That and that alone is why he has so overwhelmed both the commands we gave him and his own host's identity."

"And who is his host? What sort of man was he?"

"A peasant who looked the wrong way at the wrong time and was arrested for it. I forget his name." Master

G'Meni cursed himself for having brought himself to this point. Now he saw what Straas desired to know. If the man who had been chosen was special in some way, then he should not have been made a host to as dangerous a mask as the one of Viktor Falsche. *And I used the baron's bastard child.*

"Nothing about him struck you as unusual? Magical, perhaps?"

The alchemist drew himself up to his full height, which still left him staring up at the armored figure. "I am a man of science, not sorcery. I may delve into the basics of the latter during the course of my experiments, but it does not make me a sorcerer. I suggest you speak with the baron."

"Perhaps later." Straas dismissed the question with a wave of his hand. "When we find the host, we can always check then. Do you have a name for him?"

"He was a peasant. Of what use would I have for his name?"

The soldier's gaze swept a shelf filled with note-books. "As an alchemist, you do tend to document everything. I thought that perhaps you might have—"

"Well, I did *not*."

"A pity. I had a notion that might have worked if we only had the poor fool's name."

Despite himself, the squat alchemist was curious. "What sort of notion?"

Straas started for the doorway, the officer taking up a position behind him. "I thought that perhaps with a mask originally considered to be only temporary, there might be some overlapping of the memories. I've noted that even on a few of my drones. Had to kill a couple, they were so untrustworthy."

"You never mentioned that." snarled G'Meni. "That data would have been invaluable to me, you know. Any aberration is important to report."

"I'm sorry. I thought you certainly would've noted such cases before on your own. I'll remember that next time it happens, I promise."

"Overlapping memories, you say." The alchemist seized a piece of parchment and began scribbling things down. His mind was already awhirl with the possibilities. This false Viktor would have gaps in his original memory, gaps that the peasant Emil's memory would fill. It would make for an interesting collection of thoughts. Viktor Falsche would recall things that had never happened to him. G'Meni wondered if the baron's bastard would remember any of it when the mask was removed . . . but it was more than likely that he would be dead before there was even a chance of removing the false face.

As much as the alchemist would have liked to have studied the situation, he preferred both mask and host a burnt memory, especially if what remained was so unrecognizable that he was safe from any possible accusations by the general.

"I'll let you get back to your rest," commented the general, stepping into the hallway.

"Yes, yes . . ." G'Meni barely noted the other's departure. His mind was now racing in a number of directions, scientific curiosity mixing and sparring with concern for his own hide. The men who had brought him the peasant would have to be summoned and questioned, then their silence guaranteed.

He abandoned his notes to investigate what possible damage the general had done to his experiment. Fortunately, everything was still in place. The hair samples were held in flux between the representatives of the four basic elements and the magnetic stone hanging above still focused on the center of the sample. The solution at the bottom of the container had not formed sediments, which meant that he had calculated a perfect mix.

"Now it seems I must find you for more reasons than even before, my false Falsche, but find you I will, you know. Nothing long escapes Master G'Meni." The bent alchemist leaned farther over his device and made some slight adjustments. "Nothing."

Everything was working perfectly. He almost had to laugh. Straas had impressed him a bit with his slight knowledge of the peculiarities of the masks, but if the general believed that made him an expert in alchemy, he was sorely wrong. *Imagine if you had known what this device was, general, and how I designed it! I think you would have been rather stunned, yes?*

It was unfortunate that he could not brag about his latest achievement, but the results would garner him praise enough from he who ruled Medecia. That and the look of disgust that would grace the general's sour face would satisfy Master G'Meni.

In the first light of dawn, Viktor Falsche glimpsed what ten lost years had done to the people of Medecia.

The first hint that what one saw was a mask covering a festering sore was the refuse dump beyond the city wall. Ten years of excessive waste and cruelty by those living within the walls of Viathos lay there for all to see. The land here had once been farmland and woods; now it was a wasteland where the only creatures who roamed in numbers were the rats, wild dog packs, and carrion crows.

Actually, there was one other group, but Viktor had tried not to look at them, his shame and disgust getting the better of him. Always in the distance were the human refuse, monsters and victims both, those who could not live any other way save to scavenge in the foul land, battling rats and one another for scraps.

He had thought that darting around patrols and hiding from sentries had been a strain on him, but wending his way through the rotting filth did more to drain Viktor than even the encounter with the Amantii. Now he was not only physically ill, but weary of thought as well. Matters were not helped when he saw something among the piles of decaying matter that had once been human in life.

At first he was grateful when a careful signal by Dré had brought two of the garbage detail to their aid. The sentries here were indeed careless, not that anyone could blame them since the filth and stench likely sapped their spirit, but caution was still called for. Then, Viktor discovered that the only path in was through the sewage tunnels, which had fallen into neglect since the beginning of Mandrol's reign. The stench was even worse within and most of those forced to traverse the underworld wore some sort of protection over their faces. Water trickled through the tunnels, but it was foul already and barely enough to keep the sediment damp much less wash any of the refuse out. Combined with all else he had suffered this night, Viktor Falsche found it remarkable that he could still stand.

It was with great relief that he left the tunnels and climbed at last into the city. The relief was short-lived, however, for although the stench and decay was left behind, it was now replaced with an air of tension and apprehension so evident to him that he wondered how those within the walls could go on with their lives in so normal a manner.

His escape had been at night and so he had only seen fragments, misleading ones at that. Even in the light, a swift glance over the city would have led one to believe that under Baron Mandrol the land was prospering. The gay colors, the multitudes in the streets, the merchants and caravans passing through, all were signs of a thriving place. There were taverns and music, children running . . . Viktor almost wondered if the people *would* revolt if given the opportunity.

Then he noted the proliferation of the baron's soldiers. They were not simply present because of his escape, although the hunt was certainly chief among their duties now. No, these sentries were a normal part of Medecian life. Most folk quickly stepped out of the path of the patrols and even the wealthier merchants and aristocrats gave the men wide berth. Fear filled the air whenever Mandrol's puppet soldiers appeared, even if it was obvious that their business was elsewhere.

It was not the guards alone, however. Too many folk that Viktor saw bridled at the slightest intrusion around them. Too many arguments began over the simplest misunderstandings or accidental encounters. The most confused were the outsiders, the merchants and travelers making use of Medecia as a resting place or place to sell or purchase items. Natives would begin arguments, then halt in midstream and apologize.

Mandrol did not condone anything that threatened Medecia's trade. There were eyes and ears everywhere, not all of them human, and those who attempted to discourage the merchants from returning soon disappeared.

It was a city fraught with apprehension, a city filled with tension that should have set it afire years ago, yet somehow the lord of Viathos kept it going. Inevitably, however, Medecia would collapse under such control. From what he could see as he and Dré made their way through the crowds, the land probably had ten years remaining to it before Mandrol's rule brought it crashing down. Only the good work of his predecessors had allowed the present baron to rule so long. Viktor knew enough about Medecia's history to recognize what a hollow shell it was now compared to the past.

And Mandrol would probably simply go on, finding some new land to seize for his own. . . . Viktor had no idea how old the sorcerer baron was, but Mandrol still likely had enough years in him to bring yet another land to ruin if he was allowed to die of old age. Sometimes, sorcery allowed one to live much too long.

Viktor swore again that he would see that such would not be the case with his nemesis.

Dré led them through the city with practiced ease, knowing just where to hide whenever soldiers marched too close. At last they reached a tavern near the great market where most of the city's trading was done. Assured that no one watched, Viktor's companion led the way to a back door. Dré knocked twice in rapid succession, then a third and fourth time much more slowly.

A burly man with grease on his hands opened the door. He said not a word, but beckoned them inside. Viktor he eyed carefully. Once inside, the pair was immediately directed toward a set of stairs leading down into a cellar.

No sooner had the two descended when the light from above was cut off as the same man closed the door behind them. A lantern hanging on the cellar wall was now the only source of light, but it allowed them to see no more than a few feet in any direction.

"You've taken your chances comin' here, Dré." A woman's voice, strong and curious. "And who's this with you?"

"And good morning to you, Mara. It's an old friend I thought dead. His name is Viktor. Viktor, this is Mara."

A shape moved in the dim glow. It was a woman, but what she looked like, the sorcerer could not say, for her hair covered her face almost completely save for the tip of her nose and the lower portion of her mouth. He could not even say whether she was young or old.

"You speak of the sorcerer. You speak of the fool who went into Viathos expectin' to come out again. That was ten years ago, though, Dré. Is this to be the same man?"

"It is."

Mara shuffled back into the darkness. "There was talk among those who know that somethin' happened in Viathos the other night, some clamor that had the good baron's men runnin' around like scared rats."

Dré snorted. "That's hardly surprising, woman. Anything that your vaunted powers can add?"

"You're the one claimin' I have powers, Dré. I simply see thin's a little clearer than others at times. Right now, what I can see is that you two are in need of rest and food, am I right?"

"You are at that, my love."

"No one's been your love since that poor girl that brought you here. No one'll ever take her place, will they, Dré?"

Viktor waited for his companion to reply, but Dré Kopien was silent. At last unwilling to let the silence linger, the sorcerer said, "I thank you for letting us come here. If I could—"

"Dré, I thought there were only two of you here."

The two men glanced at one another, uncertain how to take the mysterious woman's meaning. Abandoning his sorrow for the moment, Dré finally replied, "There is only Viktor and myself."

"But I heard a third voice."

"That was Viktor and none other, woman."

"I simply thanked you," added the sorcerer.

"But it's . . ." She shook her head. "No, I can see that there are only two of you. My mind is growin' addled."

"Never, my love."

The peculiar figure waved away his compliment. "Johann has a room above that you can use. Best to get up there now, before the busiest part of the mornin' crowd comes in to eat. There's a Bruslich caravan in Medecia and its men take great stock in the concept of a hearty breakfast leadin' to a profitable day. I'll be sure to have somethin' sent up to you. When you're rested, then we can talk some more, Viktor Falsche."

Taking hold of his comrade's arm, Dré led Viktor back to the stairs. Behind them, the sorcerer heard Mara move about as if settling down. He desired to know where the other man had met such a peculiar creature as the face-less witch. What lay beneath all that hair?

The same man who had let them in seemed to be expecting them as they ascended, for he swung open the door just as Dré was about to knock.

"This way," the muscled figure commanded, sur-prising Viktor with the softness of his voice.

"She said—"

"I know what she said." That ended any further attempt at communication during the trek.

The path they took avoided the main room of the tavern. Their guide led them up a flight of stairs, down a corridor, and up another set of steps, the last old and treach-erous in appearance. However, the steps held well enough for the two men to enter a small, neglected-looking chamber.

"I'll bring something," said the taciturn man, whom Viktor assumed to be Johann. "You can speak, but do it quiet-ly." He pointed at a grimy oil lamp in the corner of the room. "Whatever light you can get from that is all you're allowed."

"I know that, Johann."

"But he don't, Dré, and I can't take no chances."

When they were alone, Dré Kopien settled down on a dingy cot. He patted the poor piece of furniture. "Ariela! I'm already missing my place."

"Who are these people, Dre?"

The other man frowned. "*Friends*, Viktor. People willing to risk themselves for us."

The sorcerer found an old stool and dragged it so that he could sit facing his companion. "Who is Mara? Is she a sorceress or a witch? Why does she hide her face? Did something happen to her?"

"I should've warned you about her. Mara's no witch or sorceress, not exactly. She just *sees* things now and then. I find her useful and a damned loyal person, man. You know, she has to stay down there almost all of the time, which is unfair to someone like her."

"Is she blind? Is that why she covers her face?"

Dré Kopien laughed bitterly. "No, she can't see well except up real close, but the hair is because she just understands how most folks are unnerved by her eye. Mara's only got one."

This stirred Viktor's interest further. "What happened to the other? Mandrol? Is that why she helps?"

"You misunderstand. She only has one eye, man! She was only *born* with one." He pointed at a location directly between his own eyes. "She's a Cyclopean in face if not in size."

As a scholar, Viktor Falsche was familiar with the legends of the creatures, supposedly the twisted offspring of humans and trolls . . . although imagining the two races mating was disturbing to say the least. "Where did you find her?"

"In the wild lands. She doesn't say where she comes from, but her accent, faint as it is, is northern, maybe Skandac. You know Skandac trolls; they mutate with each birth. Usually multiple heads, but who knows . . ."

"Why is she helping?"

Stretching out on the cot, Dré yawned. "I asked her that and she only said that she was supposed to help. She'd seen it. I never tried asking her that again. I like answers that make sense."

Although Viktor's companion faced the low ceiling, the sorcerer noted how Dré's eyes turned his direction as the resting figure spoke the last. Dré was still not satisfied with Viktor's return. Neither was Viktor. There was also the matter of the plan, which was still little more than vague fragments of memory at this point. Returning to the city had not stirred Falsche's mind as much as he had hoped.

"Best to get some sleep, man. Johann will bring us the food when he can. We won't be able to do much until late day, anyway, probably not until night can give us better cover. Then we can start on that plan of yours." Dré sobered. "And maybe finish this thing at last."

The words were a sword thrust to Viktor's heart. He could not keep Dré in the dark any longer. His friend had to know the truth, whatever the consequences. "Dré—"

Viktor got no further, for the other man's eyes were closed. Dré was already asleep. The sorcerer felt some relief; the deed was put off again. He envied his companion's ability to sleep so well under such circumstances.

There was another cot, but for the moment, Viktor was too exhausted to shift to it. The stool was close enough to the wall of the tiny room that he could lean back. Viktor stared at the opposite wall, wondering not only what he would say to Dré when the other woke, but how the other would react. Dré did not like secrets, especially those kept by people who were supposed to be his friends.

Aromas drifted up from the kitchen. The weary sorcerer inhaled sharply, wondering when the man Johann would return with something to eat.

He was still wondering when his own exhaustion seized control and sent him drifting off into slumber.

"He's asleep."

"You want me to go up there now, Mara?"

The woman shook her head, sending her thick tresses back and forth. "Not yet. I still can't read him. He should be who Dré says he is; I trust Kopien's judgment . . . but I'm gettin' another face, another man, wherever this Viktor Falsche exists."

"I remember Dré talking about Falsche," Johann muttered, uncomfortable in the dim light his companion preferred. "Big sorcerer who was going to free us all from the Mad Mandrol. The Lady Lilaith DuPrise was supposed to be his woman, but she's been pretty cozy with the baron. Didn't seem to miss her other sorcerer a bit."

"You know that thin's are never what they seem in Viathos, Johann. There're masks upon masks upon masks there . . . and one of them your brother wears."

Johann shook. Somewhere among the puppet soldiers his brother marched, taken into Viathos on some suspicion of being a traitor to the baron. The irony was that it had been Johann and not his brother Sebastian who was the traitor. The tavern keeper would have turned himself over to the Guard in the hopes of exchanging places with his brother, but Dré had pointed out that it was too late. Once Sebastian had entered Viathos, he was gone. The only chance lay in the slim hope that someday they would be able to free the men entranced by Mandrol's masks. As the years rolled by, that chance appeared slimmer and slimmer, but Johann could *not* give up hope.

"Dré has not led us astray so far, Johann. Still, somethin' is peculiar about his friend. I felt it when they arrived."

"No one leaves Viathos, not without the baron's permission."

"If this Emil is all Dré thinks he is, then he could. If only I could *see* him better I could—"

"I thought his name was Viktor."

The woman straightened, her thick hair briefly parting enough for the burly man to catch a dim glimpse of the one eye that marked her as only partly human. "It is . . .what did I say?"

"Emil."

"*Emil?* Now, why would I be goin' and sayin' that?" She paused. "Yet, it doesn't feel wrong . . . but neither does Viktor." her entire frame suddenly shook.

Concerned, Johann started toward her, but Mara shied away.

"I'm all right, Johann, I am. It's just that . . ." She grunted. "Never mind."

"Dré or no Dré, they're going to have to find another hole to hide in come the night. I'll not have you sick because of his friend's strangeness. How do we know it isn't one of the baron's spies? He can do a lot of things, the baron can."

"No!" Mara could not believe the intensity with which the word burst from her mouth. She was grateful that the walls in the cellar were thick. "That would be the worst thin' you could do."

"You know something?"

She lowered her voice to nearly a whisper. "No . . . just when you said that, I knew it was wrong to do."

"So we leave it in the hands of Dré, eh?"

"For now."

Johann made to depart. "Well, I've gotta get some food up to them. Might as well do it now."

"They're both asleep. Let them rest awhile."

He grimaced. "Someday you'll have to tell me how you do what you do, Mara."

She receded farther into the comforting darkness. "When I find out, love, you'll be the first to know, I promise."

He walked along the busy streets of the city, uncaring about the soldiers traipsing all about. People nodded to him as he walked, some calling him by name. Yet, it was not his name but another's. Viktor acknowledged them nonetheless, for he knew them all well.

His path was suddenly blocked by an elderly woman who seized him by both arms and, with tearful eyes, asked, "Where have you been, Emil? You are late! The fields are in disarray and your father needs you to plow them!"

"I am on my way to take my final test," he returned. "Today I step from student to sorcerer."

"Such nonsense when there's fields to be plowed. Your father—"

"My father is not a farmer."

The woman grew frightened. "Be quiet, Emil! Your

*face endangers you enough without you shouting it to the
world! If the keep should find out you still live, they'll kill us
all!"*

Her hands tightened on his arms to the point where
Viktor actually felt pain. He struggled to free himself, but the
elder woman clutched him as if afraid that he would blow
away in the wind.

"So! There you are, my little escapee!"

Master G'Meni stood before the two of them, grinning in triumph. He had a narrow box in one hand, a box
opened toward Viktor. Mandrol's pet alchemist shuffled forward and as he did, he grew. G'Meni continued to grow
until he was as tall as the buildings around them.

The woman gasped. "Flee, my son!"

"It's back to the box for you, Viktor! You've lost
face, you know, and I've come to claim it!"

"But I am a sorcerer! You can't stop me!" Even as
Falsche finally shook off the woman claiming to be his mother, his clothes changed from the elegant robes of his school
to the homespun garments of a farmer.

"You're not, though, you know." The huge G'Meni
reached down for Viktor, the alchemist's features shifting to
that of a Morag as he moved.

"I knew there was somethin' about you," commented the woman, only she was no longer an elder peasant but
the figure from the cellar, Mara. Now, however, Mara's face
was uncovered, revealing Lilaith's beautiful features . . . save
that there she had only one eye in the middle rather than
two.

"I believe that's mine!" snarled the Morag, who
was now Baron Mandrol. His monstrous hand caught hold
of Viktor by the chin. Mandrol pulled, but instead of the
helpless sorcerer being lifted into the air, Viktor Falsche felt
his face tear away. He screamed, but no one paid him mind.
Mara/Lilaith was tsking at his weakness and the huge Baron
Mandrol was too busy with his gruesome task to appreciate
what he was doing to Viktor.

"Into the box with you!" Mandrol slid the still
screaming countenance inside the container, then closed it,

cutting off the sound. He then eyed Viktor, who was still trying to cope with the horrible shock. "You had your chance, my friend. You failed. You are now unmasked as the failure you are." Mandrol paused. "You may take him now."

At first Viktor Falsche thought that his adversary meant the woman, but she was shying away, her lengthy tresses now covering not only her face, but her entire form. He whirled about and found himself facing a legion of soldiers, all looking and sounding like General Straas.

"Hardly worth the effort!" they all commented.

In desperation, the sorcerer sought a weapon. All he could find was a bucket of water. Viktor thought it was water, although the silvery sheen argued against that. Nonetheless, Viktor seized the bucket and tossed the contents on the soldiers. At least the downpour might momentarily catch their attention long enough for him to start running.

The water washed down on the soldiers . . . and continued to wash down on them, becoming a great storm that caught even the sorcerer. Stranger still, instead of drenching the multiple Straas, the storm burned them. They howled like hellcats, turned into smoke, then became a legion of Dré Kopiens.

"Why didn't you tell me, man?" they cried.

Viktor Falsche woke up. He stared weary and blurry-eyed at the slumbering form of his companion and whispered almost drunkenly, "That's what I need."

A blink later, the sorcerer was gone.

VIII

Only two Amantii returned.

Baron Mandrol was furious and vented that fury on his servants, for lack of a Viktor Falsche to torture. The servants quickly learned to avoid him, fearing for their very lives.

How could he not only escape an Amantii but also destroy one? How could that be possible for him? He is not even real!

He recalled the words of General Straas, who had questioned the amazing escape of the false Viktor from Mandrol's own citadel. How could this Viktor Falsche have escaped save by sorcery?

"Get me G'Meni!" he shouted at his personal guard.

The men returned with the anxious alchemist but moments later, although even that was too long for the baron's tastes. Master G'Meni looked as if he had slept sprawled over his workbench again.

"You sent for me, Baron Mandrol?"

"Obviously, you fool." The baron ran his fingertips down each side of his face and exhaled. He could not let fury override his ability to think. No matter how angry the short, disfigured alchemist made him, Mandrol had to remain in control. "Who was it that you chose to wear the face of Viktor Falsche?"

"A peasant, Baron. One of those from the dungeons, you know."

"Last night I summoned the Amantii, alchemist. Last night I set three of them on his path."

Now at last he received a proper reaction from his subordinate. Master G'Meni went pale and almost stuttered, saving himself at the last moment. "Have they taken him, then?"

Baron Mandrol leaned forward, his eyes fixed on the alchemist's own. G'Meni finally looked down. "Only two of the cats returned to me just before dawn, alchemist. Only *two*. The other . . . the other is no more." The baron leaned back in his chair and steepled his fingers. "Your peasant killed an Amantii. With sorcery."

He was pleased to see that the other could find no reply to that stunning statement. Had G'Meni done other than stare at his lord openmouthed, had he returned with some quick, witty explanation, Baron Mandrol would have had him beheaded there and then. It was only the honest shock that had saved the alchemist, at least for the moment.

Slowly, Master G'Meni found his voice. "Baron, I don't know what to say."

"You still insist that it was simply a peasant? Some sewer rat from the dungeons?"

"Yes, Baron. I admit that I gave no thought to the detection of sorcery when I took charge of him. I would not know where to begin, of course. The only sorcery I am familiar with is that which is used to first create the basic mask, and you are still the one who does that. I merely enhance them through my own humble calling."

Mandrol could not argue with that, although he would have liked to have been able to do so. "Yet you are still the one who chose the host."

"I am not, you know." Master G'Meni straightened as best he could. "The soldiers on duty in the dungeons pick them out. I give them a general request. I wanted someone similar in shape and size to the late Viktor Falsche so that the effect would be more accurate. Viktor Falsche might have noticed that he was, say, much too short or far too stout. Who they pick is then beyond my say. If he fits the criteria, then I make use of him."

"Find me the men who were on duty, then."

The soldiers moved to obey, but the alchemist surprised everyone by signaling them to remain where they were. "It will not be necessary to do that. I have already dealt with that matter. It occurred to me that very night after the escape."

The swiftness with which the alchemist had worked made Baron Mandrol slightly suspicious, but he could not fault the man for being efficient. "And where are they?"

"In the dungeons, performing their tasks. They were carefully questioned by myself. I will have them summoned here if you like, but they have nothing to add, you know. They simply chose the person most akin to the size and shape we desired. He was, as I mentioned, a peasant, a farmer, I believe. Shall we send for them after all?"

"That will not be necessary." If G'Meni was willing to have them brought up to be questioned again, the baron knew the answers would match perfectly those of the alchemist. Mandrol was wary of the thoroughness of his underling, but there was no use in pursuing this avenue. One thing that the sorcerer baron understood was that G'Meni would not plot against him. The alchemist would be left without protection. No one would follow such a man, either. The squat, horrid figure repulsed even his lord, but Mandrol, at least, was aware of the value of the alchemist.

However, if that value was ever outweighed by other, less savory aspects of the alchemist's nature, he saw no reason to hesitate putting Master G'Meni out among the lions and watching them feed.

"You are dismissed, then. Next time, however, I would appreciate knowing sooner what you are up to."

Despite the dismissal, G'Meni did not depart. "As a matter of fact, Baron, I was just about to come to you, you know, when these came for me." G'Meni would have sniffed in disdain at the soldiers if he had had enough nose with which to sniff. "You may call off the general's hounds from their useless search out in the countryside."

Baron Mandrol felt a chill run through him. Instinctively, power coursed through his hands. "What do you mean?"

The alchemist seemed rather proud of himself. "I

have achieved through scientific endeavor what the animal cunning of Straas and his lackeys has not. I have located— in general, I must admit—our quarry. He is in the city."

"*In the city?*" Mandrol rose from his chair, hands crackling with visible power. "Where?"

"I am not certain about his exact location yet, but I believe, if you give me a little more time, that I can hand you this latest Viktor Falsche in two, perhaps three hours." Master G'Meni paused, frowning. "And I believe I need one item in order to guarantee success."

"Name it, then! Anything!"

G'Meni bit his lip, then said, "I need the Lady Lilaith DuPrise."

Confusion reigned in Viktor's head. A part of him was caught up in the obsession to find the thing he needed to verify that his plan could succeed. The other part of him was trapped in contradictory memories of a life he knew and yet did not know. He knew parts of the city that during his last sojourn here, some ten years ago, he had never seen.

He was itching again, too. Every few minutes he would have to scratch one side of his face or the other. It added to his inability to focus on one problem at a time.

In his present state, it was not surprising that he jostled or even walked directly into more than one passerby. Most seemed to take him for some drunk and did their best to be away from him as soon as possible. A few remained long enough to curse him and tell him to go to his deity for a lengthy stay.

Viktor bounced against a bearded man. He raised his head and apologized. The man grunted but otherwise ignored him.

The sorcerer took perhaps half a dozen steps before pausing. He glanced over his shoulder at the man. The face was familiar. Very familiar.

Turning, he ran after the other. His prey, unaware of what was taking place behind him, walked slowly on, eyes on the various wares for sale.

Viktor put a hand on the bearded figure's shoulder.

"Excuse me."

The other turned, and snarled, "You'll get no hand-out from me, drunkard! Now let me alone; I have things to do!"

A name came to the sorcerer, a name by which he had long known this man. "Terril! It's me!"

The saying of his name made Terril hesitate, but after a brief examination of the tall, pale figure before him, the bearded man shook his head. "I don't know you. I've never seen you before in my life."

"How can you say that?" Viktor eyed his old friend with great disbelief. "You might as well forget Zura's birthday!"

"I know my woman's birthday, stranger, but I don't know you! Now leave me be!" Terril brusquely removed Falsche's hand from him. "Touch me again and it'll be a sharp blade for you."

Why did Terril not remember him? Viktor sought some solid memory of their time together. The bearded man was too good a friend to have completely forgotten him. "What about—" Something to do with horses. "What about that soldier's horse we borrowed?"

"You want to get me *killed*? Keep your mouth shut about that! There are soldiers everywhere today, ever since whatever happened up in the keep the other night!"

The keep the other night. When Viktor had made his daring escape from Viathos. Terril should have been waiting in the kitchens near the chosen exit, only he had not been there . . . and it should have been *Dré*, not Terril. Viktor did not even know this man; why then was he trying to get the bearded figure to admit otherwise? Why did he feel that he *did* know Terril?

The other man, meanwhile, was now eyeing Viktor with suspicion. In a whisper he growled, "You shouldn't know about that! Only me and . . . and Emil knew about that, and he's *gone!* They took him to the baron's dungeons. . . ."

Emil. The name struck a chord so great that Viktor Falsche's first impulse was to insist that *he* was Emil and how could Terril not know him? Then some clarity returned to the sorcerer and he wondered why he would ever want to admit to something so obviously wrong. *Who is this Emil?*

Terril had come to a conclusion of his own. Viktor barely saw the glint of metal. "You're from Viathos! You won't get me, though."

He brought the blade up to the sorcerer's rib cage.

His assailant managed to bring the point close enough that Viktor Falsche could feel it, but no farther. The sorcerer's hand caught that of his adversary and forced the blade back. Terril grunted and tried to strike him in the chin with the other hand. That attack, too, Viktor countered, but it almost cost him his life, for the bearded figure leaned forward as he struck, his weight nearly sending the blade into Falsche's body.

"I am not from Viathos!" Viktor gasped. "I'm not after you!"

The other was not listening. The sorcerer had no desire to kill a man he knew was basically good, a man Viktor's confused memories indicated was a staunch supporter of any activity that would bring down Baron Mandrol. It was fear that drove Terril now, fear that he would join those who had in the past been dragged off to the dungeons of Mandrol. There were only two fates for those taken: death, or life as one of the puppet soldiers under the command of General Straas. Of the two choices, the former was what most would have chosen, given the opportunity. Unfortunately, freedom of choice was not allowed.

Under the circumstances, Viktor could almost forgive the other for trying to kill him. Nonetheless, he had not escaped Viathos to be murdered thus. He had to deal with his attacker fast.

As if by sorcery, the man Terril pulled away. His action surprised Viktor and had the other man then stabbed, he would have surely killed the confused spellcaster. That was not on Terril's mind, however. What was on his mind became apparent as a trio of Straas-featured soldiers began moving the duo's way. The bearded man spun away from the sorcerer and raced into the crowds, which caused the soldiers to break into a run.

Viktor should have followed Terril, but the sight of the ungodly figures hurrying toward him made him pause. He had come here to find something out about them . . . *from* them. This was not how he had intended to do it, however.

The sorcerer reacted without careful thought, transporting himself away from the area.

When he materialized a moment later, the nausea was so great that he nearly collapsed. Only supreme effort enabled him to remain standing and even then all that initially met his gaze was a moist blur. It took several seconds for the scenery to come into focus. When it did, Viktor discovered himself still in the market region but in an area closer to Viathos, of all places. No one had taken notice of his sudden appearance because he stood behind one of the great tents dotting the area. Viktor had been lucky; his state of mind prior to the jump had made plotting a destination useless.

He stared up at the hated citadel. Fortunately, it was not very tempting at the moment to transport himself inside and try to kill Mandrol; the agony within him made even thinking about such an act painful.

Whether the soldiers had recognized him, Viktor Falsche could not say. He doubted that they had, or else they would have moved with more urgency. No doubt they had simply seen the struggle and had intended on arresting both men, the better to add to the numbers already in the dungeons.

For the moment, his head was clear. He stood where he was, marveling for the first time at the audacity of his search. What must Dré be thinking, to discover his companion gone with no reason given for the sudden departure? Even if Dré was asleep, Viktor was fairly certain that the woman Mara knew of his disappearance. Neither she nor the man Johann completely trusted the sorcerer and this would definitely add to their unease.

Viktor Falsche could think of no way to explain to them what he was trying to do without going through with his present search. However, doing so would increase the danger to all concerned. Did he dare go back with his prize . . . supposing that he was not killed in the process of trying to take it?

For that matter, how was he to go about the task? He could not simply go up to one of them. Here in the city, so near to Viathos, even minor magics were chancy. Transporting both himself and his prize was also clearly out of the question; the sorcerer doubted he had the wherewithal for such a feat.

Pulling his cloak tight, he cautiously stepped back out among the throngs. The merchant whose tent he had used for a shield noticed him at the last moment and warned him to keep away from his goods. Viktor pretended not to hear him. The sorcerer hurried toward the thickest part of the crowd, the better to conceal himself in the open.

He was almost there when the crowd abruptly parted, revealing in the gap a party of soldiers led by an officer. Viktor Falsche gaped, unable to believe the stream of mishap he was evidently swimming. The sorcerer quickly backed away from the patrol, trying to muster whatever strength he could for the battle.

To both his surprise and relief, the patrol continued on, the officer giving him only a cursory glance. Only belatedly did the sorcerer recall that his disheveled aspect was a mask of sorts; either that, or this was one officer who had not been informed what Viktor Falsche looked like.

Knowing that his luck could not hold, Falsche retreated farther. It grated on him that he had to hide from his enemy's forces. What had happened to the Viktor of old? In the ten years that marked his absence, he had evidently become more of a coward.

A knife pressed against his side. A voice he recognized hissed, "Keep walking with me."

It was Terril. Somehow, Viktor had chosen a destination that had brought him to wherever the bearded man had fled. Falsche could not believe his black luck. This would never have happened to him in Wesfrancia. Something ill had befallen him in Viathos Keep. He was beginning to wonder if his escape had not been planned as part of some diversion, some amusement for Mandrol and his followers. He knew the tales of the sort of entertainment that was popular among those within the vast sanctum.

Perhaps his nemesis was even now watching, slowly drawing tight the net.

It was not fear that nagged at Viktor now, only anger at his inability to control what was happening to him.

"In the building to our right," commanded his captor.

Viktor obeyed, more out of curiosity than because he was helpless. The knife was a danger, yes, but even though his sorcery had failed him again, Viktor was skilled at personal combat. He was positive that he could take Terril easily, but he wondered why the man had bothered to take him instead of simply killing him . . . which, admittedly, Terril could have done.

There was something familiar about the structure, something that again dredged up memories that should not have belonged to the sorcerer. He had spent quite some time here, yet Viktor was also aware that he had *never* spent so much as a minute in this place. The entrance indicated that this was the abode of a potter, an artisan. Samples of the man's work lined the front.

It was *Terril's* abode. He knew that, but again the source of that knowledge was unclear. Possibly he had simply made an assumption, but that was not how it felt.

The two did not speak again until they were inside. The door was closed behind them by a young man who resembled Terril enough that he was obviously a son. With his knife, the potter indicated a chair.

"I'll leave no man for the baron's dogs, but I was surely tempted with you. Still, something tells me that I should ask you some questions before I decide whether I should follow my first instinct and gut you as a spy."

Not the sort of attitude that Viktor Falsche would have expected of an artisan, but what he recalled of Terril reminded him that the man was very much as he presented himself. The potter was willing to do whatever it took to protect himself and all that was precious to him.

"Now, I'll only ask once. Who are you and why do you claim to know me when I don't know you?"

How to explain this? The sorcerer did not even know why he recalled this man that he had never met.

Telling Terril that there were memories in his head that were not his own would certainly not help. The potter would probably brand him a spy there and then, forcing Viktor to choose between hurting, possibly even killing, the man or letting Terril kill him.

In the old days before his decade-long gap, Viktor Falsche would not have had to worry about a threat so simple as this. He stared into the eyes of the potter. Much like the Amantii, Viktor should have been able to put the man into a trance simply by catching his gaze, such as now, but since his return, every attempt at sorcery had either weakened him drastically or failed entire—

Terril the potter was not moving. He was not even blinking. If the sorcerer looked close, he could see that the man was breathing regularly, but that was the only movement. Terril had frozen still.

He heard soft steps from behind him. The boy was there and in his hand was one of his father's pieces, a round, blue pot that looked heavy enough to crack an unsuspecting spellcaster's skull. Terril's son had the pot raised over his head, but that was as far as he got before a second glance from Viktor froze him as well.

Somewhat amazed by his own success, Falsche remained where he was, trying to decide what to do next. The logical notion was to depart before the trances were broken somehow. However, Terril presented a perfect opportunity to at last find some answers to the puzzle of the foreign memories.

To the potter's son, he commanded, "Lower that piece and return it to where you found it. Then go over by that bench and sit." As the boy obeyed, Viktor gave orders to the bearded man. "Now *you* sit down."

The sorcerer gave the man his chair, first removing the blade from Terril's grip. There was no sense in taking risks.

"Listen to me closely," he said, once the man was seated. "As a sign of my faith, I will release your mind from the trance. Your body will remain under my control until I deem it safe for me to free it. Now wake."

Terril did. His first impulse was to snarl and try to rise. When he saw that he could not, he opened his mouth to call out. Viktor was forced to make the other's mouth shut tight.

Ignoring the glare, the weary spellcaster sighed. "I could have killed you quite simply, Medecian. I don't want to do that. I know enough about you to know that we should be allies, not enemies. I'm no spy of Mandrol's; if I have my way, the next head propped on a pike at Viathos will be his."

Some of the suspicion faded, enough at least that Viktor decided to try once more to allow his captive to speak. He removed the spell that bound Terril's mouth, then indicated that it was safe for the man to talk.

"How do I know you're not just playing games? You might ask questions and then kill us."

"I could make you answer the questions without your permission; I have no need to allow you freedom of thought. That is not my method, however. I'm here to destroy Mandrol and free Medecia."

"You sound Wesfrancian," muttered the potter, his eyes constantly flickering to his son. "Is that why? Wesfrancia wants the trade routes?"

As far as Viktor knew, Wesfrancia had no designs on its neighbor other than removing Baron Mandrol in favor of someone more sane. That stand might have altered in the past decade, but where he was concerned, it had not. He informed Terril of this, then added, "Mandrol murdered someone dear to me. I think you can understand that." He had vague recollections of someone close to the potter being taken away, but who it had been was not clear. "I've struggled for more than ten years to bring the baron down, and not simply for her sake."

Terril eyed his son again. "I've got no choice but to answer you, do I?"

"I'll free him if you can keep him from trying to crush my skull with your fine work."

This made the potter briefly smile. "All right."

Viktor blinked. The boy unfroze. He took one look at his father and started to rise from the bench with the obvious intention of attacking Viktor with his bare hands.

"Blane! No! Stop where you are!"

The boy did, but he was not happy. "Father—"

"Please be silent, Blane. Sit back down. It's all right. He's not one of the baron's men. I've promised to talk with him, but you have to promise me that you'll leave us be."

The boy started to protest, but a look by his father made him acquiesce. He sat back down on the bench looking very murderous.

"Your son's loyalty is commendable," Viktor Falsche remarked, trying to ease things as best he could. "I promise that nothing will happen as long as he does not try to harm me. I *will* defend myself."

"I understand."

"Good." Keeping the boy in view, Viktor dragged a second chair over and sat down in front of his captive. "I understand how you must have been shocked when I called to you, a stranger accosting you and claiming to be an old friend."

"I thought you were mad, I did."

The sorcerer paused to consider his next question and also to deal with the return of the nagging itch. The latter seemed to get worse each time it returned. When it finally subsided, he said, "I believed I knew you, but now I know that to not be true. I remember a friendship that I know does not exist. In the street, I remembered some incident . . . which almost resulted in a lethal blade thrust from you."

Terril did not look apologetic. "You were blabbering about something that would have had both of us dragged off to Viathos. You don't talk about using an officer's own horse to carry smuggled items into the wild lands and then returning it while he's still in his cups at a tavern, do you?"

"You did that? Why?"

"We had to hurry and the opportunity presented itself." The potter shook his head. "Emil took a big risk considering he was never much more than a farmer. He wasn't a hero sort—too many things frightened him—but he did what needed to be done. Was almost like having a second son at times."

Viktor noted the passion with which the man spoke of his friend and felt sympathy. He understood Terril enough to know what the man was going through, retelling this. "Where is this Emil?"

"He was taken to Viathos just a few days back."

That was all that needed to be said. Once a man was dragged into Viathos, he was not expected to emerge . . . at least as himself.

Viktor scratched one side of his chin. He had more questions than answers. This was not what he had hoped for. What had happened that caused some of this man Emil's memories to overlap with his own? Was that why he could not recall the ten years of his own life?

He had the terrible feeling that something horrific had happened within the keep walls and that somehow he had been an integral part of it.

"I'm going to let you free," the sorcerer announced. "I see no reason why you should remain like this any longer. I'm sorry I've kept you that way so long as it is."

Terril the potter flexed newly released arms and legs. He made no sudden moves toward Viktor, either because he believed the sorcerer to be friendly or because it was likely that Viktor would be able to freeze him in place again before the potter could even raise a fist. "My thanks. You have my pledge, too, that I'll not be trying anything. You remind me some of Emil, although he, poor man, looked more like the baron than you. He received a lot of cursing and taunting for the resemblance, I'll tell you."

Viktor paid him little attention, his thoughts wandering. He would return to Dré without his prize and try to explain just what it was he had been attempting to accomplish. Coming on the heels of his decade-long absence, Falsche knew that he would have a task on his hands. It was quite possible that Dré would turn him away as being more trouble than aid. Certainly Viktor's insane actions had assured that none of his old comrade's companions would ever trust him again.

"I must be going. I should not have remained here as long as I did. Here is your blade."

Terril accepted the knife back even as he tried to digest what the spellcaster had just said. "You're leaving? Just like that?"

"Yes. I apologize for any trouble I caused you and your family." He turned to the potter's son. "You have a good father, boy. I know that."

"Are you going to vanish now?" asked the young man, eyes widening a bit. His hatred for the supposed villain had been replaced by open awe of an actual sorcerer.

With a shake of his head, Viktor Falsche smiled and replied, "No, I will not do any more of that for now. I have been taking chances doing that." The truth was that he was too weak to do it anyway, but he saw no need to let anyone know that. He explained, "Such powerful sorcery is detectable. To do so more than once in one area would be to beg to be discovered. I do not think that I endangered the two of you, but it would be best if I was gone immediately . . . but through the doorway."

"If you need help," Terril interrupted, "I know someone who might want to talk to you. He knows this city and has contacts everywhere. I think I can trust you. Outlander like you. His name is Dré and you can find him at—"

"I know him."

"I wish you could've told me that in the first place. It would've saved us some near violence. If you know Dré, then you're a man to be trusted. Do you know your way?"

Viktor started to say that he did, then realized that he did not. They had come in the back way and he had later departed by use of sorcery. He did not even know the name of the tavern. He admitted such to the bearded man.

"So much for magic making life simpler for a man." Terril chuckled. He gave Falsche directions, then concluded with, "And keep your eyes open. Something's stirred up a hornet's nest in Viathos. Straas himself has been out with his men. They've searched here already, so they won't be around for a while. They're searching the outer lands as well. Some would-be assassin who failed but managed to make off with his head still attached to his body, that's what I think. They'll find him soon enough, I'll warrant, and my only regret will be that the fool didn't complete the task before he died."

"My regret as well," answered the sorcerer, departing. "Who knows? Maybe he will stay and try to finish after all."

"He'd be an even bigger fool than before if he did that!" were Terril's parting words.

Outside, Viktor Falsche mulled over the potter's words as he pulled his collar tight and began wending his way toward where the tavern, known as The Red Raven, was situated. Terril was correct in calling him a fool, but even fools had purpose.

I should have asked him more. The memories that mirrored those of the man Emil still bothered him. Had he met the man in Viathos? Could Viktor have been a prisoner there, a prisoner who only a day or two ago had finally won freedom after years of confinement and torture?

Lilaith . . .

He wondered what hidden memory had caused her face and name to occur to him just then. Something about confinement?

The crowds were parting just beyond him, but it took Viktor Falsche several seconds to note the fact. When he did, he paused, still half caught up in recollection, and looked to see what had the citizenry's attention.

She rode into sight atop a pale steed, her smile, her gaze, sweeping across the gathered folk. An escort of six soldiers, five of them bearing the accursed features of General Straas, rode alongside her.

It had not been memory that had summoned her to his mind; he had sensed her nearness. Years of emptiness could not erase his love for her. She was as beautiful as Viktor remembered if not more so.

Lilaith was outside the keep walls. It was almost too much to stand. He did not question how this could have happened. It was enough that she was near. There were only half a dozen soldiers; he could surely summon up enough strength to deal with them. The officer was the only one he truly needed to fear; the puppets were always a little slower in reacting.

Flush with surprise and anticipation, Viktor Falsche

moved closer to the front edge of the crowd. Stealth was called for now. He had to plan it so that the throngs worked in his favor. Perhaps a diversion.

In the process of slipping through the crowd, Viktor bumped against a man wearing a hooded cloak. The man did not turn, but the sorcerer, acting out of reflex, glanced his way. He nearly stumbled into another watcher when he discovered who he had bumped into.

The clothing was common enough, but he recognized the hard look of one of the mercenary captains of General Straas. As if that recognition were not enough, Viktor also noted the slight but distinctive swelling of the man's torso. The man was wearing concealed armor.

Where there was one, there had to be more. Viktor quickly noted two more just a little farther down. Their hands remained by the hilts of obscured swords.

He backed away, pretending loss of interest. The trap would not be sprung. Viktor did not ask himself how they knew that he was in the city; it was enough that they did. That did not mean that they would capture him. He would simply depart and wait until another day.

Yet . . . he would allow himself one last glance at Lilaith. The sight would surely pain him, but it would also strengthen his determination. It would be a reminder of what needed to be done, as if he truly required reminding.

Viktor paused and drank in the sight of her.

As if sensing his presence, Lilaith turned her gaze toward him. Their eyes locked and a smile spread across her exquisite features.

"Lilaith . . ." he whispered.

She raised a hand . . . and pointed directly at him. "There! There he is!"

Her escort and many in the crowd turned. Only then did Viktor Falsche see that one of the drone soldiers was not a masked drone after all but General Straas.

"Seize him!" the general cried.

Around the sorcerer, a dozen forms and more dropped cloaks, unsheathed long blades, and raced to seize him.

IX

Lilaith watched the men charge Viktor Falsche, a feeling of satisfaction flowing through her. Now at last she was able to prove just how much she cared for her dear Mandrol. Now at last she could prove that nothing remained between her and the villainous sorcerer Falsche. She did not love him; she never could have loved him.

Yet . . . there was a nagging sensation in the back of her mind that belied her other thoughts. It kept leaving her with some small bit of doubt, some morsel of regret, for what she had just done.

It seemed to ask *How could you betray the man you truly love?*

She shook her head, refusing to listen to it.

Yet it would not go away and even as the soldiers closed on Viktor Falsche, it seemed to grow louder.

"Hurry, you damned fools! Get him!"

Viktor caught a glimpse of Straas charging his horse through the crowd, heedless of those caught by the hooves of his huge beast. That was the only glimpse he was allowed of the general, for the soldiers were nearly upon him and thus demanded his attention if he hoped to escape.

His first thought was to simply transport himself away, but he did not have the strength for that. That meant running, which meant he needed a diversion.

It was a simple task to make the lead man's scabbard suddenly twist around and become entangled in his legs. The soldier tumbled forward and two others fell over him. The trick failed with another of the general's men, forcing Falsche to retreat.

One of the soldiers came close enough to attempt a strike with his blade. Evidently the order to seize Viktor did not preclude gravely wounding him. Perhaps all Straas even wanted was his mutilated body. The sorcerer was not willing to give it to him, though. He ducked the blow, then kicked out with his foot in a maneuver that one of his instructors, a sorcerer from the far eastern lands, had taught him during personal combat classes. Unlike some schools, the one that Viktor had attended assumed that there would be times when a spellcaster had to rely on physical skills.

The foot caught his attacker in the leg, breaking the latter's balance. As the soldier slipped, his grip on his weapon failed. The sword went clattering to the ground just an arm's length from Viktor, who dove to the earth to retrieve it even as a second blade cut through the empty air formerly occupied by him. Falsche rose to a crouching position, matched blades with the new attacker, then stepped away as the first one returned. Although unarmed, the soldier tried to seize the sorcerer with his bare hands.

The soldier was one of the unfortunate drones, but Viktor's sympathy did not extend to risking his own life. He ran the man through the throat and prayed that he had not just killed Emil. The prayer was a very brief one, for he barely had time to turn and beat back the second man.

He could not stand here and fight them all. Despite his skill, numbers alone would overwhelm him. Also, more mercenaries were closing in, which meant swifter blades and a greater variety of tricks. Rather a dozen of the general's puppets than a trio of his hand-picked mercenaries.

Turning from his attackers, Viktor broke through the only gap left to him. There was a cart not too far ahead and a wall just beyond that. If he had the will and strength . . .

"You'll not escape, you damned ghost!" cried General Straas from somewhere behind him.

He was forced to engage a mercenary only steps from the cart. The man underestimated him, though, and evidently believed he could kill the sorcerer with a straightforward thrust. Viktor came under the soldier's blade and pushed it up with his own. In the same motion, he lunged. The sword caught the man in the narrow, unprotected gap between arm and chest. The mercenary grunted and fell to his knees, his other hand attempting to stem the flow of blood. It was tempting to finish him, but there was no time. Viktor instead kicked the man aside as he ran past.

The cart was full of hay. Not the weapon of choice, but it was all he had. There was no time to invoke the spirits of the air or any other supernatural being, so Viktor could only hope that they would take his present peril into consideration. He blew a heavy breath at the piled hay and crossed his fingers for added luck.

A powerful gust of wind tore the hay from the wagon, sending the clippings up and around. A tornado formed in the wagon, a mad whirlwind that whipped and whipped the plants about, then with unerring aim sent the shower in the direction of Viktor Falsche's pursuers. The storm had the desired effect; the soldiers froze where they were and quickly covered their faces as they were scratched and pelted. The speed with which the hay flew made it powerful enough to draw blood or blind a man.

Climbing onto the empty cart, Viktor stuck the sword in his belt, reached up, and caught hold of a jutting part of the wall. He pulled himself up, hoping that there were no archers within shooting range. The wall was more than three times his height, which made the climb precarious.

The clank of armor informed him that at least a couple of the general's men had made it to the wall. Viktor got one hand onto the top, then saw a new attacker racing his way along the top edge of the wall. The sorcerer stared at the man's feet, thinking of how treacherous a surface it must be they tread upon, especially at such a swift pace.

He watched with relief as the soldier abruptly lost his footing and fell off the wall down the opposite side, screaming. His spells were small, but each drained him. The nausea had already returned, stronger than ever. Viktor dragged himself atop the wall, then took a moment to recuperate.

Below him, the whirlwind died. That was much too soon. Viktor glanced down at his pursuers and saw General Straas in the background, bearing some sort of gleaming pendant. The pendant nudged old memories, this time truly belonging to him, concerning the general and Mandrol. A protective talisman of some kind. It made a terrible sense that the sorcerer baron would provide his commander with something capable of countering spells.

On the other side of the wall was a thirty-foot drop, that section of the city on more of a downward slope than the area from which he had just come. The twisted form of the soldier whose footing Falsche had ruined was evidence enough of the likely results of dropping that far. There was nothing to hold on to on this side. That left only sorcery, but such a spell required more of him than had the past few.

Viktor gritted his teeth and slipped over, praying again that the spirits of the air and earth would be kind.

He plummeted the first three yards and had just begun to fear for his life when his fall slowed. Air currents flowed underneath him, hindering but not halting his descent. Above him, he could hear the clamor of the first guards reaching the top of the wall. Viktor needed to reach the ground before they started throwing knives or even swords.

Something streaked past him as he neared the earth, burying itself halfway into the dirt. A long, sleek shaft. Straas had finally gotten an archer within range. Viktor cursed and broke the spell carrying him safely down. He dropped the last nine feet hoping that he had not just promised himself a broken ankle or arm.

Another bolt swished over his head as he fell, the archer having aimed true but been caught unaware by the abrupt shift of his target. Viktor struck the earth in a crouching position, the shock of his landing causing his bones to quiver but otherwise doing him no harm. He did not pause, running for the nearest cover before another shaft could finally pin him.

A third and fourth arrow accented his run, but they were farther off target than the previous. The sound of armor scraping against stone indicated that someone had located a lengthy rope. He did not need to look back to know that at least one of the soldiers must already be halfway down the wall. His margin of safety was little more than it had been before. Straas and his men were as unshakable as hounds scenting the fox.

Horns sounded, alerting others to the hunt. Viktor darted past buildings and into the streets again. He was no longer in the market district, but there were still a number of people about. They stared at him as if a troll had wandered into their midst. The sorcerer read their fear and knew that it did not so much have to do with him as it did the fact that he was bringing the soldiers of the baron into this area.

A thundering sound coming from before him made Viktor stumble to a halt. To his disbelief, a Morag tromped into sight, the monster's batwing ears flickering as he searched for his prey. Viktor did not have to ask who that prey was. He darted to the side as the creature turned his way. People began screaming and shouting at sight of the Morag, which proved to be what saved the sorcerer. The Morag's attention became fixed on the scattering bodies before him, enabling Falsche to duck out of sight before the creature's gaze could locate him.

Morags in the city! Throwing everything in to catch me, eh, Mandrol? Despite the intensity of the chase, pride swelled within Viktor's chest. Mandrol considered him such a threat that he was even willing to risk the unstable nature of a Morag in the midst of the city. It was always possible that the monster would forget its present task in order to turn to simpler pleasures, like tearing a few residents apart. Viktor Falsche desired no harm to come to those who lived around here, but it would certainly have aided his own plight if the mercurial beast presented him with the greatest of diversions.

Unfortunately, it was soon clear that the Morag would not cooperate. In fact, this one was particularly determined in its work, avoiding promising tidbits and side stepping objects as it searched. While it had not discovered its quarry, the Morag was adept at choosing just the right place to prevent the sorcerer from sneaking away. Viktor knew he did not have long before the guards arrived, which would then cut his chances of escape nearly to nil.

The Morag's ears twitched. It straightened and began lumbering in the direction from which Viktor had come. From there came the sounds of the pursuing soldiers. Falsche wasted no time; he raced from his hiding place and dashed down the street while the Morag was focused on the clatter coming toward it. With luck, he hoped that the great beast would draw the immediate attention of the general's men, keeping them from looking past and spotting him.

Cries of consternation informed him that at the very least the Morag *had* come as a surprise to the pursuers. There was a thick growl from the creature, but regretfully no sound of battle. Viktor supposed that any Morag trained for city use would have to be able to restrain itself quite well. The Morags feared their master, and rightfully so. Mandrol had even less pity for his victims than the beasts did.

Turning a corner that he knew would take him up to the more crowded and better-concealing market square, Viktor thought of Lilaith's betrayal. It was hard to believe that she was not acting of her own accord, but then that was how a spell such as the baron had placed on her would work. Mandrol would not want a zombie or an unwilling but helpless maid; that was not to his tastes. He would want Lilaith to pretend to be his even if her love was only the product of sorcery.

Still . . . it was difficult to think of her expression, her eyes, and her accusing finger and not wonder if perhaps over the years she had truly come to adore her captor and despise the man who had evidently abandoned her.

The soldiers had fallen momentarily behind, but that could not last long. Viktor Falsche turned onto yet another side street in order to better confuse any of the hunters. A smaller avenue just ahead would bring him back toward his desired destination.

It suddenly occurred to him to wonder just how he knew that. Viktor had never been down the avenue. For that matter, the escaping sorcerer recalled that he had never been down the previous path, either. During his prior sojourn in the city, Viktor had not even journeyed near this area.

Emil. I'm recalling what Terril's friend Emil knew . . . knows. He made the correction almost instantly. For some reason, it disturbed him to think of the man Emil dead. It was preferable to believe that he was still somewhere in Mandrol's dungeon, awaiting the day when the sorcerer baron's death would mean his freedom.

"Well, if your memories serve to keep me from Straas and his puppets, then my gratitude to you, Master Emil," he muttered, ever on the move. "May I be able to return the favor before long."

An arrow flashed by him. Viktor turned . . . and a second shaft caught him in the right arm.

He screamed but did not fall. A great tear and a stream of crimson marked where the arrow had struck. The angle had prevented it from embedding itself in his arm, but as if to make up for that failure, it had taken a long strip of flesh with it.

Pain goading him on, Viktor glared at the archer, who was perched on a high wall behind the sorcerer. The archer, in the midst of readying a third arrow, was suddenly pulled forward by some unseen force that sent him hurtling over the edge. The sorcerer stumbled on even as the horrified soldier crashed face-first into the street. Now the agony of his wound vied with the turmoil inside. Viktor Falsche was aware that the next spell he attempted would likely send him to his knees. He did not even have the power to heal himself.

Again the sounds of pursuit grew nearer. Either the archer had signaled his companions or they had heard the scream. Viktor did not really care. He was in grave danger now; the wound had been unexpected. The sorcerer wondered whether he would reach safety after all.

"Viktor Falsche . . . " called a peculiar, lazy voice.

He glanced to the side and through watery eyes caught sight of the Straas-visaged sentry closing on him.

"You will surrender and come with me. My master desires your company."

"Spoken just like the general," the sorcerer retorted, all the while attempting to mask some of his desperate condition. "Perhaps he will let you take his place the next time he needs to make a speech."

The drone soldier continued to close, which to Viktor meant that the puppet had as much a sense of humor as the man whose face he wore. "I will strike you down if necessary, Viktor Falsche."

Only in the last moment did the sorcerer recall that he, too, had a blade. He met the attack of the soldier, but the weakness caused by his wound made him give ground. His adversary immediately attacked again, trying to draw under Falsche's blade, but Viktor knew the trick and countered. The false countenance of Straas curled up into a very good imitation of the general's own expression of frustration.

Still, it would not be long before the soldier got through his defenses and drew blood. Viktor's right arm was now stiff and his left, which was his sword arm, was already under great strain. The puppet soldier knew that, too, and pressed hard, trying to force his prey into some fatal misjudgment.

It was then that the vicinity around the two combatants exploded with leaping bodies. Five blades and more surrounded the drone soldier. There was no call for surrender and it was clear that Viktor's opponent would not have surrendered even if offered the chance. Instead, acting as Straas would have, he turned on the nearest swordsman and tried to take him down while the others were caught by surprise.

The attack failed. Without hesitation, the surrounding figures lunged. At least three blades succeeded in finding their marks. The drone soldier gasped, then collapsed, sword still in hand.

"God, I hate that," muttered a bearded man. "Could be killing my Tobias."

"They're good as dead when the mask's on 'em, Broderin. Permanent as their own faces, they are."

Viktor forgot his rescuers and stared at the dead figure.

"Yeah, you're right there." Broderin studied the sorcerer up and down. "This's the one, all right. Mara described him perfect."

"We should leave him, he's so big a fool to go wandering around looking for trouble," snarled the second man.

"Be better off," agreed a third. Two others nodded.

Broderin shook his head. "Dré wants the sorcerer back in one piece. Now come on! Let's get rid of this . . . this *ghoul* . . . and get out of here before the rest of the baron's army comes!"

"Dump the body like we always do?"

"No." Viktor put a hand on Broderin's arm. "We have to take it with us."

"Are you daft? Do you know how hard it is to drag one of these around? If they catch us, it'll mean the ax for everyone if we're lucky! If we're not, we'll at least end up replacing this poor sod and any others you might have killed!"

"It is vitally important that I have this man to study. Dré would understand and appreciate what I'm doing."

"He didn't sound so appreciating a little bit ago, from what Mara said. Sounded ready to turn you over to the baron."

Viktor would not give in. "We have no time to argue. Please. I need help. My arm is numb or I would drag him there myself."

"What would you need a corpse for anyway?"

The men stirred uneasily. There were always tales of necromancers and anyone who had lived under the rule of Baron Mandrol was more likely to believe such tales. The sorcerer baron's puppet soldiers were, to many, the living dead.

Not having time to explain, Falsche simply replied, "He may give me the clues I need to help bring down the dear baron."

A distant sound caught the group's attention. An innocuous looking man peered around the corner and called, "They're comin'! Move on quick!"

"We can't take—" began Broderin.

The sorcerer stared deep into his rescuer's eyes. He did not use his sorcery, simply hoping that his glare alone would be sufficient.

Broderin shivered. Then, steeling himself, he nodded. "All right! You four! Grab that thing! I don't care how you do it, but get it to Dré!" As the other men bent to obey, the swordsman glanced back at Viktor. "Dré and Mara think something of you, sorcerer. I trust them even if I don't trust you."

"You have my gratitude."

His rescuer began leading him away, giving support as the wounded sorcerer needed. "Just make this whole damned escapade worthwhile . . . or I'll gut you the next time I see you."

Everyone was ready to kill him, even those who should be his friends and allies. The one exception seemed to be Mandrol himself, who had kept Viktor prisoner for years . . . which could, perhaps, have been considered a sort of living death.

"Quit dreaming!" snapped his companion. "There's at least two Morags about and if I have to leave you for bait to escape, I'll do it."

Viktor nodded, his attention shifting to Broderin's vanishing companions and their gruesome burden. Whatever else had happened, he had what he had been seeking, one of Mandrol's drone soldiers. If luck was with him, the secret to his adversary's downfall would be his within days.

He began itching again.

X

General Straas was not pleased. He was not pleased at not being pleased, either. In the past few days, he had spent much too much time feeling so. Straas preferred things to move with precision and planning. Everything was supposed to fall into place. That was how it worked in a proper, orderly world.

If one could just remove all the Viktor Falsches of the world, then perhaps things would run in a neat and ordered fashion. The Viktor Falsches, though, refused to die even when they were dead and it was always those like General Straas who were forced to bear the burden of failure.

Not this time. As usual, the alchemist's grand plans had gone awry, although G'Meni would certainly do his best to blame it on the ineptitude of the general's men. Straas would not hear of that. This exercise had been designed by an ugly little man who rarely stepped from the confines of Viathos; now it was the general's turn. He had already set some parts of his plan in motion even before the failure of the alchemist's idea. His specially trained Morags were sniffing out the false Falsche. His archers were spread over rooftops throughout the city; the odds were good that one or more of them would spot him. Other men were posted in the ground level in each quarter. By all reports, even if this puppet had command of sorcery, he had to be suffering by now. Straas wished he had talismans to distribute to his officers; perhaps this would be reason enough for the baron to finally grant that boon.

He was coordinating strategy with one of his men

when Lilaith rode up beside him. "General, if I am no longer needed, I would like to return to the safety of Viathos Keep."

Straas bit back the retort he so much desired to spit at her. Baron Mandrol would not hear of any discourtesy to the lady, even if the only reason she loved the sorcerer was due to the spell cast upon her. Despite that spell, the veteran soldier still distrusted her. Spells had too many ways of going awry. "I shall have a pair of men able to accompany you shortly. For now, you'll have to wait. We've a man to hunt."

Without a word, she turned her horse and moved several paces away. Straas tried to read her expression before her features were hidden from him, but nothing in the lady's visage indicated anything of use to him. He wondered whether she felt any secret remorse for betraying Viktor Falsche again.

One of his trusted officers, a fellow refugee from his days in Wesfrancia, rode up beside him. Despite the fact that they wore his face and tended to think along the same lines as he did, the general had no intention of ever promoting one of the cursed zombies to his staff. In the end he trusted only *true* soldiers.

"The prey's got into a hole, General! No one's spotted him since the lower district. We've got a couple of dead bodies and at least one man unaccounted for, but no sign of him."

No sign of him. That was proof again that the false Viktor had allies, possibly even the damned elusive Dré Kopien. Kopien was a thorn in the side of Straas that Master G'Meni always loved to twist. *Have you caught Kopien today, Straas? No? Maybe next year, hmmm?*

"I'll bring you both their corpses, alchemist," he muttered to himself. *Maybe have the chance to add yours to the pile, eh?*

"Orders, General?"

General Straas snarled as he gazed around the watching throngs. How many of them were Kopien's friends? How many of them knew where the renegade puppet was hiding?

"House-to-house. Every area within twenty minutes' running time. Keep the watchers at their posts. I want every spy and beggar questioned; enough gold to last them a year if they give us the key to finding Falsche! I'll pay it out of my own reserves! Tell them that!"

"Yes, general!" The officer saluted, then rode off.

Straas glanced to the side and saw the Lady Lilaith DuPrise watching him with disdain. He grunted quietly, then signaled another man. "Escort her ladyship back to the keep. Take two men with you . . . not puppets, though. Get her back in double time, understand that?"

The soldier nodded. Straas dismissed him, forgoing a salute in his desire to get the she-devil far away from him. Not only did he distrust her personally, but he bore an intense distaste for her people. They looked too unearthly, too like creatures of shadow. People were meant to be pale and sturdy, not dark and lithe. The sooner she was away, the sooner he could concentrate his full attention on bagging the fox.

"The lower sector empties out into the market at some point, doesn't it?" he asked of another man.

"Yes, General."

"Then follow me."

He would have Viktor Falsche spit on a lance yet.

"What in Ariela's name did you bring that in here for?"

Dré eyed the corpse of the soldier with open disgust. Viktor also watched as the body was dragged down the stairs to where Mara stayed. He had expected his rescuers to carry it up to the small room he shared with Dré, but Mara had evidently given orders to the contrary before he and his group had even arrived. Dré knew as little about that command as he did, but Viktor's old comrade was more concerned with what would happen if soldiers invaded the tavern.

"They find this and we're all as good as dead! Not just us, man, but all the others here! Did you think of that?"

"I did." As much as that possibility disturbed him,

the sorcerer would not be swayed. The soldier's body, or more precisely his *face*, was essential to the success of Viktor's plan. The passing of a decade meant that much of his previous information might be useless now; who knew what alterations Mandrol or G'Meni might have instigated in that time.

With Dré still raging behind him, Viktor descended to the cellar. There was more illumination in the room now, although one corner remained virtually black. A table had been set up, and as Viktor watched, the corpse of the drone soldier was dropped onto it faceup. Dead eyes stared at the ceiling.

"Thank you, my friends," called a voice from the blackness.

"This's insane, Mara," muttered one of Falsche's rescuers.

"This is necessary," she replied, echoing Viktor. The woman stepped forth. Now in addition to her thick, lengthy tresses, she wore a veil. "I know."

"What *do* you know?" Dré descended the steps as the others departed. "Did you forget to tell me something, love?"

"No. It simply occurred to me after we last talked. You were in such an unpleasant mood, I decided to wait and discuss it with you later."

"Would now be any good?"

"It's important that he has the opportunity to study this poor soul, Dré. I can't tell you anythin' more than that."

"And what about you, Viktor?" asked the graying man. "Can *you* tell me something?"

The sorcerer moved past the others to better inspect his subject. "We talked about this—" Viktor blinked in surprise. "—when we planned Baron Mandrol's assassination. I'm sorry. I keep forgetting that so much time has passed."

"I haven't, but go on."

Removing the helm, Viktor sought for the cleverly hidden seams that marked the edges of the sorcerous mask. The insidious false face was designed to blend in as well as it was able, but he had an idea of the approximate location of the border. "Mandrol's strength once rested in his own abilities, his own powers. He still has some of that strength, but much more of it has been spread to the armies under Straas. It's the armies which now maintain discipline and control Medecia for the baron."

"I remember some of that discussion, man. I remember that you sent word to Lilaith."

Lilaith had been a fixture at Viathos for some time by then. Viktor still cursed his own stupidity. He should have never allowed her to have her own way. The dark, southern woman had not really known Viktor Falsche's sister, but it was enough that the man Lilaith DuPrise loved was determined to see justice done. He should have argued against her decision to play the enchantress, but the notion had initially been his. Caught between conflicting emotions, the sorcerer had secretly been grateful for her determination.

What a thoughtless fool he had been. In many ways, he had slowly been turning into another Mandrol. The notion sickened him even as he rejoiced at finally finding the seam of the mask. "Do you remember what I said? That if we could remove the armies, the dear baron would follow?"

"And I said might as well walk in and assassinate Mandrol as try to dispose of Straas and his miserable walking dead, which is what we—" Dré glanced at Mara, who waited patiently, drinking in everything that was said. When she seemed disinclined to comment, he returned his gaze to the sorcerer. "You sent some message to Lilaith. You wanted something . . . what . . . an ingredient or some . . ."

"The solvent." Viktor Falsche straightened from his inspection of the corpse. "The solvent that would make these masks come off."

"An awakening. . . ." Mara muttered. The pair looked at her. "An awakening. I saw somethin' earlier. Somethin' to do with him, which is why I told the others to bring that creature down here. I saw faceless men waking or men gettin' up and takin' their faces *off*. So that's what it meant."

Viktor nearly rushed over to the woman and seized her, but was able to hold back. Nonetheless, he could barely control his anticipation. "Are you saying that the future shows that? Are you saying that I will succeed?"

Her voice was tinged with both sympathy and regret. "I'm sayin' no such thin', Viktor Falsche. My sights are possibilities and dreams; no more. Don't go gettin' hopes up because of somethin' I saw, spell man. That's the best way to make them not come true. Just follow through with them the best way you see fit."

"That does not help me at all. What good is it saying that when I plan to do it already?"

Mara's veiled face turned toward Dré. Kopien gave his old comrade a smug grin. "Nice to know that I'm not the only one asking her that. Just do as she says, man. I don't like it, but if Mara says you should be allowed to tinker with that tortured devil there, then I guess I'll be withdrawing my protest." He rubbed his chin with the back of his hand. "Doesn't mean I like it, now."

"I am sorry, Dré. If I did not feel that I had to do this, I would not."

"So you truly think that you can remove those masks after all? Men have tried before. I saw a soldier with his face sliced clean off. Found out that his own mother did it. She knew who he was from the scar on his neck. I think she killed him, then took the mask and face off, figuring he'd die more as himself that way."

Again leaning over his gruesome prize, Viktor Falsche nodded. "I think I can. I was close. There was just one missing factor."

"Which Lilaith said she could finally provide. For some reason, I never trusted that note, but you thought it was safe to believe."

The sorcerer frowned. "I don't recall that."

"You had visions of Mandrol bouncing around your head, man, usually visions including you strangling, gutting, or burning the good baron. I warned you about getting careless."

"I should have listened." Viktor did not look up, instead inspecting the fine line indicating the edges of the mask. It was hard to believe that such a lifelike monstrosity could exist. He would have been willing to swear that the man lying on the table was either a young Straas or at least the general's son.

Mara stepped closer to Dré Kopien. "We should leave him be if we want to give him any chance of findin' some solution, Dré. I've got some news to discuss with you. Let's get upstairs."

This surprised Viktor enough to make him look up again. "You go upstairs?"

Her laugh was more musical than the sorcerer could have believed from one descended in part from trolls. "You think I stay down *here* all the time? Most of it, yes, but I'd tear out my eye if I had to be here forever." She indicated the veil. "Not that uncommon to see a veiled lady, you know, especially a rich, young thin' interested in fun but privacy."

"Don't go making him think that you wander all over the city, Mara. She just goes for short excursions and then usually to one of the nearby safe places. Right now, we're just heading up to the room they gave us earlier."

"Just me and you alone, love," whispered Mara to Dré, imitating his manner of speech.

Even in the dim light, Viktor thought he saw his friend color. Dré and a Cyclopean? What Falsche had noted of her features indicated that, other than the one eye, she was handsome, if not beautiful. Dré had sworn never to love another after the death of Viktor's sister, and while he had dallied with other women, he had kept that vow for all the time that the sorcerer had known him. Ten years, however . . . Viktor could not blame him if life had finally caught up with his friend.

"If you need anythin'," added Mara, "there's a man outside the door to this place. If the door doesn't open, then don't force it; we might have soldiers in the tavern. If it does open, he should be peelin' vegetables. He's doin' anythin' else, then there's a problem. Understand?"

"Yes."

"How's your wound?"

"Irritating but nothing with which I cannot deal. It will not hinder my work."

"Then we'll leave you be now."

Dré shivered as he passed the corpse. "Are you sure there isn't some other way than this, man?"

Viktor tried to push the edge of his fingernail under the mask, but the foul face was sealed tight to the dead man's countenance. "As sure as I am standing here, Dré."

He was left alone after that.

Hours later, he was still sweating over the now disheveled and more than a little disfigured form. A nearby table covered with an array of stained jars, pouches, and bowls represented the intensity of his efforts, but the results of his work were so far worth nil. Dré and Mara had seen to it that he was provided with whatever he asked for, which said something about the depth of their organization, but he had nothing to show for all their aid. Viktor Falsche had kept himself from so far trying to slice the mask off, but the time was fast approaching when desperation would make him do the deed. The weary sorcerer hoped that he would be able to prevent himself from doing that, however, for such an act would thoroughly defeat his purpose by damaging the mask and face.

The mask was a tribute to the abilities of both Mandrol and the alchemist G'Meni, but the adhesive was definitely the child of the squat, disfigured servant of the baron. Viktor was willing to give Master G'Meni silent praise for his skill; the adhesive defied every solution, powder, spell, and whatnot he could devise. He had, of course, skipped the tests that he had run ten years ago, but there were others, many others, that time and circumstance had not allowed.

It was worse knowing that only one thing separated him from triumph over the alchemist. Ten years ago, the sorcerer had used his own training in the alchemical field to identify all but one ingredient in the adhesive. His samples had come from Lilaith and he was certain that at that time she had still been loyal to him.

He wondered briefly when Mandrol had discovered the spy within his own ranks; then he pushed the thought aside as useless. Mistakes of the past would not help him solve this problem.

"What did you do, G'Meni?" Viktor muttered for the thousandth time. Every combination failed when he tested it on the mask. Sorcery was very much a dead end; he could destroy the mask, but only at the cost of extensive damage to the hapless victim's head. Viktor did not want to kill the unfortunates. Not only did he respect their right to return to their own lives, but he needed the army they would make to deal with the mercenaries composing the remainder of Mandrol's forces. The mercenaries had experience on their side, but they were greatly outnumbered by the puppet soldiers.

That army would never be woken unless he outsmarted G'Meni. The alchemist was clever, but sometimes being too clever was a fatal trait. All Viktor needed was time.

He was nearly through with his latest experiment when he realized that he was repeating one of the useless tests first performed a decade prior. Cursing, the sorcerer began wiping off the pasty matter.

A small wrinkle formed on one edge of the mask. It was so tiny he almost missed it; only the accidental grazing of his fingertip against the wrinkle alerted him to its existence.

"Can't be. . . ." he whispered, almost too shocked to believe. "Can't be. It never worked before."

Inspecting the complete edge of the mask revealed that there were two wrinkles, both minuscule in size but enormous in meaning. He again rubbed the pasty matter over the sides of the mask, but achieved no better results.

This was not the cause of the wrinkles, then. Some combination of previous experiments? Perhaps saturation had finally produced a solvent. He was close to the truth, but no closer to the answer. What had he done that had caused this?

His stomach rumbled and the sides of his face itched. He found himself needing to scratch more often, which only served to continually break his concentration.

The itch appeared a permanent fixture in his life, but the hunger he could do something about. Viktor had not eaten in all the time he had been down here, which he realized must be half a day or more. Dré and Mara had both come down once during his seclusion, but the sorcerer now realized that the visit had taken place quite some time before.

Unable to calculate the hour, Viktor hoped that someone would be up and around when he opened the door. For all he knew, it was the middle of the night. He could have conjured food from the kitchen, but weariness and an empty stomach warned him of the possible repercussions of doing that. He desired to add neither nausea nor the possibility of total collapse to his ordeals. The simple way was the best way. Someone would just have to cook him some food.

A hot meal would enable him to resume his work with a fresher mind. Viktor had been a fool to work this long without sustenance. Small wonder he had found and then lost the solution.

When he reached the top, the sorcerer found the door stuck. Too exhausted and hungry to be angry, he pushed harder. On the second try, the door finally gave. Viktor stepped out and discovered that someone had placed some sacks in front of the entrance to the cellar.

Johann stepped inside from the front of the tavern, another sack in his arms. He glared at the sorcerer as if Viktor had just torched his establishment. "What're you, spell man? A fool? Get back down there before they reach this place!"

"What are you talking about?"

The burly man dropped the sack and seized Falsche by the arms. He tried to turn Viktor around to face the cellar steps, but the sorcerer would not allow him. Viktor stared at the man, his gaze at last forcing Johann to back away.

Keeping his eyes averted, the other snarled, "Listen, you damned warlock! Mara told you that the door might not open, didn't she, now? That means trouble! There're soldiers nearing this area! If they find you or that thing down there, we're sunk, man!"

Viktor vaguely recalled the woman's warning. "I am sorry. Is there anything I can do to help?"

"Just get down there, stay quiet, and pray. Mara'll do the rest."

The sorcerer glanced at the open doorway. "Won't they want to search the cellar?"

"I said Mara'll do the rest! Trust her . . . she was crazy enough to trust *you*!"

In the main room, someone slammed down a tankard and shouted, "This slop couldn't be served to my dog!"

Johann blanched. "That's a signal phrase! They're here! Get down there!"

Viktor quickly obeyed, closing the door tight behind him. He heard something thud softly against the door and knew that Johann had pushed the sacks against it again. There was another thud, likely the sack the man had been carrying.

Moments later, a thunder of heavy boots announced the arrival of the soldiers. One voice rose above the rest. "All of you will remain where you are! This tavern's to be searched! Anyone so much as rises, he'll be cut down where he stands!"

The rest sank down into an incomprehensible muttering. The soldiers tramped through everywhere. Viktor heard them overturn benches and break open doors. There were shouts, but he did not hear anything that sounded like battle.

Trampling feet neared the doorway. Viktor held his breath and readied himself. Worn as he was, he could take on a few soldiers if necessary. He hoped that Dré and the others had already departed; if they were caught with him, he did not want to think what sort of punishment Mandrol would devise for them.

"Nothing here," came the drawling voice of a drone soldier.

"Check that wall," commanded a voice that definitely belonged to a mercenary. "Make sure."

One pair of boots moved closer, then shifted away. The soldier pounded on a far wall. "Nothing."

"Come on, then!" Retreating footfalls marked the pair's departure.

There was more noise and damage, but in minutes the soldiers had departed. Viktor waited, but Johann did not come. He was just about to risk discovery when he heard the sacks being pulled away. The next instant, Dré was standing in the doorway, a grim look on his face.

"We're leaving here. We're going back to the cave."

Something in that grim expression made Viktor ask, "What's wrong?"

"What's wrong, man, is that they almost got a good number of people, Mara included, because of you. If it wasn't for her, we'd all be heading to Viathos for a fitting right now."

"You're not making sense, Dré, and I cannot leave the body just yet. I've almost got it! I've almost found the solvent that will free those men from Mandrol's control."

"Doesn't matter! I won't risk her again!" Dré Kopien shook his head. "You're reckless; you always have been. Sometimes I think you don't care that much about anyone. You risk yourself, I know, but you also risk others . . . others who don't have your power, your ability to squeeze out of danger."

"What does this have to do with Mara?"

Kopien eyed the corpse with hatred. "Mara is no sorceress, but she has abilities that blur the definitions. You know that she's a seer, but there's more. Mara can also project visions into the minds of others, but only at great strain to herself."

"The soldiers seeing the door." Now Viktor understood why neither man had noticed the entrance to the cellar.

"Right now she's up in the room they gave us, a room that she *also* had to shield, trying to recuperate. If they come back again, I don't think that she can summon the will for a believable vision. They'll see the door this time."

Viktor stepped in front of the soldier's body and confronted Dré. "I can understand your fear for her, but this is the key to defeating Mandrol. What does Mara say about this? Does she even know you came down here to talk to me?"

"She thinks I'm down here seeing if you're safe."

"I am and you can thank her for me . . . for everything. You can also tell her that I am nearly finished here—"

"Viktor—" The mustached man looked ready to strike him.

The sorcerer remained defiant. "—and success or no, I will leave here in two hours."

This caught Dré Kopien by surprise. "Two hours? I suppose that might . . . they shouldn't be back tonight, but—"

Falsche softened. "I will not let you lose a second love, Dré. I could not have that happen again."

"I don't love Mara, man! I love Cordelia! By Ariela, Viktor, I swore never to love another! How could you even—"

"You can lie to yourself, Dré, but I do not hold you false for changing after so many years. Despite the veil and hair, I can see that Mara is a handsome woman, Cyclopean or not. I know you well enough to understand that you can look beyond her differences and see the truth. I only hope that someday you will tell yourself that truth."

Dré simply stood there, mouth shut, eyes down. The sorcerer turned back to his prize. "I could use some food. Also these items." Viktor began composing a list in his head, not bothering to look to see if his companion was paying attention. Dré would remember everything. "Get them to me in an hour and I will be out of here one hour later." The sorcerer paused, touching the masked visage. "The face will not be in good enough shape to tell me anything more afterward. I'll *need* to return to the wild lands for the next step."

He heard the graying man turn toward the steps. Viktor finally glanced over his shoulder, catching Dré doing the same. The two stared.

"You *are* Viktor. No one could ever play you."

Dré departed while Falsche puzzled briefly over the remark. Then, left alone again, the sorcerer returned to the question of the mask. The list he had given Dré had been a false one; none of the items on it would help him solve the secret of the adhesive, but he had wanted to give the others something to keep them occupied so that they did not disturb him again during a crucial moment. For the information he hoped to obtain, Viktor would have to return to a track of investigation he had previously abandoned.

Sorcery. Mara's rescue had stirred his mind from the stupor created by hours of failure. Perhaps he could not discover the ingredient that the alchemist had utilized to make the mask bond so permanently, but he could use his abilities to seek the traces of just what had caused the wrinkles.

He touched the mask at one of the points at which it had wrinkled and concentrated, trying to identify through his power the various potions and powders affecting it. One by one he recognized and filed them, discarding as best he could those that seemed to have negligible effect. It was a process of narrowing things down to just those causing the rippling.

Time scurried on, but Viktor Falsche did not take much note of its passing. He continued to concentrate, weeding through dead ends and miscombinations. Even when he knew one item was involved, he still had to calculate how much of it had been involved in the effect.

Then, when the strain was beginning to tell on him, the combination revealed itself.

Both elation and disappointment swelled within the sorcerer. He knew now what mix of alchemical potions, powders, and elements he needed, but if he was correct, then his hopes for the success of his overall scheme had been set back terribly.

Potency was the problem. The combination he had created by sheer luck worked, but to create the chaos he desired, Viktor needed quantities so great he would have had to scour Medecia, Wesfrancia, and a dozen surrounding countries and kingdoms clean of the substances. To remove this one mask, the sorcerer would have had to buy out the marketplace and every alchemist in the city.

"Damn your twisted form, G'Meni. . . ." Viktor cursed quietly. The alchemist's warped but brilliant mind astounded him time and time again. The work that had gone into the adhesive was almost as impressive as the masks themselves. "This is brilliant."

The Universal Solvent was still a thing of legend, but Viktor suspected that even it would have had difficulty eating away the bent figure's creation. Still, the combination reminded him of some other, more basic, yet still incredibly potent formula, something that could do the task——

"Well, it's pins and needles out there, but here's your chemicals, man."

Dré and two others cautiously descended the stairs, vials, flasks, and pouches in their arms. Most men respected sorcery, even feared it, but alchemy stirred an anxiety all its own. There were too many tales of huge explosions and poisonous clouds, tales fairly often based on solid fact.

"Dré. There is one more item I need."

"Something else?" The mustached man looked distrustful. "I'm already thinking that you've had us wandering about just so that you could tinker with that monster there. I meant it when I said we're leaving here, man. You've got yourself just a little more time; I'd suggest you make use of it, Viktor."

The sorcerer eyed his comrade's companions, who suddenly decided that they were needed elsewhere. When the two men were alone, Viktor carefully replied, "I have the answer, Dré, but now I need to know one more thing."

"What do you mean, you have the answer?"

Instead of answering the question, Viktor Falsche asked one of his own. "Dré, what do you know of a substance called el-Khadim's Horror? We called it Plutite, too, I think."

"I know it." The graying man frowned. "I've heard men call it the Creeping Void. Terrible, dangerous stuff, man. Rare, too, thank Ariela."

"It could become Medecia's savior. Old Savas in Wesfrancia knew the secret of it, but he must be——"

"Savas is dead, Viktor. Seven years ago."

"I was afraid of that. He had two apprentices, though——"

"Also dead." Dré crossed his arms. "Let me finish this for you, Viktor. I'll be saving you some time and questions. Savas and his boys all died when his shop exploded. Anyone who knew the old curmudgeon knew it couldn't have been no accident. Two other alchemists in Wesfrancia died close to that time. One looked to have breathed in fumes from some concoction that left him looking like a sun-dried wine grape. The other one . . . well, man, they only found the bottom half of him."

Viktor Falsche scratched the side of his face. He said nothing, afraid that he knew where the tale of death was leading.

"I thought about that Plutite, too, man. I might not be the sorcerer you are or the alchemist that foreign troll G'Meni is, but I learned a fact or two. Thought it could maybe do what I think you want it to do . . . make those masks peel right off. Only there're two problems now, Viktor."

The sorcerer ceased scratching.

"I realized that we couldn't go around wiping it over the face of every damned puppet soldier. That was the first problem. The second is that it turned out, by no coincidence, I'm sure, that only one man I can locate knows its making now."

"Who is that?"

"Why Master G'Meni himself, Viktor. Who else?"

It was exactly as the worn sorcerer had feared, but the knowing enabled him to come to a decision that, however insane it sounded, was the only plausible path to take. "Then I will have to go visit Master G'Meni."

"And how do you propose to do that? You took ten years and more to escape Viathos last time, man! You don't even know how you did that, either! This time, there might not be any coming back!"

"I have to go in again eventually, Dré. We cannot succeed unless I do, you know that."

An argument was about to ensue, but before either man could say anything further, Johann appeared on the steps, a harried look on his weathered features. "You may be seeing the baron and his devil man a lot sooner, both of you!"

"What in Ariela's name are you babbling about?"

The tavern man nearly tumbled down the steps as he descended. He righted himself, glanced above at the door . . . which Viktor noted was closed again . . . and spouted, "The soldiers are back again!"

"Back again?" Dré shook his head, unbelieving. "Mara—"

"She said she'll do what she can, but that's not the worst of it, Dré!"

"What else?" interrupted Viktor before his companion could begin what would certainly be questions concerning Mara's health.

"General Straas is *with* them."

XI

Lilaith continued to stare out the window, her thoughts in turmoil. Straas was still out there, searching for the man she had sensed and pointed out, the man she had once loved.

But not anymore! the lady insisted. *The baron is my love! He took me in when Viktor Falsche abandoned me!*

A part of her believed so, but another, continually more insistent part of her denied that. It insisted that it was not so. She was having trouble coming to grips with the conflicting beliefs.

How and when had Viktor Falsche abandoned her? She turned from the window and walked slowly to the massive bed that she alone used. Mandrol never came to her. He had not come to her in years. Oh, now and then he almost seemed ready to, but something always caused him to draw back. Somehow Lilaith had offended him, but what a terrible offense it must have been to keep him away so long.

Yet there were times when she did not feel so disappointed in the baron's lack of desire. There were times when she felt almost relieved.

What is happening to me? she asked not for the first time.

"Here you are."

Lilaith DuPrise whirled at the sound of the baron's voice. The tightness that she had noted recently in his voice was worse than ever. Mandrol was under great strain.

"I searched for you. I sent servants all over Viathos just to locate you . . . and here you are in your chambers, exactly as you should be. I'll not tolerate this. Tomorrow there will be need to train several new heads."

"Please do not punish them for something I am responsible for." Lilaith flowed over to him, moving almost as silently as a phantasm. "I sought solitude and did my best to make certain that I had it."

"There must always be a guard nearby, my love," returned Mandrol, eyeing her in a peculiar manner. She wondered briefly about it, then decided that it must have something to do with Viktor Falsche. Her stomach started to turn as she thought that, which further added to her confusion. She should have *no* hesitation when it came to Viktor. "Why would I need a guard in Viathos? The danger is beyond the walls, not within your sanctum. Even now, General Straas must be near to capturing him."

Baron Mandrol laughed, but his expression afterward was anything but amused. "I've become somewhat skeptical lately of just what either Straas or Master G'Meni can accomplish. Their talents appear to involve more bluster and promise than result these past few days."

Not a willing champion of either of Mandrol's minions, the Lady DuPrise nonetheless said, "But they have come closer with each attempt. The general has men scouring the city; surely Viktor will not escape this time."

"*This* Viktor is as much a ghost as the old was, for which I have dear Master G'Meni to thank. He flits about, shows himself, and then vanishes again, leaving chaos and dead soldiers in his wake."

"Then you think the general will not capture him?" Her heart raced from both the fear that Viktor Falsche might yet come after her baron and the relief that he was still eluding Straas. It was a struggle to mask the agony her conflicting halves were creating for her, but Lilaith triumphed . . . at least for now.

"I think not at this point. That's why I've come back to you, my dearest. We spoke of something not long ago, a way for me to find Viktor Falsche with your assistance. Do you recall?"

"I do." Now she was struck by warring fears concerning Baron Mandrol. A part of her worried that she would fail him in the task he had in mind; the other feared that she would be all too worthy an aid, that her assistance would put an end to the resurrected specter that thought itself her old lover.

Again she asked herself what was happening to her and again she had no answer that satisfied her.

"Good." He came to her, took her hands in his own. She wanted to pull them away. "I know that I can at least count on *you* to remain true to me."

"Of course, Mandrol."

"I'll allow Straas a bit more time; he reports an excellent lead based on the information obtained from an honest but foolishly reluctant source. We shall see. I need time to prepare myself, too. It will be much the same as it was the first time we attempted it, only I'll have to include . . . include some animals."

"Animals?"

Mandrol pulled her close and kissed her. There was little emotion from either side of the kiss, but the baron still smiled at her, albeit a bit dourly, when they were finished. "Just a pair of cats."

General Straas marched the length of the tavern's front room. None of the patrons still there so much as lifted a tankard or even breathed too heavily. No one wanted the baron's commander to take notice of them.

"The building is surrounded?"

"Yes, General!" barked an officer.

"No one was seen leaving as the men took their positions?"

"Two patrons, sir. They've been taken for questioning."

Straas nodded satisfaction. He completed his inspection of the front room, then eyed the entrance to the back of the tavern. "The back area is also secured?"

"Yes, sir."

Without further word, the grim-faced general marched to the back. A soldier kept the entranceway open for him, his back pressed as hard against the wall as was possible. Drone soldier or mercenary, no one who desired to keep his head got in the general's path.

Behind Straas came a complement of more than a dozen men, including two officers, none of whom were G'Meni's puppet soldiers. For Falsche, even a false Falsche, General Straas wanted men whose reflexes he could trust. The drones were good for loyalty, but he was of the old school that said that a soldier was a warrior and warriors needed to be able to adjust to shifting battle situations at the blink of an eye. The drones were just a fraction too hesitant for his tastes.

It was just one of the many excuses he gave himself for being as far away from them as possible.

He paused at the entranceway and glanced back at the stairs leading up. The tavern doubled as an inn of sorts.

"The upstairs?"

The same officer who had replied earlier snapped his fingers. Five soldiers rushed to the steps and started up, swords drawn and ready.

Straas continued through to the back of the building. His eyes took note of the various supplies and miscellaneous objects stored there. The kitchen was to one side in a separate area. Sacks were piled against the wall.

"Bring him in."

One of the soldiers saluted, then retreated to the front room and out the entrance to the tavern. He returned a moment later with a bedraggled figure that Viktor Falsche might have recognized as one of the men who had rescued him from the attacking puppet soldier. The man's face was beaten and bloody and his wrists were bound. He was barely able to walk, a product of further efforts by the general's master interrogators.

"Well? Where are they?"

The man raised his arms and indicated a wall behind the sacks. Straas had two soldiers move to the wall and strike against it with the hilts of their weapons. The wall in question gave a resounding but very solid thud.

Unamused, the general turned back to his source of information. "This wall is quite real."

"Ill-illusion . . . Mara . . ."

"Nonsense." Straas raised his talisman for all to see. The glow indicated that it was functioning quite well. He stretched forth his hand in the direction of the wall. The closer proximity of the talisman had no effect. The wall remained a wall.

General Straas returned the talisman to its proper place. His face was dark as he looked down at the broken figure. "There is no magic involved here. The talisman tells me that you're lying to me. I thought that we had an understanding. I thought that you knew that if you led us to the traitors we would stop the pain."

The soldier holding the prisoner seized the unfortunate figure by the throat and squeezed. The informant gasped as his air was cut off. General Straas counted silently, well familiar with just how long a man in this condition could go without air. When enough time had passed, he glanced at the guard, who loosened his grip just enough to allow the prisoner to breathe again.

"It—not real—swear—"

The oath was so desperate, so earnest, that the general began to wonder if perhaps some counterspell strong enough to affect his baron's gift had been placed around a hidden door. He shifted his gaze back to the wall.

"It's him!" came a cry from the front room.

All thought of walls, talismans, and untrustworthy informants faded as Straas whirled about and barged his way past his men. Soldiers were already streaming out of the tavern. The men who had gone upstairs were racing down even as he crossed to the main entrance of the building.

"What the devil was that? Who said that?"

No one replied, but replying abruptly became moot as Straas caught sight of the figure standing on one of the roofs nearby. Viktor Falsche . . . the cursed puppet that looked like him, that is . . . was perched on the edge of the roof, watching the soldiers race in his direction. He looked from his pursuers to the doorway, where his eyes met those of the general.

Falsche smiled, then headed off in the opposite direction of the tavern.

"I'll slit you from head to toe, blast you!" Straas looked around him and although his men were moving as quickly as they could in pursuit, they were moving much too slow for his tastes. "What by Drayvo's Ax are you doing standing around? After him! Get him or it'll be all your heads on pikes!"

One of his aides brought him his stallion. He leaped aboard the huge beast, pulled the animal around, and urged it forward, heedless of the men who had to tumble out of his path. His aides followed, doing their best to keep up.

He had Falsche . . . and this time no tricks would save the cursed spellcaster.

There was a series of three rapid knocks, then two much more spaced ones.

"That's the signal! No time to waste!" snapped Johann. "Mara said you both leave the moment she's successful! We'll get rid of that thing!"

"My work—" Viktor began.

"Mara!" shouted Dré, trying to get past Johann. The burly man refused to budge until he was finished speaking his piece.

"She can't see you, Dré! She won't have the strength; woman was half-collapsed already when we saw them come back. You saw her; you know what she'll be like, don't you?"

"I can't leave her, man! Not like that!"

Johann looked briefly sympathetic. "She's done it for you, Dré, you and this fool of a friend of yours! It's your fault, spell man! She'll have worn herself out worse than ever, making it look like you're running away and still managing to shield both the cellar door and her own."

"Johann, if anything happens to her—" Dré tried once more to pass him and once more failed.

"It'll be on his head, Dré! I'll personally cut it off myself and throw it over the wall of Viathos if she dies." The tavern man quieted. "But consider yourself lucky, spell man. I think she'll pull through right enough if let be."

"I am grateful—"

"That you're still alive. Now follow me, both of you. We've got another way out, Dré. One you don't know. Mara had us make it but she said not to tell you until it was time."

"But Mara—"

"I'll watch her for you. She won't want nothing happening to you, Dré. I know." Johann turned then. The pair followed, Viktor with great reluctance, but the risk was too great. Still, now that he knew what it was he needed, he could plan better. His notion of entering Viathos did seem mad now that he had the time to consider it; he would not be helping Lilaith, Dré, or any of the others by rushing into the maw of death again.

Although years had gone by, he believed he knew some who still might possess the secret for making the substance he needed. The arm of Mandrol did not stretch everywhere, no matter what the sorcerer baron believed. As much as it would distress him, Viktor would have to force himself to wait until he could contact those alchemists who might be willing to deal with him. There were others in Wesfrancia, friends of Savas. Farther south, he recalled a man, a distant kinsman of Lilaith, who might at least know of an alchemist with knowledge of Plutite.

Johann's safe route was revealed to be a false stone in the floor of the kitchen area. A huge cooking pot sat atop it, but once that was moved, the stone could be lifted away. The tunnel beneath was snug but serviceable and led them under the building to the one next to it.

The path ended below a wooden floor. After deciding that no one was near, the two men pushed the boards aside and climbed up.

"Johann and the others have been busy," commented the graying man as they surveyed the empty room. There was no sign that anyone used it. "Too bad they couldn't have tunneled a few buildings farther. This is too close for my tastes."

"I wonder if she knew that we would need it," commented Viktor. He found himself constantly marveling at the strange abilities of the one-eyed woman. Her powers evidently did not fall under the title of sorcery but were some peculiar phenomenon due to her unusual ancestry. The sorcerer was especially interested in the fact that her skills were not countered by the general's very potent talisman.

"I should go back, Viktor."

Falsche shook his head. "I understand, Dré, believe me, but Mara is correct. We have to leave . . . but we will *both* be back soon."

"Damn Mandrol."

They heard a sound, possibly the squeaking of a long-unused door. A single figure furtively entered the room.

"Mara sent me," the newcomer, a woman, whispered. "She knew you'd need a way from here to the trash lands."

"That we do," responded Dré. "I know you. You lead one of the garbage carts."

The woman stepped closer, revealing to Viktor a plain, disease-marked face. She had suffered many small diseases over her life, but no great ones . . . or so the sorcerer guessed from her appearance. "And that'll be your way out. I hope you don't mind my stink, lads, because you're gonna smell a lot worse by the time we get you out."

Viktor tried to summon the strength to cast some spell, but his final efforts with the mask had left him devoid of any worthwhile amounts of power. It would have to be the garbage cart. "It would appear that we have no choice in the matter."

"Not if you want to live, no."

General Straas waved his sword in the direction he wanted the other horsemen to ride. He had already dispatched several in other directions, all with the intention of surrounding Falsche before the sorcerer could escape farther into the city. The baron's foe . . . or rather the farmer who thought he was the baron's foe . . . had not utilized any sorcery and Straas genuinely doubted that the man could anymore. Not only was the reach of the talisman long, but he also believed that the prey was exhausted. Exhaustion was the bane of spellcasters, and this one was in actuality a person not trained in the art. No stamina.

It would be interesting to see the face behind the

mask. Straas had theories about the identity. In his younger days, the baron had been a womanizer and, quite frankly, a careless one at that. Most of the bastards had been put to death, but now and then one showed his or her face . . . which was usually enough to identify them as the baron's unwanted prodigy. Somehow a few survived to adulthood.

It had to be one of the baron's children. The discovery would definitely raise questions as to the alchemist's competence since G'Meni should have checked the possibility of the prisoner being a latent sorcerer. The general smiled. What a sweet victory it would be if what he suspected was true.

Minutes passed, minutes that made the bearded veteran shift in growing impatience. His men had the building surrounded and by this time they had entered. Falsche could only fight with whatever physical means were available to him, which meant that sheer numbers would eventually overwhelm him.

At last, no longer able to stay mounted, he leaped off his horse, tossed the reins to an aide, and joined the hunters inside.

The place had been a dwelling, one of the poorer ones, divided up so that many families could live within its walls. Packing so many bodies together did not bother a veteran soldier who had spent years in tents and barracks, but the abysmal condition of the interior disgusted him. Much of the chaos was due to the zealous searching of the hunters, but the place had started out a rat hole.

The inhabitants were all packed together in one corner of the room he entered, their outright fear a satisfying sight, especially after all the chasing and dead ends that the general had been forced to endure of late. The soldiers were milling around, growing less and less efficient in their appointed tasks. Others were coming back down the rickety steps leading to the upper floors, more than one puzzled look among the faces. Even the usually impassionate puppet soldiers seemed perplexed.

"Where is he?" demanded General Straas in a quiet, calm voice that nonetheless brought complete silence to the room.

The hunters looked from one to another as if seeking some spokesman among their reluctant lot. Straas growled and focused on an officer in the back. The look was enough. The officer scurried through the ranks, stopped just out of arm's reach, and saluted nervously.

Straas took a step forward, putting the man into easy grabbing distance. The soldier swallowed.

"Well?"

"We . . . we found no trace, sir."

"He has to be here. We sighted him on top of this building. He was not seen to jump off. We have the building surrounded and men in every corner of the interior. His powers are waning and my presence means that he should have no use of his sorcerous abilities. The only things that he can do are fight and hide. He obviously has turned to the latter choice."

"We've searched everywhere—"

Straas seized the officer by the throat. "If you haven't found him yet, then you haven't searched everywhere. I want every wall prodded and every floor torn open. I want not so much as one of the fleas that populate the bodies of these scum to escape the hunt." He glanced at the people huddled together. "I want each of these vermin questioned thoroughly, and while you're at it, make certain that one of them isn't our quarry. Sorcerers'll use cloaks and dirt to disguise themselves. They aren't helpless when they're unable to cast a spell."

"Yes, sir!" gasped the officer after the general had released his grip. The hunters returned to the search with renewed effort, tearing apart the makeshift chairs and tables, breaking through weak areas in the walls, and turning up the floor wherever possible. Above, Straas could hear the same going on. It was tempting to torch the place after they were through with it, but he did not want to waste the manpower. They would have to make certain that the fire did not spread to some more worthy section of the city, such as the homes of the sycophants who supported his baron.

More time passed without any hint of discovery. Straas paced from room to room, then stepped outside to inspect the perimeter. Nowhere could he see a hole in the wall of men he had placed around the rotting structure. There were even men on the roofs of the surrounding buildings and others within, although it was impossible that Falsche could have made his way out of the building before him. Falsche had to be inside.

Didn't he?

Again the search began to wind down. Straas began to peer over his shoulder, seeking something he could not identify. The false Falsche had been sighted fleeing this way, always remaining just out of reach. It was almost as if he had been taunting them or—

Diversion! He cursed himself out loud and raced for his horse. Too many times during the chase had the figure made certain that it stayed visible rather than try to hide. It had to be a diversion of some sort, either someone dressed to look like Viktor Falsche or possibly some sort of illusion that was proof against his talisman. He had allowed himself to be tricked like some damn peasant put up on the front line in order to be sent out as fodder for the enemy. "Mount up! Back to the tavern!"

No longer did he dream of holding up the severed head of one of the baron's bastards and announcing to Mandrol that Master G'Meni had chosen this one to wear the face of Viktor Falsche. Now his best hope was that his baron would not have him flogged before the alchemist. Worse, Baron Mandrol might decide it was time that his general retired permanently.

He tried to force away the image of one of the unholy masks being placed on his own countenance but could not. It was all too possible that this latest disaster would see him joining the ranks of the walking dead as just one more puppet soldier.

No! There's still time! He can't be far! Viktor Falsche would be his even if Straas had to level the city to take him.

"What's happening?" whispered Dré to the woman leading the cart.

"Hush up, you! We're almost there! You'll be outside in just a bit unless you give yourself away!"

Viktor leaned close to his companion. "I hear horns and horses. Whatever diversion Mara used has failed. They have to be returning to the tavern."

It was the wrong thing to say and the sorcerer realized it the moment the words escaped his lips, but it was too late. Dré automatically began to rise, causing the false cover of garbage to shift.

"Stop that!" hissed their rescuer.

"Mara's in danger!" snarled Dré in what could only be termed a whisper.

The woman rapped a fist against the side of the cart, leaned close, and muttered, "You've got people starin'. Stop it or I'll leave you here, cart and all. I've got me own neck to worry about, you know!"

The cart's pace picked up. Their rescuer had just about had enough of them, Viktor decided. He could not blame her. The sorcerer was bitter; here he was once again fleeing from Mandrol instead of going to him. That he had made great progress did not sooth his embattled mind.

"Out the gates," muttered the woman. Viktor realized that she had never told them her name. "Just a few more minutes and we'll be—"

Neither man had to ask what was wrong, for both could hear the hoofbeats of horses and the rattle of armor, sounds which grew nearer by the second.

"Out of the way, you witch!" roared a husky voice. "Aside with you!"

"I can only move so fast," she snapped back. "Unless you pair want to sully your nice shiny armor and give a woman a hand."

"Have you seen anyone unusual out here?"

"In the garbage lands? Only the King of Wesfrancia, of course, and the lords and ladies of Neuland, of course. Out for a holiday I think."

"We're wastin' our time," said a second voice. "We should get back to the others. There's guards out here; he'd never come this way."

"Yeah and you saw what's out here! Those dregs in rusty armor make the zombies look lively! He could just waltz in and out of the city, what with the way they're guarding the place! They didn't even ask us why we were out here!"

While the two horsemen argued, the woman continued to lead the cart away. Viktor suspected that she would have liked to have moved faster, but her animal was a tired, mangy beast used to a pace little faster than that of a one-legged beggar. Despite subtle urgings, she could not get it to move even the least bit faster.

"Just a minute, you."

The cart came to a halt. "Now what do you want? I'd like to get this out there and dumped. Got four children and a drunkard of a husband waiting for me. This stuff stinks to high heaven, it does."

"Just don't move, hag. I want to take a closer look at this garbage of yours."

"Do you, now?" The woman shifted around to where Viktor and Dré were hiding. She moved her hands around, as if adjusting the load, and suddenly slipped a small but wicked-looking knife into the sorcerer's hand. Although both men had swords, she evidently realized that it might be impossible for one or both to draw those weapons quickly. "Some folks have strange taste. You see anything you like, you can take it home with you."

This brought an amused chuckle from the zealous soldier's companion. The other horseman ignored the jibe and urged his mount around to the side where she stood. He took his sword and prodded the top of the rubbish pile.

"Yeah, that's garbage," commented his companion. "Let's go now before Drazney asks what took us so long."

"Not yet."

The sword focused on the spot where Viktor hid. Through the carefully laid trash, the sorcerer watched the blade move ever closer. Beside him, Dré tapped his hand twice, an old signal used by the two. Viktor tapped once in return.

The soldier readied his arm for a thrust that would

cut deep into the pile and, coincidentally, the left shoulder of Viktor Falsche.

Dré tapped his hand once more . . . and the two men burst from their hiding places. Dré Kopien turned immediately, pulling free his blade as he moved. Viktor rose with the knife ready to throw. The two horsemen stared in surprise.

Viktor's adversary recovered first. He twisted his blade around and attempted to sever the sorcerer's hand, but his reactions were too slow. Viktor Falsche threw the knife with deadly accuracy, opening a scarlet waterfall in the middle of the the the soldier's throat. The man let out a gurgle of protest, then fell backward off his horse.

The battle was not so easy for Dré. His opponent, although more stunned than the first soldier, had the advantage of distance and time. Dré had to reach forward to strike, which gave the other man the seconds needed to recover. Blade struck blade with a resounding clang. Around the area, heads turned. Viktor swore under his breath. They could not hide discovery; at this point all they could hope for was to end this battle before the sluggish sentries in the distance stirred to action.

He leaped out of the cart, pausing just long enough to say to the woman who had gotten them this far, *"Run! Get away from here. Go!"*

She did not hesitate. Falsche turned from her retreating form and hurried around to help Dré. The two combatants were still struggling to draw first blood. It was clear that Dré Kopien was the better swordsman, but the soldier had the advantage of mobility and longer reach.

Somewhere a horn sounded the warning. Viktor came up on the side of the horseman and brought his own weapon into play. Harassed now by two separate threats, the soldier began to retreat. Dré jumped out of the cart, still fighting. He caught the horseman on the back of the hand, but the cut was a shallow one.

Deciding that he was both outnumbered and outskilled, the soldier took one last swipe with his blade, then urged his mount around so that he could retreat.

Unfortunately for him, the animal stumbled on the uneven ground. It was only the slightest of delays, but that was enough for Dré Kopien, who drove the point of his sword through the narrow gap on the side of the breastplate. The soldier stiffened, then slipped off the opposite side. Viktor seized control of the reins.

The other animal had fled at the death of its rider. That left them with only one horse swift enough for escape. They would have to ride double and hope that they could get through the lines and into the wild lands before the horse collapsed from the strain.

Viktor mounted, Dré following suit immediately. The sorcerer glanced over his shoulder. "Which way?"

"Not the way we came in. Go farther south. While you were busy with your work, I checked on Straas. He's thinned out the patrols; thought he'd catch you inside, I guess. The south is thinnest because the land is more treacherous."

"Then why there?"

"I know a path or two, man. Give old Dré some credit for working while you were . . . wherever you were the past few years."

"I am sorry, Dré."

The graying man looked behind them. "Apologies later if we survive this. Right now it looks like the sentries have finally stirred their stench-addled selves and are coming for us!"

Viktor Falsche nodded and, urging the somewhat hesitant mount on, headed for the south.

XII

The baron listened to the horns crying out in the distance. He turned from the window of his private chambers and paced the length of the massive room.

Mandrol's spies among his general's aides gave the same report over and over. The search continued, but the impostor Falsche continued to make Straas look like an addled fool, leading him around by the nose and then disappearing. The debacle with the chase, the chase that had ended with the general leading his men back and forth over half of the city, was simply too much. He could no longer trust either Straas or G'Meni to do anything correct. Even his own efforts had failed, but that was because until now they had been the half hearted work of a slothful, jaded fool filled with fear and too much rich food.

No more. He had not gone far enough with the Amantii; he had wasted their efforts earlier by not giving them what they needed to make their task possible.

"Summon the Lady DuPrise," he commanded a servant. "Inform her that it is time."

She was quick in coming to him. Years ago, Mandrol would have been grateful; now, he only found her swiftness useful. Lilaith could be trusted to be efficient, unlike his lackeys of late.

"I am here to aid you, my love."

The sorcerer baron ran his fingertips along each side of his head and exhaled. Feeling much more at ease after the exercise, he held out his hand to the dark-skinned enchantress, then led her to the bed. "Sit here, my dear one."

Once seated on the edge, she peered around the expansive chamber. "Where are the animals? You mentioned that some would be involved?" Lilaith tried not to look revolted. "We aren't to sacrifice them, are we?"

He laughed at that, enjoying her puzzlement at his strange response to her fear. "No . . . far from it. Don't worry yourself, Lilaith. The cats will not be harmed."

"Cats?" Her brow furrowed as if some memory were trying to force its way to the surface. "Cats?"

"Never mind." He sat down next to her. "Give me both of your hands, close your eyes, and we can begin. You will notice a few little differences in what I'm attempting, but nothing harmful to you . . . just to Viktor Falsche."

She did as she was bade, ever loyal. Mandrol's eyes lingered over her smooth skin and perfect features, then shifted to the hands. He closed his eyes and concentrated.

"Listen to me, my love . . ." he began.

Everything proceeded as it had before until the sorcerer reached her innermost mind. There he found resistance that he had not expected.

"Open yourself to me," he commanded. "Let your memories become mine. Give to me that which I ask for. Let me see Viktor Falsche as you know him."

An image formed, a ghostly pair entwined together. Man and woman. By her coloring, Baron Mandrol knew the woman to be Lilaith. The man . . . the man could only be Falsche. The baron focused his interest on the image of his long-dead but still dangerous foe.

"Lilaith . . ."

She looked at him, smiling.

"Come to me."

She released Viktor, who remained motionless. Arms outstretched, Lilaith DuPrise drew nearer and nearer until she was almost upon him.

That was when the ghostly Lilaith became a Morag wielding a huge, spiked club.

Mandrol tried to retreat, but the link between Lilaith and himself would not be broken. *She* would not allow it to break. Despite the spell that kept her loyal to the baron, the dark-skinned woman was trying to *kill* him with her thoughts.

He knew that if the club struck his mind self, it would feel the same as if he had been physically hit. She had to know that, too. Somehow, he had fallen into a trap. Where Lilaith could not compete with him in the realm of sorcery, she could easily do battle in the world of the mind. He knew how strong her will was, spell or not.

He *would* die if he did not stop her first.

"This is foolish, my love," he called out, trying to reach a place beyond the advancing Morag. The thing's bat-like ears twitched, but other than that there was no response. He dodged a swipe by the creature and retreated farther. There was not much play left in the link. Soon he would have to stand his ground.

"My will is greater than yours, Lilaith. My will *is* your will. You will obey me. You have no choice. Cease the theatrics and open the way to me before I'm forced to punish you, my dear. This can only end that way."

She would not listen. This was not truly her conscious mind at work, he decided. This was a bit of her subconscious that had buried itself deep when he had first taken her will from her. It must have waited here all those years, patient. Now its patience had at last been rewarded. It had him where it wanted him.

Mandrol gathered his will. He would have preferred a less violent answer, if only because he still had fondness for her, but Viktor Falsche's specter was out there somewhere also waiting to kill him. Compared to that, Lilaith DuPrise was a minor irritant.

"Very well, my love. You force my hand."

The Morag raised its club, readying for what would certainly be a fatal strike.

"Come in, my children."

The Amantii entered the link. Summoned through by the baron, they took on form in the realm of the mind, standing as his champions against Lilaith's Morag.

"I hope you will not suffer too much because of this, my love. Remember, it's all in your mind."

The hellcats lunged at the Morag. It swung the

club, but the massive weapon passed over the heads of the two beasts. One Amantii clamped its jaws on the arm of the Morag. The other darted around and took hold of a leg. Roaring, the huge beast tried to free itself of the two monsters, but they held fast. Under the pressure of the two attacks, the Morag lost its footing and fell back.

It did not take long for the Amantii to finish Lilaith's champion.

"Thank you, children."

The hellcats retreated to the back of his mind, but they did not depart completely. The two beasts were still needed.

"Lilaith?"

A new image of the dark-skinned enchantress formed. This one, however, greeted the sorcerer baron with great emotion and obvious devotion. "My love! I was so worried about you! Can you forgive me?"

Mandrol opened his own arms to receive her. "All is forgiven, Lilaith. You need only give yourself to me to make everything well again."

Seeking to obey, she came into his arms . . . and *melted* into his body.

Mandrol's mind became filled with images. He was now a part of her innermost memories. All memories, all dreams, and all desires were open to him.

"Give me Viktor, Lilaith."

She did. Mandrol found himself surrounded by an infinity of Viktor Falsches, each a little different. Here was Falsche eating. Here was a younger Falsche studying. Yet another Falsche was casting a spell. Another, slightly older one, laughed at some joke.

"Children."

The Amantii materialized again.

"Know him. See him. Be him. Discover all there is to being Viktor Falsche."

Leaping forward, the Amantii attacked the visions, who did nothing to stop them. The hellcats tore apart and ate the figures one by one, swallowing the pieces and running to the next. Each devouring would link them to Falsche in a

way that would make escape impossible. No matter where
he hid, the Amantii would now find him.

They would also know him better. His tricks would
be insufficient to save him this time. The beasts would know
him as well as his former love had and by doing so, they
would become perfect trackers. His very presence would
draw them. This was where the baron had failed earlier.
Had he not listened to G'Meni, the ghost of Falsche would
have been long dead . . . again.

Only when the last of the images had been devoured
did the Amantii cease their efforts. They turned to their master, as frightening now as in the mortal plane.

"Find him. Kill him. Let nothing stand in your
way."

The cats started to move . . . then paused in confusion. One sniffed the air near Mandrol and snarled.

"What's the matter with you? Find Falsche!"

This time the Amantii moved nearer, almost as if
they intended to pounce on Mandrol's mind self. The sorcerer baron grew furious. "The wild lands, you fools! Search
the wild lands!" No report had as yet reached him that had
indicated Falsche was no longer in the city, but Baron
Mandrol was somehow certain that such was the case. Straas
would waste time as long as he continued to search the city
and not the countryside. "Go!"

Giving the pair of demonic felines a destination
broke the confusion. The hellcats vanished from Mandrol's
mind, but he could sense the two preparing for the hunt. It
was not yet night, but the day was fast waning. As soon as
the sun set, the two would be off on the trail. There would
be no pausing for other activities; Mandrol had given the pair
a compulsion. They would find the mad puppet who thought
himself a renegade sorcerer.

The Amantii on their way, Mandrol began to retreat
to the real world. He was satisfied that Lilaith would attempt
no further betrayal. The core of rebellion had been eaten
away by the mind assault of the hellcats. She was completely his now and soon there would be no further memory of
Viktor Falsche to weaken the loyalty he asked of her.

Her love, on the other hand, he no longer expected or even desired.

Dusk was near, but the dark of night that would soon follow did not necessarily give the two riders any advantage. Viktor knew that Straas would be far better equipped for a night hunt than the last time. The only advantage he and Dré did have was that many of the hunters were still inside the city, which meant that the lines they had to cross were much thinner.

The sounding of the horns actually proved to be to their benefit. Alerted by the noise, sentries in the outer perimeters focused their attention on what was happening within the walls. Hence, those nearest to the craggy rise did not note the horse and riders until it was nearly too late.

Dré was the first to notice that they could be seen. He leaned in to Viktor and whispered, "Over that other hill. Three men with horses."

The sorcerer glanced that way and nodded. One of the men in the distance turned, saw them, and gestured to his companions.

"That tears it, man! No more tiptoeing! We've got to get this nag moving again!"

Their mount, who had struggled well despite the heavy load, shook his head as if to refuse, but Viktor's urging made the beast pick up speed. The going was treacherous, but thanks to Dré Kopien's knowledge of the area, they were able to pick their way up and through the worst regions.

However, at the moment it would still have been preferable to have had two horses. Their own horses fresh and bearing only about half the weight of that of the fugitives' mount, the sentries chopped away at the distance between the pair and themselves. Viktor glanced at the nearby hills and woods ahead of them and estimated that he and his companion had a fair chance to reach the edge of the wild lands, but beyond that he doubted that their sole steed would have much strength left.

"Not around that way!" warned Dré. "Turn him to the left."

The horse stumbled as loose rock and dirt flew through the air. Rocks tumbled downward. This side of the rise was precarious. A little steeper and Viktor Falsche would have called it a cliff.

"Now ease around to the left some more."

He obeyed as best he could, wishing now that his companion had sat in front rather than himself. Behind him, Viktor could hear the fast-approaching animals of the soldiers. Somewhere, another horn sounded.

"This is narrow," Dré whispered in his ear. "We may have a chance, man."

The wary sorcerer did not understand until the first of the horsemen began to descend after them. Then, while he was still struggling to bring the mount to the bottom without sending both riders flying, Viktor heard a rumble. A horse whinnied in sudden panic and a man cursed frantically.

"Don't look back now! We've our own necks to worry about, Viktor!"

Even as Dré spoke, a cloud of dust swept over the area to their right. A landslide began just to the side.

There was another shout, this one more frantic . . . then the landslide became a raging river of rock that caused their own mount to start to panic. The sorcerer drew from deep within him some of the energy riding had allowed him to regain. It was not much, but it was enough to enable him to calm the animal.

Their pursuers had no such power to aid them. Viktor heard a horse cry out again, followed by a terrible scraping sound and a scream of agony, the latter cry originating from human lips.

Amid the ever-increasing rock slide the helpless bodies of a soldier and horse tumbled past to the bottom. There was no hope for either man or beast; both were tossed about like rag dolls.

"The other two've fallen behind." Dré Kopien exhaled. "I nearly lost my own life trying to figure a safe path down this side. Nearly the whole thing is loose chips and dry, cracked dirt. It's a death trap, which is why they don't guard it too much. If we'd had the time, I would've made us climb down on foot." He paused to consider. "I hope that path hasn't changed much since I was here last."

Thankfully, it had not. When their horse put the first hoof down on more-or-less flat ground, both men and steed shuddered with relief. Their relief was short-lived, however, for now they had to worry about losing their pursuers in the wild lands. The nearing sounds of horns indicated that others had been alerted to their location.

"Ride toward that copse of trees, Viktor. A trail starts there that'll lead us to the most tangled part of the wild lands. We might be able to lose them there." Left unsaid was that there was also a good chance that the pair might lose their lives as well, for Morags frequented such areas. While few of the wild ones would be this near the city, the baron's Morags tended to remain close enough so that they could be summoned quickly. Viktor did not know if he had the strength to even stand up before one of the horrific monsters, let alone fight it.

They reached the trees ahead of the two soldiers, but not by much. Valiant as he was, their mount was nearly spent.

"We have to dismount here and take the two of them. Perhaps we can gain a second horse," the sorcerer recommended. Dré nodded. The two men dismounted and Viktor sent their horse off with silent thanks. He hoped that it would find its way to the city or, better yet, to some outland farm like the one on which he had grown up—

Viktor shook his head. Another of the man Emil's memories. Yet another mystery to which he had to attend when time permitted.

"Here they come!" Dré hissed, blade drawn. He disappeared behind a tree. Viktor followed suit.

The two horsemen materialized a moment later, swords drawn and eyes wary. They slowed their animals and peered around at the darkening forest. The horses snorted anxiously, perhaps smelling traces of Morag or wolf.

The pair waited for the soldiers to ride just beyond their places of concealment, then attacked.

Their attempt to take the riders by surprise failed.

The horsemen swerved and deflected the blades with their own. Viktor found himself facing an expert swordsman who had the distinct advantage of sitting upon a well-trained mount. His adversary threatened to run him down if he did not run him *through* first. The sorcerer was forced to retreat rapidly.

Glimpses beyond the overshadowing form of his opponent revealed that Dré was also in dire straits. His adversary, too, had him retreating. On foot, it was likely they would have beaten the soldiers, but mounted the men were virtually unstoppable.

Once more Viktor Falsche drew from his meager reserves. What little energy he had been able to recover while riding was nearly depleted. He would have to use it sparingly.

A shrill sound pierced the air, a shrill sound that sent the horses rearing and twisting in panic. The soldiers suddenly found themselves hard pressed to stay in the saddle. The shrill sound repeated itself, causing the steeds to struggle harder to free themselves of their masters' control.

Viktor took advantage of the situation to run his opponent through from the side. The man grunted, tried to swing his sword, and finally dropped backward off the saddle.

The sorcerer tried to catch the reins of the horse, but the mount was too panicked. It kicked at him, almost removing his head, then raced away into the darkness.

Dré was struggling with the reins of the other animal, his adversary also having fallen to him during the panic. Viktor moved to help him, but with a last twist, the mount broke free and raced after the first. The two men watched the form recede into the darkness.

"Eyes of Ariela! I don't believe that happened!" Dré kicked at the ground. "I thought that we'd at least get one of those blasted animals!" His eyes suddenly widened. "The Morag! We have to get away from here before it shows—"

"There is no Morag. I created that cry. It was the only thing I could think to do."

"You—" Dré started to laugh, then immediately sobered. "Well, we'd better be going before one really does come along. It's a long, treacherous way back to the hole and I'm sure more of the good general's men will be following this poor pair's trail."

"How far?"

"Far enough that you don't want to ask how far it is."

The two trudged on, Dré Kopien leading the way. Viktor studied their route, but if he had ever been this way prior to now, then that memory was lost. The memories of Emil were also of no help. The only impressions he picked up when thinking of that faceless man was fear at being out in the wild lands after dark. Viktor could sympathize with such thoughts. He had been fortunate with the Morag and the Amantii once, but he had no desire to repeat either experience.

They traveled without incident for quite some time and were just beginning to relax a bit when they saw the torchlight in the distance. Viktor noted it first. He counted more than seven separate flames and stopped when at least that many more materialized behind the first group.

"On foot," muttered Dré. "That's good and bad. They won't be as fast, but they can track us where the horses can't go, which means they'll be harder to shake. We'll have to go deeper into the woods."

The number of flames had more than doubled in the time it had taken him to speak. Now they could also make out voices, although nothing intelligible. Viktor and his companion picked up their pace. If they stayed on their present path, Mandrol's servants would certainly see them. By turning to the deeper woods, they risked attack by things more vicious than the soldiers, but at least they had a chance of completing their escape.

The torches grew fainter as the duo moved away from the hunting soldiers. Around them, the woods thickened, cutting off the last vestiges of the dying day's light. Worse, a mist was forming. Viktor squinted, trying to make out detail, and finally decided that if he survived his vendetta he was going to live somewhere where trees were few and far between. All he ever saw of Medecia were trees, it seemed. That and tavern cellars.

"Horsemen!" Dré whispered, pointing to their right. The sorcerer could see nothing, but he, too, heard the rapid hoofbeats of several heavy animals. The clink of metal was enough to identify the riders, not that anyone other than Straas and his men would be out in the wild lands during nighttime.

A shout rose above the din, a shout which caused the riders to come to an immediate halt. Viktor and Dré fell to crouching positions. The woods grew silent.

For several moments, the riders milled around. Various mutters indicated some lengthy discussion. The two watchers remained motionless.

One voice stronger than the rest barked out an order. To the sorcerer's surprise, the soldiers turned and headed back the direction from which they had come.

"I don't like this, Viktor."

"How much farther? I still do not recognize this area."

"I don't think we ever came over this way. We're making progress, but we likely still have a couple hours traveling . . . and that's at a steady pace."

Viktor glanced back in the direction of the now invisible torches. "The noose is tightening. Straas is learning. It might take more than a couple hours. . . ." He scratched the side of his face; it was bad enough that he was once more running from Mandrol's dogs, but now the itch was becoming constant. "I do not know what I am doing anymore, Dré. It would have been better if I had stayed lost."

Dré stared at him. "I'd like to agree with you, man, but the truth is you also got me moving again. No matter what I said about getting things going, we've done nothing more than harass a few soldiers and merchants. The past five years especially have given us nothing. Mandrol's still baron and the people are still hurting." The graying man shrugged. "At least you have Viathos jumping around more than it has in years. I'd love to have seen Mandrol's face these past few days."

A cry rose in the darkness. It was not the cry of a Morag, but something worse . . . and something familiar. Now the mist that surrounded them made terrible sense.

"You didn't do that, did you, Viktor?"

"No." He estimated the direction and distance of the cry. "No, Dré, I did not."

"It's that thing again, isn't it? That hellish feline?"

The call had been far away in the general direction of the city gates, but Viktor Falsche knew how swift an Amantii could be. The beast could be upon them in mere minutes if it knew where to look. "Not the one we fought, but another. Maybe even two."

In silent agreement, they started moving. "What do you mean by two?"

"I think I mentioned it before. Amantii come in trios. Two females and one male. We faced a female. The other two will be better prepared and likely very upset."

They began to run.

"The soldiers are still out," Dré gasped. "Why aren't they at least gone?"

"I do not think Mandrol cares. I think he wants me at all cost."

"Straas will be pleased, won't he?" Dré stumbled momentarily over an upturned tree root. "Well, that's something to be happy about . . . I suppose."

The Amantii cried out again, this time much closer.

"They're guessing pretty good where we are."

"I do not think they are guessing." Even for the hellcats, this was too swift a hunt. They were excellent trackers, but not this exceptional. It was as if they already knew where he was.

"Dré . . . if you know any trails . . . narrow and treacherous of foot . . . take us there. The Amantii look immaterial, but they must follow some physical laws. We can slow if not stop them on such a trail."

"I can't think . . . think of anything around here more treacherous than what we're taking. It gets a little worse up ahead, but . . . I don't know."

"Then we had better run faster."

As if to encourage them in that respect, another Amantii cried out from a different direction. This one sounded nearer.

They were not going to make it to the sanctum in time. Viktor searched within himself and found that he was wanting in power. Worse, he stumbled more and more with each step.

"I don't think . . . we're going to get there, man," Kopien breathed. "I don't think that I can keep up this pa—"

The darkness came alive. Three huge shadows shifted before the pair.

"Sssorcererrr . . ."

"Prey."

"Morags!" Dré shouted uselessly.

A triple set of eyes glowed faintly in the dark, the only part of the monstrous creatures that did not seem simply formed of shadow. Viktor noted a club and two huge axes, one of the latter of which came down in his direction but a moment later.

The sorcerer jumped out of range just in time. Dirt flew as the edge of the weapon buried itself in the ground. The Morag hissed frustration.

"General wants head," snarled a companion creature.

"Head," agreed the less-articulate third.

"Wants dead," reminded the first. "Dead first."

The two humans had split, each coming around opposite sides of the tall shadows, The club-wielding Morag joined the first in pursuing Viktor, while the third chose to concentrate on Dré. The trio was after the sorcerer, but perhaps it felt that anyone accompanying him had to also be of some importance to General Straas.

"Little rabbit," mocked the first Morag. It brought the ax down again, but Viktor twisted to the side. The blade cut deep into a tree, sending massive, sharp splinters flying. The tree tilted under the impact but did not fall. Viktor, however, wisely moved to a safer location.

The Morags, rather than growing impatient, found the antics of their quarries amusing. The massive creatures liked a good hunt, especially when they were certain that eventually the prey would fall to them.

"Viktor!" Dré was invisible in the darkness, but beyond the pair of Morags hunting him, the sorcerer heard what had to be his friend battling the third. The pattern of thuds indicated that Dré was trying to fight back, but unless he managed to stab the leviathan in either eye, the Morag was likely to consider any wound it received as little more than a pinprick.

"Ha!" The Morag with the club smashed it into the earth. At first Viktor wondered at the monster's aim, the attack having missed by a wide margin, but the shock of the creature's strike caused the ground to shake. The sorcerer stumbled and fell to his knees.

"Morag meat," it rumbled, using what seemed to be a popular and unsettling phrase among its kind.

"Not yet," muttered Viktor. "Not yet."

He concentrated, trying to draw strength from within both him and the natural forces around him. Viktor called on the powers of the air and earth, fire and water, willing to take aid from whoever would give it. He stared at the shadowy Morags.

Nothing happened. He was drained.

He was about to die.

Beyond his attackers, there was silence. Whether Dré was dead or had fled from his hunter, Viktor did not know. All he did know was that both Morags had now flanked him and were readying their weapons, aware that even if the little human dodged one, the other would end him as any sort of threat to Viathos. All the Morags evidently cared about was that the head would still be identifiable.

A howl that no Morag could have ever produced cut through the night. Viktor's attackers paused and looked around, their ears twitching. An uncomfortable look crossed their trollish features, but neither retreated.

From behind Viktor came the low growl of an Amantii on the hunt. The rumble made it clear that the hellcat did not care for those who poached on its territory. The Morags were clearly distraught, but they were not ones to flee from an enemy, especially when the odds were two to one.

"Cat," muttered the one.

"Morag meat," snarled the other.

The hellcat gave them a warning growl.

"Ours."

The Amantii took a step forward, clearly indicating its opinion on the matter. The Morags glanced at one another.

Weapons raised and war cries cutting through the night, they charged the Amantii.

Viktor wasted no time watching the struggle. Even as the Morags howled and attacked, he was up and running in the direction he had last seen Dré. Neither man nor Morag was in sight, but ruined trees and overturned shrubbery left indication of the chase. The sorcerer followed the path of destruction while behind him the battle cry of a Morag turned to a howl of pain and the sound of a club crashing against a tree echoed again and again.

He climbed over a small ridge and discovered the third Morag stalking through the woods, the beastman's breathing rapid from exertion. While dismayed at running into the murderous creature, Viktor was at least glad to see that the Morag was still hunting. That meant that Dré was still alive.

An angry shout from where the battle raged caused the shadowy form of the monster to pause. Viktor ducked down as the Morag turned his way and stared. The faintly glowing orbs fixed on his location. Slowly, the Morag swiveled around, then headed toward his hiding place.

Viktor prepared himself for what would certainly be a futile struggle, but to his relief, the Morag changed paths, turning to a wider trail leading past the waiting human. As the beastman moved, it picked up speed. It was returning to its companions.

Whether the Morags would be enough to stop the Amantii was not a concern of his. He harbored a faint hope that perhaps the two groups would destroy one another, but that was unlikely. One or more of them would be on his trail again soon . . . probably too soon.

He renewed his search for Dré, for the first time sighting vague shapes that struck some chord in his memory. Dré had estimated wrong; they were nearer to the hidden sanctum than either of them could have hoped. Possibly his old comrade had planned to take a more circuitous route, the better to avoid leading pursuers to their one sanctuary, but Viktor Falsche no longer cared. He had to find Dré.

All the while, the itch burned. Unable to concentrate any attention on it prior to this, Viktor scratched away as he worked through the foliage. First one side, then the other. The left side felt rough, as if something had happened to his skin. The sorcerer gritted his teeth, trying not to think about what might be the cause. It was possible that his constant use of potions and powders had affected him, but the itch had been with him far longer than that.

He could not worry about that now. An itch was certainly not as great a priority as the survival of both he and the one loyal friend he still had.

To remind him of that fact, the din of combat renewed. Viktor was startled that it had gone on as long as it had, but while the Amantii were likely to triumph, Morags *were* hardy. They were also cunning in an animal way.

Fight all night if you can! he thought to the trollish creatures. Let them at least delay the hellcats, if nothing else.

He stumbled on a little longer and because of the darkness did not see the stream until he had walked into it. The splash was much too loud, but fortunately nothing took notice of it. The exhausted sorcerer almost continued on, then realized how thirsty he was.

Deciding that the risk was worth the time needed for a single sip, Viktor Falsche found a dry bit of land, put his weapon aside, and cupped his hands. His first sip was sweet, but not nearly sufficient. He had another and then, still not satiated, reached down for a third.

A large splash downstream brought him up short. He reached for the blade, but paused when he saw the outline of a man. Hand hovering over the hilt, he whispered, "Dré?"

"Viktor?" Another splash, followed by a curse.

Still whispering, Dré Kopien muttered, "Haven't been able to see a blasted thing! I escaped that Morag by sheer luck. Hoped you could do the same with the others. Have you seen it?"

"It turned to help the others. The Amantii showed up."

"Damned bad luck keeps getting worse, doesn't it?"

Viktor stuck his hand back into the stream, then wiped his forehead with the moistened fingers. He then ran his fingers along the side where the skin had grown rough. The water did nothing to soften the skin but did soothe the itch a little. "They may have actually saved my life. They did not care for the Morags trying to lay claim to me."

"Well, I hope those blasted troll cousins crush their skulls. At least I know I've got some vague hope against the Morags. I was only guessing against the—" Yet another splash. "Ariela take this darkness and— I've got to risk some light, man!"

"Let me. It will be softer, less noticeable." More to prove that he still had some will than because he truly wanted to do it, Viktor called on the power. At first nothing happened. Then, realizing that his hands were still moist, a counter to the sort of element he desired, the sorcerer wiped them dry.

"No luck?"

"I'm growing careless. Let me try again."

This time, he felt a response. A faint blue spark formed in his left palm, but its light was less than that of firefly. He concentrated further, forcing all outside influences, including the incessant itching, to the background.

The spark blossomed into a low blue flame that illuminated the region just around him. It was a coloring of light that would not be as evident to something with eyes like a Morag or an Amantii. The two humans still risked discovery by utilizing it, but the simple success and the lack of nausea pleased Viktor so much he almost forgot his exhaustion.

He held it up so that Dré could make use of its light.

"Ariela be praised. There are times, Viktor, when I find sorcery absolutely— *gods!*" Dré Kopien blurted out the last word, in his obvious shock forgetting the need for silence.

"What is it, Dré?"

"Viktor . . . man . . . your face . . . what *happened*?"

"What?" The sorcerer touched his face, running his fingers along in an attempt to find blood or some wound. When the Morag had struck the tree, splinters had scattered everywhere. He could recall no injury then, but . . .

Viktor bent over the stream and stared at his distorted reflection, the blue glow illuminating his features.

His own shock was so great that he canceled out the light without thinking. The image had been indistinct, but he would have sworn that his skin was loose on the one side of his face.

He brought the light back into being, but Dré walked toward him at the same time, his steps disturbing the water. He knelt next to the sorcerer.

"Let me see that. It looks bad."

"I do not feel anything . . . except this damned itching."

"Itching?" The second man paused, studied Viktor's expression, then slowly reached toward the damaged side. "Can you bring the light closer?"

Viktor raised his hand close to the area in question. "Is this better?"

"Better." Dré touched the flesh. "It doesn't feel right, man. Viktor, do you feel any diff—"

The sorcerer waited for him to finish his question, but when Dré did not continue, Viktor Falsche finally asked, "What is it? Is the wound bad?"

Dré had pulled back; in fact, he was stepping away from Viktor as if the latter had just transformed into a Morag. "You're one of them . . . you're one of those dead things. . . ."

"What are you talking about? I'm one of what, Dré?" He touched the ruined area. "What's wrong?"

From the shadows Dré Kopien somehow produced his sword. He kept Viktor at bay before continuing, "I should've known. Ten years was too long. I should've known better than to think that in the end you'd somehow tricked Mandrol! You're not Viktor Falsche, whatever you might claim or remember. You're nothing but a puppet, one of the walking *dead*. . . ."

"You make me sound like—" Why did the wound feel familiar? What was it Dré had said? The walking dead? A puppet?

"I'd run you through, but I don't know whether you're one of the baron's men or someone dragged out of his dungeons."

"Dré—"

"*Just stay away from me!*" Backing away, Dré Kopien disappeared into the darkness. His footsteps faded away but moments later.

Viktor watched him run, then cautiously, fearfully, he began to run his fingers along the edge of his countenance, concentrating not just on the damaged area but all around his face.

Small wonder, he discovered, that his own comrade should fear him so. The slight line he could feel, a line that coursed around his entire countenance and would have been virtually unnoticeable if he had not evidently worn away part of it with his scratching, was all the evidence he needed. Now he understood the itching, too.

He wore a mask. A mask of his own features. There was only one reason for him to be wearing so lifelike a copy of his own countenance. It was also the reason that he shared the memories of one peasant named Emil.

Viktor Falsche was dead and now existed only as one of Baron Mandrol's parasitic masks . . . a mask that was now falling apart.

XIII

He was *dead*.

Mandrol, General Straas, Master G'Meni, the Amantii, and a horde of Morags could have come upon Viktor Falsche at that moment and he would not have noticed them. All he could think was that he was *dead* and probably had been dead for the past decade.

The images he had experienced in Viathos, the images that had hinted at his betrayal and defeat, they had been memories of his death. He recalled the gnome G'Meni leaning over him and covering his face. That must have been when they had taken the imprint, the death mask.

I am a shadow . . . nothing more than a shadow possessing another unfortunate's body and mind.

Viktor knew who Emil was now. Some peasant chosen from the dungeons to be the host for his mask. Mandrol did not care about who he abused for his amusement. *And I was to be the center of entertainment at his ball.*

He knew the tales surrounding the baron's masques. Food and merriment to reward those of station who continued to support his dark reign, then the highlight, the rehumiliation of one of the sorcerer baron's defeated foes. From the baron's collection of masks would come one representing an enemy defeated and dead. That mask would be placed on the chosen one, generally someone with close enough build so that the illusion would be very accurate. The person wearing that mask would then become the one whose face it represented.

Mandrol would allow them to believe they were

who they now resembled. He would allow them to plot against him; then, just as the masked impostor would be about to strike, the baron would triumph. His beaten and defeated adversary would be paraded before his followers . . . then generally executed by beheading or some other method favored by Mandrol that evening.

Viktor was to have been the other night's entertainment.

The sorcerer stared at the shadowy forms of his own hands. So caught up had he been in his vendetta that he had never looked closely at himself. There were probably hundreds of obvious differences between Emil and himself, but who would have thought to have looked for them? Who could ever have imagined themselves in such a terrible, mind-numbing situation?

He was dead. All that existed of Viktor Falsche was a memory and a false face. At some point soon, however, the mask would slip completely off and when that happened, he would cease to exist even as yesterday's thought.

I am nothing, Viktor thought. *I should tear it off now and save Emil, at least!*

And yet . . .

Mandrol would still be alive, though, and he would not only have Medecia still under his iron rule, but he would also continue to control Lilaith. The murderer of Cordelia would continue his life of dark pleasure while Viktor Falsche would rot away, the last remnant of his being a few tattered fragments of a mask.

His hand froze. He wanted to tear off the false face, yet he could not. Not yet.

He was dead, yes . . . but he could not allow himself to pass quietly away. Baron Mandrol still had to pay for what he had done, and pay he would. Before he ceased to be, Viktor would set into motion the events and elements needed to see to it that Mandrol would not be long in following him to the afterlife.

I cannot die without your company, Baron, he thought as he rose, all notion of self-destruction fading. *Not this time.*

The adhesive that held his mask . . . his life . . . in place was obviously weak in comparison to what G'Meni used on the drone soldiers, but Viktor was certain that this formula he could duplicate. That would only buy him a little time, however, for the mask was deteriorating. Soon it would not matter how well it was sealed on; the mask would be so tattered that whatever shadow of his personality G'Meni had succeeded in imprinting on it would fade.

Mandrol had to die before then.

Stumbling away from the stream, Viktor Falsche started after his companion. Dré had warned him to stay away, with good reason, the sorcerer had to admit, but Viktor needed his aid. Dré had the network and supplies that he needed. There was no time to seek out another alchemist who could create Plutite; he had to go to the one source readily available, and that meant journeying into Viathos. Odds were that he would never emerge from that accursed place, though, which was why he had to have everything else prepared ahead of time.

The shock of discovering his terrible fate had, for some obscure reason, jarred loose other, older memories. Bits and pieces of his grand plan finally fell into place that had been missing even after his sojourn in the city. Now he recalled how he had sought to deal with the armies of Mandrol, how he had hoped to turn the sorcerer baron's legions of puppets into a two-edged weapon.

Dré had to help him. Viktor could not have more than a few days left. Just as important, he could not leave the man Emil to suffer such a fate as this. Emil deserved his life back and someone would be needed to help him readjust after such an ordeal. Viktor had made a sorcerer out of him and that would never change. Dré or someone else with some knowledge of the calling would be needed to show him how to make use of the power.

This was all assuming that things did not unravel further before Viktor was able to set his plans into motion.

How long he ran, hand pressed tight against the side of his head, he could not estimate. Viktor only knew that through a combination of memory and pure luck, he finally found the hidden entrance to Dré Kopien's secret sanctuary.

There was no sign of the other man, but if there had been, Viktor would have suspected something wrong. Dré had not survived out here for ten years by becoming sloppy and leaving a trail for all to see. Even the sorcerer, as confused and weak as he felt, had managed to mask his trail.

The way was sealed. He should have expected that after the horrific discovery. Dré wanted nothing to do with him.

"Dré!" he called, planting himself close. Viktor did not want to call outside attention to his presence. There were still hunters, both human and inhuman, searching the wild lands for him.

No response. It was possible that his comrade of old had sealed the entrance and then left for a safer location. In truth, that was probably what Viktor himself would have done. However, despite the knowledge that he was very likely wasting his effort, the exhausted sorcerer called out again.

He was inhaling for a third try when the sword point pricked his back.

"One more shout, man, and I'll run you through, no matter whether you're a soldier or an innocent."

"Dré—" Viktor began, trying to turn.

"No moving, either." To emphasize the command, the other man pushed the point in just enough so that if Viktor did anything but breathe normally, it would sink into his back. "I knew after I ran that it was idiotic to think you wouldn't come here, so I set things up a little for you."

"Listen, Dré—"

"No, *you*, whatever you are, listen to me!" A pause. "We're going to go inside and have a little talk. I want to find out everything you know about the original Viktor. Now hold your hands behind you, tight together."

The sorcerer obeyed. He felt something wrap around his wrists, something that moved as if almost alive.

"That'll hold you, ma— that'll hold you. Now inside."

Dré touched a small rock formation, twisting two of

the pieces in a short series of patterns. Now the entrance was open to them. Viktor glanced at the other man.

A ghost of a smile materialized briefly on Kopien's features until he realized that it was not the true Viktor Falsche to whom he was talking. "You don't remember that, do you, *Viktor?* I didn't bother to mention it when you returned. Even when I thought you were the true Viktor, I just couldn't bring myself to trust you completely. I hoped that I was wrong, but there were just too many unanswered questions." He prodded his prisoner forward. "Didn't expect an answer like this, though."

Once inside and with the entrance secured, Dré Kopien steered the bound Viktor to the center of the small chamber. He pushed the sorcerer to the floor, making him kneel. Viktor did not struggle, understanding that cooperation was his only hope of obtaining the other's assistance.

"There were a few physical changes that I noticed. The memory, too, Viktor always had a sharp memory. You also weren't always as arrogant as he could be." Dré gave his captive a grim smile. "There were times when you showed me enough to convince me that you were him, but that you might have been changed by whatever had happened to you in Viathos." He snorted. "Now I know what happened. Viktor wasn't back; he'd died ten years back, just like the rumors I'd heard then."

"But it *is* me, Dré! The mind is *me*—"

"Just be quiet!" The tip of the sword rose, tracing a path over Viktor's . . . or Emil's . . . throat. "You're pathetic! You're nothing but a monstrous creation by Mandrol and that misfit creature he has for an alchemist!"

"Perhaps I am," Viktor replied defiantly. He looked at Dré as if daring him to cut his throat. "Perhaps I am only the faded memory of the original Viktor Falsche, but you should then think about this. So long as I have existed, so long as I *still* exist, my hatred for Mandrol and his cohorts remains as fiery as it did the night . . . the night I died."

The sword wavered. Dré Kopien eyed him as if trying to read how much truth there was in the words. "Eyes of Ariela, man! Why did you have to go in there that night? I warned you about it, but you didn't listen!"

"I was always headstrong, you know that, Dré."

"And now you don't even have a head," muttered the graying figure. He leaned back, removing the sword as a threat, but made no attempt to remove the bonds. "God, I'm sorry for saying that, Viktor, it was in bad taste—"

"But typical of your humor."

The other man stiffened, then studied his captive with more attention than previously. "There's something peculiar about the way you speak and act, though. You're too *you*. Not just a shadow of a personality like those poor wretches with the general's features, but I'll be damned if you aren't exactly the Viktor Falsche I knew. You also can work sorcery, which you shouldn't be able to do now. That's not the way it's supposed to work. What was it you told me once?"

Viktor recognized the test hidden within the innocent question and sought desperately for the answer he had given Dré those many years ago. "The masks contain only imprints, reflections of the person, not the real personality. They have some limited awareness, but must be instructed."

"Good enough for the baron's grand entertainment at his masques, but not good enough to escape and replot revenge?"

"No," the sorcerer responded automatically. Then he understood what Dré had just said. "*No*. Within a certain range the masks might be able to operate in such a way, but not to the depth that I have. As for being able to perform sorcery . . . I am not certain how this mask was created. Perhaps it is different from the others in that respect or perhaps . . . perhaps my host had the potential. That would explain my earlier nausea whenever I attempted to cast a spell or why those spells sometimes went awry. I know it is not the best explanation—"

"But it's close enough. You shouldn't be this real, though. You should be little better than those blasted drones, but every word, every thought, screams out *I'm Viktor Falsche*, man! Until this night I would've never had a doubt."

"Then help me. Help me succeed before it's too late."

Dré leaned on the sword. "What do you mean?"

Viktor rose. As best he could, he indicated the damaged side of the mask . . . of *him*. "I'm dying again, Dré. The mask is deteriorating. What's left of me will be gone when it fails to hold. I do not know why I am different from the others, but that difference will not be enough to save me. Before that happens, though, I *have* to rescue Lilaith and finally bring Mandrol to task for his crimes."

Putting aside the sword, Dré came around Viktor and removed the bonds. Viktor, finally able to see them clearly, noted that they would have been proof against his sorcery. He had brought them himself in the now faded hope of dragging a helpless Mandrol back to Wesfrancia for a proper execution. That was before he had come to realize that simply killing the sorcerer baron was the safest thing to do.

"Can nothing be done for you, man?"

"Only temporarily. Do you have anything that can act as an adhesive?"

"This." Dré stepped to the far wall and located a small container. "I use it when I need to hide my features with a disguise of some sort. Will it work?"

Viktor looked the contents over, then applied some to his face at the point of damage, being careful to keep the mixture from spreading beyond where the edge of the mask would be. When he was satisfied that he had applied a sufficient amount, the sorcerer slowly put the somewhat tattered portion back into place. The mask sealed. "Yes, this will do. For now. I have only bought a few days at best. I do not think that the mask will last more than a week. I have to have Mandrol before then."

"A week?" Dré looked stunned. "But Viktor! We can't possibly organize anything in a week! We've barely escaped the patrols and they're still out there!"

"I do not have time to wait. It must be in the next day or two, no later."

"You just said—"

Viktor turned from his old friend. "In three days, I may not have the concentration to make this succeed. The mask will last about a week, but the last day or two I may not even be able to speak. You will find yourself in charge of a man named Emil, by the way. There is another man you know, a Terril the potter, who can tell you of him."

Silence hung between the pair, silence that reigned for several minutes. Then Dré Kopien walked up to Viktor and started to hug him. He paused in the midst of the act, possibly recalling that this was not truly his friend, but finally completed it.

"You're the brother I needed, Viktor. The friend who was there to help, who let his own pain wait while he comforted someone who had loved and lost his very sister. I should've been comforting you, you two were so close."

"You came with me, Dré. No one else had the courage, or maybe the audacity, to think that we could succeed. Just you."

"And Lilaith, Viktor." The other man's face hardened. "And Lilaith." He walked away from Viktor, sat down by the small wooden table where they had shared meals, and asked, "What can I do?"

Viktor breathed a sigh of relief, then cleared his mind for the task ahead. He had been telling the truth when he had said his time was limited; therefore, it behooved him not to waste it on too much sentiment. Still, even as he organized his thoughts, memories of Emil reminded him that there was one innocent person caught up in his machinations, one person with no choice in the matter.

He could not let that bother him now. "You have a map of the city and the surrounding area?"

"Of course." Dré did not even have to rise, instead reaching below the table and retrieving a battered roll of paper. "I updated it just before you . . . you returned."

They spread out the map, Viktor already perusing it even as Dré finished straightening it. The map was weathered but very detailed. Typical Dré Kopien. Dré had always been an organizer, but not so good a planner or instigator. That was yet another reason why he and the sorcerer had gotten along so famously. Their skills complemented one another's.

Viktor saw what he was looking for almost immediately. He poked a finger at different locations in and beyond the city walls. "Here. Here and here. These five locations also. Can you remember them?"

"Of course."

"I need a fire burning at each location. Keep each of them going from the time you last see me until it becomes impossible to keep them lit. I'll be giving you a sack for each fire. Toss a handful of the contents into the flame every quarter hour until you either run out or the fire cannot be kept burning."

The other man peered closely at the map. "What's this about? What're you planning?"

"The same thing I have always planned. I will explain after I finish telling you the specifics, Dré. I simply want to make certain that you know what to do right away . . . in case. You may have to do this without me."

Dré Kopien said nothing, but his gaze flickered from the map to his old comrade.

Ignoring the glance, the sorcerer continued with the explanation. "Get everyone ready. It is all or nothing here, Dré. We bring Mandrol down now."

"So far you have me setting bonfires and tossing who knows what into them. What about Straas and the soldiers? What do we do about them?"

"Have no fear. If all goes well, they will deal with themselves. Listen to me again, Dré. Even if I do not come out, I want you to keep those fires going until you cannot."

Dré leaned over the table, his arms burying Viathos Keep. "What do you mean, if you do not come out?" His eyes narrowed. "I know what you're planning. You're going after G'Meni. You want that foul mixture after all. I thought we—"

"There is no other way. The Plutite is what we need. It and it alone will have sufficient power to destroy the masks. Somehow I will get it to you. Just keep the fires going."

"Then what?"

Viktor gave him a grim smile. "You will know. When the army falls into chaos, then you strike."

"Which is still no guarantee of success."

"There are never guarantees, Dré." Viktor began to scratch his face, thought better of it, and instead tapped his finger on the map. "The plan is relatively simple—"

"And we're relatively simpleminded for doing it."

"—but one question remains for me," finished Viktor.

His companion laughed sardonically. "Only *one*? Ariela, man! I've got a thousand to add to that one!"

Still ignoring the comments, Viktor Falsche stared off into the ether. "How do I get in?"

"At last some sense!" Dré swept his hand over the map, specifically Viathos and the inner city. "It's one thing to get past the city walls, man. After all, it is a trade route. But to get into Viathos? Gods! Why don't you just walk up to Straas and hand yourself in! You'll get a pretty thorough tour of Viathos that way, Viktor! That's the only way I can think of."

The sorcerer closed his eyes in thought. Perhaps there was a way in . . .

"Now, wait a minute, man! I don't like the way you're—"

The entire sanctuary shook. Both men toppled over in surprise.

"What in Ariela's name—"

The chamber shook again. Picking himself up off the ground, Viktor listened. A rough scraping noise, a noise which sounded distinctly like an animal digging away at the walls, informed him as to exactly what was going on.

An Amantii had located them. The Morags had lost the battle for rights to his head. He knew it was one of the hellcats and not a Morag for the simple reason that the huge trolls would have simply tried to batter the cave to pieces. They were not diggers and they were especially not *thorough* diggers like the creature outside. Louder and louder the scraping became, evidence that the Amantii was making excellent headway in its mission to unbury its prey.

"Damned cats! Has to be them!" snarled Dré, going to one wall and seizing a worn but serviceable lance. "I got this for possible use against Morags, but maybe it'll help against one of those, do you think?"

"Maybe." The sorcerer was doubtful, but did not want to sound fatalistic. He glanced around, searching for anything he might use against the Amantii's weaknesses. This one would certainly not be as easy to destroy as the first . . . as if that *had* been easy. If Mandrol was sending them out again, it was only because they were better prepared than previously.

Nothing seemed right. There was water, but in the confines of the cave he would not have time; he was doubtful he even had the energy. Some of the ploys he might have utilized would only work in the open, but the moment they stepped out, the cat would have them.

Were there two out there? Only one could be heard digging, but the other might be watching the entrance. The two men were trapped like rabbits in a burrow, save that they could not dig another path out and escape.

"It's starting to break through!"

Dré's words were punctuated by scattering chunks of rock and earth that pelted the pair. A snarl cut through the sanctuary as the hellcat poked its head into the hole it had made. The dry mist that marked its coming filled the chamber, dimming all illumination.

"I'm getting damned sick and tired of these things!" roared the sorcerer's friend. He jabbed at the exposed head, but the Amantii pulled back out of range. It was questionable as to whether the lance would have actually hurt the demonic beast; likely it had simply learned not to trust any weapon used by either a spellcaster or a spellcaster's companion. Sorcery it feared very much.

Sorcery was something Viktor had very little control of at the moment.

The Amantii roared again and tried to catch the eye of either human. Both were wise to its tricks now and avoided staring directly at it. There was enough of the monster to see without having to look into its eyes.

Despite the intensity of its assault, Viktor did notice

that the hellcat was not as steady or as swift as it should have been. He recalled now that the creatures could, with great effort, be physically damaged and so perhaps the Morags had not fallen without inflicting injuries to the winners. There might even be only one Amantii out there after all, although even one was too much.

"The hole's getting bigger! It'll be inside in a matter of minutes, man!"

The fear that originated from the mind of Emil suddenly swelled up, nearly making the sorcerer panic. Viktor struggled to keep Emil suppressed, but all he could think about now was that he wanted to go home, back to the farm where life had been peaceful. Images of the farm were contradictory, however. Sometimes he saw the man who he knew to be the father, other times he saw a younger man, possibly a brother, although the memory was not distinct enough. The former image seemed older, less distinct.

"Here it comes again!"

The Amantii tore away at the cracking wall, the hole it had made now large enough not only for its head to fit through but one paw as well. Dré jabbed at it again, nearly losing the weapon in the process.

Home. The sensation was overwhelming. Home was haven, a place where the darkness did not dwell.

Viktor began to feel strange, but it took him several breaths to realize why the sensation felt familiar. When he did, the sorcerer desperately made his way to his companion.

The Amantii snapped the lance in two. Dré stumbled, falling out of Viktor's reach. His stomach wrenching, Viktor Falsche did the only thing he could do; he threw himself forward, falling on his friend even as the hellcat burst full into the devastated chamber.

Their surroundings shimmered as Viktor's power . . . and Emil's subconscious . . . sent them away from the Amantii's taloned grasp.

But to where?

"At last! He's waking!"

Viktor blinked. His last memory had been of the

claws of the Amantii just grazing his back. Then it had felt as if he had been turned inside out. Someone had removed his stomach and replaced it more than once, seeming to use only brute strength to do it. After that, the oblivion that had followed had seemed like a godsend.

Now he rested in an old farm bed, his upward gaze catching the concerned expressions of both Dré Kopien and a younger man who looked familiar.

Dré looked haggard, as if he had not slept in days. Something about that nagged at Viktor, but he was still too dazed to follow through with the thought. Instead he asked, "Where am I?"

"You remember our friend Emil, don't you, man?" Dré put a grateful arm on the young man's shoulder. "This's his cousin, Isaiah. Isaiah's run the farm with his wife since Emil left for the city about . . . oh . . . a little more than a year ago, I guess."

"About that," said the farmer in a surprisingly deep voice.

"How long have I been unconscious?"

"About a day and a half."

Bolting upright, the sorcerer stared wide-eyed at Dré. "Surely you jest?"

"I don't. I tried to wake you once or twice, but it became obvious that you'd have to wake up on your own. I'm sorry, Viktor. I know how important time is to you."

The look on Kopien's face was enough to prevent any further outburst by Viktor. It was not his companion's fault. Emil's reflexes had taken over, but in a sense Viktor's host had saved all three of their existences.

"Thank you for your hospitality," he finally told the farmer.

"You're Emil's friends."

The eyes of the two fugitives met briefly. "Yes, we're close in some ways."

Isaiah indicated Dré. "He said that you knew my cousin better than he did. He's not contacted us in some time." The young farmer's eyes narrowed. "Has something happened to him?"

"What do you mean?"

With a sigh, Isaiah leaned against the bed. He ran a hand through his dark hair and smiled ruefully. "Sarah's outside. I asked her to find some fresh eggs . . . the baron's men don't leave us too much, but this far out they sometimes forget to come for their due and so we have a few extra eggs. It's always been hard, which was why Emil ended up going to the city. He hadn't been the same since his mother and then his father died. There was always something not quite right between him and his parents."

Viktor wondered what this had to do with the farmer's question, but wisely did not interrupt.

"My cousin's never been a brave man, but he hated the baron with more passion than anyone I've known. Always thought that was a little funny, considering that from what I've seen of the banners, they look something *alike*."

From his tone, the sorcerer was certain that Isaiah was hinting at something. *Looked something alike?* What could—?

A sharp intake of breath from the side matched his own. Dré had come to the same conclusion at the same time. One possible reason why Viktor could still perform sorcery was that his host might have been one with a potential for the magic arts. The ability was often one passed on from generation to generation. The children of Viktor Falsche . . . children that would now never be . . . would have stood a great chance of following in his footsteps. So would the children of any great sorcerer, even the bastard children of a careless sorcerer like Mandrol.

Too often royalty was careless when it came to siring offspring. Who was it to say that Mandrol in his earlier years had not sired a few off of both willing and unwilling maids and wives? It would have been interesting to see just what Emil looked like if not for the fact that it would have meant Viktor's end in the process.

"I know what he's been doing in the city," continued Isaiah. "I know what he's a part of. But he always contacted us. Not anymore. We should've heard something by now."

Viktor tried to control his expression. "He is alive.

He is at risk, but I will try my best to see that he does not come to harm."

The farmer had a questioning look on his face. "I've heard rumors and seen riders. Something's happening, isn't it? Something major against the hounds of Viathos. You don't have to tell me; I see it in your faces."

"You must believe me when I say that Emil will be safe—"

Isaiah raised a hand. "I'll ask no more of you. I know that Emil, though not the bravest, would willingly do what he could if it meant the baron falling."

"That's good to hear, that is," commented Dré in an innocent voice. Viktor said nothing but gave his companion a warning look. The sorcerer felt no better about using his host so, but if Emil truly desired an opportunity to help destroy Mandrol, then he was about to receive that opportunity.

"You'd best stay here for a few days. It'll be safe. My Lord Jakaly is departing tomorrow for Viathos itself and most of his personal guard will be with him. That means that you could walk freely around this region."

Viktor was about to tell the younger man that they could not stay, but then the import of Isaiah's words touched him. "Jakaly? Renfrew Jakaly?"

"Of course."

"You recall Jakaly, Viktor. He was Mandrol's court representative in Wesfrancia before the baron's atrocities made it impossible for him to stay. Tall, gangly fellow, although I think he's got a paunch growing these days. Not much hair left on his head, either. He's still one of Mandrol's favorites."

The sorcerer nodded. He knew Jakaly now. "Why is he going to Viathos?"

"For the masque, of course," the farmer replied.

Viktor was confused. "The baron just held a masque. Why would he have two so close to one another?"

"Jakaly finally convinced Neuland to send an emissary to Medecia. Neuland's having troubles with Wesfrancia, who seems to be put out by Neuland's desire for the eastern edge of their country." Dré looked apologetic. "You've missed a few changes in diplomacy these past ten years, man. The masque is in the ambassador's honor. It was arranged rather quickly and I figured it would've been canceled after what went on in Viathos, which was why I didn't mention it before."

"But you knew about it."

"As I said, didn't seem any reason to tell you."

Isaiah obviously wanted to ask just what had happened in Viathos, but Viktor interjected with, "Jakaly will have, of course, no trouble in gaining admittance."

"Viktor, man, you're not thinking—"

"I have no choice, Dré, and Jakaly makes a good key." To the farmer, he asked, "When does Jakaly depart?"

"Late afternoon. He wants to arrive just as the masque is beginning, but not so soon that he'll have to wait around for others. That's his way. Our great Lord Jakaly is not always a patient master." Isaiah looked uneasy. "What d'you plan to do?"

"Too much." Viktor Falsche lifted himself out of bed. "Dré, can you contact the others?"

"I think I can. The patrols have grown more since last night, but—"

"Then listen, because I have to tell you the rest. You need everyone ready . . . and I'll need Mara. I'll try to make certain that she remains safe, I promise."

"As safe as Emil, I suppose."

Viktor cursed his friend's temper when it came to Mara, but he also understood. "Please, Dré. This is it."

Hesitation. Then, "All right, damn you. Tell me what else I have to do." Dré Kopien pointed at Isaiah. "What about him?"

The sorcerer tilted his head and caught the farmer's gaze. Isaiah started to speak, but the intensity of Viktor's eyes froze him with his mouth still open. "He will join his wife in taking care of this farm. He will remember no talk concerning our plans for tomorrow. Is that not correct, Isaiah, my friend?"

"Yes." The blankness vanished from the farmer's

expression. He glanced at the two men. "I'll leave you be. It's time I helped my wife. We share the load equally here."

The pair watched the bearded young man depart. The moment Isaiah was gone, Viktor turned back to his companion.

"Here's what you need to know before you depart—"

"Before *I* depart?" Dré folded his arms and glared at the weakened sorcerer. "And where do you think you'll be, man? You *can't* be thinking what you're probably thinking!"

"I will remain here. I need to rest for the journey."

"Still Viathos?" When Viktor nodded, Dré could not resist also asking, "And how will you get in there?"

Viktor Falsche touched the damaged side of his face. The mask still held, but for how long he could only guess.

"I said, *how* will you get in there, man?"

The sorcerer stared into thin air, already planning for the next day. Half-distracted, he still managed to reply, "With Lord Jakaly's fine help, of course."

XIV

"**V**iktor Falsche will be at the masque this evening."

Baron Mandrol studied his subordinates from his chair. The dais upon which the chair was positioned allowed him to look down on the duo, which was as it was supposed to be. Both G'Meni and Straas did not reply, knowing all too well that at this point their reputations, their *lives*, teetered on the brink. Baron Mandrol made certain to remind them of that fact now and then with carefully placed barbs in his conversation.

He did not try to reflect on his own constant failures. The Amantii hunt could still not be termed a failure; the cats had not yet returned from the wild lands. The sorcerer baron could no longer sense either of the demonic beasts, but that did not necessarily mean they had been destroyed. He chose to believe that it meant they were beyond range, but still hunting the fugitive.

"He will come and we must put an end to his haunting or else we not only risk the treaty with Neuland set up by Jakaly but also our very lives. Viktor Falsche will not rest until he is either dead or we are, my so cunning and capable servants."

"The mask cannot last longer, Baron," started Master G'Meni, his pride overwhelming his common sense. Beside him, Straas continued to stare ahead. Mandrol knew that the general was hoping that his rival would hang himself with his words.

"The *mask* . . ." The baron ran his fingers along his

temples, then eyed the bent alchemist with exaggerated indifference. "Yes, you keep telling me that, G'Meni. You keep telling me all sorts of things about masks, but you cannot tell me why the mask persists and why we cannot stop it . . . *him*. Yes, him. Viktor Falsche. This is no mere reflection, no shadow, my loyal ones; this *is* the true Viktor Falsche, make no mistake. Only Viktor Falsche was ever so troublesome."

"But you defeated Falsche, Baron," insisted G'Meni. "He died at your hands, great one."

Baron Mandrol straightened the collar of his high-necked dress uniform, momentarily proud of that accomplishment, but then he recalled the details of that struggle. "And nearly lost my own life at the same time. I will not give Falsche a second chance, alchemist. He nearly succeeded too well on his first try, wouldn't you say?"

The disfigured G'Meni said nothing, which the baron thought was perhaps the wisest comment the man had made in days.

Straas shifted. "My baron, if this Falsche does come, he'll use his sorcery to disguise himself. He'll walk in among the courtiers. My talisman is limited; I cannot be everywhere. If I had more—"

"You would waste them, Straas, that's what you would do. You do not understand the subtleties of sorcery, either. If you use your talisman, it will possibly reveal Falsche, but it will also disrupt other spells I have set into motion. More important, I want him where he can't possibly escape. The talisman is a range artifact; even if he should be at the very edge of its range, it will affect him . . . and give him warning that he is undisguised. I do not trust that you and your men will prevent him from escaping again unless he is in this room standing before me."

Straas wisely did not argue with his baron's logic. Mandrol cared not whether his explanation answered everything; he only cared that Viktor Falsche would come close enough so that the baron could be assured of his capture, yet far enough so that this too-solid ghost would not manage to complete his decade-delayed vengeance.

"Falsche must be in the center of the ballroom,

where he should have ended up in the first place." He gave the alchemist a brief glare. "Only then will I be satisfied. Only then will I be able to rest, gentlemen. Only then . . . will your lives be restored to you."

Both men flinched. Mandrol decided that they had been reprimanded enough. What was important now was to assure that Falsche was caught.

Baron Mandrol snapped his fingers. A liveried servant stepped from behind his chair and walked down to where the alchemist and the general waited. In the servant's hands was a black pillow on which rested a pair of small emerald and gold rings. The servant displayed the rings for both men, but finally positioned himself only before Straas.

"In lieu of what you ask for, General, I do have these. They are . . . old. Take the one on your right. The other is mine . . . and before you take your ring, I must ask you to remove the talisman and place it in this special container." Another liveried servant joined the first, a small, intricately carved lead box in his hands. After Straas had obeyed and the box had been closed, the baron inhaled deeply and continued, "Now, General, I shall teach you a little about those subtleties I spoke about." He turned his gaze to the alchemist. "And you, G'Meni. I also have something for you to do, too."

"We want everything just perfect for our guest of honor."

The masques at Viathos were a time of high, albeit occasionally dangerous entertainment for those who followed the baron and for his special guests, such as the dignitaries from Neuland, but for all others the masques were a time of fear. The dignitaries were led through a special corridor of the city, never to see the truth about Medecia. Most knew the truth, but their function was to promote their own land's causes, and in Neuland's case, the truth would have mattered little. Neuland had an agenda, one that required the cooperation of Medecia.

Mandrol was occupied with other matters and so it fell to Lilaith to greet those arriving for the masque. Most she knew by name, although never did she encourage their companionship outside of the balls. Fortunately, neither did her love, who only cared that he had their allegiance and their fear. Mandrol despised them almost as much as she did.

Jakaly was among the worst, but in his case, the baron found him useful and so she was forced now and then to suffer his foul company. He had not yet come and after facing so many fawning courtiers Lilaith had no desire to see him, much less welcome him to Viathos.

She excused herself from one short, overweight guild leader with sticky fingers and, hardly caring how undignified her actions looked, darted across the great hall toward the stairway leading up to her chambers. On her way she noted General Straas, clad in his very best dress uniform, wandering around the area, a goblet in his hand. Several people attempted to speak to the soldier, but the general merely gave them a few quick words and then moved on. He seemed to be looking for something.

Viktor. He looks for Viktor. That was, truth be told, her other reason for not wanting to remain among the guests. Mandrol was expecting Viktor. Viktor would come, too, even though he knew that the baron would be waiting for him. To Viktor, this would be the opportune time, for she suddenly recalled him saying long ago that an enemy such as Mandrol was at his most vulnerable when he thought he knew what was happening. *But that always worked both directions, my love. You suffer from the same ego as your adversary.*

Lilaith paused in her flight and blinked. *My love?* She meant Mandrol, of course. Never Viktor Falsche. It was Mandrol she loved.

Unfortunately, her pause put her in perfect line-of-sight for Straas. He cut through the crowd, actually barging his way through a few disconcerted aristocrats, and confronted her just before the stairway.

"My Lady DuPrise. Are you all right? Your place is back that way, greeting our baron's guests. It's essential that you are here; all of the guests should see you." He meant Viktor, of course. Straas considered her bait, nothing more.

"I have greeted many of them, General, but my head throbs. I fear that I must return to my chambers for a few minutes." She tried to step around him, but he casually shifted in front of her again. Her expression of growing annoyance the veteran campaigner ignored completely.

"If it's a problem with your head, I have with me a small vial containing one of G'Meni's few useful concoctions. It'll clear your head."

"Thank you, but I simply need a few minutes of quiet . . . if you please."

Holding his goblet out, Straas bowed and stepped aside. As he did, Lilaith caught sight of the unusual ring on his hand. It gleamed almost as if on fire.

Despite her need to be away, Lilaith DuPrise was fascinated by the unusual piece of jewelry. The gem changed as if it had a life all its own. She leaned forward, wanting to touch it to see if it was as warm as it appeared. The general saw her interest and glanced down at his hand.

"Damn!" he muttered. He looked up and scanned the crowd behind her. Straas swore once more, then, completely forgetting Lilaith, barged back into the crowd.

Glancing over her shoulder, she watched as the general wandered around the great hall, growing more frustrated by the moment. Lilaith continued to watch for several seconds, entertained by anything that put Straas so ill at ease.

Her fascination was shattered when she recognized an overdressed figure who must have just arrived after her departure from the greeting line. Jakaly. If anything, he repelled her more than ever. He was not alone, either. With him was not only an entourage as great as any king's, but also several blond, gray-uniformed men who could only be the emissaries from Neuland. Jakaly had probably made certain to arrive just as they did, to further emphasize his part in the diplomatic coup that had brought the Neulanders here.

Mandrol would be furious with her for having missed greeting such august guests as these, but she could not remain any longer. The tale she had told to Straas was now truth; her head did hurt her. It throbbed as if she had been struck soundly by the gauntleted hand of the general, an act which he probably dearly would have liked to have performed. Turning away before Jakaly or his cohorts could see her, Lilaith hurried up the steps toward her chambers. All she needed was a few minutes . . . but if Mandrol did not notice her absence, the Lady DuPrise intended on remaining hidden for the rest of the evening.

While Viathos above filled with the baron's faithful, Viathos below continued with its own, less urbane and much darker tasks. The dungeons, Baron Mandrol's source for both amusement and experimentation, still needed to be overseen, and now and then new guests were brought in by the soldiers trying to weed out both the malcontents or anyone who simply did not look right to them. There were farmers, tradesmen, beggars, and the occasional lone travelers whose wealth was enough to attract the watching guards but small enough that their disappearance would not be questioned by anyone save a few distant, desperate friends and relatives.

At the lower gateway leading into the belly of the keep, the sentries on duty noted the latest arrivals. Two guards with a trio of prisoners, all men, who looked just slightly better than beggars. There was a chance that the masks might be used this evening and so the guards in the dungeons noted the general appearance of each new prisoner. One never knew what type Master G'Meni wanted for his baron's entertainment.

Another soldier dragged in a harmless-appearing old man who babbled half the time. He had been nearly trampled by the horses of Lord Jakaly, then had also had the audacity to beg from the aristocrat. Since they had already been well on their way to the city, Jakaly had decided to make an addition to the baron's dungeons. He had doubted that the old man was worth a mask, but knowing both Mandrol and G'Meni as he did, Lord Jakaly was certain that they would find *some* use for the prisoner. Besides, it meant less refuse cluttering his own domain.

The officer in charge of the dungeons never argued about extra prisoners. If the cells grew overcrowded, it was only a temporary state at best, nothing to concern him at all.

The ring was aglow.

Straas glared at the gem, cursing it. He had been careless in confronting Lilaith DuPrise; her decision to defy his baron was inconsequential compared to allowing the false Falsche into the masque. The glow meant that a sorcerer was within range. The ring had been created so as to ignore the presence of the baron, so that left the possibility of it being anyone other than Viktor Falsche slim. The ring was attuned to the presence of a sorcerer of great ability and the only other such person in the city was Falsche.

Straas casually slipped over to one of his staff, who was in conversation with a pair of minor aristocrats. The officer abandoned his conversation the moment the general joined him.

"Keep smiling and nodding, Clevell." General Straas took a sip from his drink. "The fox may be within the walls now. After I'm through with you, speak for another two minutes to those two fawning creatures, then excuse yourself and depart the hall. I want you to have every man alerted to Falsche's presence. Do not attempt to close the noose yet. There is still a level of uncertainty. Falsche must still be identified. Got all that?"

Clevell smiled broadly, as if just having heard some grand joke. "Yes, General."

"Very good." Straas nodded back to the man, then belatedly included the aristocrats for the sake of form. They, having no idea what was going on, flushed with honor, for everyone knew the general was one of the baron's most trusted subordinates. The general wanted to laugh; these same men would have even bowed to Master G'Meni if only because of the slim hope that he might recall them to Mandrol someday.

Jackals. No, much too ferocious. Mice. That's what they all are . . . mice. Mice following the scent of cheese. It was hard to believe that his baron needed such people, but General Straas knew enough about politics and governing to know that even such as these had their places in the scheme of things.

And among them is one fox, he reminded himself. Goblet hand twisted so that he could just see the gem in the ring, Straas wandered around the room. The ball had not yet officially begun, but nearly everyone was here. Jakaly, too, he saw. The baron's favorite stood with several of the gray-suited Neulanders, evidently sharing some bit of humor. The general paused in his search to briefly study the foreigners. Their military bearing was admirable and what he knew of their campaigns filled him with the desire to talk with them about strategy. That would have to wait until the would-be assassin was eliminated.

Turning away from Jakaly and his guests, the general continued to sweep across the vast room. The nearer he came to the sorcerer, the more brilliant would become the ring's glow. All he needed was a bit of time; Falsche could not go anywhere now. If he attempted to leave Viathos or even this chamber, he would find his way blocked.

Straas still wished that he had his talisman, but the ring could not work within the range of that object. The masks could, for they were part the child of sorcery and part the creation of alchemy. Still, it mattered little, for Mandrol never allowed Straas to wear the talisman during these balls since there were other spells in place it sometimes disrupted.

He could not focus on the sorcerer. The guarded doorways were the only way into the masque now; the baron's spells prevented materializations and any flying object would have been spotted by the general's men.

In frustration he did a nearly complete turnaround. All about, the gadflies and toadies that came to pay homage to Baron Mandrol talked, ate, and drank . . . and they did all three with gusto. Even the Neulanders seemed much too at ease in the court; Straas had expected more disdain, more aloofness. He was somewhat disappointed.

Mandrol would be down soon. By this time he was finished with whatever business he had with the horrid little alchemist and was being dressed for his grand entrance.

That gave Straas anywhere from a quarter hour to a half. Not nearly enough time, he suspected.

As he glanced about, he noted that Jakaly had now left the Neulanders completely alone. Straas surveyed the vast room in all directions, but the noble was nowhere to be seen. Yet another potential disaster. Someone should have been here until the baron could make his entrance. Either Jakaly or Lady DuPrise should have remained in the room. Straas certainly had no time to play host to a legion of pampered wastrels, the Neulanders excluded from that grouping, of course.

Twisting his hand around, the general studied the ring for what seemed to him the thousandth time. He was truly beginning to despise the thing. It was so damned imprecise. It had not glowed brighter, despite his having circled most of the room by this point; in fact, now the gem appeared just a little dimmer. Did that mean that somehow he had started to walk farther away from the sorcerer?

For some inexplicable reason, Jakaly came to mind. Straas did not know why, but when such sudden notions had occurred in the past, usually he had found some connection between events and his thoughts. Yet how, he wondered, could the aristocrat be related to his present task?

Forgetting the ring, the general marched over to the Neulanders, who took in his appearance with some growing interest. Jakaly had no doubt pointed out the general to them. He stopped before them, clicked his heels, and said, "Gentlemen. I am General Straas. I regret that our first meeting must be on such a disorganized note, but I'm hoping that you might be able to tell me exactly where I might find Lord Jakaly."

The uniformed men muttered among themselves in their harsh tongue. Straas understood just enough of the language to know that two of the men were explaining to their counterparts just what the general had said and what he wanted of them. At last, one older soldier bedecked with countless medals uttered something to a younger man who had the look of an aide on him.

The young officer turned a strict face to him. "My

General Straas. My greetings through my interpreter, Haufmann Dreckel." Here the aide indicated himself. "I hope to have a discussion with you later joint military exercises to the benefit of both regions concerning. As to your question, the Lord Jakaly, he asked excused to be, but did not say where he had to go."

Straas tried to hide his disappointment.

"However," continued Dreckel in a more casual tone, "I must tell you personally from me, my general, that I believe I saw him those stairs ascend."

Following the Neulander's lead, Straas found himself looking at the same stairway the Lady Lilaith DuPrise had ascended only minutes before. Again the general was not certain of the direction of his own mind, but a few points of information were already jelling together.

"Thank you. I sincerely hope to speak to all of you later. If you'll excuse me . . ." He did not wait for the Neulanders to finish their bows. Baron Mandrol had given him a task and he still needed to complete it.

He had to find Clevell. Straas had new, possibly delicate orders to give his subordinate.

Lilaith sat in her chambers, only one dim set of candles illuminating the vast, elegant room she now occupied. Despite the silks, the colors, and the softness of her surroundings, the dark-skinned woman could find no peace. Every time she nearly relaxed, unbidden and forbidden thoughts crept into her mind. She had already tried to shut them out with drink, but that was the way of cowards. Sleep was also of no use, for the thoughts drove it away. Even reading, one of her favorite pastimes, gave her no shelter. Each passage she read reminded her somehow of her troubles.

Her Mandrol had assured her only recently that such thoughts would bother her no longer, but, contrary to his promise, they seemed more rampant than ever. Oh, for a short time after his promise she had lived without them, but that reprieve had been so brief that it barely counted. It seemed that once she had come to know that Mandrol and the others expected Viktor to appear at the masque, Lilaith had been unable to think of anything but that. She hated and loved Viktor Falsche and the conflict was again driving her near to insanity.

She was thankful at least for the quiet her chambers afforded her. The constant patter of oil-drenched flattery was almost as maddening as the dilemma within her head, but not nearly so significant in nature. All anyone down there could do was tell her how magnificent the baron was and how stunning she looked. *It is almost like listening to a room full of parrots all taught the same phrases!*

She rose to pour herself a drink, her servants having been dismissed the moment Lilaith had arrived. They could whisper all they wanted; she did not want *anyone* around her.

Her goblet filled, the dark-skinned woman returned to her place and once more attempted to sort out the conflicting notions. Mandrol was her love, but sometimes she utterly loathed him. Viktor had been her love once, and while she now loathed him, she also still loved the renegade sorcerer.

I will *go mad!*

"Lilaith?"

The goblet fell from her hand as she first took the voice as that of the very man of whom she had been thinking. Then her face hardened as she saw who the uninvited newcomer was. "Lord Jakaly."

The tall figure of Renfrew Jakaly swept into her chamber. Lilaith had not even heard the door open. The overdressed aristocrat quietly closed the door behind him. Lilaith was too stunned by his audacity to react until he had walked all the way over to her and had bent over to pick up the goblet.

"What are you doing here?"

"You're fortunate, my good lady. The wine spilled only on the floor. It would've been a shame to ruin so enchanting a dress." As he rose, Jakaly's eyes lingered on the low front. "It is positively beautiful."

Blandishments from Renfrew Jakaly were not what she desired now . . . nor ever. He was the worst of the lot, ever fawning and ever grasping, but never before had he dared to come to her chambers. "What is it you wish, Lord Jakaly? I am not feeling well at the moment and would like to rest, so the sooner this conversation ends, the better, I am sorry to say."

He did not seem at all put out by her words and in fact her defiant tone almost appeared to entice him. Lilaith could not recall Jakaly ever being like this. He had admired her at times, true, but now it was almost as if he intended on making her his own, no matter that she belonged to his baron.

"I'd prefer that this conversation never end, myself, Lady DuPrise. I could not keep myself away. I've something to tell you and I think that you will find it of great interest." He took her by the arms and drew her nearer.

Lilaith DuPrise waited until she was close enough, then slipped out the small, jeweled dagger she often carried secreted in her gown. Elegant it might have looked, but the point was honed fine, perfect for marauding lords. "Your stomach presents an unavoidable target, Jakaly. Pull me closer and I will let some of that hot air out of you. Release me, I say."

He did, but under confusion and protest. She would have been willing to swear that he found her reluctance to fall prey to his so-called charms astonishing.

"But Lilaith! You can't be serious! If I could just tell you, explain to you, I'm certain that—"

The door to her chambers was thrown back.

"Stand where you are, my *Lord Jakaly!*"

Through the doorway rushed nearly a dozen well-armed soldiers followed by the foreboding figure of General Straas. It was perhaps the first time in all the years that she had known him that Lilaith was actually pleased to see her baron's hound.

The soldiers swiftly surrounded the shocked and quite befuddled Jakaly. Lilaith backed away. She did not know why Straas suddenly found the aristocrat a threat, but it would not have displeased her to see him removed even if he was a favorite of Mandrol.

"Straas, man! What the devil are you doing? Stop this insanity now!" shouted the prisoner.

The soldiers were keeping a respectful distance from Jakaly, almost as if they thought him dangerous even while unarmed and at bay. *Do they expect him to sprout talons or pull a pair of rapiers out of thin air?* Lilaith wondered.

"If you *are* Lord Renfrew Jakaly, then my apologies for having to do this." It was clear from his tone that General Straas seemed to think that the man before him was in fact someone other than Jakaly. "If not, then be warned that if you move so much as an inch without my permission, my men will cut you into a dozen different pieces."

Jakaly was intelligent enough to take the general's warning to heart, but he grew more furious by the moment. In his position, it was doubtful that anyone had ever treated him so commonly. "This is absurd, Straas! You know me! Who the blazes do you think I am if not me?"

Taking a few steps forward, Straas reached up and cupped his prisoner's chin in his gauntleted hand. Jakaly almost moved then, but the rustling of weapons kept him from making what would have been a foolish and fatal mistake.

"I think that you might be a sorcerer. I think that you might be *Viktor Falsche*, perhaps."

"What? Viktor Falsche? I've never heard anything so absurd in all my life! Viktor Falsche is dead . . . *dead!* Even his bloody ghost must be by this time!"

"You protest too much." Straas continued to calmly study his prisoner's features. "I have reason to believe that you are." The general raised his free hand and revealed to both Jakaly and Lilaith a ring in which was set a gleaming gem. The dim candles in the room could not be the sole reason for the gleam. "This tells me that you might be other than you appear. It didn't glow until you entered the main hall. Then the glow weakened when you left the hall and headed here. Now the gem gleams again. Not as bright as I would've thought from what my baron said, but bright enough. I think you're a sorcerer, and since the true Lord Jakaly is not, then it is fairly safe to assume that you might be the sorcerer I'm looking for."

"You've gone mad, Straas! If you harm me, the

baron'll skin you alive, then turn you over to Master G'Meni for his experiments! I'm needed to speak with the Neulanders! You know how important that is to Mandrol! Wesfrancia is vulnerable and if he can manipulate the goals of the Neulanders, we can own the blasted place in just a few years."

"Knowledge easily obtained by the use of sorcery will not sway my decision. You may be who you claim to be and then again you may not be."

"By what right do you interrupt my work, Straas?" grumbled a new voice. The alchemist G'Meni shuffled into the chamber.

Lilaith, all but forgotten, observed the tableau with growing amazement and not a little concern. Jakaly had been trying to say something to her, perhaps to reveal that he *was* Viktor. After all, everyone had been expecting her former love to return despite the obvious danger, and how like Viktor to openly risk his own life by coming to her. Jakaly had been acting most unlike himself. . . .

She almost spoke then, almost denied that Jakaly was anyone but Jakaly. It would not have been because she was trying to save the arrogant and self-serving aristocrat, but rather because she feared that Viktor had indeed been captured again. Sorcery could readily be utilized to alter one's entire appearance. Lilaith could not bear to see him killed a second time.

But Mandrol is my love!

Unable to come to a decision, Lilaith DuPrise simply stood and watched, hoping and praying that some other force would make the decision for her.

Followed by two sentries, Master G'Meni waddled over to Straas and his captive. "What are you playing at, Straas? Why have you seized our good Lord Jakaly?"

"This is why." Straas thrust the ring toward his rival's ruined countenance.

G'Meni sniffed, a horrid sight considering what remained of his nose, then peered closely at the bit of jewelry. His eyes narrowed. "Interesting. This does not look good, you know, Lord Jakaly."

"Surely you of all people aren't going to side with

this trumped-up sewage guard!" roared the furious prisoner.

A sinister gleam appeared briefly in the general's eyes, but neither Jakaly nor G'Meni noticed it, although the latter did smile at the comment.

"I side with the evidence. What other proof have you, Straas? The baron will not take kindly to having Lord Jakaly condemned as Viktor Falsche. Data, my good Straas, data is what we need."

"I have proof enough." Straas repeated his statement concerning the aristocrat's entrance and the intensity of the gem's glow. "He then came up here and his actions contradicted the Jakaly we know. Jakaly would never be so foolish to approach the Lady DuPrise and try to steal her from the baron. His words were more those one would expect from the mouth of Viktor Falsche."

"Small enough proof to go on," chided G'Meni. He rubbed his chin. "Still, not exactly in your character, you know, Jakaly. Also, the ring does seem to indicate a closeness to a sorcerer, although I admit that I'm not so adept in that field of study as I am in alchemy."

"Do I look like Falsche, you blithering gnome?"

Now G'Meni, too, looked at Jakaly a little more harshly. Lilaith knew that the aristocrat was hurting his cause with such insults. Both the alchemist and the general were the type of men who would use the excuse of suspicion to teach Jakaly proper respect for their positions.

Master G'Meni carefully inspected the captive, first testing the clothing at various points, then running his gnarled fingers over and around Jakaly's snarling face. The alchemist muttered to himself and prodded the other's visage time and time again, sometimes with more enthusiasm than Lilaith suspected was needed.

"As I said, I am not as versed in the ways of sorcery as I am in alchemy. That is still the baron's field. The fabric of your clothing seems real enough, but then creating a piece of clothing is hardly a tremendous effort for a sorcerer of ability. Your face—"

"Is obviously my own, you pompous baboon! You prodded it enough to discover that, I hope!"

The alchemist's mouth curled upward, but his expression could hardly be termed a smile. "Yet I am also aware that an illusion cast by a sorcerer not only can look real, but also may *feel* real on closer inspection." He shook his head, his mouth still set. "I am afraid that we shall just have to run some tests, you know."

"*Tests?*" For the first time, Jakaly seemed uneasy.

"Oh, yes. Even sorcery can be detected by tests. I've been working on a few, but I have yet to use most of them in the field, so to speak. I do have one test of importance available now, however. One that our baron aided me in creating." From a pocket, he produced a small mechanism consisting of gems, wires, and a tiny, transparent flask of some blue solution. The flask was sealed tight save where two wires entered at the top. He held it near the prisoner. "This won't hurt, you know. The idea behind it is fascinating. Spells, specific spells, radiate a specific aura. Now, if this detector works the way it is supposed to, then we can see if there are any spells cast upon you. In this case the most obvious would be the illusion that you look as you do now. You could actually be a tiny woman, you see, but an illusion spell would make you look just like you—"

"Get on with it!" Straas barked. "Spare the lectures for later."

"Yes, I suppose so. Now, here . . . now, this *is* interesting."

"What is?" asked the general, anxious for results.

Lilaith could not help but lean forward in anticipation.

"There are at least two spells covering you, you know, *Lord* Jakaly, and one, hmmm, yes, one does appear to be an illusion spell." The alchemist chuckled. "Well, it seems my apparatus is functioning properly, I think."

"I demand to speak to the baron! This is preposterous!" Renfrew Jakaly started forward, but Straas suddenly had a long knife at his throat.

"In due time," said the general. "But as he cannot be disturbed right now, anyway, we might as well try some of the good alchemist's other, more definitive tests." He pulled the knife back. "You have the choice, Jakaly. Armed escort or dragged in irons. If you are Viktor Falsche, even your vaunted powers won't help you this close, so consider well."

"This is absurd!" shouted the prisoner. Then he took a close look at the sharp blades around him and the steady glares of the soldiers . . . all men personally chosen by Straas with not one puppet among them. "Very well, though. The sooner we are done with this, the better. I demand that someone be sent to wait for the baron, however, so that he can be notified immediately about the situation!"

"Oh, you may be assured that he will be notified," said G'Meni. "Shall we be going now? I'm anxious to begin, you know. I have so many things to try."

Renfrew Jakaly shivered.

With the soldiers to escort them, the alchemist and the furious aristocrat departed. Lilaith waited impatiently for all of them to depart and was surprised when General Straas did not follow the rest.

"Are you not going to assist Master G'Meni with the interrogation, General?"

"Master G'Meni has things well in hand. He will get the truth out of your visitor, my lady. Are you concerned about that?"

"Whether or not you lose your head over Jakaly's impertinent advance is not my concern, although I am grateful to you for being timely for once."

The general gave her a mock bow. "My pleasure, my lady. When I know the results of Master G'Meni's tests, I'll have them relayed to you."

"I couldn't care less about what happens to Renfrew Jakaly, thank you."

"But what about Viktor Falsche?" asked Straas as he departed.

Lilaith was still trying to answer the last question long after the general was gone.

XV

The officer currently in charge of the dungeons, a gruff, bearded dog named Severin, leaned back in his chair as the guards who had brought in the latest prisoners came to report in before returning to the outside. He did not recognize the faces of either of the two mercenaries and it was a waste of his time even bothering to look at the drone soldier with the nearest of the two men.

"Anything unusual to report?" he grumbled, reaching for a scrap of paper. The general wanted everything written down, which was bothersome work for an officer who had trouble spelling his own name. Severin generally had his subordinate, who could spell better even if he took longer to write, take care of the reports. The man had vanished, however, even though he had been around when this trio had first appeared. Either down one of the corridors watering the prisoners or just goldbricking. Either way, Severin planned to give him a hiding when he came back. This was not senior officer work. He was a soldier, damn it, a *warrior*, not some court scrivener.

It was not until after he had gathered the paper and something to write with that he recalled that no one had as yet given him an answer. "I said, did you—"

The drone soldier was leaning over the table, a long knife in his hand. The point of the knife was inches from the officer's unprotected throat.

"Not a word if you want to live, man."

Severin opened his mouth to shout the alarm even as his right hand went for his own weapon.

He failed in both attempts.

"Damn, bloody damn!" hissed the drone soldier in Dré Kopien's voice. "What a fool! I was hoping to avoid having to do that!"

"It couldn't be helped," returned one of the other guards in a voice identical to that of Mara. "Some are just not born with brains, love. He should've been dead a long time ago, thinkin' like that."

"Never mind about him. You and the others have given me all the help I need, Dré," interjected the third. "You should take the prisoners out of here and get to safety. There are still the fires to tend."

"Which are being tended to by others, Viktor." Dré confronted Viktor. "I'm beginning to think that you might have a death wish, man. You think that I'm going to let you wander Viathos by yourself? Do you expect to bring down Mandrol alone? Maybe you've forgotten all those soldiers and toadies of his above us. Why, we're right under the great hall. Straas has men all over. Just about everyone above our heads *wants* our heads and you plan on going up there by yourself!"

"Hush, love! There're still other guards down here! We can't go bickerin', with them around. The others need time to free and arm some of the other prisoners."

Viktor put a hand on her shoulder. "Drop your images, Mara. Conserve your strength for yourself. You have already done more than I requested of you, but I have one more task if you are willing." He waited for her to nod before continuing, "The guards down here will be trapped if we just close the outer gate. You two take care of that while I survey the area."

"All right." In place of the three soldiers now stood Dré, Mara, and a man not at all resembling Viktor Falsche. Dark hair and a short beard, a common enough style among all classes of men, did much to obscure his features and cover the ragged side of the mask. At first glance, most would have mistaken the sorcerer for a servant in Viathos, which was what he planned. No sorcery had been involved in his disguise; Viktor had assumed that it would be troublesome enough to disguise the fact that he was a sorcerer without adding magical trappings to himself.

That was where the great Lord Renfrew Jakaly had come in. What Viktor needed to make his entrance into Viathos less noticeable was to give Mandrol's minions someone else to focus on. With the aid of Mara and one of her most theatrical and daring of associates, they had set a distraction in the form of an old beggar. His mind on the distasteful figure before him, Jakaly never even sensed the carefully laid spells enshrouding him as he rode with his retinue toward the city: One to make certain that he did not kill the beggar but turned him over to the first soldiers that he found. One to give the false indication that his appearance was the result of illusion. Another, a compulsion, that would make Jakaly seek out Lilaith. He would give her a message and, since she was still under Mandrol's control, she would betray him to the guards.

Renfrew Jakaly had proven to be quite susceptible to sorcery. The spells had set with only slight effort on Viktor's part.

In the meantime, Viktor and his companions, with the further aid of Mara's peculiar abilities, would enter Viathos by its rotting underbelly. He did not think her abilities were detectable in the same way that sorcery was and so hoped that any detection device or spell put together by Mandrol and G'Meni would fail. Viktor had planned contingencies if that assumption proved incorrect, but he had hoped he would have to turn to none of them . . . at least in the beginning.

Mara took charge of Dré, preventing any renewal of his argument with Viktor. The sorcerer made his way down the corridors, seeking out those guards not yet dealt with by the invaders. So far, the invasion of the dungeons had been a surprisingly quiet one. The men they had brought in with them, including a pair who had been involved in Viktor's rescue in the city, were silently freeing the last few prisoners. Weapons normally set aside for the guards were now in the hands of their former captives and more than a dozen sentries now occupied cells. Viktor had ordered them bound and gagged for now. He did not like straightforward killing, with the exception of Baron Mandrol. So far, the sorcerer counted three dead among the guards, including the fool of an officer Dré had been forced to dispatch. One of the men with them had been able to provide bits of information about the network of cells because of a relative who was an overtalkative servant of the keep, but even though they were well informed, Viktor considered his group as having been very, very lucky so far.

"Hold it! Who're you?"

He froze at the sight of three sentries marching down the corridor from the opposite end. "Just brought some food down to your captain. Orders from above. Don't know nothin' else."

One of the men started to lower his weapon. "Severin's getting food from—"

"You couldn't be from up there!" snarled the foremost, silencing his companion with a quick wave of his free hand. "To do that, you'd have had to walk right past us earlier, and I know we didn't see you."

He stalked toward Viktor, his two companions belatedly following.

"You're mistaken," retorted the sorcerer, but it was too late. He reached for his sword as they closed in on him, forgetting that in his present disguise he only carried a dagger.

"Get him!"

With his companions too far back, the battle was strictly in the hands of Viktor. He had to use sorcery, but in as subtle a fashion as possible lest he ensure that Mandrol take notice of him.

Like to like. One of the simplest forms of sorcery. He had a dagger, which was a small blade. Daggers were actually small swords, which meant that he was carrying a sword. Of course, in a battle, one carried a longer sword, so that was what he had in his hand.

The blade transformed just as the lead man swung. The look on the soldier's face would have been humorous under other circumstances. His eyes bulged as the short dagger that should not have even been able to slow down his sword grew to match his own weapon.

"Sorcerer!" he gasped.

With his free hand, Viktor struck the guard across the chin. As the man fell back, he collided with one of his companions, who paused to catch him. The third man came forward, but his progress was also slowed by the one who had fallen. Blades clashed as the two opponents tried to take one another out quickly. The soldier was an adequate swordsman, but Viktor knew that he had the advantage ... so long as only one man faced him. Acting swiftly, he brought his blade under that of his adversary and pushed up. As the soldier's arm rose, the sorcerer thrust.

He did not severely wound the man, but the thin cut and the shock of nearly having the point of a sword in his face caused the guard to step back a pace or two. This caused him to partially block the duo behind him, who had finally managed to move forward again.

From behind Viktor came the sounds of men running. His first thought was that he was now surrounded on both sides, but then another man, a prisoner, leaped past him and crossed swords with one of the guards. Two more men and then another broke by the sorcerer, suddenly leaving him bereft of opponents.

Swamped by the newcomers, the nearest soldier went down almost instantly. One of the others managed to gut an overanxious prisoner, but he, in turn, was run through by two blades. The third guard turned to run, but was not swift enough. One man caught him by the legs, bringing him down. Before Viktor could stop them, a human pile had formed on the unfortunate soldier. The sorcerer turned away from the sight, shivering at what little he had been unfortunate enough to see before the soldier had vanished underneath. The prisoners were justly bitter with their captors, but even so, the guard's death was far too unsettling. A simple sword thrust should have been satisfactory.

More and more it was impossible to keep the level of noise down. Men were shouting, some in happiness and some in anger. Weapons clanged against weapons, a sign

that other, deeper parts of the dungeons were not yet liberated.
Viktor started back, then paused. He wanted to help finish the
struggle down here, but there was actually little he could do.
The sentries were not only outnumbered, but also fighting
men driven by bitterness and anger. The sorcerer eyed some
of his fellows. Scars attested to their whippings. There were
also burns and more than one prisoner had been mutilated in
some way. Even the women had not escaped torture.

Yet these were the lucky ones, the fortunate ones
who had, for the most part, suffered only a short time. Many
others ended up either in Master G'Meni's workplace, the
baron's sanctum, or as mindless soldiers in the army of
General Straas. It was impossible to say which fate was the
worst.

Dré had told Viktor that the fires were already burning. By now those assigned to the fires would be adding the
mixtures he had concocted to the flames. That meant that
the skies would be clouding up very soon. His companion
and the others already knew what steps had to be taken once
they achieved the liberation of the dungeons. All that
remained was his own part to play, a part which was integral
to the success of all.

Viktor began racing toward the steps leading to the
upper levels.

Guilt raged within him. He had not wanted it to be
like this. A rebellion should have been allowed enough time
for planning and preparation. Thanks to Viktor, one had
been thrown together in less than two days.

No, that wasn't true. Most of the preparations and
planning had been in place since his death; all the rebellion
had needed was a catalyst. His guilt stemmed from the fact
that he had rushed this attack because he had found himself
with but a day or two left of life. He could not bear the
thought that Mandrol would survive Viktor's second life. He
was throwing Medecia into turmoil for the sake of his own
vendetta. Viktor Falsche did indeed want freedom for the
people of this land, but that was secondary to his chief
desire. Before the mask lost control, he *had* to deal with
Mandrol.

Only when he was on his way up did he recall that he now carried a sword, not a simple dagger. He sheathed the weapon in his belt, hoping that none of the soldiers or other servants he encountered would think it strange. Considering Mandrol's likely state of mind these days, perhaps it would not seem so strange for one of his servants to be going well armed.

At the top of the steps Viktor confronted a locked door. His first test. There would be at least two sentries guarding the path down to the dungeons and one of them would have the key to the prisoner's freedom. Viktor had no intention of transporting himself around Viathos; that would be inviting disaster. He was certain that Mandrol had planned for such sorcerous activities.

Taking a deep breath, the sorcerer banged on the door. It was thick and wooden, which was probably the only reason that there were not hundreds of soldiers streaming downstairs. The baron probably wanted it thick so that annoying noises from the dungeons would not disturb either him or his guests. Viktor silently thanked his adversary even as a tiny window in the door, workable from both sides, slid open and a guard peered through.

"What?"

"I'm done down here. Let me out."

The sentry looked him over. "I don't remember lettin' you down there."

"I came in through the dungeons' outer gateway with a guard. Now open the door; I'm supposed to be helping with the masque, you idiot."

"I don't know. . . ."

Viktor concentrated on the guard, willing him to believe.

"Let me see," said another voice. The guard that Viktor almost had mesmerized was shoved aside by a taller, burlier figure with a bushy beard who looked the supposed servant over from head to toe. "Yeah, you look okay."

The window closed, but moments later the heavy door swung back to welcome him into a much brighter corridor. Viktor walked through and saw that besides the two men he had met there were no other guards. He turned and faced both men.

"My thanks. I hate the dungeons, don't you?" As he spoke, the sorcerer touched each man on the shoulder.

There was no chance for either man to question his peculiar gesture, for both soldiers stiffened, then slumped together. It was a risk using his sorcery yet again, but the other choice would have been to fight the two hand-to-hand. He could not mesmerize both of them at the same time.

The side of his face began to itch again, reminding him how quickly his time was running out.

He had just positioned both men so that they would not be immediately discovered when the scuffing of boots against stone made him whirl.

"Seems I'm always having to track you down," muttered Dré Kopien. "Seems you're always running off without telling me exactly what you're doing."

"I have no time for arguments, Dré. I am running out of time."

"Well, I'm coming with you, man. You need someone to watch your back."

Viktor sighed. "Perhaps you are correct, Dré." He smiled at his old comrade and looked him square in the eye. "Perhaps you are correct, but I think it would be better if you kept control over the others, don't you think? They need your guidance."

"Yes, they need my guidance, don't they?" Dré stared back. His eyes grew wider but less focused.

"They do, friend. One of us has to remain around if I fail in this. I am expendable, Dré; you are not."

"I'm not."

"Go rejoin Mara and the others. You will know if the plan has failed. There should still be time then to escape." Viktor Falsche pulled back.

"Should be time to escape." Dré blinked. "All right, Viktor. Have it your way. Ariela knows, someone has to keep that bunch down there under control until we know whether we have a chance or not." Kopien retreated back to the steps leading to the dungeons. "I'll send some men to watch the door. You'd better be going, man, and remember, you're not just risking your own existence. There's Emil."

"I will try to bring us both back," the sorcerer replied with a touch of sadness. He hated having had to mesmerize his oldest friend, but it was the only way to ensure that Dré would have hope of surviving. As for Viktor and Emil . . . if there had been a way to avoid endangering the farmer, the sorcerer would have chosen that way. Regrettably, he knew of no other course but the one he was already on.

Left alone again, Viktor Falsche made his way through the vast halls of Viathos. It was an undeniably beautiful structure, but some of its masters, most notably Mandrol, had left their taint in its walls. He could sense the madness, the dark sorcery, and the deaths of many years.

Tall marble columns lined each hall. The corridors were stark here. Mandrol was not an admirer of art; his collection in the main halls was more for the benefit of his admirers. Here, where few other than servants and aides came, there was little.

The sounds of music and merriment informed him that the masque was well under way. Servants darted fearfully through the halls. Servants who failed to perform their tasks to the standards the baron set suffered. No one paid special notice to one more figure rushing along on some assignment, which was exactly as Viktor had hoped.

As he ascended from one level to the next, the sorcerer at last came across a window. Pausing despite the urgency of his mission, he gazed outside. The day was darkening, but the darkness was not entirely due to the coming night. Black clouds were forming in the heavens, black clouds that especially hung over Viathos and the city.

Nearly time, he noted. *Nearly time.*

"You there! Why are you standing there? Have you nothing better to do?"

A chill ran down the sorcerer's . . . or rather, Emil's . . . spine. Keeping his surprise in check as best he could, Viktor turned.

Baron Mandrol stood just down the hall, six armed

guards accompanying him. He was dressed in a dark blue uniform with black cape and high leather boots. Anyone else would have looked dashing, but Viktor not for the first time thought the man resembled more a baboon someone had dressed for the entertainment of an audience.

Quickly taking on a most servile manner, Viktor replied, "My most humble apologies, my baron! I was out of breath and simply paused—"

"Spare me your excuses!" Mandrol started forward, then paused as if reconsidering. There was no indication that he recognized Viktor under the disguise that Dré had supplied. "If you value your life, make yourself useful and fetch me my gloves. Do it quick enough and I may not have you *whipped*."

"Yes, my baron! Thank you, my baron!" Although he had no intention of fulfilling Mandrol's request, Viktor moved along in the direction he hoped that his foe's apartments lay. He would have dearly loved to confront the baron there and then, but this was not the proper time. First Viktor had to strip Mandrol's might from him, and that meant removing the armies that kept his subjects in fearful check. Only then could he face the murderer and tyrant.

Evidently satisfied that he had put terror back into the heart and mind of a negligent servant, the baron resumed his trek to what Viktor assumed must be the masque. Mere steps later, however, Baron Mandrol paused and glanced back at him. The disguised sorcerer pretended not to notice, hoping that if he continued on, the baron would forget him.

"Stop!"

Still in his role, Falsche turned and bowed to the other sorcerer. "Yes, my baron?"

"Look at me."

"My baron?" Viktor focused on a location just below Mandrol's eyes.

"The black gloves, not the blue ones."

"Yes, my baron!"

"Bring them to me at the masque. Quickly, now!"

With great relief, Viktor Falsche bowed low and hurried off. He did not slow at all until he was up the next flight of stairs and well on his way down one of the lengthy corridors. Memories of his previous, fatal visit to Mandrol's stronghold were the only clues he had to where his destination lay. He was not after his adversary's apartment, however. Rather, Viktor hunted the personal chambers of the twisted little alchemist who was in great part responsible for many of the travesties the baron had visited upon his people and even others beyond Medecia.

A possessive creature such as Master G'Meni would keep a substance of Plutite's potency in his own private chambers, the better to make certain that it was safe and secret. In fact, G'Meni's chambers likely doubled as a secondary laboratory. Viktor only hoped that he was correct about the substance being stored there.

The masque continued to work to the sorcerer's advantage. Although there were guards posted all about Viathos, for surely Mandrol expected Viktor to be here as much as Viktor had planned to be here, none of them truly gave him a second glance. Mandrol had grown complacent and overconfident over the past decade, Viktor thought. The baron was too confident in his already-established power, so much so that he could not see someone else making use of that show of power to cover his own deeds.

That will be your downfall, dear Mandrol! Too much soft living and overconfidence!

His face continued to plague him, demanding that the itch be scratched. Doing so would only wear away the mask further, which Viktor dared not do. He carried with him a small vial of adhesive, but the more he was forced to repair his face, the more chance that at some point it would finally fall apart.

Scents tickled his nose as he rushed, but for the most part he paid them no mind. It was not until he passed one closed door where the scent of flowers graced his senses that Viktor froze. He whirled, stared at the wooden door, then finally inhaled.

It was indeed the scent of morning flowers, the same scent that lived in his memories of Lilaith.

He almost opened the door and rushed inside.

Almost. What held him back was the knowledge that she would likely scream if he appeared before her. For now, the woman he loved was a puppet to Mandrol. If she even knew of his presence, she would give the alarm, alert all Viathos to his location.

Viktor Falsche stepped back from the door and quietly continued on. When he had dealt with the other part of his mission, he could return to her. No sooner. First came Mandrol.

There was a great chance that G'Meni might be in his chambers. The alchemist was not one for masques, save when he was in charge of the special entertainment or when the baron simply demanded his appearance for form's sake. The squat figure was not one whose presence inspired merriment in the baron's followers. Viktor suspected that it was in part due to the way Master G'Meni eyed each and every one of them as potential test subjects for his experiments.

When at last he found it, the doorway to the alchemist's personal chambers proved unmistakable. Even after ten years, Viktor was pleased to see that his information was correct. *Trust a creature like G'Meni to be consistent. He has probably not cleaned the place out since he first came here.*

An air of neglect surrounded the part of the hall where G'Meni roosted. It was doubtful whether servants cared to wander too close. Dust and cobwebs spoke of the extent of their fear; no one had bothered to clean the hall and the alchemist was certainly not one to care. The adjoining rooms were likely empty, if they had not at some point been usurped for further work space.

Now that he had reached G'Meni's abode, the question Viktor Falsche had to ask himself was whether he dared risk seeing if the alchemist was within. That G'Meni would have what he sought the sorcerer did not doubt now; in his work on the baron's masks, the horrific little figure would require substances like Plutite in case there was an accident with the adhesive. Plutite was rare even among alchemists, which meant that G'Meni had hidden within his sanctum a treasure as great as any his master owned.

Viktor put one hand on the hilt of his sword. He was not averse to the thought of killing the alchemist if he had to do so. Master G'Meni had twisted his craft into the tool of evil. He was as much a murderer and sadist as either Mandrol or General Straas.

The sword it might be, then, or even a spell if Viktor dared risk it. *Strange that there are no guards, though.* . . .

He took a step forward, but was brought to a halt by a slim hand on his arm.

"It *is* you, Viktor. It is you. That disguise might fool even Mandrol, but I know the face beneath it too well."

Lilaith stood behind him, her eyes wide in wonder . . . and perhaps fear?

His mind blanked. The sorcerer could only stare at the dark-skinned beauty, the woman he had sworn his love to time and time again. It was the same woman who had helped him in his grief and who had more or less taken it upon herself to act as his spy among the foul devils of Viathos.

It was the same woman who had later betrayed him, a victim herself of Baron Mandrol's considerable power.

"I beg your pardon, my lady?" he finally stammered. "I'm on a task for my baron. He—"

"You are Viktor. You cannot lie to me." She looked at the floor. "To think that I almost wondered whether Jakaly was actually you."

"Jakaly?" The comment gradually registered. His diversion had worked, then.

She was suddenly in his arms. No longer able to remain in his role, Viktor enveloped her in his own arms. They held one another far longer than was safe, but the sorcerer did not care. He knew that he had no future, but at least he could savor a few last moments with her.

"He is not in there, Viktor. He's farther down in the area Mandrol set aside for his real work. They were questioning poor Renfrew Jakaly, thinking for some strange reason that he is you." There was true amusement in her voice as she said the last.

"Lilaith, I . . . Lilaith, how. . . ." He could get none of the questions out that he wanted to ask. Her very presence had him aflutter.

"It started with Jakaly. After they took him, I could not help thinking that I had possibly betrayed you again . . . yet, I was supposed to be loyal to Mandrol. I sat in my chambers, trying to reason it out, when . . ." She shook her head. "I can't explain it, Viktor. I thought I sensed you out here and everything fell into place. I knew who it was I loved and who it was who had *used* me. I stood up, walked out into the hall, and saw your back. The sense that I knew you grew even stronger. I *had* to follow, and the more I followed, the more I knew that it *was* you."

He wanted to kiss her, to hold her forever, but then she would see the mask and how it was falling apart. Forcing her back to arm's length, Falsche said, "It is time, Lilaith. It is time to end Baron Mandrol's bloody reign. I am ten years late in doing so, but things are *ready*."

She tensed, feeling his excitement. "What do Master G'Meni's chambers have to do with that?"

"The good alchemist has something of which I can make use, a way to strip Mandrol of much of his might and leave this a more personal battle . . . one I intend to win this time."

Lilaith looked away, tears coursing down her face. "Viktor, you cannot know how I feel about—"

"You were under Mandrol's influence, Lilaith. His will is strong."

"But I should have been stronger!" She paused, straightened, and wiped away the tears. "But my crying will not help you. Viktor. Before you go in there, I think that you should come back to my chambers. I think that I have something there which will help end this even sooner."

"What is it?" His eyes strayed to G'Meni's door. So close to his prize, but if Lilaith had something . . .

"It would be too difficult to explain. You have to see it for yourself. Something Mandrol gave me. A token of his love. A particular talisman that is tied to him. I know you, beloved. I think that you could use it to strike directly at him when he least expects it." She leaned forward and kissed him, an act which nearly made the sorcerer forget his entire quest. "I think that the talisman could mean the difference between success and failure, Viktor, even more so than anything that monstrous gnome might have secreted in his chambers. It will only take a few minutes. Come."

He took one last glance back at the door, then Lilaith was pulling him along. Viktor suffered her directness and authority with resurrected pleasure; this was the Lilaith DuPrise that he had known, the woman who did what she felt was best and was not afraid if it meant stepping into a lion's den.

This was the woman who had voluntarily walked into Viathos and presented herself to Baron Mandrol . . . all for Viktor's sake.

They were at her door before he even realized it. The sorcerer was surprised at how few people they had run across on their way here, but as she had pointed out and he had thought countless times already, most of them were busy with the masque. General Straas was no doubt stalking around the grand gala, pretending to enjoy himself. G'Meni was probably still busy with the unfortunate Jakaly, and Mandrol—

Lilaith, still tugging on his arm, led him inside the dim room and immediately shut the door.

"Here we are, Viktor. He makes me keep it by my bed—"

He heard movement from behind him, exactly where an open door would have obscured the form of a man.

Pushing Lilaith away, Viktor drew his blade just in time to parry the strike of a guard with the face of Straas. The puppet soldier pushed forward, forcing the sorcerer back but not breaking through. Continuing his backward flight of his own choice, Viktor caused the guard to stumble toward him, and as the man straightened, Viktor ran him through.

From another room charged two more soldiers, one identical to Viktor's first opponent, but the other an officer with a crafty glint in his eyes. Almost as soon as the two engaged him, yet another pair entered from the opposite side.

"Lilaith!" He looked for her, fearing that one of the guards had taken her, and was horrified to discover the dark-skinned woman standing resolute in the background as the soldiers surrounded him.

She had betrayed him again.

The sentries pressed him back, leaving him no more room to maneuver. Two more joined the fray. Weaponplay alone would not save him now; he was not so magnificent a swordsman that he could take on six men, and Emil's arm had a tendency toward awkwardness as it was. Sorcery was his only savior.

Sweeping his blade across in a reckless but effective attempt to push his adversaries back a step, Viktor mouthed pleas to whatever powers could sense him to grant him the strength for his spell. If he could take out three of the guards, he stood a chance.

The power swelled within him . . .

. . . and faded away as quickly. Someone or something had countered his attempt. He was fairly certain that he knew the source.

As the guards closed again, the harried sorcerer glimpsed Lilaith calmly walking to the door. Then one of the soldiers got around his guard and cut him on his sword arm. Viktor grunted in pain and lost hold of his sword, all thought of Lilaith's second betrayal forgotten as armored bodies crushed him and pitiless hands nearly wrenched his arms from their sockets. Each moment he expected a blade to at last pierce the heart, but instead Viktor was dragged to his feet and held a prisoner.

Lilaith still stood by the door. Once she saw that her one time love was secured, she opened it.

Baron Mandrol walked in, on his heels General Straas and Master G'Meni. The baron wore an expression of sadistic pleasure while Straas had the satisfied look of a soldier who had just won a long, hard campaign. The alchemist simply looked curious.

Leaning over, Mandrol kissed Lilaith. "Thank you, my love."

"Anything for you, Mandrol," she replied, smiling.

Viktor tried to speak but could not.

Walking over to his captive, the sorcerer baron smiled. He reached forward and carefully removed Viktor's disguise. "A pleasure delayed is a pleasure doubled. I think that's a proverb of some sort, but even if it isn't, it has a ring of truth to it. Speaking of rings, have you seen this one?"

Viktor Falsche glared at the ring on Mandrol's finger. At first he saw nothing extraordinary about it, but then he realized that the gleam was not due at all to the illumination in the chamber.

"This ring senses the presence of any strong magical force other than my own. When I suddenly found it glowing so bright that I could have used it to illuminate a darkened room, I recalled the servant I had sent to find my gloves. A quick search revealed that you were going not in the direction of my room, but rather that of the good alchemist here. It was enough to convince me that what I suspected was in fact truth."

"What did you want in there?" demanded Master G'Meni.

"Never mind that," the baron snapped. Returning his attention to Viktor, he continued, "I knew somehow that you had at last returned to me. Then it was a simple matter of deducing what would be the best bait to draw you into my web." With a sweeping gesture, Mandrol indicated Lilaith, who looked oddly pale for one of her dark complexion, then leaned close enough so that nearly all of his captive's view was taken up with the baron's long, simian countenance. "You spoiled my last masque, Viktor, but then you always were one to cause unnecessary trouble, weren't you?"

"Anything for you, Mandrol."

"Aah! He has his voice back. Strong words, Viktor, especially for one who's failed not only in life but now also in death. You've provided me with the most entertainment yet, but I'm afraid your career is at an end."

"With all due respect, my baron," interjected Straas,. "I feel that we might be better in waiting. Something's wrong, I tell you, and he knows what it is."

"I, too, would like to do some tests—"

"*Be still, both of you!*" The baron's very form shook with anger. He reached up with both hands and slowly ran his fingers down both sides of his face. As he did, his breathing slowed and his expression calmed. "I've not forgiven either of you for your treatment of Jakaly. It was fortunate for you that I discovered what you were doing before it was too late." Mandrol stared Straas down. "You'll just have to deal with any emergencies that arise, General. That *is* why I keep you. With Viktor Falsche removed, Dré Kopien and his fellow criminals return to being the minor nuisances they were before."

Straas did not look convinced, but he nodded.

"As for more tests . . ." The alchemist gave Mandrol a hopeful look. "The only test I want to see is how quickly one of the masks *dissolves*."

Summoning what strength remained to him, Viktor Falsche tore one arm free. He sent one guard sprawling with a punch and another back with a kick to the stomach, but before he could touch Mandrol, the other guards regained control.

"It ends *here*." With a flourish of his cape, Mandrol stepped back and snapped his fingers. "I've decided that I'd rather see you gone now than risk another incident."

G'Meni walked forward, hands briefly burying themselves in the folds of his garments. From some unseen pocket he produced a small bottle with a peculiar, springy top.

The baron laughed mirthlessly. "This game is over. Good-bye, Viktor Falsche, for the second and final time."

Raising the bottle to the prisoner's face, the alchemist pressed the top.

A harsh, foul-tasting liquid covered Viktor from forehead to chin.

Noooo! he tried to cry. His mouth would not work.

The world began to slip away. Everything was twisted, melting. Mandrol continued to laugh, his face stretching longer and longer. G'Meni was a squashed pile of cloth. General Straas spread apart. Lilaith—

Lilaith was his last sight before the world ended and Viktor ceased to be.

"One of *my* mongrels, are you?" asked the baron as he looked over the face so long hidden by the mask. "I thought I'd rid myself of all of you long ago." He turned from the shocked and unwitting peasant so closely resembling him and looked at the cursed and crumpled piece of false flesh resting in the alchemist's hands. The liquid in the bottle had made the mask slide off almost instantly, but the face of Viktor Falsche still looked much too lively for Mandrol's tastes. "Did you bring the solution with you?"

Master G'Meni shook his head. "In my haste to make amends to Lord Jakaly and still arrive here in time, I'm afraid I did not, Baron. The solution is in my laboratory, you know. I can simply take this there now and have it done in less then five minutes."

"Never mind. I would have preferred to watch his face slowly dissolve away in the acid solution I *requested* you bring, but the mask will just as easily burn, won't it?"

"Yes, I believe it will. The masks can exist in temperatures of up to—"

"Spare me a lecture and bring me a torch."

Straas signaled one of his men to do just that. Mere seconds later, the soldier returned with one of the torches from the hall. Another man secured a bowl from one of Lilaith's marble tables.

"Hold up the mask over the bowl, master alchemist."

"Yes, Baron." The mask was temporarily lost in the folds of G'Meni's garment as he replaced the bottle in the pocket. Then the disfigured G'Meni raised the crumpled mask as far away from him as his arm would permit. In the light of the torch, the twisted face did not even look like that of Viktor Falsche.

Mandrol reached out and took the torch. He held it just underneath the face, then, when he saw that the alchemist was ready, the baron raised the torch just enough so that the flames licked the bottom.

The mask burst into flames so swiftly that G'Meni

barely released it in time. Even then he yelped in pain as the intense heat singed his fingertips.

Already a charred wreckage, there was little left of the face by the time it struck the bowl.

To the side, Lilaith DuPrise fainted. A sentry went to her aid, but the baron waved him away. "Leave her." Mandrol watched the fire eat away at the last remnants. "Even dead a second time you still hold sway over her, I see."

When only ash remained, General Straas doused the already-dwindling fire. He looked up at the still horrified prisoner. "And what's to be done with this one?"

The baron was already turning to the door, a sense of quiet elation coursing through him. He barely looked at his bastard son. "Put him in the dungeons. I'll deal with him after the masque . . . and I'll deal with you then, too, Master G'Meni. I will be interested in hearing about your reasoning behind so interesting a choice for Falsche's host."

"It was not meant to turn out this way, Baron! I—"

"We will talk of this later. I've important guests to consider. Kindly also reconsider your garb, Master G'Meni, and join us downstairs. General . . ."

Smug at his rival's downfall, Straas saluted. "Coming, my baron." To the guards he commanded, "Take him below. Give him a special place until the baron requires him." His gaze drifted to the unconscious form of Lilaith. "And her, my baron?"

"Have a man inform her that when she is ready I desire her company at the masque." With that, the baron departed.

The guards dragged Emil away, leaving only the general and the alchemist. G'Meni took one last look at the ashes, shook his head, and abandoned Straas.

Now alone save for a guard outside who was to inform the servants of Lilaith DuPrise of his baron's wishes, the general walked over to the bowl and kicked it over, spreading the contents everywhere. Straas carefully ground the ash into the floor. The Lady DuPrise would see it until someone took the time to wash it away.

Satisfied with the turn of events, he hurried off to join the baron.

XVI

"**W**hat happens now?" someone asked Dré again. He had grown long sick of the question, mostly because it had been going around in his own head for the past several minutes. Dré could not put his finger on it, but he felt something was dreadfully wrong. Call it intuition or paranoia, but he was certain that their plans were now in disarray. He was certain that something terrible had happened to his friend.

Viktor had told him to escape with the others if the sorcerer did not succeed, but Dré could not bring himself to do that. He was still berating himself for having allowed his old friend to go on alone . . . but there was suspicion in his mind that perhaps Viktor had used sorcery or mesmerism on him. That would be just like the Viktor Falsche he had always known.

"Damn him!" he muttered.

"Viktor again?" asked Mara, coming up behind him. She wore a veil so as not to frighten anyone around her. There were too many people who would have found one of her kind almost as terrible as Baron Mandrol.

"I think something's wrong, Mara. I can feel it in my bones, woman."

"I'd like to be arguin' against that feelin', love, but I've got one of my own. Somethin' is definitely wrong."

He turned and held her close, ignoring what any of those who knew them might think. "What do I do, Mara? These folks are willing to fight, but Viktor might be dead and Mandrol has an army up there, not to mention his own power."

"Do you think we should just leave, then? Be

happy that we emptied out his dungeons . . . at least for a little while?"

That settled it for Dré. Mara had, as usual, struck the point he had tried to ignore. If they left now, they would have indeed been successful in embarrassing Baron Mandrol, but that would have been all that they had done. Like so many past strikes, the final results would be more annoyance than pain. Straas would simply clamp down on Medecia for his baron and in the end more innocent people would suffer than would have if Dré and his companions had simply let the dungeons be.

It was, as Viktor had often said, time to bring Mandrol down once and for all.

"Dré!" One of the men that Mara had disguised as an incoming prisoner stumbled down the corridor. "Dré!"

"Stefan! What is it, man?"

"Three soldiers, including an officer, bringing a prisoner down. The men you left at the door are stalling them, but we'll have to let them in or do something!"

The men at the door were clad in armor borrowed from imprisoned guards. Dré, similarly clad, was grateful to Ariela that his mind had worked well enough to recall that part of the plan. "Everyone get back. Let them come to this point, then we can surround them. If they surrender, I want no killing, do you understand? We're not Mandrol's boys, after all. Besides, you might end up killing the prisoner, who could be kin to some of you, right?"

They moved with more swiftness and efficiency than he would have given them credit for, but Mara was not so surprised. "It's you, love. They've faith in you and that makes them work at being better."

"Like I have faith in Viktor?" He could not help asking.

She did not answer, instead pulling him to the side. A minute or two passed, then the sentries Stefan had spoken about came marching down the hall, the prisoner between two of them and the officer leading the small band. Dré noted the man's rank and face and frowned. This was one of the general's aides. Who was the prisoner?

He had no time to study the prisoner, for at that moment the officer, a man Dré recalled was named Clevell, stopped cold and looked around. Clevell's eyes grew narrower with each passing breath.

"Severin! Damned fool! Where are you?"

Severin's dead! Dré silently replied, assuming that the man Clevell was shouting for had to have been the idiot in charge of the dungeons. Several other men had donned armor, but watching the officer, Dré Kopien knew that only he had the skill to buy the necessary seconds. Despite a great desire to be doing anything else, he stepped out as if just having heard the officer's voice.

Dré saluted. "Sir, sorry. Severin's ill and some of the other men are busy with some . . . reluctant . . . prisoners."

"I shall speak to the general about this," Clevell responded, still gazing around at his surroundings. He did not look completely satisfied with what appeared to be going on. What little Dré had gleaned about the man was that Clevell was one of the general's more competent aides.

"Shall I take the prisoner from you?"

"I've not turned him over to the officer in charge yet, or have you forgotten the procedures set down by Straas himself?"

At times, Straas had an obsession with procedures and protocol, something which Dré had, over the years, found both humorous and frustrating. There was something to be said about the sense of order the general desired, but it was something that Dré could not always say in mixed company.

"Of course not, sir!" he returned. "It's just that I'm acting officer." He indicated the small markings on his breast plate. The armor had belonged to Severin's second, a man who would have been much more competent in the senior officer's position. At present, he was residing in one of the cells. Unlike his superior, the younger officer had known when it was wise to surrender.

"Very well." Clevell signaled his men to turn the prisoner over to Dré.

As the men obeyed, the disguised rebel received

his first good look at the poor soul they had brought in.

At first glance he would have thought him Mandrol himself.

"Quit your gaping," snapped the officer. "I can see that you know who he resembles. Try not to think further about that, understood?"

It was fortunate that Clevell had misread him, for the resemblance was not what had stunned Dré.

Viktor was dead. Bereft of his host, he could not exist.

Viktor was dead. . . .

"Ariela take you!" he roared, throwing Emil behind him. Taken aback by his stunning change, the two guards simply stood and stared. Dré took advantage and, drawing his sword swiftly, ran one of the pair through the neck.

The others charged out from the corridors and unlocked cells, beleaguering Clevell and the remaining man. The officer managed to get his own weapon out, but when he saw that there was no hope, he immediately dropped it and raised his hands so that everyone could see that they were empty. Next to him, the surviving guard quickly imitated his efforts.

"Keep back!" Mara's voice froze the frenzied mob before they could slaughter the two unarmed men. Taking charge, she had the two men quickly secured.

Meanwhile, Dré concentrated on the new addition to his ranks. "Your name is Emil?"

The farmer still seemed confused about everything. "Yes . . ."

It was hard to look in his face and not think about Baron Mandrol. The disgust Dré had felt earlier when seeing him gave way to sympathy. Others might not have noticed the resemblance as much, but he had lived with Mandrol's features etched into his mind for years.

"What happened? Quickly, man! What happened up there?"

"I don't . . . I woke up . . . there was the baron and I was just there! How . . . how did I get—"

"Never mind that!" Dré tried not to grow exasperated. Emil was trying to answer him. "Just tell me what happened. Who was there?"

"The baron . . . the general . . . a dark woman, a southerner, I think . . . and"—he shuddered—" . . . the baron's devil . . . the mask man . . ."

"G'Meni the alchemist. Go on. What happened?"

"They were burning something. I don't . . . it was . . . it was . . ." Emil looked up, his eyes wide with innocence. "Who's Viktor? I keep thinking of the name."

Suppressing an urge to scream, the rebel leader leaned closer. "*What* were they burning?"

In a small voice, the dazed farmer replied, "The mask . . . I think it was the mask. The one they put on me . . ."

There it was. Confirmation of his greatest fear. Tearing himself away from the other man, Dré stumbled back to where Clevell and the guard awaited his questioning. Through tear-wracked eyes, Kopien noted the look of wariness spreading across the officer's countenance. He sheathed his sword and drew his dagger, placing the edge against the cheek of the senior soldier.

"If you want to live, man, you'll tell me everything I want to know. If you don't answer to my satisfaction, I'll flay you a little at a time."

"Falsche is dead again; I'll tell you that." Clevell sneered at his captor.

Twisting the dagger, Dré cut under the skin.

Clevell grunted in pain, but did not cry out. Dré cared not. "I'll peel your face off like a mask, Clevell. Now, will you answer my questions or shall I begin again?"

"Dré . . ." Mara tried to pull him back.

"Viktor's gone, Mara! Viktor's gone and Mandrol, Straas, and that twisted gnome G'Meni need to pay! I know what I'm doing!"

"Don't become just like them in the process. Isn't that what you always wanted to warn Viktor about? That you feared he would become just like Mandrol in the process of bringing him down?"

She was correct of course. Still, even if he found he agreed with her, Dré could not show that to Clevell. He needed the information the officer could provide. "She makes some sense, man, but I don't care about sense right now." He jabbed the wound briefly, causing his prisoner to flinch. Thanks to Mara, Dré doubted that he could torture Clevell any more than that; fighting a man was one thing, but torture . . . Mara was just right. "Anything to say before I get to work, man?"

To his relief, Clevell began to talk.

Master G'Meni returned to his chambers and changed to what he thought the baron would consider more appropriate clothing for affairs of state. He did not, however, journey immediately on to the masque. Instead, bundling up his old clothing, he carried it along the halls and through Viathos until he reached his true sanctum, the place where his grand experiments were performed.

Mandrol and the others would not be missing him so soon, which meant that he had time. Had the baron been aware of what he was up to, G'Meni knew that he would have been executed on the spot. Still, there were some things more important. The alchemist was a hunter of knowledge and sometimes that hunt would lead him into regions others dared not go. Mandrol would appreciate his decision someday . . . not that the bent figure had any intention of telling his master what he had done just yet. A few years from now would be good, say ten or twenty.

There were a pair of guards at the door, but these were men hand-picked by the alchemist. They saluted as he carried his bundle past, but did not otherwise look at him. G'Meni paid them well to miss a few things that would have made even the baron uneasy had he known of them. He vowed to give them a little extra next time. Good men were hard to find.

When at last he had the door closed and bolted, the alchemist dared to unroll his prize. The clothing he immediately tossed aside, not caring about such frivolous things as where they landed or how grime and powder-ridden the floor was.

"We have much to learn still, you know," he informed his prize. "The baron, great man that he is, is not

an alchemist, I should explain. He would not understand the
thirst for knowledge that makes one an alchemist, nor would
he understand how important this is to him. We must constantly delve into places others take for granted. They cannot often see the value in what we do or sometimes, you
know, they even think we are mad to take such risks." He
chuckled. "I'd rather be an alchemist than a sorcerer,
though. Too much dependency on unpredictable and unreli-
able sources, like sprites and water elementals . . . I ask you,
is that any sort of proper calling? Of course, I imagine
you're somewhat prejudiced, just like the baron."

The wrinkled mask of Viktor Falsche stared blindly
back at him from the worktable.

"I still intend to destroy you, you know. The solution is easily re-created." He indicated a container of clear
liquid sitting on another table just beyond. "The acid is
strong. I will, of course, time the process when I finally dissolve you." Gently he picked up the torn face, pausing only
to wipe a bit of dust off of it. In some ways, he was proud of
it despite . . . no, *because* of how it had reacted. He had seen
its like only once before, but now he had verification of how
the process could be repeated. Yet another achievement to
further the science of alchemy. "But for now, I must keep
you safe until I have the time to properly test you."

The container from which he had drawn the face of
Viktor Falsche still sat nearby, a sign of how harried
G'Meni's last few days had been. He *tsked* at himself for
having left it out; the containers were expensive to create.
With great care, the alchemist placed the mask inside and
locked the lid in place.

The baron would never know. The unfinished mask
that G'Meni had secreted in his clothing and then switched
for the true face had resembled Falsche enough so that no
one would grow suspicious. He understood his master's
obsession, but the renegade mask was too rare an item not to
study. There were possible clues in it to research that not
even Mandrol knew about . . . and never would, if G'Meni
were to keep his head.

What was another day or two, perhaps even three,

before the mask was truly destroyed? The moment it had been removed, the personality of Viktor Falsche had ceased to be an active entity. That was the way it was with the masks.

He returned the container to its proper place, then shut the huge case. *And that is that!* he thought with satisfaction. *Once this interminable celebration for the Neulanders is over, I can return and begin my research.*

Smoothing his oily mustache, the alchemist departed. He looked forward to studying the mask and its contradictory properties. The baron would never know, but what G'Meni had done, he had done because of his loyalty to Mandrol . . . just as he had done so much else in the past. G'Meni would do whatever needed to be done to see that the baron remained on the throne; without him, the alchemist had little hope of a future. Too many misunderstanding people desired his death.

Yet, if Baron Mandrol discovered that the mask of Viktor Falsche remained intact, it was also true that he would see to it himself that the alchemist's future was very, very short indeed.

Lilaith woke to find her closest servants hovering around her, looking like so many condemning spirits from above. At times like this she was reminded that their true allegiance was to Mandrol and not her.

"What . . . what . . ."

"You fainted, my lady," replied the eldest, a dour, gray woman named Elsbith. In all the years that she had tended Lilaith, the dark-skinned woman had never grown close to her. For that matter, Lilaith had not grown close with any of the servants the baron had provided for her. "The guard outside said that you fainted after some dreadful incident in here. There was an intruder or Lord Jakaly, he was not clear which."

The women circled nearer, obviously hoping for some clarification of the event. Their presence made it impossible for Lilaith to think. She could feel their eyes burning through her. It was unbearable.

"Leave me! I will summon you when I need you! Go!"

"My lady, you might need—" began Elsbith.

"If I do, I will certainly call you! Is that understood?"

Elsbith looked around at the others, who immediately withdrew. The elder servant curtsied formally, then departed after. "As you wish, my lady. The baron did say that he would like to see you down at the masque as soon as you are able."

"I will be down when I am ready."

"Yes, my lady."

It was not until they were long gone that Lilaith's head began to clear and her thoughts reorganized. Now she slowly remembered the scene in her chamber. Mandrol had commanded her to betray Viktor again and his will had been too strong. She had brought Viktor into the chamber, there had been a struggle, then he had been captured.

What happened after that? Was he a prisoner in the dungeons? She recalled something about a prisoner, but . . .

The last scene, the blazing fire and the horrid object Master G'Meni had held over it burst full-bloom in her memory.

Although a strong woman, she nearly fainted again.

Viktor, the last trace of Viktor, the man she had loved, had been burned. The mask had been burned by Mandrol himself with the alchemist's assistance.

Mandrol . . . but she loved him, too, did she not? Yet, he had destroyed all that had remained of Viktor Falsche, the sorcerer who, despite the baron's words to the contrary, had never truly betrayed her. She could recall no memory of that. Only her baron's own word about what had happened.

She, on the other hand, had betrayed Viktor at least twice. Now he was gone forever and it was her fault. Her fault.

"What have I done?" Lilaith whispered. Unbidden, tears rolled down her face. "What have I done?"

Without realizing it, her hand ventured near the very

dagger that she had used to halt Renfrew Jakaly's advances.
Lilaith DuPrise slowly drew out the blade and, through red,
tear-soaked eyes, gazed at the sharp point. All these years,
she had kept it so. Only three times had Lilaith drawn it and
the worst of those times had been Jakaly's visit. It was as if
she had kept it honed for another reason lost on her all this
time.

Now she knew. It had simply been waiting for the
proper moment. It had waited for the day when the Lady
DuPrise would awake to her terrible error and come to grips
with what had happened.

She drew the dagger closer.

The world was darkness, complete and overwhelming.

He called out but had no voice. He tried to see but
had no eyes. He tried to hear but his ears were deaf.

He could not move at all.

Yet there was one link, one thing that allowed him
to finally stretch beyond the black confines to the world he
vaguely recalled. His will. It was all he had and so he used
it, thinking of what he wanted and silently crying . . . no,
demanding . . . that he be heard in that way if not the other.

It was all he could do.

XVII

The weather worsened outside, but Baron Mandrol did not care. His mood was high, the highest it had been in days. The apparent loss of his Amantii, the chaos within and without Viathos, the ineptitude of his underlings . . . hese and more faded to insignificance now that he had at last purged his life of the last vestiges of Viktor Falsche.

I should have dealt with that matter long ago, he pondered. *I should have commanded G'Meni to burn that mask before it was ever used.*

Thinking of false faces, he turned his attention back to the ball, which was only just now officially under way. Servants were passing out masks to his guests, the masks that he always chose for them. The Neulanders looked both suspicious and bemused by the fanciful features. For them, the baron had chosen from among the *canis* family. Wolves and hounds. Jakaly had explained to the foreigners about his baron's masked balls and so they had a right to be suspicious even if they were certainly in no danger. The Neulanders would unwittingly be his pawns for expanding his own domain, which had gotten too small for him, and so he needed to treat them well for now.

Others were already donning their masks, wearing faces of creatures of all sorts, including Morags, for some of those who had fallen out of Mandrol's favor, to fanciful designs over otherwise human features. There were also more macabre masks, representing the grotesque nature of humanity. The baron considered himself an authority on humanity.

Each and every mask was symbolic, although the fools who wore them could not know that. If there was one regret Mandrol had concerning the death of Viktor Falsche, it was that he of all the people would have understood the joke, the mockery, inherent in the false faces. He would have seen the grand trick that the baron played on the fawning masses before him.

A few of the masks were more than symbolic; they were weak variations of the ones the drones wore. Those who wore them would be forced to follow a compulsion, sometimes humorous, sometimes not. The stimulus of the compulsion varied with each mask. It could be a word or a sound, an image or a time. Whatever Mandrol had chosen. These faces were not always used. Sometimes weeks would pass before one of them was passed out to an unsuspecting guest. It made for a more interesting game that way.

It was a mark of the baron's power that they still came to pay him homage despite knowing the risk they took. It was a mark of their fear of him.

The baron himself did not wear a mask. That was his right. Everyone else in the room wore masks, even Straas and G'Meni. Neither was ever pleased about having to wear one, but Mandrol cared not. They, the servants, and even the guards all had to wear the false faces. It was the baron's way of reminding them, especially his two subordinates, that *no one* was exempt from his power. Baron Mandrol was Medecia.

As usual, General Straas stalked about the room, ever looking like a hungry hawk seeking its prey. Tonight he looked even more hawkish, for Mandrol had given to him just such an avian face to wear over his own. The mask was open under the beak so as to allow the general to drink and eat and so the sorcerer was able to see the dour frown. Straas had men searching for the way in which the false Viktor entered into Viathos, but as yet no one had come to report its discovery. Mandrol was not overly concerned; after Viktor Falsche, there was no one who was a true threat to him. To be sure, Kopien was still out there and might even have been a part of the false Viktor's plan, but without his sorcerer friend, Kopien would either go slinking back to his hole or die in some foolish heroics that would likely cost the baron little more than a few easily replaceable soldiers.

It was a grand night for him and, feeling in such a jubilant mood, he decided to announce so to his guests.

He rose just as an aide masked as a crow came scurrying over to Straas. Mandrol ignored the man . . . aides were always scurrying over to the general . . . and raised his hands.

Thunder and lightning rumbled through the room. Blue and red flashes accented the miniature storm.

Everyone fell silent, rightly stunned by his display of power. It was always good to remind them that he was a power in his own right and not simply baron because Straas and his men kept rein on the kingdom.

"My most loyal friends! My dear subjects! This is a night of triumph! There were those who questioned, those who wondered about the events of the past few days, when even the thought that my power might be failing was dared to be pondered by a foolish few. . . ."

Many quickly shook their heads, nervous, no doubt, that he might think them to be among those foolish few.

He smiled. It would frighten them further. "But the time of uncertainty has passed! The challenge was met and easily crushed! I stand here as proof of that. Now there are new challenges, new alliances." Here Mandrol looked at the Neulanders and toasted them. "I am Medecia and Medecia is me, and together . . ." To his annoyance, Straas moved in his direction, his haste an indication that he cared not whether he disturbed the concentration of his master. ". . . together *no* challenge will ever be too great!"

They cheered and applauded, as was correct, but Baron Mandrol was angry. The speech had been only a pathetic shade of what he had wanted to convey, and he blamed Straas. He seated himself and stared at the general as the tall soldier joined him.

"Forgive me, my baron—"

"You've been asking that a lot of me lately, Straas. I find my ability to forgive your blunders has reached its limit."

"If you will hear me out, I . . . Damned thing!" General Straas tore the hawk mask from his face. "My baron, *we* are under assault!"

Mandrol leaned forward, expecting some sort of joke. The veteran soldier was not one with much of a sense of humor, though. "What do you mean *assault?*"

"The . . . it . . . forgive me, my baron, I find this unbelievable, but the dungeons are evidently in the hands of rebels."

It was so ludicrous a thought that Mandrol nearly laughed despite the news. Still, any defiance to his reign had to be dealt with accordingly. No one could be allowed to think him weak. "The dungeons?"

"Yes, my baron. I—"

"Then deal with it, Straas. That *is your* function, isn't it? To keep Viathos . . . to keep Medecia . . . secure for me? I think it about time that you did just that, don't you think?"

Straas clicked his heels together. "Yes, my baron."

"Surely the dungeons are not the most practical place for these rebels. There are only two entrances. Shut off both and they are trapped. Then it's simply a matter of time, isn't it?"

"None will survive, my baron."

Mandrol considered this, at last shaking his head. "If you can, save a few. There may be some questions I wish to ask. Who knows? Tonight we may also have for our pleasure Dré Kopien. Then the book may be closed on Viktor Falsche and his legacy."

"I'll have my officers take special care to watch for Kopien, then, my baron. It will be difficult; only I and a few others would know him on sight."

"If you can't take him alive, bring his body. I've not added to my collection in some time."

The general tensed, but otherwise hid his distaste for the collection. "Yes, my baron."

"Well? What are you waiting for?"

Straas saluted, then quickly departed. As he rushed along, he signaled his officers and men. By the time the general abandoned the room, he had an entourage greater than the one Jakaly always brought with him.

Better and better, the sorcerer baron decided as he sipped some wine. *Squash the fools once and for all. With Dré Kopien dead, resistance will crumble. Medecia will remain secure.*

The room had grown more humid during the past few minutes and in his dress clothing the baron became too warm. The one thing that would make the evening truly perfect was if the rain would finally fall. All he asked was that. Perhaps there was something G'Meni could do about it . . .

He looked around, but the alchemist was nowhere to be seen. Mandrol frowned. G'Meni had slipped away, probably to tinker on some experiment. The alchemist's disappearance did not sit well with the baron, who still planned to discuss in depth the horrific little man's choice of host for the Viktor mask.

Outside the night sky rumbled.

The darkness still prevailed. His efforts had so far gone for naught, but he continued. There was nothing else to do but to keep trying.

There was nothing else to do but keep hoping.

"Stefan! I want you to take two others in armor and make your way out of Viathos. I've told you how to act, man, so don't worry. The guards aren't that clever. When you're out, find a place and give the signal we told the others in the city to watch for. Our best hope of success is still if we force them to confront us both inside and outside of this damned pile of stone. We'll give you ten minutes, then start our assault from within. With luck, we may catch most of them in the ballroom."

"Aye." Stefan summoned a couple of other men clad as guards and headed for the outer entrance. Dré watched them go, exhaling in exhaustion as the men vanished from sight.

"Dré."

Mara's voice. He turned to the veiled woman, wondering at the ominous tone. "We're almost ready, Mara. As soon as Stefan and the others set the signal, all hell breaks loose in the baron's house. I'm going to try and skewer the blasted baboon myself, for Viktor's memory."

"Dré, I saw somethin'."

When she spoke in that tone, the graying fighter knew that the Cyclopean woman was not speaking of normal sight. Mara's visions came when they chose, not when she wished them.

But why one now?

"What did you see?"

"Too many thin's." She shivered, sending her veil briefly swinging. "Contradictory thin's. I saw you killin' Viktor. I saw Viktor killin' you. Then I saw Viktor killin' Viktor. *None* of it makes sense, but it's all possible somehow."

Now it was his turn to shiver. "I'd sooner kill myself than Viktor, woman, and he's likely dead already. Not all your visions come to pass."

"Not that we know," she corrected. "There's more, though. I also saw Viathos fallin' on us. The *whole* damned keep, Dré. It fell on us, buried us, but we were in pieces as if we'd been cut up by it first. I don't—"

"Dré!"

It was Stefan. By this time, the man should have been well on his way out of the dungeons.

"What are you doing back here, man? We need that signal!" Looking disheveled and sweaty, Stefan shook his head and gasped for air. "We can't get out! We barely got back inside! There're soldiers everywhere out there, even a Morag or two, I think!"

"What? Soldiers? They shouldn't know yet."

"They've got the outside entrance blocked off. Gods, Dré! There's a wall of soldiers all with the general's face on them staring at the gate!" Stefan grew more pale with the telling. "I've never seen anything so . . . so . . . so damned horrible!"

"We'd better be checkin' the steps," Mara said quietly, her tone indicating the gravity of doing so.

They had barely started toward the corridor leading to the interior entrance when two men came racing down. Their words and tone were much akin to those of Stefan.

"Dré! There's soldiers in the hall! They killed Ivan and Dask! We barely got the door locked! They've got a Morag with a ram out there and they're trying to beat the door down!"

The two men killed had been the pair that Dré had placed as false guards outside the dungeon entrance. He had hardly known either man, but their deaths weighed on his conscience.

A resounding thud echoed down the corridor.

"They keep that up like that, they'll break through in no time!" a man nearby cried.

"Then we've got to make certain that they stop!" Someone had discovered them and now the dungeons had become one great cage. It was a risk they had all feared, but for a time it had seemed that they would be fortunate. Now Dré cursed himself for having been so hesitant. He should not have waited for the launching of the signal. If they had simply broken into the rest of Viathos, at least Mandrol and his toadies would have felt their presence. Now he wondered whether those attending the masque would ever even notice that the keep had been invaded.

"Dré, love, I'll keep them from comin' down through the inside. You take the gate! I can't help feelin' that somethin' still has to happen!"

"Ariela, but I hope you're right, woman!" He already knew that one of her visions had come true. Viathos *was* falling on them and the cutting made sense. Straas would see to it that they were slaughtered down to the last man and woman. The only one the general might try to spare was Dré himself, and that would only be so that the rebel leader could be prepared for a worse fate.

It occurred to him suddenly that they had one potential wild card. Quickly he looked around, searching the dungeons for the farmer. "Where's Emil?"

"Over there," Mara supplied.

He was barely able to spot the top of the man's

head. Emil leaned against a wall, but that was all he could tell. The farmer's cousin had said that Emil was not a brave man, but that where Mandrol was concerned, the baron's bastard son was willing to do almost anything that would hurt or even bring down the beast that had sired him.

Emil was a sorcerer. An untrained one, true, but from what Dré had seen during the farmer's time as Viktor's host, Emil was powerful. All he needed was guidance. Dré Kopien knew enough about the basic tenets of the calling to give him just that guidance.

"Get some heavy planks! Tables or benches even! Get them up to the door to use as counter against whatever those soldiers are trying to knock it down with! Get other tables and drag them to the gate. We need a barrier. I want any lances or spears, and if anyone can find a bow here somewhere, I'll marry them! Bows to the gate!"

With that said, Dré made his way through the hurrying mass of men. He tried to ignore the growing fear and frustration among them. For many, freedom had only just been restored to them for the first time in weeks, months, possibly even years, and yet now it was gone again.

"Emil!"

The farmer ignored him, evidently fascinated by something in the cell across from the mossy wall against which he leaned.

"Damn you, turn and listen! We need you, man!"

The baron's son continued to watch the cell. He did not so much as acknowledge the other man's presence even when Dré stood before him. Desperate, Kopien looked to see what it was in the cell that fascinated the farmer so.

There was nothing. The cell was empty and, as such dank places went, quite ordinary otherwise.

Dré looked Emil in the eye. "Just what do you think—"

Only now did he see that the farmer was quivering. Emil's entire body shook. Dré grabbed him by the shoulders and tried to break whatever had a hold on the other man, but the trance was too strong. Emil continued to stare blankly ahead, all the while quivering uncontrollably.

"Emil! Can you hear me at all?"

No response. Some force had completely snared the baron's son, which meant that the wild card that Dré Kopien had been hoping for would not be available to him. That meant that it was now up to *him* and him alone to free all of them from the dungeons.

Dré did not give much for his chances of success.

The crash from within Master G'Meni's workroom sent both guards jumping. The alchemist was at the masque and no one else was supposed to be inside. Although bribed quite handsomely by the disfigured alchemist, the guards had a quite reasonable fear of what went on behind the door. They, more than most, understood that the stories passed on by servants often paled in comparison to the truth.

The senior of the two pointed at his compatriot. There was no protest, only resignation. The first guard unlocked the door, then held it open for the second, who was reaching for a torch on the nearest wall.

"Are you daft?" growled the senior. "You want to blow up Viathos?"

"There's no light in there!"

"There's candles near the first table, right where the master always puts them, you cowardly fool. Means you just have to walk in the dark a little. Bring a torch in there and you could set off some of those concoctions! Now get in there! I'll be here, watching the corridor. I'll leave the door open, too, if you like. It'll give you some light inside."

Feeling ashamed at his own fear, the other guard readied his weapon and went inside. His comrade, sweating and pale himself, glanced back and forth between the corridor and the room. He bit his lip as the other man vanished into the darkness of the room.

Several seconds passed. The guard inside remained invisible.

Then . . . "You said the candles were on the table!" came the voice suddenly. "There's . . . *gods!*"

The first guard tore his gaze from the hall and

leaned into the laboratory, trying to make out the form of the younger soldier. "What is it?"

Silence.

"Where are you? What is it?"

From within, he heard a cough. Then, "Come here! Quick!"

At first the guard started forward, then something made him pause. There was something wrong with his companion's voice. He held his weapon before him and replied, "Come out here and tell me what it is first."

He expected hesitation, but the voice immediately replied, "All right."

Relaxing just a little, the senior guard watched as a figure clad in armor identical to his formed from the darkness. A chuckle escaped him; what had he expected to come out, some monstrous creation of the alchemist's?

"Now, what was it you—?"

The face that stared back at him from within the helmet was not that of the younger guard, but rather that of a man now twice dead. A face that the veteran soldier recalled well.

"*You're*—" was all he was able to spit out before Viktor Falsche stabbed him with the blade concealed in his left hand. The senior guard stared at the knife sticking in him, then at his own weapon, which at that moment dropped from his twitching hand.

As the man fell, the sorcerer caught hold and dragged the body back into the alchemist's work chamber. He came back a moment later, retrieved the lost weapon, then, with one last glance down each end of the corridor, closed the door from the inside.

XVIII

It had still not rained, but the air within Viathos had become so thick that Baron Mandrol found himself coughing every once in a while simply to clear his throat. Around him many of his guests did the same. He began to wonder if the weather was not the cause but rather some problem in the main ventilation shaft of the keep.

Air circulated among the many levels of Viathos through various shafts the original designers had put in place. The main shaft also served as the method by which the baron's citadel was kept heated. At the bottom was a fire manned by guarded prisoners. The fire was constantly kept high enough so that the heat would rise and spread throughout the central portion of Viathos. It was not entirely efficient, but it kept Mandrol's chambers and the great hall warm enough, which was all that mattered.

The shaft itself extended all the way to the top, with openings on each level. Secondary shafts with their own fires heated other areas, but all of those eventually merged into the main one. There was also a shielded grate on top which was opened or closed depending on how much heat was desired within. At present the grate should have been open, but some servant might have erred. If that was the case, he would have the miscreant whipped.

Mandrol reached for his goblet in the hopes that yet another sip of wine would clear his throat for the time being. Nothing else helped at all.

A faint, inhuman mind touched his own. He nearly toppled the goblet. It took him a moment to recognize the touch as that of one of his Amantii.

The hellcat, one of the two females, was badly injured and much depleted in strength. He did not ask her where she had been nor what had happened to her mate. The Amantii had disappointed him more than either Straas or G'Meni. The cats' failure was again a reflection on his own power, something that did not sit well with the sorcerer.

"So you come crawling back now," he muttered. "You sensed a little rain and came back to beg to be let inside, did you?"

To his surprise, the cat acted as if she had not felt his displeasure. Instead she appeared insistent that she was still obeying her orders, that she still hunted Viktor Falsche.

"Falsche is dead. The hunt is over."

The Amantii insisted otherwise. He could sense it striving to continue the hunt inside, something the baron could certainly not allow her to do. There was too great a risk; the hellcat might accidentally kill an important guest, such as one of the Neulanders, with whom he had yet to speak. Jakaly was still preparing them for their audience with him.

"I said that Viktor Falsche is *dead*." A few of the nearest guests looked at the baron. He clamped his mouth shut.

Still the Amantii remained determined. She had lost the trail, but had sensed him in here . . . at this very moment. He was there in the hall.

"Return to your den," he commanded at last, impatient to be done with the futile conversation. Mandrol almost expected defiance, but the creature obeyed without further complaint. That she did so was a sign of how weak the Amantii was.

When his mind was at last clear of any trace of the hellcat, Baron Mandrol pondered the demonic beast's persistence. While less than satisfactory in their efforts this time, the creatures were generally competent. The additional spell he had attached to them should have made it impossible for Viktor Falsche to remain hidden from them for as long as he had.

Falsche was dead now. He had seen to it himself.

Yet . . .

The torch. The mask. Master G'Meni holding the mask over the flames. The mask burning to ash before the sorcerer's very eyes.

Falsche has to be dead. For some reason, it did not ring true, despite it having to be so.

He slammed his fist on the arm of his chair. "Find me G'Meni!"

A pair of sentries standing nearby leaped to obey. They soon had the alchemist, who had secreted himself in a safe corner until he could escape the ball permanently, bowing before the baron.

"You summoned me, Baron?" The question ended with a cough.

Ignoring the stares of many of his guests, the sorcerer leaned forward. "What happened to the mask of Viktor Falsche?"

The alchemist looked confused. "You yourself burned it, Baron. I held it over the flame for you, if you recall."

Mandrol considered the answer, then considered the man who had given it to him. Master G'Meni was obsessed with his craft, never missing an opportunity to garner some bit of knowledge that might be of use later on. His methods were questionable and often his theories haphazard, but in general he had been invaluable to the baron. However, there had been times, now and then, when he had overstepped his bounds in pursuit of some knowledge, even going so far as to disobey Mandrol . . .

"I'll ask again, G'Meni, and you would do well to consider your answer, for if I find at some later time that you've lied to your master, then I will have you beheaded. Is that simple and straightforward enough for you?" A cough accented his threat.

The alchemist nodded. "I assure you, baron, that—"

"Think *carefully*, G'Meni. It would not bode well for you if I chose to have your quarters and your laboratory searched once you gave your answer."

His horrid little face twisting suddenly in open fear,
Mandrol's alchemist sputtered, "I . . . the mask is in the case,
baron. It is perfectly harmless, I assure you! The mask cannot function without a host and once a few tests, whose
importance I must emphasize, have been performed, then I
will dissolve it as you requested earlier, but—"

The last bit of his protest was cut off as the baron
waved his hand and a green mist covered the fearful
alchemist's mouth. G'Meni froze, knowing that if he
attempted to claw off the mist, his master might choose to do
more than simply silence him.

"So the Amantii saw true." He coughed again, took
a sip from his goblet to clear his throat, and remarked, "Time
and time again you've failed me of late, G'Meni, and I've let
you do so. Now you compound your failures with betrayal.
This will not do, not at all. Of late I've wondered if perhaps
you were even worth the trouble."

Mandrol rose. The musicians continued to play and
the guests continued to make merry, but no one missed what
was happening. No one wished to acknowledge that it *was*
happening, however. Those who had earlier played up to the
alchemist now looked for Lord Jakaly or General Straas.
One never desired to be associated with someone receiving
the baron's wrath.

At Mandrol's signal, two members of his personal
guard broke ranks and surrounded the alchemist. Although
they took up positions as escorts, it was clear that G'Meni
understood they were also watching him.

"This pair will go with you, master alchemist. They
will escort you safely to your laboratory, where they will
then watch you remove the mask and, after it is verified to be
the true features of Viktor Falsche, *dissolve* it in the solution
I requested you mix. Then, when that is finished, they will
bring you back to me. I will then decide just what, if anything, to do with you." The baron coughed again. "Is that
all very clear?"

G'Meni nodded, his mouth still sealed. However,
before being escorted away, he indicated that he wished to
speak. Mandrol waved his hand, dissipating the mist.

The alchemist gasped in air, coughed twice, then began, "Baron, I'm concerned, you know, about the weather. This is not natural—"

Mandrol had no desire to listen to the short figure's prattle, not at least until it was verified that G'Meni had, this time, destroyed the treacherous mask. To the guards, he commanded, "Escort the master alchemist to his destination."

The two guards took hold of G'Meni by his arms and fairly dragged him off. The alchemist clamped his mouth shut, tore his arms free, and marched out as if the idea were his own.

Mandrol observed him departing, thinking that although he was still of use, Master G'Meni would need to be taught a lesson in obedience. Perhaps it would be proper to enlist the services of Renfrew Jakaly in that matter; such a notion certainly seemed fair, and Jakaly could be imaginative at times.

He coughed again, but when he sought another sip, he saw that his wine goblet was empty. Holding it up for his servants to see, he patiently waited while the one pouring the wine tried not to spill despite shaking hands.

Outside, it at last began to rain.

In the depths of Viathos, in a place even below the dungeons, prisoners who still knew no freedom strived to keep the fires to the level commanded by the overseer. The baron did not want his guests chilled, therefore the fires had to be fed continuously. The heat was searing, but the whips of the guards were even worse and so the prisoners braved the heat.

One prisoner, wiping his brow, noticed a small bag fall into the vast fire at the bottom of the main shaft. A moment later, a second bag joined the first in the inferno.

"No standing around gawking or you'll be fed to the fire next!" shouted a guard. He cracked the whip in warning.

Quickly returning to his work, the prisoner all but forgot the two bags. It had not been the first time that someone had thrown garbage down the shaft. The prisoners gen-

erally welcomed refuse, for most of it fed rather than damp-
ened the blaze. What the contents were was never a concern.

Working as they were simply to stay alive, neither
the suffering prisoners nor their sweating guards noticed the
smoke from the flame growing slightly blue in hue. Nor did
they notice how the blue smoke rose faster, more deliberately
into the air, almost as if with purpose.

The archers readied.

General Straas gave the signal.

A stream of arrows fluttered toward the dungeon
gate, porcupining the wooden entranceway, but otherwise
doing little damage to those within. Straas was not discour-
aged. The volley had been for effect; the rebels inside would
be reminded just how dire their situation was and just how
many men the general had at his disposal.

Two Morags waited impatiently nearby, a huge battering ram between them. They were well trained, as was the
one trying to bash its way through the interior entrance, but
even training had its limits. Morags were not patient in the
first place and these two had been exceptionally quiet
already. Now the rain that had threatened Medecia all
evening had finally begun to fall and it looked to be at least a
steady downpour, if not a full-fledged storm.

"Ready the ram," he commanded to a subordinate,
who signaled the monstrous pair.

The two Morags grinned and lifted their toy. This
to them was a special treat. They were being allowed to
wreak havoc within Viathos itself.

"Begin."

The officer waved them on, telling the two where to
strike. Straas watched the Morags with interest, knowing
that, like the volley, the beastmen would have their effect on
the morale of the rebels.

"At last, Kopien . . . at last."

The rain grew steadier. Straas was pleased that he
had ordered lanterns to be used instead of simple torches.
He wanted to see as much as possible. He wanted to see Dré
Kopien's face when the gate finally gave way before the

Morags' onslaught and his rebel friends were cut down.

One of the Morags snarled and drew back, dropping his end of the ram at the same time. A moment later, the officer commanding the monsters toppled over, the shaft of an arrow seeming to sprout from his throat. The Morag tore at another shaft which had gotten lodged in the fleshy part of his arm. The creature's wound was minor, but enough to annoy him.

"They have a bow, sir," one of the younger officers needlessly informed him.

"One bow will not save them, especially if the next fool up there uses a shield to protect himself." As he said this, he looked directly at the officer who had just spoken.

Swallowing, the officer retrieved a shield from one of the men and went up to join the Morags in the hopes of convincing them to continue. Two other soldiers retrieved the body of his predecessor.

The beastmen resumed their work. The gate began to sag inward. Straas dared take a few steps forward so that he could be heard by those within. "You've nowhere to go, Kopien! You've led these people to their deaths! Stay in there and they all die! Only a matter of time! All they've got to do if they want to live is surrender, Kopien! Surrender and turn you over to me!"

Something huge hissed past his ear. Behind him, a soldier cried out.

Whirling, Straas discovered one of the soldiers bent over, a shaft buried in his upper arm. Those nearest seized hold of him and while one of his compatriots began trying to work the shaft out. The strike had been a lucky one for the unknown archer, who had no doubt been aiming for the general instead.

Straas decided to take a few steps back, just to be on the side of caution. He coughed again, then glared at the pair of Morags still battering away at the gate. "I want that damned thing down now or I'll be feeding the dogs fresh meat tomorrow!"

The creatures put in renewed effort. The gate caved in a little more, this time a loud *crack* accompanying the blow.

Around him, officers readied the men. Once the gate was down, they would enter one squad at a time. Drone soldiers first, of course. They could always be replaced and their presence would add to the horror of the rebels. Their own dear friends and relatives would be coming to kill them and no matter how many those within managed to slaughter, Straas could send more. Morale within would fall to less than nothing.

There was a second massive crack as the gate caved in even more. A shaft flew from within the dungeons, but it went wide of the Morags. Straas knew that there would be no time for the lone archer to loose more than two, perhaps three arrows before his men began pouring into the dungeon and commencing with the mop-up.

He started to give the command to advance, but again a cough interrupted him. Despite the rain, or perhaps because of it, the air was thick. Straas tried once more to advance his troops, but once more he fell prey to a coughing fit, this one worse than the last. Others also coughed, some of them so horribly that they were doubled over.

Swallowing yet another cough, the general looked around. A good third of his men were suffering from coughs of varying intensity. Most of them were puppet soldiers; the masked slaves were suffering almost to a man in some squads. A few clutched their faces as they tried to hold back the attacks.

"What the devil?" Straas looked up at the dark heavens. It was rain— a thick, misty rain, to be sure, but it was still rain. Yet . . . he could not put his finger on it, but the veteran soldier felt that there was more to the weather than there appeared to be. The coughing was too rampant, too quickly spread. It had not been a problem until the rain had begun.

The Morags' ram shattered the last bits of the gate to splinters. Straas had no time to worry about insistent coughs.

"First squad forward!" He would not let a little weather dampen this moment.

The first squad moved, but their order was ragged,

and several stumbled. A drone soldier fell out of the ranks and bent over double. A second puppet warrior followed suit. Several men coughed, but none of them was as affected by the rain as the drone soldiers appeared to be.

"Get them forward!" the general roared at one of the mercenaries.

The soldier tried, but the puppet men would pay him no heed. All over, the same thing was happening; his mercenaries and loyal guard suffered little more than coughs, but the drones were in physical agony. Straas watched one tear at his face, the general's own distorted features staring back at him as the soldier tried to relieve whatever pain he was suffering.

Before his very eyes, his forces were collapsing. The ranks were in havoc and the number of combat-ready men had been cut at least in half. Suddenly, Dré Kopien's resistance no longer looked so futile. What was happening?

Spell! Straas thought. *Spell or alchemist's trick!* Besides being a master of sorcery, Viktor Falsche had known some alchemy. Yet . . . Falsche was dead again.

Was he?

The slave soldier who had been scratching at his face screamed . . . and then tore part of the face *off*.

The general's eyes widened. That was not possible. It could not be possible. G'Meni's less-than-trustworthy promises aside, the baron had assured Straas that the masks the men wore were permanently sealed to their true features. The adhesive was supposed to be so strong that only a few rare chemicals could remove it without killing the host.

A second mask began sloughing off. As it did, the gaze of the host met that of the general.

The pain in those other eyes gave way to open hatred at sight of the commanding officer. Straas stared into the eyes of a man whose life he and his baron had usurped. Now that man lived again, lived and yet still *remembered* what they had made of him. One hand reached down for a blade dropped earlier.

Straas ran the man through before the latter could rise.

His reprieve was short. The masks, his face, melted as the rain poured. One by one and then faster still, the puppets became puppets no more, but rather men who had lost days, weeks, months, and years because of the baron, the alchemist, and, of course, Straas.

A scream made him spin. One of his senior officers fell to the wet stone, a sword through him from the back. A thing with half the face of pockmarked farmer and half the twisted, melting features of the general stood over the corpse, eyes darting this way and that.

They never told me that the men would remember, pondered Straas. Of course, it had not been a question on his mind. He had assumed that the personality of the hosts would simply cease to be while they wore the mask, and since the mask was permanent, there had been no need to wonder further. Now he saw that he had assumed too much. They had all assumed too much.

He was in danger of being butchered by his own army.

"Drash! Verlinsk!" The men were the two of the most capable officers he had nearby. "Reorganize the mercenaries and our own specially picked! Slaughter all drone soldiers! Now!"

Drash moved to obey, but Verlinsk had not taken more than a step when one of the puppet men swung a blade at him. The officer, a fire-haired veteran with Straas since the general's arrival in Medecia, parried what looked to be a crude thrust. Much to the officer's surprise, though, the other's blade was no longer where it should have been. Instead, it had looped around the soldier's blade, caught Verlinsk's weapon, pushed the other sword aside, and ended with the point in the officer's throat. Verlinsk went down, but Straas cut his killer down in turn.

His hand shook as he watched himself die. It was not out of any shock at watching a man with his own face perish, but rather because the general recognized the style with which the drone soldier had fought. There was no mistaking the maneuver; he had used it himself many times.

The man had fought with the general's own skill

and knowledge even after the mask had become useless.

They remember everything . . . even the skills I spent years to perfect!

Drash had the other officers re-forming their ranks as best as possible, but a pitched battle was already being fought all around them. The drone soldiers outnumbered Straas's loyal forces and they were waking quicker than ever. Each one was as skilled, or almost as skilled, as he was, which meant that his own men were at an even worse disadvantage.

"Sound the horns!" he roared, hoping that someone capable of obeying would hear him. "Alert the rest of the keep!" It occurred to him to wonder how extensive this rain was. From what little he could see in the night sky, the clouds spread to the horizon in every direction.

The clouds covered all of Medecia.

He had to warn his baron. He had to let Baron Mandrol know that somehow, even in death, Viktor Falsche had set into play the possibility of his master's downfall.

Not to mention the general's own.

His loyal troops, now re-formed into squares, fought and kept the waking men at bay. Drash steered the general into one square consisting of the commander's own crack guards and his best remaining officers. So far, some advantage still lay with Straas and his men, but only if they killed most of the drone soldiers before the cursed things fully regained their former identities. It took a minute or two for their recognition to return and another minute or two to refocus. That could be enough time. Straas would lose some of his own valuable men, but victory still hung within his grasp. He also had the two Morags, which he had yet to make use—

What had happened to the Morags? They should have come to his aid by this time. With them at his side, the vengeful puppet men would be wiped out in a matter of minutes.

Only too late did he recall Dré Kopien, a man who, while not the devil that his sorcerer friend Falsche had been, still knew when to take advantage of an opponent's sudden turn in luck.

He glanced over his shoulder and through a small gap between the wary forms of his guards saw that his fear had come to life. The rebels from the dungeons had chosen to make their stand outside. They were even now swarming through the opening, their numbers and their weapons, causing the Morags and the few soldiers left up front to retreat.

Straas's men could not fight both forces, not without reinforcements. This battle was lost.

For now. . . . Straas pulled Drash and another trusted officer, Harskinov, over to him. "We leave now! We must make contact with the others posted to the north of here! We must protect the keep and the baron!"

"What about the otherssss?" hissed Harskinov, indicating the rest of the harried squares.

"They'll be our shield! They'll hold off these rabble!"

Neither the sibilant Harskinov nor Drash argued.

"Let them have their little victory, man! It'll be a bittersweet, short-lived memory for them!"

The general's square moved away from the battle.

Coughing, G'Meni quickened his pace, leaving his two unwelcome companions to do their utmost to keep up with him. Despite appearances, the alchemist was swift and agile when he desired to be. Speed suited him now, for he sensed something strange in the air, a slight scent that disturbed him greatly. The alchemist wondered why such a scent should exist. There was no reason for its being there; the scent was not even native to this land. It recalled to him something familiar, something that he himself had mixed together. One of his most powerful solvents. . . .

A solvent? Could someone have put—

He laughed silently at himself. Paranoia. *Perhaps I'm becoming too much like Straas! He looks at the universe all the while thinking that it seeks to cross swords with him! Not I! I simply pursue the fleet specter of knowledge, a quieter yet more worthwhile venture—*

His thoughts paused as he stared at the unmanned doorway of his laboratory. First the familiar scent and now this. There should have been two men guarding the door. They would have known the penalty for leaving their posts.

"Something is wrong. Something is dreadfully wrong."

His two companions were, of course, distrustful of him. They glanced at one another but did not otherwise comment on the alchemist's fears.

Master G'Meni shook his head. Unimaginative, that was what the sentries were. "Two men stood watch over this door when I last left it. Now they're gone, you see. This doesn't seem correct, does it? Some might even question what had happened to them, don't you think?"

"Perhaps they're inside," suggested one. Then, dropping the subject as unworthy of their time, he added, "The baron said that we were to watch you destroy the mask. To do that we have to enter."

"Something might be waiting inside for us, you fool."

"Our baron commanded that you destroy the mask. We are here to make you do that."

Gazing up at the pair, G'Meni could not decide which was greater, their determination to follow Baron Mandrol's commands to the letter or their plain, simple stupidity. Both were intertwined, he finally concluded. "Very well, gentlemen. Then, after you, please."

"We will follow."

He almost demanded to know who they thought they were, but he already knew the answer to that. At this point, they had the authority to dispatch the alchemist regardless of his previous standing with the baron. They had no proof other than his own word that there had ever been sentries there. They likely thought that he was stalling, a not unrealistic conclusion, he was painfully aware.

Hands tightened on weapons. Knowing that his time was limited, Master G'Meni reluctantly turned to the door. He would deal with these two when he was once more one of the baron's favorites.

The situation was ironic. There was no one more loyal to Baron Mandrol than he. He wished that he dared to prove the great extent of his loyalty, but that could never be. Mandrol was just as likely to have him beheaded for that.

Cautiously, he opened the door.

Nothing happened. There were no traps, no explosions. However, G'Meni was not satisfied. "Find me a torch."

One of his guards returned a moment later with a wall torch, which he then nearly thrust into the alchemist's contorted face. G'Meni took the torch without a word and stepped inside, careful to keep the torch away from all walls. Unlike the guards, he knew where all the volatile items were kept.

All seemed in order, but as Master G'Meni lit the candles situated in calculated positions around the chamber, he had the feeling that some things had been moved. He scanned the shelves of his more precious chemicals, trying to decide if one container had been sitting more to the right or if another seemed just a little too far back. The alchemist reached for one of the containers, curious as to whether the contents still remained within, but one of his undesired companions abruptly prodded him in the back with the side of his sword, nearly causing the short figure to push a particularly explosive powder over the side of the shelf.

Containing his anger, he turned. "Yes, what is it?"

"The mask."

"Really, I have other—" He could see that they would not be swayed even for a moment. "All right. They would be this way. Mind those swords of yours. You might knock something over that will leave a hole where Viathos used to stand."

From their expressions, his warning had burned deep into their minds. As he turned his face from theirs, the alchemist allowed himself a brief smile. There was no such mixture in his laboratory, but his reputation was such that almost anyone would have believed him capable of leaving such dangerous potions just lying around. The worst he presently stocked would have destroyed only a few rooms.

His pleasure at having unnerved his watchers died when his foot struck something large and hard that should not have been lying where it was. The alchemist forwent lighting the candles and quickly lowered the torch to see what it was he had touched.

It proved to be one of the guards he had left to watch the doorway.

"The case!" he snarled, forgetting that the two soldiers with him were his keepers and not his servants. Ignoring how the flames of the torch flickered much too closely to certain jars and containers that he would otherwise have avoided, Master G'Meni rushed to the case where the mask of not only Viktor Falsche but countless others had been stored. Even before he made it to the case, though, something crunched beneath his feet.

It was glass. To be precise, it was the glass lid from one of the special boxes used to house a mask. The rest of the container lay in fragments just beyond the pieces upon which the alchemist had stepped.

The master case was open, which made it quite easy to see which mask was missing. Falsche's.

"Someone's taken the mask!"

The guards looked at one another as if questioning whether to believe him.

"Look for yourselves, you imbeciles! A man dead! The box shattered to pieces! Do you think I did this as some sort of elaborate game?"

After some hesitation, the first finally agreed. "The baron should be alerted."

At last they chose to believe him. Now he was once more master of the situation. That he had had to wait as long as this for reason to return amazed G'Meni. "By all means we must inform the baron! You!" He pointed to the first guard. "Let Baron Mandrol know all that you've seen, you understand? Someone's stolen the mask! Tell him that it cannot have been very long. Tell him that I'll need more men. This entire set of corridors must be searched. Now go!"

The soldier actually saluted before he departed, a sign of how things had changed for the alchemist. The remaining guard anxiously awaited his next words.

G'Meni ignored the man at first, stooping to inspect the damage. The case had been shattered and someone had taken the mask, but not before killing the guard. Where was the second man? Stuffed away elsewhere, G'Meni supposed. He would locate the second corpse when there was time. First he had to consider who would steal the mask. As far as he knew, no one had noticed him switching the unfinished one for Falsche's, but someone obviously had discovered his ploy.

The baron had deduced what he had done, but who else knew? Straas was generally informed of such matters. Although the idea that his rival was responsible for all that had happened was enticing, G'Meni knew the general well enough not to consider accusing him.

However, there *was* Lilaith DuPrise.

On the surface, he could not find fault with her. She had proven herself more than once to be truly under the baron's spell. She had turned in Viktor Falsche yet again. Not only that, but Lilaith DuPrise had also witnessed the burning of the mask and G'Meni could recall her reaction then. Very real. She could not have known that he had placed the cursed mask in a hidden pocket, the same pocket from which had come the false one.

Still . . . one cannot dismiss her fainting spell, can one? There are still emotions at play within her. He rubbed his chin in consideration of this fact. The Lady DuPrise made a fine suspect, although it was, of course, possible that the thief was some unknown person. However, Master G'Meni chose to set his sights on Viktor Falsche's former love. If she was not responsible for the theft, it was quite possible that she still might be used to trap the one who was.

"Leave this for now," he commanded the remaining guard. "And come with me. We've not a moment to waste!" He wished that he had more than one soldier with him, but the baron needed to know what had happened. In a strange way, the alchemist decided, it was good that he had saved the mask; now they knew that there was a traitor in their midst.

He marched swiftly down the corridor toward her apartments, his trek hindered only by the ever-increasing coughs. If the theft proved to be the woman's doing, then perhaps at last the baron would come to his senses and dispose of Lilaith DuPrise once and for all. Her meddlesome presence was one of the few points that he and General Straas agreed on. The woman was a danger to them. Even under the compulsion, who was to say that she could be trusted where either the alchemist or the general was concerned? She was a southerner, strong-willed and touched a little by the power herself, although never had she revealed any true mastery over sorcery. Lilaith DuPrise also despised both him and Straas. Perhaps this was some plot to rid Mandrol of one or both of them.

Idle speculation and likely not at all true. Still, it would be worth investigating.

Turning into a new corridor, G'Meni again regretted not having more than this one lone guard with him. Lilaith DuPrise could be dangerous. There was also the possibility that she had a confederate. While he was not without his own tricks, especially the items he carried secreted in various hidden pockets, the alchemist had no desire to fight an open battle. He would have to leave it to stealth and deception, areas in which he was far more adept.

His uneasiness melted a bit when he noted a guard leaning over one of the ventilation openings, evidently in search of something. With double the manpower, he was less likely to have trouble with the treacherous woman, even if she had someone to help her. Perhaps there might be a few more along the way.

"You there!" he called, picking up his pace yet more. "Cease whatever it is you're doing and join us! I've need of you!"

The guard, whose back was to him, straightened but did not turn around. In a gruff voice he responded, "The baron's ordered me to check the vents. He thinks there's something wrong with the air."

Coughing again, Master G'Meni cursed the limited flexibility of soldiers. Give them one order and they remained fixated on it even when conditions warranted otherwise. "Never mind that! I'll deal with that when I've the

time! This is most important! The baron will understand!"
His anger grew as the man refused to face him. Near enough
now to almost touch the armored figure, the alchemist
roared, "Now turn around and listen to me, you lout! We
have—"

The guard finally turned.

It was Viktor Falsche.

As if confronted by a spitting serpent, Master
G'Meni drew back, hands before him to ward off the sorcerer. Behind him, the other guard slowly realized just who
faced them. His sword ready, he charged.

Falsche met him with his own blade, which he drew
with expert grace. The alchemist continued to back away
even as the two swords met. He knew from the past how
skilled a swordsman Falsche was. The guard was competent,
but certainly no match. At best, he was a delaying tactic, but
that suited G'Meni. All he needed was a safe place and a
few moments. Viktor Falsche might think him the easier of
the two adversaries, the alchemist's battle skills laughable at
best, but he was not going to face the sorcerer on that front.
Rather, he would deal with Falsche in the role of alchemist.

Twisting around the corridor, G'Meni hurried down
a path that would take him into one of the subcorridors.
From there he intended on coming around and returning to
the battle, but from *behind* Falsche. From the shadows, so to
speak, the alchemist intended on striking with a combination
of creations he kept on him in case of need. Straas always
assumed that his rival went unarmed, but that was because
the general only understood weapons with long, sharp edges.
The weapons of an alchemist were far more subtle yet far
more deadly when used by a practiced hand.

It was something Viktor Falsche was about to discover.

G'Meni had estimated that the struggle would still
be ongoing when he returned and so was pleased to see that
his calculations were, as usual, correct. The damnable sorcerer had the guard retreating. Another minute, maybe two,
and the duel would be over.

More than enough time for what he planned.

You've had two lives too many, Falsche! Time to bury your memory forever!

From his pockets, he removed a small device consisting mainly of a hollow tube. A clever series of strings and a trigger mechanism much like that on a crossbow would allow the alchemist to shoot a special needle completely through the armor and into the figure's back. The needle itself would not necessarily kill Falsche, but the chemical solution it had been treated with would do so almost instantly. Of course, if he managed to puncture a lung or even the heart, G'Meni would accept that, too. He knew that the weapon worked; he had experimented with it enough.

The mask was a small target, but all he needed to do was kill the host. The mask would be helpless, then. G'Meni did not ask himself how the guard had come to be wearing Falsche's visage; that was a question for later. Mandrol would not mind the death of one soldier if it guaranteed the renegade sorcerer's final death.

It was at that moment that Viktor Falsche killed the guard. G'Meni centered his weapon on the back of the sorcerer even as the guard collapsed and Falsche withdrew his blade. There was no possible reason why the alchemist could miss from this distance. Even if his intended target noticed him now, he could not move swiftly enough to escape the needle.

He could not resist calling out. "Good bye for the final time, Viktor Falsche."

The sorcerer started to turn.

G'Meni's finger tightened on the triggering device.

XIX

It was a miracle.

A miracle with Viktor's signature on it! decided Dré as he helped one of the freed prisoners fend off the savage attack of a desperate soldier. The soldiers were being pushed back, their morale in chaos due to both the sudden turn by the puppet soldiers and their own general abandoning them.

Dré's army had multiplied not only in strength, but also in skill. As he watched the awakened figures in armor fight, he noted how each of them moved with the dexterity and experience of veteran soldiers. In fact, they moved as if all had been trained by the same man.

Straas? He knew that they could not all be swordsmen; most of them were peasants who had never lifted a sword during their normal lives. Yet here they were now, handily defeating men with battle experience, men who should have been slaughtering them.

They must remember something. They must remember something of what Straas himself knows. It's the only explanation! Perhaps there was another, simpler answer, but Dré did not care. He only knew that though he had expected a heroic yet futile death for all of them, he found he was now in command of a force that had the enemy on the run.

It could not last, of course. Straas had not departed out of cowardice. Not him. There were still many elements of Mandrol's armies who were paid or loyal men, not entranced puppets. True, they were greatly outnumbered now, but they were still a threat. The skills and memories of the freed soldiers were those of a Straas much younger and somewhat less experienced. The masks had also been poor copies of the general. Dré could not hope to win simply because of their aid.

"Stefan!" he cried. There was no answering shout until his tenth or so try, when Mara joined him. She wielded a weapon as well as any man he knew, but he did not like having her here amid the thick of the fighting. Her veil was pulled back, but in the still-increasing darkness, it was nigh impossible to see that she was not quite human. "What are you doing here? You should be in the back!"

"Stefan's dead, love! Sword in the stomach!" She parried a cut that might have reached him. "I'm not goin' to stay in the back now! We need every man!"

He forwent the obvious concerning her gender, instead choosing to make the best of a bad situation. "I've got to take some men and try to stop Straas from linking with the rest of the army, but we still need to send the signal! The others have to know that the time is right!"

"And you want me to be the one to do it."

"That's why I love you, woman! You've got a quick mind, you do!" He gave her a grin that the darkness all but obscured. "Take whatever men you need to get to the point, but we need to see it done quickly now!"

"I've all the men I need. You take the rest, love." She ran off before he could protest. She had all the men she needed?

He blinked. Four swordsmen had joined Mara, creating a protective square around her. Dré cursed. If the four men had seemed to come from nowhere it was because they had done just that. Mara was exerting herself to her limits, creating four mobile images that were, unlike the images she had cast on the parties entering the dungeon, linked only to herself. The extra cost would drain her, possibly leave her weakened and defenseless.

There were limits to what he would allow her to do. He grabbed hold of the nearest pair of men. "You two! After Mara! See to it that she doesn't get herself killed, understand?"

They nodded. Dré gathered his men. The remaining soldiers had begun to retreat. One of the Morags was dead, the other wounded and retreating with the soldiers. The new army was too great even for the Morags. The freed drone soldiers and several former prisoners would deal with the remnants. That left him the time to deal with Straas.

"To me, men!" Without waiting, Dré charged in the direction the general and his guards had fled. There was still time to catch them. Straas had to be dealt with before he could even think of confronting the baron. If Stefan had been able to signal the others when Dré had first sent him off, the general would have found his outside forces already harried and therefore unable to assist him. Now Dré had to pray that either Straas moved too slowly, not a likely bet, or Mara could set off the signal before the general gathered his resources together. Straas still could raise an armed force capable of turning possible victory for the rebels back into utter defeat.

Dré could not allow that. Viktor had given him this much with which to work. Now it was up to him to stop Straas or die trying. Mandrol would be terrible enough a foe to face without an army to aid him.

And what do I do about Mandrol if I do manage to stop Straas? How do I defeat him, Viktor, when even you failed twice?

He could not allow himself to think about that. Dré would deal with the problem of the sorcerer baron once he had settled with the general. He dared not think any further ahead until Straas was stopped, lest his own confusion be the key to the rebels' destruction.

In the night sky, a flame that defied the storm shot high above the walls of Viathos. It was bright enough to be seen throughout the city. Dré's heart briefly soared. Mara had managed to set off the signal, yet one more creation of Viktor's. It should have been sighted as far as the wild lands, but the city was what mattered most. Whoever controlled the city when this was over controlled all of Medecia.

The flame served one more purpose. Ahead he could briefly make out a mass of armored figures fighting their way to the wall gate. Straas.

"Aaah, General," he muttered. "Wait up a little longer, man. We're not through with each other yet. Not yet."

They had taken his life, but they had not taken his will. Once woken, Viktor Falsche could not rest again. Even after G'Meni had removed the mask, the sorcerer had existed. He knew that he should not have and yet it had happened. More, the longer Viktor had struggled, the stronger he had felt. There was power to draw upon, power that should not have been his to command. With that power, he had shattered the very glass box he had been stored in, sending the mask to the open floor.

It was not until after, not until he had drawn the guard with his will, made the man pick up the tattered mask from the floor and place it on his own face, that Viktor had been able to understand. Only when he had become human again did he sense the source of his power. He was still linked to Emil, still linked to the baron's unacknowledged son.

The mask remained in place long enough for him to deal with the second guard, then a little adhesive borrowed from the alchemist's stock assured that Viktor would not lose face again . . . at least not until he had killed Mandrol.

Everything he had needed was there in Master G'Meni's laboratory. From what he found among G'Meni's possessions, Viktor was fairly certain that the alchemist had already created the potent solvent in the past. It would have been easier if the sorcerer had run across a supply of it, but such was not to be the case. Still, it had been simple enough to put together the proper ingredients, then divide them up into the necessary amounts. From there, the sorcerer had made his way to the air vents, depositing into each one or more small bags containing the mixture. The fires would destroy the bags and release the contents into the hot air, where everything would rise and spread throughout Viathos. From there, it would go into the heavens.

The mixture was potent. Master G'Meni would have admired Viktor's ingenuity, he was certain. From the

fires outside rose the other portion of his alchemical creation.
That portion, when combined with what he had deposited,
created a rain and mist from which no one could escape.
Most people would suffer no more than an irritating cough
and a slowing of the reflexes, but the burning Plutite, first
carried into the air by the fires of Viathos and then brought
back to the ground by the rain, would create a solvent especially adapted to the adhesive created by the baron's
alchemist. It would permeate the air, spreading even into
Viathos itself.

The reaction was swift, the results astonishing even
to him. He had only been halfway through his work when
the first sounds of battle, the first sounds of his success, had
risen above the din created by the revelers at Mandrol's
masque. It had taken him all the speed that he could muster
to carry the remaining pouches to their appointed shafts.
Had he been too slow, it was possible that his mist-borne solvent would have dissipated too early or would not have
reached out beyond the first few blocks of the city. He had
to make certain that the city and hopefully even much of
Medecia's outerlands were enveloped by his creation.

It was with great satisfaction that he had released
the last two sacks down the ventilation shaft. Viktor even
allowed himself to savor his success. He had watched as
they plummeted to the fires below, his heart . . . the guard's
heart, he reminded himself . . . pounding harder and harder
as the flames engulfed it. Viktor had at last brought chaos to
his adversary's domain. By this time, Mandrol would be
noticing the initial effects. All Viktor had to do now was—

"You there!" a horribly familiar voice had suddenly
called. "Cease whatever it is you're doing and join us! I've
need of you!"

Master G'Meni. The alchemist's timing could not
have been worse. Viktor, his back still to G'Meni, had made
some excuse, but the squat figure would not have that. He
had ordered Viktor to turn around, and with no other choice,
the sorcerer had obeyed.

G'Meni, of course, had recognized him. So had the
guard with the alchemist. Viktor had suddenly found himself

fighting for his life just as it had seemed victory was at hand.

The guard was good and briefly pushed him back, but Viktor soon had proved himself the better swordsman. However, as he had forced the soldier back, his thoughts had turned again to Master G'Meni, who had vanished as soon as the duel had begun. G'Meni was not a warrior, but neither was he a coward. He might have gone for help, but for some reason, Viktor had found himself unable to believe that.

At last he cornered the guard and, slipping under the man's own blade, ran him through. Breathing heavily, Viktor paused for a second in order to sort his thoughts.

From behind him, the gloating voice of Master G'Meni called out, "Good-bye for the final time, Viktor Falsche."

The sorcerer whirled about, aware already that it was too late to prevent the alchemist from attacking.

A thin needle flew past his shoulder and embedded itself in the stone wall. At the same time, Master G'Meni, instead of firing again, gasped. From the twisted alchemist's hand fell a peculiar tube covered with tiny ropes and mechanisms. A device imitating a crossbow was Viktor's only guess.

G'Meni fell to his knees, eyes staring upward. He tried to say something, but the words would not come out.

The alchemist fell forward then, his disfigured face striking the floor with a resounding crack. Blood flowed over his back, a crimson rose blossoming from a ghastly chasm more than the width of Viktor's hand.

"I had to do it. I could not lose you again. When I felt you moving, it was all I could do to keep from crying aloud."

Standing behind the alchemist's crumpled form was Lilaith. Her face was drawn and weary and in her hand she held an elegant dagger now red with the life blood of Baron Mandrol's dark servant. The southern woman was shaking from effort. She had been forced to overcome the renewed compulsion of the baron and overcome it swiftly enough to kill one of his most trusted subordinates.

"He kept strengthening it, telling me that I would

learn to hate you and love him, but his love was always a lie and once I realized that I had again betrayed you, I could not listen to his false words. When the mask burned, the spell died, also. He could not hold me anymore after that."

"Lilaith . . ."

Holding the dagger high, the dark-skinned woman eyed the stained weapon. "I was going to bring this with me to the masque. I was going to take it and when the baron's attention was elsewhere, I was going to drive it through his heart right in front of that legion of toadies."

The dagger fell from her hand. Viktor raced forward, leaping over G'Meni just in time to catch his love before she could faint.

Lilaith looked up into his eyes and shuddered. "It is you, but the eyes say more, do they not, Viktor? You have come back to me, but it is not for long, is it?"

"No, not long."

She touched his face, noting where the mask was most damaged. Lilaith had no knowledge of alchemy save what she had gleaned now and then from Master G'Meni's convoluted explanations, but even she could see that the mask was fast becoming undone. "Only a short time . . . there is no way to keep the mask whole?"

"Not for very long."

"We could create another from the original mold."

He shook his head. "It would not be me, Lilaith. It might not have any personality at all. I believe that what was left of me merged with this mask and this mask alone."

Straightening, she glared down at the alchemist. "Well, I am still glad I was able to do what I did! This was his doing just as much as it was that of Mandrol. He made the masks what they were; he made them as much his creation as they were the baron's. All the things that he did, that I *witnessed* and could do nothing about . . ." Lilaith pulled away from Viktor and, with great relish, kicked the body. "I wish that I could kill you again, Master G'Meni!"

She pulled her foot back in sudden shock as a faint moan rose from the still form. Viktor quickly bent down and turned the alchemist onto his back.

Master G'Meni was not dead, not yet. There was no hope for his survival, but he still had a few moments of life left. He slowly opened first one eye and then the other, gradually focusing on the two faces above him. The alchemist coughed.

"I was . . . correct . . . I was . . ." whispered G'Meni, referring to something that neither of the two understood. "Fascinating, Viktor Falsche. I would . . . dearly . . . your face to study, but the baron . . . he knew . . . I don't think he realized just how much he knew that . . . that you lived still . . ."

"Leave him, Viktor," suggested Lilaith, her tone growing cold. "He deserves his slow death, besides, Mandrol must still be reckoned with!"

"Cruel . . . cruel woman . . ." the dying alchemist mocked. "You must be care—" a cough, "careful that you do not get your wish!" His head twisted so that he could stare directly at Viktor. "Whether you win . . . or lose . . . you lose, Falsche! I've seen to . . . that, you know! Be killed . . . and you . . . die! Kill the baron and you . . . die, too! A grand . . . jest . . ."

"What does that mean?" demanded the sorcerer. He knew Master G'Meni too well not to take heed of the alchemist's mocking statement. "What do you mean when you say I die whether I win or lose?"

The blood-soaked figure shook his head, an action which was clearly an effort for him despite its simplicity. G'Meni tried to chuckle, but the mocking laugh degenerated into another coughing fit. "I planned so well . . . didn't I? No one knows the . . . the difference . . ." The master alchemist smiled triumphantly. "That is why I am—"

G'Meni passed out. A moment later, his chest ceased moving. Viktor carefully checked for signs of life, but found none. Master G'Meni was most definitely dead.

"At last he dies," whispered Lilaith. She picked up the dagger and slowly wiped it clean on the disfigured alchemist's clothing. When she was finally satisfied with its cleanliness, she slipped it back into her gown.

Viktor could not blame her for her seeming coldness. She had spent ten years in Viathos, her will usurped by

Baron Mandrol. She had no doubt witnessed things that would make even the sorcerer shiver, especially the experiments of the baron's pet alchemist.

He took hold of her again. She did not struggle, but neither did she soften. Viktor was content to hold her against him until he was reminded that the arms that cradled her were not his at all.

A coughing fit struck Lilaith. She fought for control for nearly a minute before succeeding. "Gods! What is wrong with me? I feel as though I have the plague!"

"The time has come, Lilaith. What discomforts you now is the beginning of the end for Mandrol's army."

"You mean . . . ?" The dark woman gave him a hopeful look. "You found a solution!"

"Yes, but the solution means nothing so long as Mandrol lives . . . and I have little time, Lilaith. From the sound of things, Dré and his people have Straas busy. Now is my opportunity to confront the good baron once and for all."

"But he is surrounded by his faithful. There are guards and even a Morag within. You cannot simply walk up to him. Let me. He thinks I am still his puppet, Viktor! He thinks that I will bow to his every need." She pulled the dagger halfway free of its hidden sheath. "Let me have my revenge."

He shook his head. "Mandrol is mine, Lilaith. He is not a fool and I will not risk you. Mandrol's power is at least as great as mine. You would not have a hope if he discovered your treachery." Viktor touched his face and felt the rough edge of the mask. "I have to do this while I can. You must let this be between the two of us."

Her other emotions faded as she suddenly gripped him tight and cried into his chest. "Gods, Viktor! I cannot keep losing you! I cannot let Mandrol take you away again!"

"Just one last time, Lilaith." He wiped the tears from her face, then kissed her. She responded. Her hands rose to caress his cheek, but the sorcerer caught hold of them before they could touch the worn sides of the mask. "I cannot risk any more time. I still have to deal with the disposal of our good friend the alchemist here."

"Leave him to me." Lilaith DuPrise pulled herself together, drawing shut the emotional doors. They both knew that there was no future for them; there was only the drive for revenge. The list of Baron Mandrol's atrocities had grown yet longer. It was time for an accounting. "He's small; I will have no trouble moving him myself, my love. I will find a place to put him. No one will find Master G'Meni when I am finished hiding him. You go on. The longer you hesitate, the more time Mandrol has to organize his power and his servants."

He did not want to leave her to this distasteful task, but the sorcerer knew he could trust Lilaith to accomplish it. She now knew Viathos better than almost anyone, even including the baron himself. If there was a place where she could safely dispose of the alchemist's body, Lilaith would uncover it.

Viktor Falsche sheathed his blade. It was time to confront Mandrol, but as his companion had pointed out, he could not simply walk up to the baron and kill him. His face was too well known to those loyal to his foe.

Of course, it was a *masque*.

"I have to go, Lilaith. I have to find one final item and then I go to see Mandrol."

"What is it? What do you need?"

"A new face," was all he could say in explanation. He was not even certain if what he wanted existed, but knowing Master G'Meni's thoroughness and Mandrol's vanity as he did, he suspected the alchemist had everything he needed.

"I may never see you again," she whispered.

"I will always be there for you." He kissed her, then turned and quickly departed for the late alchemist's abode. Viktor could sense Lilaith behind him, watching his receding figure, but he dared not look back for fear he would decide to simply run away with her and spend what little time he had left in relative peace.

Guilt-ridden peace.

He forced his thoughts from images of a tear-ridden Lilaith to the sanctum of Master G'Meni. Unbidden, the alchemist's final words returned to haunt him. He understood that if he was killed, he would be dead. That much of G'Meni's nonsense was true, of course, but what did he mean in the other statement? How would Mandrol's death cause his own? Had it just been the alchemist's last attempt to leave doubt in Viktor's mind? If so, the sorcerer had to admit that the devil had succeeded there.

Does it matter? Viktor finally asked himself. *You are dead regardless of the outcome. Dead.*

But what *had* the damned alchemist been hinting about?

The guard sent by G'Meni found himself waiting with his terrible news, for Mandrol had other things with which to concern himself at that moment. Although the revelers still remained oblivious to all but their desires, the baron was now aware of just what was happening both beyond and within the walls of Viathos.

He was not at all pleased. Long hair bordering his visage like some hood, Mandrol glared down at the two officers before him. They were imbeciles just like all the rest. He tried to teach them, tried to guide them, but all they could do was stumble all over one another and then come to him when trouble began.

"Find Straas!" he hissed, trying to keep his voice low enough so that he would not create a panic. Enough of the rabble here were aware that something was not completely right, but so far they were all behaving normally. "Find Straas and tell him what I told you!" He coughed. "I want—" Another cough. "I *want* G'Meni!" Where is he?"

The guard sent by the alchemist dared to step forward. "He sent me, my baron! There is—"

"Has he destroyed that accursed mask yet? If not, tell him that I've changed my mind! Something is happening and Viktor Falsche can still tell us what it is. All we need is the mask and the proper host, which—"

The soldier shuddered. "My baron, the mask is missing."

Mandrol coughed again. His face was contorted

from the effort of staving back yet another attack while he confronted the guard about this latest news. "What . . . do . . . you . . . mean?"

Trembling, the man told him.

Mandrol cursed quietly. "*Stolen?* The mask stolen? Someone has Falsche's mask."

He could think of only one person who could have performed the deed, one person who, despite his efforts, ever chose to follow his rival rather than him. Mandrol looked at the guard. "Take as many men as you need, but bring me the Lady Lilaith DuPrise." He folded his arms. His mouth was set. "The Lady DuPrise has disobeyed me for the final time. I want her brought here even if it requires dragging her here in chains."

The guard was quick to obey. The baron turned his attention back to the two officers. His green eyes widened in disbelief. "Well? Why do you still wait?"

"My baron," began one. "If you could see what it is like outside! If you could only—"

Mandrol's eyes took on a sinister glow. His hands sparked with pent-up power. "Find the general and tell him what I told you. Tell him that if he fails in his part, it will not be Dré Kopien or even Viktor Falsche whose power he need fear. He will fear *mine*. Now go!"

The masque continued, but Baron Mandrol hardly took note of it anymore. He signaled one of the men of his Guard to step closer. "Draw in the keep guards. Surround this hall as best you can. Bring up whatever Morags we have available as well."

"Yes, my baron."

The pressure was becoming unbearable. Mandrol ran his fingers along the edges of his face, calming himself. He had to be fully in control. Viathos, perhaps the entire city, was in an uproar, but it was only a temporary situation. Dré Kopien could not maintain complete control over his little rebellion for long; he was not Viktor Falsche, after all. It was simply a matter of time. Straas merely had to better coordinate his own efforts.

Meanwhile, there was one last thing the baron had

to do. He braced himself. This would drain him temporarily.
"I will return shortly."
The soldier started to reply, but the baron's chair
was suddenly empty.

XX

Lilaith DuPrise sealed the garment cabinet, then allowed herself a deep breath. It was not the choice she would have made for a resting place for the alchemist, not at all, but time was against her. No one would look for him in there, at least for the present. Later she could dispose of him permanently . . . if there *was* a later.

She had almost thrown him down the main ventilation shaft, but then recalled that the fires would be well attended this night. Too many might see the corpse before it was engulfed in the flames or, worse, Lilaith might have missed the fire completely, leaving a dead and twisted form for the guards below to discover. The garment cabinet was the best short-term solution under the circumstances.

A dead man in her cabinet. Lilaith did not care. The clothing she wore had all been gifts of Baron Mandrol, things she wanted no part of anymore.

There was a knock on her door.

Lilaith stiffened, then realized that by behaving oddly she would certainly make her visitor suspicious. Smoothing her gown, which she had by some miracle avoided getting any blood on, the dark-skinned woman sat regally in one of the plush chairs Mandrol had provided for her private chambers. "You may enter."

The door opened and five guards, some of them still wearing the false faces required of all at the baron's masque, marched into her room.

Lilaith held back any visible sign of her growing alarm. "What may I do for you?"

The lead guard, an unmasked officer, approached her with an ominous expression on his face. "My Lady DuPrise, you will accompany us to the baron."

"I will be down in a moment. You may tell Mandrol that—"

"No, my lady," interjected the officer, drawing his weapon. "I have orders to bring you to him at once. In chains, if necessary."

"In *chains?*" She could not believe what she was hearing. "Surely not by Mandrol's order?"

"By his very order, yes, my lady." The soldiers moved in, circling her. Each had their hands on their blades, but only the officer's weapon was out. "Will you come now?"

She rose, giving them an imperious glare that hid the rising fear within. "I shall most certainly come with you. I would have words with my Mandrol about your attitude. You had best be careful how you act from here on, my good man, or it may be your head."

Her reputation and expression were enough that the officer looked momentarily uneasy. Then his own expression tightened. He sheathed his sword. "I obey my baron's orders, my lady, something perhaps he may choose to also discuss with you."

Armed escorts on all sides of her, Lilaith was herded from her chambers. As she and the soldiers entered the corridor, Lilaith caught sight of her servants watching from their own chamber doors just down from hers. There was more than one wide-eyed look and even one or two satisfied expressions. Further evidence of exactly who they truly obeyed.

None of the other servants she passed met her gaze. They recognized, no doubt, that she was under armed guard, and wished to distance themselves as much as possible. It was the same with the few guests who happened to be nearby when she reached the great hall. One glance at her escort and their looks of pleasure turned to absent expressions focused in any direction but where she walked.

By the time she faced Mandrol, Lilaith expected the worst. Not only was she shunned by all, but her escort grew by another three masked guards when she reached the bottom of the stairway. To her surprise, however, she found that she did not care nearly as much as she thought she would. Viktor was out there somewhere, completing his mission, but even if he brought down the baron, his time was limited. He would cease to be. Without him, Lilaith found all else pointless. She only hoped to see some sign of Mandrol's downfall before he had her executed.

The guards brought her to the baron's chair, but to her surprise the chair was empty. All but the officer and a man at her back departed, the other sentries returning to their watch duties. Mandrol liked his guests to feel secure . . . or perhaps wary . . . and so guards always lined the hall during the masques.

Neither of her companions asked or even seemed at all curious about Mandrol's disappearance. Lilaith's hopes rose. Perhaps he had run into Viktor already and the soldiers were waiting for a master who would never return.

She could not resist coughing again. Several guards, mostly the slave soldiers of the baron, also coughed, as did various guests. There was something thick in the air, something the rain outside evidently had not washed away. It also seemed more humid than she recalled from earlier.

The masque was, for all practical purposes, at a standstill. The pretense of unabated merriment had ended with her arrival. Now all they awaited was their master's return.

There before her, Mandrol himself suddenly appeared in the chair.

She could recall only twice having seen the baron transport himself like that. It was a strain, so he said, one that even the greatest sorcerers most often chose to forego. Yet here was Baron Mandrol now flitting about as if such spells were, for him, of the utmost in simplicity. She grew suspicious.

The baron did not look at the crowd, but rather directly at her. His expression was one of comic utter disappointment, as if he stared at not a grown woman, but a small, disobedient child.

"My darling Lilaith . . . I tried so much to give you the love and caring you deserved. Time and time again I forgave you your small desires, your obsession with distorted memories."

"Mandrol, I do not understand. Why have I been brought here? If it is because of what happened earlier when we captured the villain Viktor Falsche, it was simply a momentary lapse, I assure you. You are my love."

The expression of disappointment vanished momentarily, to be replaced by open anger and—she could scarcely believe it—pure jealousy. Mandrol was actually jealous of her love for Viktor. Once free of his compulsion, she had assumed that he had kept her only because she represented yet another triumph. Now she saw that there had been more. It might have been pitiful, almost tragic, if not for the fact that it was Baron Mandrol before her. The sorcerer had never had an ounce of pity for anyone else, not even his own flesh and blood.

"The good Master G'Meni—who still has not returned, I might add—informed me earlier that a certain mask was not destroyed as I thought. He made what will be a costly error for him. It seems I burned a mask that was not the mask I sought to burn. It seems that he saved the original mask in order to study it further."

"He should be punished, then," she replied, trying to imitate the tone of intense loyalty that she had used when fully in thrall to him. Now that same tone disgusted her, but she was aware that there was little enough hope for her at this point. All Lilaith could do was stall, possibly giving Viktor a few more precious minutes with which to work.

"He will be." The tone indicated that any further talk would not include mention of the alchemist's future or lack thereof. "I'm going to ask you this just once, my dear." He coughed, then continued, "I asked the same question of the good alchemist and he was wise enough to answer truthfully the first time. *Where* is the mask of Viktor Falsche?"

"Darling Mandrol, I did not know that the mask still existed. The last I saw of it was as it burned to ash before my very eyes. How could I steal something that I believed no longer survived? How could I do that, my love?"

"There is no one else, darling Lilaith. It must be you. I know it. There is a link of some sort. His mind and yours. We share one to some extent, but not nearly as deep as the one you share with him. You can sense him, can't you? Not physically, but his presence, his being . . ."

"Mandrol, my love—"

"You were *never* my love, Lilaith. I tried to make it so, but it was not meant to be." He steepled his hands. "Very well. You leave me no alternative, Lilaith. I must know what you've done with it."

"Mandrol—" Suddenly she could neither speak nor move. Mandrol's eyes became her entire world. Lilaith DuPrise struggled, but, although her own will was not insignificant, it was not sufficient to long combat one with the strength of the baron.

"Your will is mine, Lilaith. Your dreams are my dreams."

A thundering crash shook her from the trance into which he had drawn her.

"See to that man! What's happened to him?"

She tore her eyes from Mandrol's hypnotic presence and looked in the direction of the harsh sound. Two masked sentries stationed on the steps of a lesser stairway, one with the face of a bird of prey and the other with the red, laughing countenance of a fox, were aiding a third, who looked to be having trouble standing. A sword and shield lay scattered on the floor.

"Another one, my lord," replied the bird-visaged guard. "Another down."

"Damned drone soldiers! What's happening to them?" Mandrol coughed again. In fact, more and more people around him were coughing continuously. "Get him out of my sight."

"Yes, my baron." The guard with the bird mask removed his collapsing counterpart while the fox put the sword and shield out of sight.

Unwilling to return to the service of Baron Mandrol, Lilaith turned her gaze anywhere else but his face.

Unfortunately, she could not escape his features, for one of the sentries wore a mask that looked much like a distorted image of the sorcerer baron's own countenance. It was stretched long with wide cheeks and sunken eyes. Very much a caricature of the dark baron. She wondered what Mandrol thought of it. Such a mask was not to his tastes. This one looked too much like a baboon for Mandrol to tolerate it for very long. Was the guard suicidal?

"What is—" The cough continued to wrack him. "Where is G'Meni? You there! Check all the ventilation shafts in Viathos. Take men and descend to the fires. It may be there that you'll find it . . . or at least the evidence of its coming!"

The soldier designated to check the shafts saluted. "My baron, what is it I look for?"

"A sack or pouch, possibly something else." Mandrol cleared his throat. "There is . . . something in the air. Look at the flame and smoke; you may notice something different. Hurry!"

With sluggish movements, the soldiers obeyed. Lilaith watched them depart, relieved at the momentary delay. As the guards vanished, however, her eyes again drifted toward the still stationary sentry wearing the mask she thought of as the caricature of Mandrol.

"Now, Lil—" Mandrol's abrupt cessation caused the dark-skinned woman to look his way without thinking, but instead of finding his eyes and will focused on her, she found him staring at the sentry wearing the traitorous mask.

As she had thought, the baron was not one to take any such slight easily. He rose and faced the guard, who finally realized that the tall, maned figure was staring at him. The man's hands began to shake so hard that Lilaith thought he was going to lose his grip on his weapon.

"Remove that mask." Mandrol spoke in a quiet monotone, a voice more frightening in its own way than when he raged. He reached forth with one hand and repeated the command. The guard clutched at his throat, then finally nodded. The baron released him from his control, but kept his hand out as a reminder.

With his free hand, the sentry reached up and slowly removed the false face.

The countenance beneath was that of a young, scarred man, one to whom violence and dark tastes seemed very familiar. There was no arrogance in this face, however, not now, at least. Only fear of his master's attention.

A great wave of disappointment washed over Lilaith. She could not say why, but perhaps because of the choice of masks, she had assumed that the face behind the caricature would have been that of Viktor Falsche.

From his expression, it was clear that Mandrol had assumed the same.

The mask flew from the shaking guard's fingers into the waiting hand of the sorcerer. Mandrol pulled wide the mocking features, stared at them, then again at the hapless soldier. "Is this your idea?"

"N-no, my baron, I—"

"Where did you get this mask? It is not one of the regular ones. This is—" His expression tightened. "Never mind. Just answer my question."

"My—my lord, I don't know! That's not the one I was given! I've been wearing another . . . I don't know when I could've put on that one . . . I . . ."

"What was your mask?"

"A reynard, my baron . . . you know . . ." The soldier was almost on his knees. "A fox. On my life, I cannot say why, but I never noticed the change!"

"A fox?" No longer paying heed to the man's ramblings, the baron shifted around so that he now faced another of the guards, a man who stood alone on the steps. He had been one of the two guards aiding the sentry who had collapsed.

Without awaiting a command from the baron, the guard reached up and slowly discarded the animal mask.

"Misdirection, Mandrol. The best weapon against the overconfident, I think."

"Falsche!"

Around her, the crowd of guests flowed quickly backward, leaving only the two sorcerers, the guards, and

Lilaith. The officer near her snapped his fingers, summoning others to surround the dark-skinned woman, preventing her from attempting any escape now that Viktor was here. Out of the corner of her eye, she saw the Neulanders gathered separately from the rest. They watched the events unfold with great interest but did not appear ready to interfere.

Viktor threw the fox mask to the bottom of the stairway. "I've waited ten years and three lives for this moment, Mandrol. Even death could not keep me from you. Master G'Meni discovered that the hard way. You will have to find yourself another alchemist, by the way." Viktor cocked his head to one side. "And perhaps a new general, if what I hear outside is indeed the sound of battle."

There were murmurs from the throng. Lilaith knew that most of the guests still did not know what was going on outside.

This knowledge seemed to amuse Viktor. "You have not told them about what is going on outside . . . and even inside, Baron? You have not informed them that Viathos and the city are caught up in a battle between your dwindling forces and those who would free Medecia of your evil? Have you even informed them that Straas must now fight not only the rebels, but also much of his own army, nearly every drone soldier now freed from your accursed masks?"

Now the murmurs of the crowd grew quite audible. Several nobles in the back attempted to depart the room, only to find the doors bolted and guarded by soldiers willing to kill even them rather than risk letting in any rebels. Renfrew Jakaly had returned to the Neulanders, his tone and gestures indicating that he was trying to convince them that this was a very minor inconvenience, not a full-scale rebellion.

"Viathos is secure, Falsche. I do not rely on the strategy of Straas alone, not of late. For now, your little friends are probably enjoying their supposed victory, but within a few minutes more, they will be crying for mercy, I promise you. You, meanwhile, will be unable to save them, for you'll be dead, Falsche, dead for the *final* time."

The two guards nearest Viktor suddenly charged

him. Their movements, however, were much too slow, much too weak. Their attack was almost laughable and their deaths at the point of the sword that swept up so quickly were predictable. The duel was over in little more than a single breath.

Mandrol had not moved during the combat. Now he backed to his chair and, rubbing his chin, nodded understanding. "You *have* done something to the air! I was correct."

"I have."

The sorcerer baron nodded again, then straightened. As he did, he not only appeared to grow, but also to crackle with energy. Lilaith gasped and stepped away, but Mandrol had eyes only for his old adversary. "You know that I'll not be slowed. You know what you face in me, Falsche."

Sheathing the sword, Viktor raised both palms so that not only the baron but everyone else could see them. They, too, crackled with power. "I know very well."

For the first time, the arrogant veneer slipped from the dark figure's expression. "You should not be able to do that. Your host cannot also have such abilities. None of my guards has such an affinity for sorcery; I would have known it. How is it possible for you to do that?"

"I will do anything it takes to bring you down, Baron. Even the impossible."

Mandrol twisted around so that his chair now stood between Viktor and him. Lilaith was puzzled; why was the baron retreating so much? He was not so fearful of the other spellcaster. What could it be?

The baron smiled. "Come to me, my loyal ones."

His forest-green eyes ablaze with power, Mandrol stared at the open area between the two foes.

Smoky forms erupted from the floor, forms that coalesced immediately into two huge, almost human figures twice the size and width of any man. They wore helms and breastplates of black iron and kilts crimson as the setting sun. Their eyes gleamed with anticipation and a sense of intelligence and guile that Lilaith had never seen before in their kind. Their teeth were as sharp and savage as any of their brethren.

They were the two most monstrous Morags that she and probably everyone there had ever seen. The only thing Lilaith DuPrise found more frightening than the Morags was the fact that the baron had been able to transport not just one but both of them to this spot without any visible effort. The exertion should have almost sent him collapsing to the floor.

Had he fooled her all these years?

"Ten years is a long time, Viktor. In ten years, I've made some changes and some improvements on the Morags."

"Kill the little man, my baron?" asked one of the creatures in perfectly pronounced words. It raised an ax almost as tall as Lilaith.

"These are why your friends will fail, in the end, Viktor. These and a hundred more like them. You were actually the catalyst for their indoctrination. Ten years ago you proved that I could not entirely trust the puppet soldiers. Certainly I could not trust them to guard Viathos from your last living intrusion, and by all means I wondered about their fitness should I decide to . . . expand . . . the borders of Medecia. Oh, they would be the bulk of my forces, but for certain tasks, they were deficient.

The Morags have always been more durable if somewhat unrestrained in their activities. They simply needed focusing, the proper training. The results, as you can see, are magnificent. I'd hoped to first reveal them to our honored guests from Neuland and so this little demonstration couldn't come at a better time." The smile vanished from Baron Mandrol's face. "Yes, Klytos, you may kill him now."

"As you command, my baron," responded the second. He carried an enormous blade with an edge so honed that it looked capable of slicing through marble.

As the two advanced, Viktor pointed a hand at each. Energy crackled. A hail of arrows rained down . . . and faded just short of the Morags. Viktor tried again, creating whirlwinds that danced madly toward the monstrous attackers . . . then broke up within two feet of them.

Lilaith gasped. The baron's followers murmured their approval. The pair of Morags were bespelled somehow.

Some unseen shield or incantation protected them from Viktor's sorcerous assaults.

"Pathetic, Falsche," mocked Baron Mandrol. He remained behind his chair, doing nothing but staring intently at the tableau before him. "Spend what you will; I tell you that you'll never kill them, but you're welcome to try . . . up until *you* perish."

Lilaith watched as the creatures approached her love, their weapons ready to cleave him in two. Viktor had not yet given up, though; even now he summoned up the power needed for a third attempt. She did not know what reserves of strength he had from which to draw, but this would have to be his greatest attempt because it would almost surely be his last. The Morags were nearly within range to strike.

Viktor had cheated death yet again only to now risk perishing as Mandrol had originally intended, as entertainment for the baron and his followers. There was no one to save him, no one, at least, save for Lilaith herself . . . and she had no idea what she could do against a sorcerer as powerful as Mandrol.

It was nearly impossible to tell friend from foe in the dark, but Dré Kopien went on the assumption that anyone not trying to kill him was an ally. Not all the puppet soldiers had been freed by whatever potion Viktor had managed to mix into the rain. Now and then the pasty features of Straas materialized in front of Dré, the figure's intent being either to sever his head from his body or run him completely through. So far, the graying fighter had stemmed off both, but his arm was growing so very tired, and Straas always seemed to have one man left just for him.

Worse, despite the fact that they were beating the general back, they were unfortunately beating him back in the direction of the gate, where Straas evidently desired to go.

Something flew down past Dré, something that made the man beside him scream and fall. There were still archers here and there despite the fact that the former puppets stationed on the battlements had almost immediately turned on their former masters. It was only the swiftness with which the drones recovered from their enchantments that had so far saved the makeshift rebellion. Trust Viktor to know that . . . unless, of course, his friend had merely been guessing. Viktor had always been willing to take chances and make wild guesses when it came to Mandrol.

He pushed away his latest foe, who was then swallowed up by the battle, and glanced over the general's lines. Not once had he caught sight of Straas himself, and that was beginning to worry him. Straas was the key; cut him away and the elements left under his control would splinter.

Someone sounded a horn. The enemy suddenly ceased their retreat and began pushing the rebels back.

Dré pulled back from his own line and tried to peer over the combatants. The darkness made it impossible to be certain, but he thought that the gate was moving.

"Don't let them get the gate open!" he roared, trying to steer men around in the hopes that they could break through. It was already too late. Now he knew where Straas had gotten to; the man had left the battle to his subordinates and had himself concentrated on reaching and opening the gate. Behind that gate were no doubt fresh reinforcements, loyal or paid troops originally encamped there earlier.

Fires had broken out in one section of the keep yard, possibly torches or lanterns knocked over during the battle or dropped by a dying man. Even the steady rain, which was only now beginning to lessen, was not enough to completely douse the flames. The flickering light became just strong enough for a weary and fearful Dré to see the gate slowly open wide.

The horn sounded again.

Straas had his reinforcements . . . which meant that the tide was about to take a nasty turn against Dré Kopien and his friends.

I should've kept shaking Emil until he woke, Dré decided, wondering what choices he still had left to him now. Then it occurred to him to wonder just what *had* happened to the farmer-turned-sorcerer. *Ariela! In the excitement, we left him in the dungeons!*

By this time Emil was either dead or a prisoner and therefore no option that Dré could consider. A second later, as more armored figures poured through the gate, it occurred to him that he had *no* options whatsoever left. The only option remaining to the rebels was to fight. By some miracle, some of them might escape Viathos in the confusion. That was truly their only hope . . . but first they would have to battle through a sea of seasoned troopers.

If only he had been able to make use of the farmer. Even untrained, the man would have been a great weapon.

The farmer-turned-sorcerer was indeed in the dungeons, but not for long. Ignoring the soldiers charging past him, soldiers who appeared as oblivious to his presence as he was to theirs, the stiff figure of Emil ascended the steps leading to the interior halls of Viathos. His eyes stared directly ahead and although he clearly saw nothing of his surroundings, Emil did not even stumble. The farmer moved as a man drawn, or perhaps as a man called.

He walked slowly but steadily toward the great hall.

XXI

The world outside the doors of Viathos was in bloody chaos, but typical of his kind, Mandrol was confident about his security. Viktor Falsche might have found such a way of thinking even more outrageous if not for the fact that he was in imminent danger of becoming the crowning climax to Mandrol's latest masque. Small wonder that the baron's sycophants grew at ease once more, becoming positively boisterous, in fact, as time rushed on. Their baron was proving to them that nothing was beyond him and in moments they expected to see his archrival slaughtered for their amusement.

One of the Morags took a lazy swing at Viktor, more to shake him up than to kill him. They were playing with him, drawing the event out for both the crowd and themselves. Mandrol wanted him to see how helpless he was.

Twice now Viktor had struck with his might and twice now the foul creatures had barely noticed his attacks. Viktor was confused; he knew that in the days before his death his power and that of Mandrol's should have been almost equal. Who might have had the advantage, it had been impossible to say. The baron had defeated him through subterfuge, not skill. Now, however, the mistitled lord of Medecia had transported two fully armed Morags to this chamber from who knew where and at some point made them impervious to Viktor's sorcery. What did that say about his chances against his old foe even if he did somehow succeed in defeating both monsters? Not much, he was beginning to think.

Yet when he caught sight of Lilaith, her own fear for him spread wide across her exotic features, Falsche knew that he could not simply give in and die. Even if he wore himself out fighting Mandrol's beastmen, leaving nothing which he could use against the baron, Viktor would go down fighting.

He mustered his strength yet further. His third strike would have to be the one.

Lilaith wanted to help Viktor, but although she still carried her hidden blade, the guards around her prevented the woman from doing little more than watch the man she loved die yet again. It was almost too much for her to bear, but she had sworn that she would not faint even when . . . if . . .

In desperation, Lilaith studied Mandrol intently, seeking some weakness. She knew him better than anyone, or so she kept insisting to herself. One never completely knew the sorcerer baron; Lilaith had already discovered that. That his power had been great, she had already known, but not that it was this great. Mandrol did not look at all weary from effort; in fact, he was no more tense than if he had cast but the lightest, simplest of spells.

There was an eager look on his long, ugly face, a face that she had once gladly kissed. Lilaith shuddered with distaste at the memories. Never of her own volition would she have touched someone like Mandrol. He was more of a monster than his Morags.

Her eyes flickered back to Viktor. He was still drawing upon whatever reserves he had . . . and from what source she could not say . . . for one last great strike against the approaching creatures. The Morags were still toying with him, moving nearly close enough to strike, but making certain that their weapons came up short each time they swung them. All the while Mandrol watched from behind them, his eyes fixed on what his adversary was doing. The more Viktor drew in strength, the more eager the baron became. It was almost as if he wanted Viktor to cast as great a spell as was possible for him. Was he that confident in the protection he had given his beastmen?

Was it something else? What? What devious ploy was hidden by that mocking smile?

Could it be . . .

It was only knowing Mandrol as she did that made Lilaith take the chance. If she was wrong, Viktor was dead, but if she was correct, if what she wondered was true, then he might have a chance to survive even if she herself died in the effort.

From her gown she carefully slid free the dagger with which she had killed Master G'Meni. The guards, transfixed by the scene, were not watching her very closely. If she tried to run, they would, of course, stop her before she managed even two paces. Lilaith did not plan to run, however. She only hoped to throw.

She was not an expert at knife throwing. Such things had never been taught in her home. The Lady DuPrise could handle a weapon in hand, a skill she had learned outside of the protection of her parents' abode, but no one had ever taught her how to toss a knife with any accuracy. She wished they had; then she would have tried for the baron's chest. As it was, all Lilaith hoped to do was throw the dagger well enough so that it hit one or both of the Morags. Whether the blade struck point first or landed flat against them did not matter. All it had to do was hit at least one of them.

Readying herself, she peered surreptitiously at her escort. The guards had spread a little farther apart since the appearance of the Morags. Their eyes followed the battle with anticipation. She estimated that she might have enough time to take one step forward and throw, provided that she started her toss as she moved forward.

It was very probable that one of the guards would cut her down when they noticed the knife. They would be afraid that she meant it for their master.

"Come, come!" roared Baron Mandrol, mocking Viktor. "Where is the impetuous Falsche of old? Where's the man who swore that he alone would bring me down? Where's the man who continues to fail even with chance after chance to redeem himself? Come, Viktor, my Morags grow tired of playing with you! Either strike or they will put

an end to this charade by cutting you into tiny gobbets that
I'll be feeding to my dogs . . . after these two get their share!"

Viktor was preparing to strike. Lilaith had to act now.

She leaped forward as far as she could, her arm
already cocked back. The gown made it awkward to throw,
something she had not considered but could now do nothing
about. There was movement around her and arms reached
up to prevent her from releasing the dagger, but Lilaith
avoided them long enough to complete the throw.

"Viktor!" she cried, feeling the hands clutching at
her, dragging her down. "Watch the dagger!"

It was possible that she was wrong. It was possible
that she had indeed underestimated the sorcerer baron's
power. Perhaps he did have the might to transport huge, living creatures back and forth time and time again, but if so,
why use these against Viktor? Mandrol would want to personally see to his adversary's death; both he and Viktor were
similar in that way. Of course, Mandrol was the type who
preferred the advantage to be his; a weakened foe was more
to his taste. He was never one to fight fairly, not when ploys
could also achieve his final goal.

Yet somehow she was certain that all was not as it
seemed. Mandrol would not have wasted time bringing such
leviathans here when he had a score of soldiers already at his
command, not to mention another, albeit less trustworthy
Morag already positioned within sight.

Her view was partly obscured by her attackers, but
the Lady DuPrise could see the dagger itself and where it
would land. It would not be as high as she had hoped, but if
the Morag nearest to her did not move, it would strike him in
the leg.

She was fortunate. As she . . . and hopefully
Viktor . . . watched, the spiraling dagger did indeed land flat
against the massive leg of the Morag . . . and then continued
on *through*, unhindered by what should have been flesh as
hard as stone.

The Morags were nothing but illusion.

Illusion. The Morags he had been facing were nothing more than illusions . . . illusions against which Viktor had been wasting his precious strength, both physical and sorcerous. He barely kept his pent-up power in check; unleashing it as he had planned would have taken much out of him. He would have weakened himself enough to give Mandrol the advantage the baron had obviously been after.

Illusions! I fell prey to illusions! It had taken Lilaith to open his eyes, Lilaith, who might even now be paying for her love and loyalty with her life. Viktor wanted to turn and deal with her captors, but that would leave him open to the baron's attacks, which would defeat the purpose of her sacrifice.

"You may dispense with these creatures of shadow, Mandrol. They have failed in their appointed task." To show his faith in his words, Viktor walked up to the nearest of the two and thrust his hand through its midsection. The Morag swung at him, but the weapon passed harmlessly through the sorcerer's neck.

The almost merry mood of the baron's followers faded. Noises of uncertainty again rose among the aristocrats.

"Very well." The baron stepped from behind the chair, and as he did, the two Morags faded into oblivion. The floor between the two men suddenly became charred and cracked. Mandrol had also masked the damage Viktor had done to the hall in order to hide the fact that his warriors were nothing more than illusion. "You were always impetuous, Falsche, and I simply played on that. Twice you struck hard and those strikes will cost you. Whatever well of strength you've drawn from cannot last you."

"Illusions cost, too."

"But not nearly so much, as you know." Baron Mandrol reached up and ran his fingers along the outer edges of his face. His expression calmed. "The advantage is mine. I'll kill you, then display your body . . . the body you wear, anyway . . . and destroy the morale of your pathetic criminal friends."

Viktor could not believe the audacity of the baron. "Do you not understand what is going on out there, Mandrol?

Straas is outnumbered. Your slave soldiers are slaves no longer. Even the ones in here are being affected." It was true. While still under the spell of the masks they wore, the puppet men within were fighting to keep on their feet. Already several had been taken away. The potions that Viktor had put into the air were not as strong in here, but they would still eventually do their work if given the time. "Time and fortune have run out for you at last, Mandrol. The servile bunch who follow you may still surrender, if they do so now. You, however, have only one choice left to you." Falsche's hands clenched together in anticipation of what was to come. "You may die."

"You've been entertaining, Falsche, but that's all. I shall enjoy killing you for the last time."

Both men pointed at one another.

If their attacks were not immediately visible to those who watched, then at least the effect on each was. Viktor and Mandrol shook as each sought to tear at his adversary from within, a favored method in such duels. Sweat poured over Viktor's stolen body, but he was pleased to see that Mandrol, too, suffered. The baron's clothing was wet with his own sweat. Mandrol reached with his free hand to open the collar of his uniform.

They broke off almost at the same instant, their breathing ragged. Everyone around them was entranced, even the true Morag still guarding one of the entrances. This was a battle as none here had ever seen. Mandrol did not generally face his foes in the open.

There was a movement behind Viktor. He heard someone gasp.

He reacted with his power just soon enough to prevent the lance from piercing his back. With grim determination, Viktor Falsche caused the lance to swerve until it faced the direction from which it had come, then released it. The sinister missile flew straight and true and at a speed far in excess to that at which it had been hurled. The guard who had dared the cowardly attack turned to flee, but he might as well have stayed where he was. The lance struck with such force that it completely pierced the soldier in the stomach, at the same time throwing the hapless man a good ten feet.

Even as the guard's lifeless form clattered on the floor, Viktor was turning back to Mandrol. Just as he feared, the baron had taken advantage of the distraction to renew his attack. A savage crack appeared in the floor between the two, a crack that swelled into a chasm vast enough to swallow Viktor. It was a daring and dangerous feat; the very citadel shook as Mandrol undermined some of its support in order to deal death to his adversary. Because the keep was already riddled with underground dungeons and air vents, the baron's spell caused new, longer fissures to spread from the one intended to engulf Viktor.

People began to scream, but Viktor could only concern himself with his own life at the moment. The quaking floor left him fighting for his balance even as the crack spread to beneath his feet. Unable to counter the spell quickly enough . . . uncertain even that he *could* counter it . . . Viktor Falsche simply threw himself to his left and hoped that he would be able to find a fairly stable surface before anything else happened.

The spreading fissures caused columns to shift which in turn created cracks in the ceiling of the great hall. Large chunks of masonry broke from the ceiling and came crashing down, some of them striking unsuspecting guests. People started to struggle toward the doors, where the armed guards were again forced to keep them from opening the interior of Viathos to the threat of the battle outside. The guards were hard-pressed this time, however, outnumbered as they were and facing an ever-panicking mob.

"Are you insane, Mandrol?" Viktor shouted as he regained his footing. "A poor victory it will be for you if you bring all of Viathos down on your head!"

"I'd bring all of Medecia down if that's what it takes to finally put you back in your grave, Falsche! Viathos will suffer, but it will still be standing long after I have your face shredded before the masses!"

The floor was now an uneven series of precarious levels, many of which were unstable. Viktor leaped to one nearer to where members of the baron's Guard still held a struggling Lilaith. It was dangerous to focus on more than one goal during a sorcerers' duel, but he still hoped to free his love from her captors while there was still hope of escape for her.

Mandrol evidently understood what Viktor was planning, for the baron twisted and pointed at the guards and their charge. A cage of stone drawn from the ruined floor enveloped the party. "She will die unless you surrender yourself."

"She will die, anyway, Mandrol. I know you. Kill her, kill them all if you desire, but it will not keep me from you. Lilaith knows what is at stake."

Lilaith did, Viktor was thankful to see, but the baron's guards were staring at their master with pleading eyes. It had not occurred to them that he might repay their loyalty with death by sorcery.

The baron chose to spare the entire party, but not out of any pity for his own men. "No, I think instead that I'll save her for after your death. I think that I'll finally take the time to teach her who is her master . . . very slowly, of course. I've been much too kind to her, although I don't know why." His gaze returned to Viktor. "But her pleasure must wait."

Despite his attempts to keep his thoughts clear of conflicting emotions, Viktor Falsche found his control slipping. The baron's words reminded him of what Lilaith had been forced to suffer these past many years. Mandrol's leering, simian face did nothing to ease his anger, either, for the baron's expression openly hinted at what the southern woman would be facing if Mandrol survived.

Viktor attacked. It was a thoughtless, haphazard attack using pure sorcerous energy, and although it at first pushed Mandrol down to one knee, the baron recovered almost immediately. He did not strike back but simply allowed Viktor to keep attacking until fury gave way to common sense.

The wild energy further shook the already battered hall, stirring the panicking aristocrats to renewed attacks on the unfortunate guards. One guard was pulled away from the doors and battered to the ground. Others followed. No longer willing to simply stave off their attackers with the flat of their blades, the remaining guards began cutting down the nearest figures regardless of their status. Swords clashed and shouts filled the chamber, making it seem as if the battle outside had indeed made its way into inner Viathos.

Gasping, Viktor cursed his own stupidity. He had further worn himself out. Mandrol was weary, too, but not nearly as much as he was. The baron straightened, then glanced at the Morag still holding its position despite the pandemonium.

"Kill him," he commanded of the creature.

The Morag had already witnessed the great forces unleashed by both puny-looking humans and so although it did not hesitate to obey, a look of uncertainty covered its inhuman visage. It raised its weapon, a twin-bladed ax, and descended the unstable floor toward an exhausted Viktor.

Viktor had no real choice. Physically, he was now certainly no match for the gigantic creature. Sorcery was his only option, but by choosing so, Viktor further weakened himself.

Recalling his escape from Straas and the soldiers, he stared intently at the Morag's footing. The floor was indeed unstable, parts of it lower than before and deadly chasms coursing throughout. If the huge beastman was not careful, he was likely to slip. . . .

Influenced by Viktor's concentration, the Morag abruptly lost its footing. Cracked marble gave way. Roaring, the creature fell forward, the ax slipping from the massive, clawed hand.

Before the Morag could recover, Viktor summoned a lance from the hands of an unsuspecting soldier. One would not be sufficient, however, and so he tore from the grips of other soldiers more than half a dozen of the long, wicked weapons.

The first lance speared the Morag in its left leg. Unlike its phantom counterparts, the monster was not impervious to Viktor's efforts. It howled and tried to pull the head of the weapon free, but the second lance flew around and caught it in the back. The third and fourth lances quickly followed, pincushioning the monster, yet still the Morag would not fall. It gave up trying to remove the deadly missiles and sought its ax. The fifth lance caught it in the chest even as it gripped the ax handle. Two more sunk deep into its right side below the rib cage.

Viktor, fighting to stand, glared at the stubborn creature.

The Morag exhaled, then collapsed.

His remaining missile Viktor directed toward the baron.

Mandrol deflected it, albeit a little less easily than he would have earlier.

Viktor's legs nearly buckled. He needed much more time to recover, but doubted very much that his opponent would give him that time. Deep within, his anger was refueled by the knowledge that Mandrol continued to rely more on weakening his adversaries than on his own power. He was even angrier that he had allowed himself to be manipulated into such a position. The fault for his failure so far was not all due to the baron. "What next, Mandrol? Soldiers? Another illusion? You cannot win a duel save by constant subterfuge! Your own strength is a joke!"

"I win as I see fit, Falsche. The important thing is that I *do* win, don't I? I always win."

A wall of force buffeted Viktor backward, sending him rolling against a stairway. Guards scattered from the area so as not to be in range of their master's attack. Mandrol picked his way across the shattered floor, ignoring the slowly collapsing ceiling.

"Viathos is and shall always be mine, Falsche, and I'll continue to spread my power out over wherever I please. You should've left well enough alone. What use was the young girl you called sister? Nothing but blood tied you together, but you insisted on coming here regardless. You made your choice. Now you've done nothing but waste your own life over and over."

Again Viktor was tossed backward, this time against one of the stone walls of the room. He grunted as the air was jarred from his lungs. It felt as if his entire spine had shattered, and yet he still tried to rise.

Mandrol raised his hands and pointed at his adversary's chest.

"Father . . ." someone called.

The calm yet firm voice broke through the din, causing the baron to falter. His gaze shifted from Viktor to a lone figure standing not too far from the battling sorcerers. There had been no one there moments before, but now a man both familiar and strange to Falsche stood watching them, the newcomer's eyes half-shut, as if he slept while still awake.

It was the farmer Emil. The long face and dark hair were fair enough indication of whom he called father.

"Get away from me!" roared the baron, focusing on his son. Disgust and not a little fear crept into his voice. "You are not mine! None of you are mine! I reject all of you!"

Baron Mandrol could not, *would* not, acknowledge the truth, Viktor saw. Perhaps he feared their potential to be his downfall, especially those who inherited his aptitude for sorcery, as this one had. Perhaps there was even some reason behind this refusal. Had the baron turned on his own progenitor, perhaps?

Emil did nothing to stop the spell that Mandrol then cast. Viktor tried to recover faster, but he was still not swift enough to protect the newcomer. More important, it suddenly felt as if he could no longer cast a spell, anyway.

The farmer glowed red. Tendrils formed around him. He stumbled, but did not fall. Mandrol pressed harder, but to Viktor's surprise, Emil still stood.

It then occurred to him that he was failing to take advantage of the baron's own mistake.

Rising, Viktor started toward Mandrol. Since the farmer's arrival, he had lost all ability to perform sorcery, but he believed he knew why. Emil was his link. He had stirred the potential for sorcery within the baron's bastard son and formed a bond. That bond had now been severed, though, for Emil needed his strength to protect himself. Yet, the link had been strong enough that it had let the peasant know that

Viktor Falsche needed him, and so Emil had come.

Left with only what remained of his physical strength, Viktor drew the blade that had hung all this time at his side. A sword through the chest would kill Baron Mandrol just as readily as a spell.

Caught up in his desire to eradicate all trace of his bastard child, Mandrol did not hear the warning cries of the guards trapped with Lilaith. However, there were others who did hear them, the few among the baron's guests who were not struggling for release from the hall. Viktor looked up to see Renfrew Jakaly and another extravagantly clad popinjay cut him off from the baron, their elegant but quite functional swords out and ready to do him in.

Unwilling to fritter away the time that Emil had bequeathed him, Viktor dove into the battle. The overperfumed popinjay fell quickly to Viktor's sword, perhaps in part because Jakaly suddenly backed away, leaving the other noble suddenly without the assistance he had expected. The sorcerer pulled free his blade just as Jakaly tried to stab him in his sword arm.

"You tried to play me for a fool!" snarled Jakaly. "You made them think that I was you! I was almost tortured by the squat little toad and it was your fault! You're mine!"

"No," returned Falsche, parrying an attack. "No, I'm Mandrol's if anyone's."

He pushed down the other's sword with his own, then killed Jakaly before the latter could bring it back up again. To the end, Renfrew Jakaly had talked too much for his own good.

Now at last perhaps I can have you, Mandrol, Viktor thought as he pushed his worn and wounded body toward the baron.

Luck continued to fail him. Emil, still in his trance, began to buckle. Mandrol, gasping from effort, caught sight of Viktor as Viktor edged toward him with the sword. It was clear that the baron did not want to stop his assault on his son; perhaps he feared that Emil would eventually retaliate for everything Mandrol had done to him. Yet, he could certainly not ignore Viktor Falsche.

"I would've preferred that my hand be the one to extinguish your life, but circumstances demand otherwise, don't they? That you've dealt with Jakaly shows that I can't trust you to stay put. How much power can you still muster, I wonder?"

"Enough for you," returned Viktor. The baron did not realize that Emil was Viktor's sole source of strength. "Although cutting out your black heart will do just as well for me, I think."

"Yes, I'd thought as much." One hand still focused on his offspring, Mandrol pointed in Viktor's direction. The baron's eyelids fluttered. "One last chance for you, my precious," he said to the air. "One last chance to redeem yourself." Mandrol coughed. The air grew mistier, even more than Viktor's spell should have caused it to be. "Take him."

The mist before Viktor coalesced, but this time what formed was not an illusionary Morag, but rather a single massive shape almost as much mist as it was solid. It was worn, beaten, but not at all subdued, and once it had completely solidified, it roared its eagerness to seek its proper prey. This was a very real monster.

The last of the Amantii.

Viktor halted, but kept his sword pointed directly at the hellcat. The Morags who attacked the hellcats might have died, but now he clearly saw the wounds that they had managed to inflict. There were scars and gashes, even a dried substance that he assumed represented whatever the Amantii called blood. The monstrous cat favored its left front leg over its right and some of its vicious teeth were missing.

There was, only the one. Viktor was fairly certain that if Mandrol had any more at his command, then the baron would have summoned those also. This one was even more solid than the first Viktor had encountered, which meant that it had spent much of the time since he had last faced it on the mortal plane. The longer the hellcats remained earthbound, the more real grew their forms. It allowed them more mobility and resistance, but it meant that they could be better dispatched by physical means. The Morags had already proven that.

Could Viktor? He hardly had the strength to battle Mandrol, much less yet another of the sorcerer baron's servants.

It was not as if he had any choice.

The Amantii looked from Viktor to its master and back to Viktor again. Feline eyes studied both men with great interest.

"He is yours at last! Rend him, tear him up!"

The hellcat again glanced at the two humans. Its expression bordered on what Viktor would have sworn was confusion.

"Do as I command!" snarled the baron, his own gaze shifting continuously from the demonic cat to the silent, staring form of Emil. "You cannot know rest until you fulfill the task given you! Kill Viktor Falsche! That is my command, damn you!"

Indecision still evident in its mannerisms, the Amantii crouched and roared. One ear flattened . . . the other no longer existed . . . as the monstrous creature prepared to leap.

Viktor readied himself, knowing that this last of Baron Mandrol's seemingly endless legion of servants would likely be the other sorcerer's weapon of death. Viktor could not face up to the hellcat, not without sorcery.

Something changed in the Amantii's expression. She had come to some decision.

The great beast leaped . . .

. . . and, twisting around in a way no earthly cat could, fell upon *Baron Mandrol*.

They were trapped. Even with as many of the freed slave soldiers as he had at his command, Dré Kopien knew that. Straas had men pouring through the open gate, veteran mercenaries and handpicked, loyal troops, all ready to do his bidding. Even now the rebel band was being pushed back. Straas's men fought with a frenzy that Dré found astounding. They seemed more like men possessed. . . .

Then more and more men came pouring through the open gate, and although the unsteady light caused by the fires made it impossible to observe any scene in detail, he thought he noticed one soldier turn on another. The scene then repeated itself.

Could it be?

He could not take the chance that he was mistaken. Rallying some of his men around him, Dré called out, "Push back! Push back and we have them!"

Whether or not they believed him, his own effort seemed to encourage better on their part. Kopien's men held, then began to squeeze the soldiers back ever so slightly.

Dré killed the soldier in front of him and leaped straight up. The glance was but momentary, but this time he saw enough to verify what he had almost thought he had imagined earlier.

The latest wave of soldiers *was* attacking its fellows. The first wave, the one obviously loyal to Straas, was now forced to turn around and do battle with the soldiers flowing through the gate. Why the rebellion among Strass's own men?

Dré laughed, disconcerting a soldier who tried to jab at his shoulder. It occurred to him that there was a very reasonable explanation for what he was seeing. The drone soldiers from beyond the outer walls of Viathos—they were the new wave pouring through. Caught up in the battle, he had forgotten for a time that they, too, would be freed by Viktor's work, not just those within. From the looks of things, they had already been harrying the general's men outside before Straas had even gotten the gate open.

Straas and his men were pinched between two forces. Slowly the realization spread among Dré Kopien's forces, and as it did, a new enthusiasm, a new determination, spread with it. They fought harder, their confidence rising with each step back the enemy soldiers had to take. Dré no longer had to shout to encourage his ranks; they were now well beyond needing his guidance.

Straas's soldiers began to surrender rather than face certain death. A few were killed nonetheless, the rebels' newfound confidence overriding decency. Much to his relief, however, Dré noticed that most of his men were willing to take the prisoners without further bloodshed.

Then, seeming to stand out in the dancing light of the flames, he saw General Straas.

Straas and five of his officers were fighting their way up one of the sets of steps that allowed soldiers to reach the battlements. One of the officers fell even as Dré watched, but the remaining four continued to protect their commander from threats both above and below.

Whether Mandrol's general had some new plot in mind or whether he was simply making good his escape, Dré did not care. He could not let the general escape. In some ways, Dré understood how Viktor felt toward the baron. Every soldier left to Straas might surrender or die, but the victory would somehow feel hollow if the cursed general made good his flight.

"To me!" he shouted at the nearest men, some of them former prisoners from the dungeons, others still clad in the armor forced upon them for their roles as warriors of Baron Mandrol. "Straas is there!"

That was all his men, especially the former slave soldiers, needed to hear. Accompanied by more than two dozen ready swords, Dré cut his way through the depleted ranks of Mandrol's troops. One of the prisoners next to him went down and a former puppet soldier became entangled in a duel with a minor officer, but the others remained with him all the way to the steps.

By this time, Straas had battled his way to the top. Two of his former slaves tried to kill the general, but their skills were no match for the more experienced campaigner and the three officers now left. Still, the delay cost Straas much time. Pushing ahead of the others, Dré charged up the steps.

The nearest of the officers kicked out, trying to boot this latest attacker from the wall. Dré, in turn, seized the foot, twisted it by the ankle, and sent the man over the side headfirst. He then barely had time to duck a killing strike by one of the other soldiers, a thrust which impaled the unfortunate man behind Dré.

As Dré pushed aside the blade, his gaze met that of

the general. "I'm here for you, Straas! Dré Kopien! I'm here for you, man! You've wanted me these past several years . . . well . . . now you've got me!"

"And I'll see your head on a pole, Kopien!" swore the bearded figure. Nevertheless, Straas continued to retreat, not turn back and fight.

One of the men behind Dré engaged the officer who had tried to murder him. The remaining soldier paused at the very top of the steps, indicating that any rebel who wanted Straas would have to face him first. Dré was astonished at the loyalty of the general's officers, that they would sacrifice themselves so. He would never understand how a man like Straas could invoke such loyalty, but then he still did not understand why men were willing to follow *him*.

"I'll presssent your head to the general myssself, Kopien," hissed the officer.

The sibilance was enough to identify the officer for Dré. Harskinov, a man more trusted by Straas than Clevell and far more capable with a sword. Yet Dré had no time to engage Harskinov, not if he wanted to keep Straas from escaping.

It grated him to do it, but he had one chance of ending this quickly . . . and with his life still intact. "Surrender now, man, and I'll see to it that you live. I'll even see you safely out of Medecia. You've got my word and I'll swear by Ariela that I'll uphold the promise. What do you say, man?"

The other's blade pinpointed Dré Kopien's heart. "Do you think that you can buy me with that? Do you think that I would truly sssurrender rather than die for my general?" There was a pause . . . then Harskinov suddenly threw aside his sword. "All right. I sssurrender. I will not fight for the sssake of hisss hide. He runsss while I am to face death! Bah!"

"Put him somewhere safe and make certain that no harm comes to him," Dré commanded to the nearest men. They nodded their understanding.

As Harskinov turned himself over to his captors, Dré rushed past him, eyes frantically searching for some sign of Straas. The darkness beyond combined with the general's armor would make Straas an almost invisible specter, but Dré knew that the wall path allowed the general only one direction in which to run. Sword before him, he darted along the narrow walkway, avoiding the corpses of men and the occasional duels still raging. Nothing could deter him. Straas had the lead, but also wore armor both heavy and noisy.

The walkway ended in a door leading both up to the top of a watchtower and down to the ground level. Dré paused, then kicked it open. He had not expected Straas to be behind it and therefore was not disappointed when the door swung back unhindered. Stepping inside, a wary Kopien glanced first up, then down. He could hear nothing. By this point, he should have been able to hear the general running. Was Straas still that far ahead or had he stopped somewhere?

Fearful that he was losing his quarry, Dré started down the steps. He had only begun descending, however, when an unsettling sensation caused every hair on his neck to stand on end.

Damnit, no! I couldn't have done such a idiotic thing! Dré spun around and looked back up the steps.

General Straas stood several feet above him, blade out. Despite his armor, he had managed to come almost within sword's reach of his intended victim without Dré hearing him.

"Your little rebellion may succeed, Kopien, but you and I won't be around to see what happens. I'll be on my way to Neuland, I think. They'll be interested in someone of my skills."

"Someone with the skill for skulking away during the heat of battle?"

"As for you," the general continued, ignoring his opponent's jibe, "you'll simply be dead."

Dré readied his own blade. "Now, there, man, you'll have to rethink things a little."

"I doubt it very much." With those words, Straas attacked.

Fighting uphill against an opponent was not something that Dré cared for, especially against a skilled adversary such as the general. He had been a fool to fall for so simple a ploy as this one. General Straas now had the upper hand and was making the most of it. From hunter Dré had swiftly transformed into the hunted.

Step by step they descended, Dré Kopien not only having to battle the general but also his own footing. Straas seemed perfectly at ease fighting on such an uneven surface. His long blade darted here and there, a demon of steel.

Halfway down, Dré stumbled. Straas was in immediately, trying to gut the other man before he could recover. Dré, only hope was to back down more and hope that in the process he did not completely lose his balance. They were still high enough that a tumble down to the bottom of the steps would kill him.

The general's blade slashed him across his sword arm, leaving a trail of blood. Kopien gritted his teeth, not wanting to give his adversary the pleasure of his pain. The wound was not deep, but it stung badly. Now each clash of swords sent the pain vibrating through the rest of his body.

"You're a buffoon, Kopien," remarked General Straas almost indifferently. "You're nothing without Viktor Falsche, nothing at all. A footman trying to lead a battle, that's what you are."

"And you're a general without an army, man. Even your mercenaries and personal troops are surrendering rather than fight for your so-called glory."

"I'll raise a new one in Neuland." Straas slashed at him, sending Dré stumbling down several more steps. "Perhaps I'll even bring them back here for a visit." He lunged again, nearly breaking through the other's defenses. Dré almost slipped, but managed at the last to grab hold of the rock wall, albeit at the cost of some skin from his fingers.

Where, by Ariela's guiding hand, is the blasted bottom? The rebel leader wanted to know. He had some small chance if the surface would just even out. This fighting down the steps was maddening.

When at last he did reach the bottom, the change

was so surprising that he almost fell. Straas continued to press, striking closer and closer with each attack. Dré was tiring and his arm was nearly numb. Both knew in which direction the battle was leading.

"Just lower your sword and I'll make it quick, Kopien. You're only prolonging the pain and anticipation."

"I'll live with that, man." He could not tell whether Straas could make out his face that well, but Dré smiled at the end of his comment just in case.

"As I said, a buffoon." Straas lunged.

Dré threw himself back, shoving open the door that he had known must be there. Suddenly the two duelists were again out in the open. It was a small victory, but a victory nonetheless. Encouraged, Dré Kopien fought harder, actually scoring a small flesh wound on the general's bearded chin.

The veteran soldier touched the bleeding mark. "Better than I would've expected. At least you're making this fairly interesting."

"I'll make it even more interesting before you die, Straas."

"Hmmph." Pushing, the general suddenly had Dré on the run backward. Now his blade moved in ways Dré had not faced on the stairway, possibly because the angle of the steps made the moves as deadly to Straas as to him. Now Straas could fully unleash his years of practice.

He's got me! Dré finally realized. He was no match for the man.

Straas caught him again on his sword arm. This time, the blow was too great to ignore. Dré Kopien's arm twitched and his grip on his blade slipped. The sword went clattering to the ground.

Holding the point of his own weapon in line with his rival's chest, the general chuckled. "The game's ended. Had we more time, I might've given you a second lesson. You were improving toward the end there."

"I'll be glad to pick it up where we left off."

"A buffoon." Straas readied his blade for a killing stroke, then froze as he caught sight of something over Dré's shoulder. "What in blazes are you doing just standing there?" he shouted at someone out of his defeated opponent's line of vision. "Get some horses! We're leaving for Neuland!"

Soldiers. Dré Kopien's hopes sank. He had hoped that some of his men had discovered them, but if they were simply some soldiers still left from the battle—

Still eyeing the newcomers, Straas suddenly lowered his blade into a defensive position. "So it's to be that, is it?"

To the other's surprise, the general began to back away. There even seemed to have been a touch of fear in his voice.

Dré waited until he was out of range of the general's sword, then dared to peer over his shoulder. Several soldiers—eight or nine—had come up behind him. To him they were identical to any of the general's other men save that they had no interest in Dré, their attention and their weapons fixated on the retreating Straas.

Only belatedly did the rebel leader realize who these must be. Straas's *former* puppet soldiers, not his mercenaries as Dré had first imagined.

"It *is* him," muttered one in a voice dripping with loathing.

"Straas . . ." snarled another.

"Straas . . ." echoed several more.

The general glanced around, possibly seeking the door to the tower, but the duel had led him too far from it. The only thing behind him now was a wall.

"Straas . . ." repeated the freed drone soldiers, turning their former master's name into some dark litany.

Dré shivered. Even in the dark, he could sense their fury, their utter hatred. He almost sympathized with the general.

"You fools . . . I made more out of you than you would've ever been on your own! Your lives were nothing of consequence before you were brought to me."

"I don't think that's the right thing to remind them about, Straas." Dré retrieved his sword. To the stalking figures, he called, "Hold on! We might need him to—"

He ceased when he noticed that they paid him no

attention whatsoever. They only wanted the general's blood. If Dré interfered, it was just as likely that they might turn on him. Nothing could be allowed to hinder their revenge.

Straas saw that, too. He stopped before the wall, crouched, and pulled out a small dagger to accompany his other blade. Then, as the human pincer closed on him, the general attacked.

One man went down with the tip of a sword in his throat; a second was badly scarred by the dagger. Now, however, the freed slave soldiers attacked in turn. Straas fended off several strikes, but a pair of blades cut him on each arm. He snarled and jabbed with the dagger, but missed. Another blade caught him in one leg. The general stumbled.

It would have been a mistake to think Straas defeated yet. Another man died as the general brought his sword up from his half-bent position, the lengthy blade gutting the hapless attacker. Unfortunately for the general, the twisting body pulled the blade from Straas's hand, leaving him only the dagger.

As Dré watched, he flattened against the wall, awaiting the inevitable. Two more men moved past Dré, reinforcing the pack.

"I'm waiting . . ." challenged Straas. The challenge would have been even more impressive if not for the tremor at the end.

More than half a dozen blades came at him. Straas fended off two and actually seized a third with his gauntleted hand, but at least three plunged into him. The general gasped, the dagger falling.

Left alone, he would have bled to death in minutes, but his executioners were not satisfied. This time, every blade plunged into the general, skewering him like some macabre bird ready for roasting. Straas roared.

Any further strikes proved unnecessary. The general slid to the ground, blood pooling around him. His arms fell limp to the sides and his head tilted to one side. One man stepped forward and thrust his blade through the hated general's throat, but by then it did not matter. There was no doubt that Straas was at last dead.

His opponents stood there, staring at his lifeless body. It was as if they now did not know what to do. The man whose face and personality they had been forced to bear was dead. Now what?

What, indeed? One very obvious thing came to mind. Dré glanced back at the main structure of Viathos. The grounds were his, but Mandrol and his followers still hid within the great hall.

"Straas is dead," he called to the men who were gathering, some of them prisoners from the dungeons, others more freed drone soldiers. They muttered as they noticed Straas's body. Everyone was pleased with the general's death, but wanted more. They began listening. "But the evil he obeyed is still inside Viathos!" Dré pointed at the main doors of the keep. "Mandrol is still in there, Mandrol and all those who used you as if you were less than their dogs and horses!"

The apathy around him turned swiftly into renewed fury as the soldiers suddenly recalled that Straas himself had been only a servant. The men who had executed the general nodded to one another. One of them whispered Mandrol's name and *Mandrol* became a litany, a chant to spur Dré Kopien's men on.

Dré knew that by the time they reached the doors, he would have an army behind him. "Follow me! Straas is dead and Mandrol is next!"

A roar coursed through the gathering men. As Dré moved, they followed him, once more his to command. The moment was both exhilarating and chilling. Many of these men would still die. Sycophants and toadies many of the baron's followers might be, but the nobles in general were still dangerous. Most had been long trained in swordplay. Many might surrender, but many would certainly fight

Straas had fallen, but the war was far from over.

XXII

Viktor stood where he was, stunned beyond belief. Mandrol had ordered the Amantii to kill him and instead the hellcat had turned on the one who had summoned it.

The vision of the traitorous monster leaping upon her master was enough to send what few brave souls remained into the same panic that had overwhelmed the rest there. Guards fled or gave way to those fleeing. The followers of the baron poured through the open doors, not caring what awaited them beyond. The only ones to remain behind with Viktor were Emil, Lilaith, and the guards trapped with her. The party could do nothing but watch and pray that they would not yet be included in the destruction.

Shocked into immobility by the cat's turn, Mandrol was buried beneath the Amantii as she landed. Viktor almost turned away, expecting now a horrific tableau of bloody gobbets tossed about as the demonic beast tore apart its former master. Before he could do so, however, it became suddenly clear that the cat was doing no such thing. In fact, although she had the baron trapped beneath her powerful claws, the Amantii seemed unable to proceed further, try as she might. She kept Mandrol at bay, true, but each time she raised her claws to tear, something caused her to slowly lower them again.

This did not mean that Baron Mandrol was out of danger. Any moment it was possible that the hellcat would finally free herself of whatever caused her to hesitate. Then it would be the matter of a single swipe to eradicate the sorcerer baron.

Perhaps Mandrol was aware of this, for suddenly he gripped each forepaw of the Amantii and muttered under his breath. As he did, the cat shrieked and again sought to rend him.

Viktor moved forward. He knew what Mandrol was doing.

The baron shouted, "Into this realm I did call you, beast of the nether regions, and out of it I now cast you! Return to the pit! Return, damn you!"

Glowing bright green, the Amantii raised her head back and unleashed a loud, mournful cry. She began to fade in and out of existence.

Sword raised, Viktor Falsche neared the pair.

The hellcat dissipated in a puff of dry smoke, still howling to the end.

Baron Mandrol looked up at Viktor, eyes wide. Even as the blade came down, however, Viktor's rival rolled under him, causing Falsche to lose his balance. He fell to the floor next to the baron.

From his belt sheath, Mandrol drew a crooked dagger. He lunged at Viktor, who shifted barely in time to avoid the point in his shoulder. The two men glared at one another from the floor.

A dagger instead of sorcery? Has the baron finally worn himself down? Has it come to the two of us relying solely on mortal weapons any skilled warrior could probably make do with better than either of us?

"Why won't you die, curse you?" snarled Mandrol. "I put an end to you again and again and somehow you still keep coming back! Why don't you die?"

"Not until you join me, Mandrol. Not until you join me."

"It would almost be worth it." The baron thrust. Viktor slipped out of range, trying to locate his sword. Unfortunately, he had thrown it far when he had lost his balance. There was no hope that he could reach it before Mandrol buried the dagger in his side or back. Summoning it by sorcery was also not an option available to him; his link to Emil was severed, he now knew. Now all that remained to him were the physical abilities of his host body.

But Mandrol does not necessarily realize that, does he? His own show of great power had been partly bluff; would such work for me?

It was worth the chance. It was perhaps his only chance.

"I have saved something for you, Baron." He rose as he spoke, trying to add credence to his words by his show of confidence before the dagger. "The sword would have been the swift method, but I am glad it failed. Now I can treat you the way you should be treated. Now I can punish you properly for Cordelia, Lilaith, and all the others you have harmed or killed."

Was that a glint of fear in Baron Mandrol's eyes? Viktor could not say. He clenched his hands tight, caused every muscle in his body to tense, and locked gazes with his rival. Every movement, every inflection, indicated a spell of great magnitude being cast, so great that it might kill its caster . . . *after* it killed his target. He moved nearer a step at a time, ever keeping Baron Mandrol's eyes trapped by his own. Mandrol could not be hypnotized without great effort, but what Viktor Falsche attempted to do was not quite hypnosis. He was counting on what he knew of the baron's personality.

Perhaps it was because of Viktor's return after each defeat, perhaps most because of his refusal to die, but Mandrol hesitated. The dagger lowered, not completely to the ground but at an angle more in line with Viktor's knee, and the baron's head moved slightly back and forth as if pleading for his life.

Viktor Falsche lunged at his quarry, his own hand reaching for the hand which held the deadly blade.

Mandrol tore his gaze free just as his old enemy caught hold of his wrist. The baron growled and tried to twist the arm loose, but he could not break the other's grip. The pair grappled, neither sorcerer with any discernible advantage over the other save, of course, for the blade.

"I'll skin that mockery of a face off when I'm through with you, Falsche!"

Viktor smiled, knowing how much the smile would shake the baron. "Then I will come back again and again until I have you, Mandrol. You can try to burn it, tear it to shreds, or bury it beneath Viathos, but this face will always haunt you, will it not? I will always be there in your dreams and in your waking hours. Why not avoid the terror? Why not let me finish this now?"

"Oh, it will be finished now, I promise you that!" Mandrol's eyes flared.

He was trying to summon enough power to unleash one last spell. Viktor cared not whether the baron had the strength left to do so or was simply trying the same ploy that both he and Falsche had used already. Mandrol had to be stopped now. Viktor's own physical strength, the strength of his host, was failing.

Throughout the battle, he had kept the helm of the soldier on, not so much because of its protection, but because he had simply not thought to take it off. Now it was his best, his only, weapon. It was the one attack he doubted Mandrol expected at this point.

Bending his head back as much as he could and still keep his foe in check, Viktor Falsche, master sorcerer, then snapped it forward and struck the baron in the forehead. Unhelmed, he would have been just as likely to injure himself, possibly even damaging the upper portion of his mask. Even with the helm on, Viktor's head vibrated, every beat resounding again and again. He silently cursed his rival and the alchemist for making the masks so alive that they felt every ache and agony.

Still, as painful as the strike was for him, it was a hundredfold worse for Baron Mandrol. The baron grunted in shock and pain. The dagger slipped from his grasp, but Viktor managed to seize it before it could fall. Mandrol could not stop him; for that matter, Mandrol could hardly even stand, so stunned was he.

With little care for his rival's well-being, Viktor threw the other sorcerer to the floor and crouched on top of him, Mandrol's own dagger pointed at its master's throat. The blade seemed almost unnecessary; Baron Mandrol was still incoherent. Yet, knowing the cunning of his adversary as he did, Viktor Falsche could not take the risk.

"Now, Mandrol . . . now at last, we—"

There was something amiss with the baron's forehead where his long, black hair usually covered it. A peculiar yet somehow familiar scar . . . no . . . .cut? It was in the approximate location where Viktor's helm would have caught the baron's head. It was an odd sort of cut, though, more like a tear than—

Viktor straightened in shock, the dagger falling to the floor. It could not be . . .

Hands shaking, he took the baron by the chin and studied the face. It was the baron; it had to be.

Yet as he held the chin, the skin began to slowly slide upward. Mandrol's face became squashed and distorted. The baron's visage did not look at all human anymore. It resembled nothing more than *a mask*.

A mask.

"You cannot be!" Viktor muttered, trying to push the face back into place. "You cannot be someone else, damn you!" His attempts to make Mandrol whole again only served to twist and tear the face further. The potion he had put into the air had affected the baron, but at a slower rate than it had the drone soldiers. Viktor's own mask only remained because he had resealed it not long before and thus the adhesive was still strong and fresh. Mandrol's mask had to have been not only designed to be permanent, but created stronger and capable of containing a full personality print of the original subject. The stronger a mask, the longer it lasted. For such a mask as this to exist, however, meant that the one whose features it represented had to be . . . *dead*.

Mandrol was . . . had long been . . . dead.

Dead.

Then whose face was underneath?

Viktor began frantically tearing the mask away.

Mandrol screamed in sudden fury and brought both hands to Viktor's throat. The sound issuing from the baron's mouth was nothing a human should have been able to make. It was a purely animal howl, the howl of a creature in most dire agony. The strength in Mandrol's hands threatened to crush his rival's windpipe, but Viktor could only use one hand to defend himself. The other continued to tear at the mask. If he was correct in how the masks functioned, he had a chance. If not, then Baron Mandrol might still triumph even in defeat.

The world swam. It was almost impossible to breathe. The hand that Falsche had been using to defend himself dropped to join the other. The only thought left in Viktor's mind was to tear away Mandrol's mask. Only with the mask gone could he free himself. Only with the mask off could he survive . . . for at least a short time longer.

Baron Mandrol's hands shook, then without warning slipped from Viktor's neck and dropped to the floor.

Gasping for air, Viktor again cursed the perfection with which the false faces had been created. The pain might as well have been from his own true throat rather than the throat of the host body he wore. *How ironic that I should still fight for a few more minutes of life even knowing that I am already dead!*

His vision, the vision of his host, gradually cleared, the last speckles of darkness fading. Viktor's breathing settled into a regular pattern again. Beyond him, the sounds of battle returned, the sounds of battle and the cries of one woman. From where she still stood prisoner, Lilaith called his name, but not even her call was enough to draw his attention from the face below the mask of Mandrol. Only a host with an aptitude for sorcery could have allowed the baron to continue to cast the spells he had. Viktor's own case had been a strange exception, possibly because of his great will, the circumstances of his death, and the inherent power buried within the farmer Emil. He could not say for certain.

But who was Mandrol's host? Who had been chosen—by Master G'Meni, no doubt—to take up the mantle of baron?

He cleared away much of what remained, then looked at the still partly obscured features, the very pale face made so pale by years of being hidden . . . and almost passed out on top of the false baron's form.

It could *not* be true, yet it was.

Viktor Falsche stared down at Viktor Falsche.

G'Meni's dying words came back to him. *"Whether you win . . . or lose . . . you lose, Falsche! I've seen to . . . that, you know! Be killed . . . and you . . . die! Kill the baron and you . . . die, too! A grand . . . jest . . ."*

If not for his accidental discovery of the tiny rip, Viktor would have killed Mandrol right there. He might never have known that he had not died, but rather been made the host for the baron's foul specter. A grand jest, indeed.

And here am I, not even a ghost. I am nothing but a copy, a reflection of you, Viktor Falsche, with no real life, no real past. A last great laugh from the alchemist, eh?

Now he understood why the Amantii had finally turned on Mandrol. She had sensed as no one else could that Viktor Falsche had been hidden behind the face of the man who had summoned her. She *had* obeyed Mandrol; unfortunately for him, he had also been Viktor Falsche.

So caught up was he in the terrible truth that Viktor simply sat where he was, peering down at himself. He did not hear Lilaith continue to call to him, nor did he noticed the lull in the chaos. It was not until a familiar voice cut through the fog that he stirred.

"Ariela, man! What's the meaning of all this?"

Dré Kopien stood at his side, his eyes wide at the sight below. Viktor's old comrade glanced from copy to original, not comprehending the truth.

"Viktor, for Ariela's sake, man! What trick is this? Where's Mandrol?"

"He is dead, I think," the listless figure replied. "I think he died in a struggle with me . . . *him*. Ten years ago. It is the only thing that makes sense to me."

"What is that? Another mask?"

Viktor shook his head. Dré still did not understand. "That is the true Viktor Falsche, Dré. Something must have happened that night he went into Viathos. Mandrol trapped him, but somehow perished himself." Things began to fall into place . . . at least in Viktor's mind. "I can only surmise that the alchemist discovered his master dead. I don't know whether they had taken the mask of Viktor Falsche yet, but whatever the case, it must have occurred to G'Meni that without his baron, he and the others were lost."

He could see the alchemist working. An unconscious Viktor, perhaps wounded, perhaps not. Maybe conscious but unable to move, as the vague memories he carried had earlier indicated. The mask of Mandrol had to have been taken not long before. How fortunate the alchemist must have felt himself to be. He had the perfect host for his baron. *Typical of Master G'Meni. I might never have woken so fully if he had not chosen one of the baron's get, a man with at least as much potential for sorcery as either Mandrol or myself. There he finally became too clever for his own good.*

Had Mandrol known? Somehow, it was doubtful. G'Meni had found some way to trick his reborn master into not seeing the truth. That was more likely and much the way of the alchemist. There had been signs, though. There were the movements, the running of the fingers along each side of Mandrol's face. A way of relieving his tensions, but also of assuring that the nearly invisible seams remained tightly pressed.

I had won. I had killed Mandrol as I had hoped. Then G'Meni had to twist that victory around! For a decade I have enslaved Medecia . . . and all due to that damned, crooked little man!

No, he had not ruled Medecia, Viktor Falsche had. *He* was only a copy.

Medecia . . . "Dré. General Straas—"

"Straas is dead and most of his men either in the netherworld along with him or in cells. There's still elements of Mandrol's forces out in the edges of the city and the wild lands, but they're in chaos." Dré sheathed his worn blade. "Most of Mandrol's followers from the masque are also our prisoners. Several died, though, not that I'll have any pity for them. The city's essentially ours."

"Good." Viktor felt some satisfaction. Perhaps he was not the true Falsche, but at least he could be proud of the feats he had accomplished. Perhaps when his other self woke, they could converse a few minutes. The true Viktor, he felt, would be proud of him.

"Is he all right, man?"

"I do not know. He collapsed when I tore apart the Mandrol mask and has yet to wake. It will be up to you and Lilaith to help guide him for a time." Thinking of the dark-skinned woman, Viktor rose. "Lilaith!"

Lilaith and the guards waited silently, all witnesses to the eerie scene. Tearstains streaked her face, but she did not step back from him as he approached, for which Viktor was grateful. He hoped that his true self would treat her well. She had suffered long for him.

"Viktor."

"He will wake eventually."

She grew perturbed. "I was talking to *you*. You are Viktor as much as he is."

"Only for a time." He inspected the cage Mandrol's . . . his . . . power had wrought. "The spell was well worked. The cage is strong."

"It'll take us hours to chip through that." Dré walked around the cage, then eyed the men inside. "And whether we let these boys out depends on if they come to their senses and surrender. What do you say?"

"Our swords are yours," replied one of the soldiers. The others nodded and began throwing their weapons through the openings.

"Glad that's settled. I'll get some men, smiths, if I can, with war hammers. Maybe they'll—"

A sudden twinge made Viktor look around. "No, I do not think that we need them. There is someone who can help us."

They followed his gaze to see a confused and shaking figure rising near the body.

"I . . . I had to come here . . . but . . ." Emil's eyes were wide with wonder and fear, "this is . . ." He caught sight of the still form. "V-Viktor?"

"All will be explained in time, Emil." If there was anyone who could understand what the baron's son must be feeling, it was Viktor. "Please come here. We need your help."

"Mine?"

"Yours. You have a skill, a special talent, my friend."
Emil's expression was blank. "I don't understand."

"You will. Come here."

The farmer did as requested. His eyes darted
around the ruined hall as he stumbled to the cage. Emil's
complexion grew more pale with each passing moment. He
finally paused just before Viktor and asked, "Baron
Mandrol? Is he—?"

The full truth would have been too confusing for
Emil to comprehend at this time. Later someone could explain
the secret of the baron to him. For now, simplicity was best.
"Mandrol is dead, Emil. You helped bring him down."

"I . . . did?" Emil's face brightened. "He was—"

"We know. No one holds it against you. That can
wait, though." Viktor brought him to the cage. "You inherited abilities from him, Emil, abilities that Mandrol abused but
that you can use to right his wrongs. You are a sorcerer,
Emil, albeit an untrained one. Do you understand me?"

"I . . . yes, I guess so. You want me to do something?"

Viktor nodded. "I want you to put your hands on
this stone structure. I want you to feel it. Then I want you to
close your eyes and imagine it no longer there."

"I can't do that!"

"Yes, you can. Here." Viktor guided the farmer's
hands to the stone cage. "You feel it?"

"Yes."

"Now close your eyes. Imagine that the cage is no
longer there. You can do it, Emil. Trust me."

Still uncertain, Emil obeyed. As he closed his eyes,
Viktor concentrated, trying to reach the young sorcerer with
his mind. The new link would fade again, this time permanently, as Emil came into his power, but for now it should
have still been possible for Viktor to influence him.

The cage does not exist, he thought to the other. *It
does not exist. Those standing before you are not imprisoned, but free. What you feel is nothing. It is the empty
dream of a dead man. There is no cage.*

"No cage . . ." whispered Emil.

The air crackled, sending all of them jumping. Viktor was the first to recover. He was also the first to realize that a stone barrier no longer separated him from Lilaith.

"Viktor!" She ran to him, kissing him before he could push he away. Her lips were soft. He could not help lingering over the kiss, the last one he would know.

Dré slapped Emil on the back. "You did it, man!" He then abandoned the farmer and signaled to his men, who came and took Mandrol's guards away.

"I . . . did . . . it." The baron's son gaped at the place where the cage had once stood. "I did."

"It will come even easier as time passes," added Viktor, Lilaith still in his arms. "It will . . ." He trailed off. Out of the corner of his eye, he could see something moving. Uneasy, Viktor turned to where they had left his true self.

The body was shivering. Random spasms, but definitely strong movement. The first sign of activity since he had torn away the mask.

Forgetting the others, forgetting even Lilaith, Viktor rushed toward the body. He could vaguely sense the rest of his party chasing after him, but they were inconsequential for the moment. All he could think about was the man lying before him.

The true Viktor stared up at the ceiling, the spasms now all but ended. He stared up and did nothing more, not even blink.

Viktor leaned over the still form. "Viktor?"

The other continued to stare. Still there was no blinking. If not for the movement of the chest, he would have almost sworn that his true self was dead. "Viktor Falsche. Can you hear me?"

Still nothing. He leaned close, inspected the eyes.

Lilaith, Dré, and even Emil joined him.

"Viktor?" Lilaith called.

He ignored them, continuing to search for some sign of recognition. All the other Viktor would do, though, was stare up. He did not even see the figure looming over him.

A chill coursed through Viktor as he finished

inspecting his body. "Emil. I have a request of you."

"What is it?" There was no hesitation. Emil wanted desperately to help the sorcerer in any way he could. It was simple gratitude, but Viktor was touched.

"Emil. Put one hand on his chest here. The heart is here. Then put the other on his forehead."

The farmer obeyed, crouching down beside the still form. When he had done as Viktor requested, he asked, "Now what?"

"Now call to him in your mind. Call to the soul, the spirit, of Viktor Falsche."

"But you're—"

Viktor raised a hand to halt the coming questions. "Please. Just do as I ask."

Nodding, Emil closed his eyes. He began mouthing Viktor's name, calling to the sorcerer. Even as untutored a spellcaster as the baron's son would be able to sense the stirring of the true Viktor's spirit.

Yet, after more than a minute, Emil finally opened his eyes and asked, "Am I doing it wrong?"

"Do you sense anything?"

"No . . . yes . . . *no* . . . I . . ." Emil took his hands from the body. "There's . . . nothing? It's . . . a hole . . ."

The chill returned. Viktor looked up at the others, avoiding Lilaith's gaze. "There should be some presence, but there is not."

"What are you saying, Viktor?" Lilaith demanded.

He looked at Dré rather than face her with the news. "There is nothing left inside. There is a body, but nothing else. The true Viktor is no more. It was not from losing Mandrol's face, however. This happened long ago, I think. Probably when the mask of his . . . the mask of his own face was taken. The shock was too much."

"He's dead, man?"

"The body lives, but yes, I suppose for lack of a better word it would be termed death." Viktor could stand it no more. He rose and stared at the woman he and his other self loved. "I am sorry, Lilaith. I know how much you meant to each other."

"How much—" To Viktor's surprise, she looked more bewildered than upset. "Viktor, you keep talking as if you are someone else!"

"I am only a copy of the original Viktor Falsche, Lilaith, nothing more!"

"That's absurd!" She took him by the shoulders with more force than he would have thought possible from her. "That is absurd, Viktor! I have had enough time to study you. You are not simply a copy of a man. Everything I recall of Viktor is evident in you! Every nuance, every passion." Lilaith DuPrise forced her gaze down to the staring figure. "The masks were supposed to be taken as the victim died. The Straas masks were not the same; they only created weak copies. To fully reproduce Straas would have required that he was first dying before the imprint was taken. I know that. Master G'Meni liked to preach on the masks at great length."

"That changes nothing, Lilaith."

"But it *does*, don't you see?" Again she looked into Viktor's eyes. Her own hinted at something other than sadness, something akin to . . . hope? But what hope could there possibly be? "I think that when the alchemist took the imprint of your face, Viktor, he took something more. I think when you lay there, *not* dying, a sorcerer of great will and power, that Master G'Meni took much more than he planned. I think he also took what might be called your soul."

He wanted to argue with her, but what she said made too much sense. As intricate and fascinating as the masks were, they should not have been able to reproduce his personality so perfectly. Viktor had discovered that information in the course of his search for a method by which to destroy the poorer masks the drone soldiers wore. None of the other special masks had ever behaved as he had.

The mask absorbed more than simply the personality? A notion, an insane notion, blossomed. Was it possible?

"Dré! Are we truly secure? Is Viathos . . . for that matter, Medecia . . . secure?"

"There's still some pockets of enemy resistance, but, aye, we've won, man. What is it you have in mind?"

"Get some strong men. I need them to gently carry him to Master G'Meni's laboratory. Lilaith knows where it is. I will meet them there."

"Viktor," Lilaith held him tight. "Are you going to do what I think you plan to do?"

So she had been thinking somewhere along the same path that he had. He thanked the heavens for a woman so quick-witted and decisive as her. Without Lilaith, Viktor knew that he would have given up long ago. "You know what I plan?"

"I . . . I had some vague hope. There is a body and a mind, merely separated. . . ."

Dré folded his arms and looked at the pair in frustration. "Would someone tell me? Something's doing and I know it's important, but I *don't* know anything more! Do you understand them, Emil, lad?"

The farmer shook his head. That reminded Viktor of the one other factor required for his mad plan. "Emil. I know I've abused your abilities. You cannot have ever dreamed of all of this. I need you for one last thing, however. I would not ask this, but you are the only one who can help me."

Pride filled the novice sorcerer. "What can I do for you now?"

"Give me time to study Master G'Meni's notes. Knowing the alchemist, he kept very thorough ones. Try to rest and maybe eat. Dré, can you bring us food? Good." Viktor felt an insistent itch spreading across the damaged side of his countenance. "We begin in one hour, whether or not I discover what I am searching for. There is no time to waste."

"But what is he supposed to do, Viktor? Dammit, man, you still haven't told us."

Viktor Falsche gave his old friend a hopeful smile. "Master G'Meni took something out that he should not have taken out. I plan to put it back in . . . where it belongs. Now hurry! I do not have much time remaining."

Dré summoned men to carry the body. Lilaith kissed Viktor. Emil waited expectantly.

They all have faith, he marveled. Viktor wished that he could have informed them of one danger to his plan. He hoped to put himself into the empty body, to make the form and soul of Viktor Falsche one again. It should be possible, given the design of the mask and Emil's great potential. All that had to be done was place the mask on his true visage and let Mandrol's son meld the two together.

If it worked, he would be whole. He would *live* again. If it did not, that would be the end of the matter, for in the process of melding, the mask would be used up one way or the other. There would be no second opportunity.

There would be no Viktor.

XXIII

Master G'Meni's notes were not promising. Viktor had not known what to expect, but he had not expected to find so little on the actual process by which the mask drew forth the personality imprint. He had always known the alchemist to be fastidious in the recording of information, and everything that Lilaith had told him had indicated that G'Meni had not changed during Viktor's decade-long absence. The hour that he had set aside for searching the alchemist's papers grew into two, then three, then on until Lilaith came in to see what was the matter.

"Viktor! Are you all right?"

He looked up from the latest notes, notes that had hinted about the secrets he desired but that had revealed no more. Viktor shoved aside the papers and the scowl on his face, meant for the late alchemist and not for his love, sent Lilaith several steps back in fear.

The sorcerer's expression instantly softened. "I am sorry. I wish that I knew more about the masks. I would be tempted to make one of Master G'Meni simply so that I could ask him a few questions. His specific notes must be hidden away somewhere, curse him!"

"So you have found nothing?"

"Not enough to satisfy me, but it will have to do. It has been much more than an hour, I fear—"

"It is nearly morning."

"Mor—" Viktor touched his face, the mask. "Where is Emil?"

"Asleep in a room not far from here. You know he

would not sleep in here, not after what happened to him."
She looked beyond him to the body resting on the very platform where the alchemist had always applied the dreaded
masks. "How . . . I mean . . ."

"There is no change. There is nothing left inside
that *can* change." Viktor rose. "We must begin. It itches
more and more. I do not think that the mask will . . ." He
blinked. "What was I saying?"

"You itched."

He shook his head. He could not even remember
mentioning that, although it was certainly true. The itching
had continually disturbed his concentration, causing him
often to reread passages in the alchemist's notes. "The mask
is fast deteriorating. I cannot take the chance. I need Emil in
here now. Also a pair of strong men."

"Strong men?" Her concern grew.

"When this mask is removed, the guard I possessed
will wake. Someone must be there to deal with him."

"I understand." She departed.

Viktor walked over to his other self and stared at the
face. The fact that the mask was deteriorating faster meant
the risk of failure was even greater than he had earlier feared.
It was possible that it was already too late for a complete
transference. What would happen then?

Lilaith returned with not only Emil, but also Dré,
Mara, and the two men that Viktor had requested. Viktor
was especially pleased to see Mara, who had been among the
missing the last he had heard. Dré had been frantic the first
hour that the sorcerer had been working, then had gone in
search of the woman, finally giving Viktor the complete
silence he had required.

"So this is what it meant when I saw you killin'
yourself or you killin' Dré. Mandrol was also you," she said
to Viktor.

"Any new visions?" he asked of her.

"Nothin'." She did not wear the veil now, but no
one, save perhaps Emil, was bothered by her single eye. On
Mara, the lone orb looked proper—beautiful, in fact.

Viktor hoped that at least Dré and Mara would have

many years together. "Time to begin, then. Emil, I explained to you before I began my researching exactly what I thought you might have to do. Do you remember, or should I go over it again?"

"I remember, Viktor, but . . . but you said that the notes might make you have to rethink the steps."

He sighed. "The steps will remain the same. Lilaith, I have to ask you to be the one to remove the mask. It must be done with delicacy, as should the application, too."

"I understand, Viktor."

"Dré, if you could ask your friends to hold my arms tight. The guard may struggle when he wakes. The weapons I have already set aside."

Dré gave the command. The two men, both former prisoners of the dungeons and trusted not to speak of what they were about to witness, took hold of the sorcerer's arms, squeezing so tight that he almost thought they would tear the limbs free.

"Do it, Lilaith."

She stepped forward and, hands shaking slightly, took his head by each side. Then, to Viktor's surprise and gratitude, she suddenly pulled him forward and kissed him.

"I love you," he whispered.

"And I, you." Her fingers worked at the edges of the mask.

He was cast into utter darkness.

Lilaith stepped away from the dazed figure held prisoner before her. It took the guard, a young man, a moment or two to recover, then he stared in dismay at the scene around him. His mouth opened and closed, but no sound escaped.

"Put him with the others," Dré commanded.

She did not watch the trio depart, instead already walking over to where Viktor's empty form lay, eyes now closed. In her hands, the mask, what truly was Viktor Falsche, was cold. He had warned her that it might be so, but she could still not believe just how chilling the mask could be. How could he still be alive?

No! It was wrong to think that way. Viktor *had* to still be alive, even in this terrifying state.

"Shouldn't there be some sort of adhesive, woman?" Dré asked from behind her.

"Not for this. He said it might cause the mask and body to not meld together properly. We want the two to merge, otherwise he might simply end up wearing the mask for a time before it crumbles." Crumbling was already a problem. A tiny fragment from the damaged side fell off even as she held the false face over the true. The mask had not been designed to survive the rigors that Viktor had been forced to put it through. "Emil, are you ready?"

The farmer came over to the other side, standing exactly opposite her. She still had difficulty looking directly at him whenever they were close. He looked so much like his father, although that was certainly not *his* fault. "As soon as I release my grip on it."

"I know, Lady DuPrise."

Holding her breath, she placed the mask on the face. It had to be positioned perfectly. Another fragment broke off as she positioned it, causing her more anxiety. She dared not lose any more pieces.

It was done. Gingerly the dark woman removed her fingers from under the edges. "Do it, Emil. Call us when you are done."

The process had to be performed alone. Untutored as he was, the baron's son needed complete silence so that he could concentrate. If he slipped even for a moment . . . her Viktor would be gone forever.

She hurried out of the room, not wanting to consider such a horrible future.

Dré and Mara joined her in the corridor. The Cyclopean woman took hold of her. "Come, Lilaith DuPrise. There is nothing that can be done now. We must wait elsewhere until Emil is finished."

Lilaith did not answer, her gaze fixed on her now-empty hands. There were small fragments of the mask on them, fragments she had not noticed in the laboratory. Even less of Viktor had survived than she had thought. Would it be enough?

What would she do if he did not survive?

He was trapped between darkness and light. Forces beckoned him from all sides and he could not tell which was the one to follow. One of them had to be Emil, but they all pulled with equal force.

Then, slowly, he felt a warmth, a touch of life. It drew him as nothing else could. Slowly at first, then much faster, he journeyed toward it.

Images, vague images, appeared before him. He thought they were of a man leaning over him, yet they also resembled a man lying on his back, a man with his face.

Closer . . . something pleaded. *Come closer* . . .

He obeyed, knowing that he was at last heading to where he needed to go.

Closer . . .

The journey was long, but each time the voice guided him until at last he came to a place where the darkness seemed a little less overwhelming.

Come! the voice cried.

He grew uneasy. For some reason his guide suddenly sounded fainter, less distinct. Why the change?

Then he noticed that the power guiding him was beginning to fade. The path abruptly grew less certain. He wavered in his choice, tried to seize hold of the voice again, but found it already too weak for him to follow.

Emil! Not yet! It must have gone on longer than he had estimated. Time had a different meaning here than it did in the physical world. Emil must have assumed that he had failed. The baron's son could not be blamed for his assumption, but if only he had waited a few moments more, he would have completed the transference and brought the sorcerer back.

Emil! Viktor flailed in the deepening darkness, trying to continue on. He could not even be certain of his direction by this time. Only hope guided him now.

Three hours . . . it should not take three hours, Lilaith thought, pacing the room in which she, Dré, and Mara waited. Dré had departed on and off in order to coordinate efforts to deal with the remaining elements of Mandrol's forces, but for the past quarter hour he had remained with the women. All three were uneasy. All three felt that something should have happened by this time.

The door opened. The trio rose as one.

Emil stepped inside. He was pale, weary, and the drawn look on his long face told them enough.

"Viktor! No!" Lilaith tried to run past the farmer, but Emil still had the presence of mind to stop her.

"Lady DuPrise! There's nothing! I . . . I tried! I thought I felt something . . . but then it vanished! I tried again and again, but I couldn't find it!" He buried his face in her hair. "Forgive me, my lady . . . forgive me, please . . . I . . ."

She should have been the one being comforted, but his almost childlike ways made her feel instead the need to comfort Emil. He, of all of them, had been an innocent pawn in all of this, yet in his way he had given as much as any.

"You . . . you tried," she whispered. Behind her, she felt Dré put a hand on her back, the most he could do at the moment to relay his own regret.

Lilaith would have said more, but then the howl reached them.

The mournful cry echoed throughout the corridors. No one moved, so struck dumb were they by the ghostly wail. Lilaith was the first to finally stir. She pushed Emil to the side and darted through the doorway.

The second howl came as she reached the entrance to G'Meni's sanctum. It was animal . . . yet human.

Lilaith flung the door open.

Viktor lay on the platform, half bent to the side. His eyes stared blankly ahead and his mouth was still open from the last scream.

The broken fragments of Viktor's mask lay scattered across the floor next to the platform.

"Gods, Viktor! No!"

Rushing to his body, she flung herself on top and cradled his head in her arms. She was still positioned in that manner when the others arrived.

"Lilaith, darling," whispered Dré. He started

toward her. "Lilaith . . . there's nothing to be done."

"No . . . no, I cannot believe it!" She looked down at the pale, distorted face. "He cried out! I cannot . . ." Yet it seemed so empty, so very lifeless. There would be no more howls.

It had to be true, then. They had failed. Failed.

Lilaith reached up with one hand and gently closed Viktor's eyes, resigning herself to what had to be the truth. At least he had succeeded in finally defeating Mandrol. At least they had that for which to remember him.

Hollow memories. She closed the mouth, then, because it would be the last time, Lilaith kissed Viktor good-bye.

His body tensed beneath hers. She jumped away, gasping. "Viktor?"

Nothing. He was as still as . . . as death.

"Give up, woman, he's . . . Ariela!"

Viktor's eyes opened . . . and they focused on her.

"Lilaith . . ." he gasped.

He lived. He lived, thanks to her. So close Viktor had been to his destination, but in the end it had only been because he had heard her voice, sensed her presence, that he had been able to cross the final segment. Only because of her had he been able to reach his goal.

She kissed him again, threatening to take his breath away in her enthusiasm. The sorcerer was at last forced to push her softly to one side. "A little more . . . time, Lilaith. Then . . . then, I promise I will make it up to you."

"He needs rest," Mara reminded them for him. "He needs to heal."

Viktor tried to rise. The pain that coursed through him almost made him lie back down, but he refused to give in to it. "I almost wish that I had been more gentle with Mandrol. I never dreamed I would be injuring myself."

"Let me help you, man." Dré helped the sorcerer stand. Viktor's comrade was all smiles. "Ariela, but it's good to have you back . . . in one piece, yet!"

Viktor Falsche began to cry, so touched was he by

their care. His eyes drifted to Emil, who looked very much ashamed.

"Master Falsche . . . Viktor . . . I let you down. I abandoned you when you needed me."

"You did more than I asked. I was the one who did not realize how difficult it would be or how long it would take." He reached out and shook the novice sorcerer's hand. "I will always be in your debt."

"And I in yours."

"We need to talk. You need to be trained to understand your abilities, Emil."

The baron's son smiled tentatively. "When you're better."

"No more dawdling," Lilaith insisted, taking hold of Viktor from the other side. "Rest and food. Everything else can wait."

He nodded, too exhausted for anything else. With Lilaith's and Dré Kopien's aid, he headed toward the door. Rest and food sounded wonderful.

Only a few steps from the door, Viktor abruptly called a halt. Freeing himself from his companions' grips, he looked first at the platform, then at the vast case in which his mask, in which *many* masks, had been stored. Last he stared at the crumbled, nearly unidentifiable wreckage that was all that remained of his death . . . no . . . *life* . . . mask.

"I'll have this place cleaned out," Dré offered. "We'll burn all the masks. It'll have to wait until we've got Medecia organized again . . . and don't be surprised if you find yourself nominated for new baron, Viktor. More than a few folks know what you've done. Reminds me. Have to get someone to escort the Neulanders back home. They were smart enough to stay out of the way, even offered to make an alliance with whoever comes up on top, not that I'd trust the bastards."

"We'll deal with the Neulanders later, Dré," returned Mara. She stared at Viktor with her one beautiful eye. "You don't want us burnin' the masks yet, do you?"

"No, not until I have a chance to study them. I want to make certain that none of them . . . that none of them is like I was."

"Do you think that might be possible?"

"Not likely, but I want to be certain." His eyes remained on the fragments of his own face. There was little left. "But that you can remove. Burn it, please."

Mara nodded. "I'll be takin' care of it as soon as you're gone; I promise."

"My thanks." Viktor turned back to the door. He put one arm around Lilaith's waist but turned down Dré's offer of assistance. "I will walk on my own."

"Are you certain, man?"

"Yes." He smiled at Dré, then turned to the woman at his side and kissed her. "Are you ready?"

"If you feel strong enough to walk. Viktor, are you certain that Dré should not—"

"I can walk well enough, Lilaith." He took a tentative step which, while slow, was still steady. The sorcerer smiled again.

He was ready. It was time to face the world again . . . and face it as himself.

ABOUT THE AUTHOR

RICHARD A. KNAAK lives in Bartlett, Illinois. Besides the Dragonrealm novels, among which are the titles *Firedrake, Dragon Tome,* and *The Dragon Crown,* he has also been a longtime contributor to the Dragonlance® series, having penned several short stories and two novels including the *New York Times* bestseller *The Legend of Huma* and its sequel *Kaz the Minotaur.* His other works include the Chicago-based fantasies *The King of the Grey,* and *Frostwing.* Chicago will also be the setting for his next novel, *Dutchman,* coming in summer of 1996 from Warner Aspect. In the future, he plans more fantasy, science fiction, and also mystery. Those interested in finding out more about future projects may write the author care of Warner Books.